Praise for *Before I Let You Go*

"Kelly Rimmer skillfully takes us deep inside a world where love must make choices that logic cannot. Ripped from the headlines and from the heart, *Before I Let You Go* is an unforgettable novel that will amaze and startle you with its impact and insight."

—Patti Callahan Henry, *New York Times* bestselling author of *The Bookshop at Water's End*

"*Before I Let You Go* is a heartbreaking book about an impossible decision. Kelly Rimmer writes with wisdom and compassion about the relationships between sisters, mother and daughter…. She captures the anguish of addiction, the agonizing conflict between an addict's best and worst selves. Above all, this is a novel about the deepest love possible."

—Luanne Rice, *New York Times* bestselling author

"Rimmer's timely novel captures the unbreakable bond of two sisters and humanizes the difficult intersection of the opioid epidemic and the justice system…. A heartrending tale."

—*Publishers Weekly*

"Get ready for fireworks in your book club when you read *Before I Let You Go*! One of the best books for discussion that I've read in years."

—Diane Chamberlain, *New York Times* bestselling author of *The Stolen Marriage*

"[A] shimmering and poignant new novel."   —*Library Journal*

"Strongly worded, cautionary and honest to a fault, *Before I Let You Go* is raw and unerringly truthful. Do not expect to put this book down until you get to the very last page. *Before I Let You Go* is that compelling."

—*Fresh Fiction*

"Thanks to Kelly Rimmer's authentic voice, *Before I Let You Go* is a heartwrenching story about the love between sisters, the complexities of women, and the lengths we'll go for those closest to us. Thought provoking and deeply affecting, I couldn't put this one down until it was finished."

—Karma Brown, bestselling author of *In This Moment*

Also by Kelly Rimmer

BEFORE I LET YOU GO

The Things We Cannot Say

KELLY RIMMER

GRAYDON HOUSE

**GRAYDON
HOUSE**

Recycling programs
for this product may
not exist in your area.

ISBN-13: 978-1-525-82356-5

The Things We Cannot Say

Copyright © 2019 by Lantana Management Pty Ltd

For questions and comments about the quality of this book, please contact us at
CustomerService@Harlequin.com.

GraydonHouseBooks.com
BookClubbish.com

For Daniel, who always has the best ideas.

The Things We Cannot Say

PROLOGUE

Soviet Union—1942

The priest presiding over my wedding was half-starved, half-frozen and wearing rags, but he was resourceful; he'd blessed a chunk of moldy bread from breakfast to serve as a communion wafer.

"Repeat the vows after me." He smiled. My vision blurred, but I spoke the traditional vows through lips numb from cold.

"I take you, Tomasz Slaski, to be my husband, and I promise to love, honor and respect you, to be faithful to you, and not to forsake you until we are parted by death, in fear of God, One in the Holy Trinity and all the Saints."

I'd looked to my wedding to Tomasz as a beacon, the same way a sailor on rough seas might fix his gaze upon a lighthouse at the distant shore. Our love had been my reason to live and to carry on and to *fight* for so many years, but our wedding day was supposed to be a brief reprieve from all of the hardship and suffering. The reality of that day was so very different, and my disappointment in those moments seemed bigger than the world itself.

We were supposed to marry in the regal church in our hometown—not there, standing just beyond the tent city of the Buzuluk refugee and military camp, *just* far enough from the tents that the squalid stench of eighty thousand desperate souls was slightly less thick in the air. That reprieve from the crowds and the smell came at a cost; we were outside, sheltered only by the branches of a sparse fir tree. It was an unseasonably cold day for fall, and every now and again fat snowflakes would fall from the heavy gray skies to melt into our hair or our clothing or to make still more mud in the ground around our feet.

I'd known my "friends" in the assembled crowd of well-wishers for only a few weeks. Every other person who'd once been important to me was in a concentration camp or dead or just plain lost. My groom awkwardly declined to take communion—a gesture which bewildered that poor, kindly priest, but didn't surprise me one bit. Even as the bride, I wore the only set of clothes I owned, and by then once-simple routines like bathing had become luxuries long forgotten. The lice infestation that had overrun the entire camp had not spared me, nor my groom, nor the priest— nor even a single individual in the small crowd of well-wishers. Our entire assembly shifted and twitched constantly, desperate to soothe that endless itch.

I was dull with shock, which was almost a blessing, because it was probably all that saved me from weeping my way through the ceremony.

Mrs. Konczal was yet another new friend to me, but she was fast becoming a dear one. She was in charge of the orphans, and I'd been working alongside her on compulsory work duties since my arrival at the camp. When the ceremony was done, she ushered a group of children out from the small crowd of onlookers and she flashed me a radiant smile. Then she raised her arms to conduct and, together, she and the makeshift choir began to sing *Serdecnza Matko*—a hymn to the Beloved Mother. Those orphans were filthy and skinny and alone, just as I was, but they weren't sad at all in that moment. Instead, their hopeful gazes were focused on me, and they were eager to see me pleased. I wanted nothing more than to wallow in the awfulness of my situation—but the hope in those innocent eyes took priority over my self-pity. I forced myself to share with them all a bright, proud smile, and then I made myself a promise.

There would be no more tears from me that day. If those orphans could be generous and brave in the face of their situation, then so could I.

After that I focused only on the music, and the sound of Mrs. Konczal's magnificent voice as it rose high above and around us in a soaring solo. Her tone was sweet and true, and she scaled the melody like it was a game—bringing me something close to joy in a moment that *should* have been joyful, offering me peace in a moment that *should* have been peaceful and dragging me back once more to a faith I kept wishing I could lose.

And as that song wound on, I closed my eyes and I forced down my fear and my doubt, until I could once again trust that the broken pieces of my life would fall into place one day.

War had taken almost everything from me; but I *refused* to let it shake my confidence in the man I loved.

CHAPTER I

Alice

I'm having a very bad day, but however bad I feel right now, I know my son is feeling worse. We're at the grocery store a few blocks away from our house in Winter Park, Florida. Eddie is on the floor, his legs flailing as he screams at the top of his lungs. He's pinching his upper arms compulsively; ugly purple and red bruises are already starting to form. Eddie is also covered in yogurt, because when all of this started twenty minutes ago, he emptied the refrigerator shelves onto the floor and there are now packages of various shapes and sizes on the tiles around him—an increasingly messy landing pad for his limbs as they thrash. The skin on his face has mottled from the exertion, and there are beads of sweat on his forehead.

Eddie's medication has made him gain a lot of weight in the last few years, and now he weighs sixty-eight pounds—that's more than half my body weight. I can't pick him up and carry him out to the car as I would have done in his early years. It didn't feel easy at the time, but back then, this kind of public breakdown was much simpler because we could just evacuate.

Today's disaster happened when Eddie reached the yogurt aisle. He has a relatively broad palate for yogurt compared to his peers at the special school he attends—Eddie will at least eat strawberry *and* vanilla Go-Gurt. There can be no substitutions on brand or container—and no point trying to refill old tubes, either, because Eddie sees right through it.

It has to be Go-Gurt. It has to be strawberry or vanilla. It has to be *in* the tube.

At some point recently, someone at Go-Gurt decided to improve the design of the graphics on the tubes—the logo has shifted and the colors are more vibrant. I'm sure no one at Go-Gurt realized that such a tiny change would one day lead to a seven-year-old boy smashing up a supermarket aisle in a bewildered rage.

To Eddie, Go-Gurt has the old-style label, and this new label only means that Eddie no longer recognizes Go-Gurt as food he can tolerate. He knew we were going to the store to get yogurt, then we came to the store, and Eddie looked at the long yogurt aisle, and he saw a lot of things, all of which he now identifies as "not-yogurt."

I try to avoid this kind of incident, so we always have a whole shelfful of Go-Gurt in the fridge at home. If not for my grandmother's recent hospitalization, I'd have done this trip alone yesterday when Eddie was at school, before he ate the last two tubes and "we are running a little low on yogurt and soup" became "holy crap, the only thing we have left in the house that Eddie can eat is a single tin of soup and he won't eat soup for breakfast."

I don't actually know what I'm going to do about that now. All I know is that if Campbell's ever changes the label of their pumpkin soup tins, I'm going to curl up into a little ball and give up on life.

Maybe I'm more like Eddie than I know, because this *one small thing* today has me feeling like I might melt down too. Besides Eddie and his sister, Pascale, my grandmother Hanna is the most important person in my world. My husband, Wade, and mother, Julita, would probably take exception to that statement, but I'm frustrated with them both, so right now that's just how

I feel. My grandmother, or *Babcia* as I've always called her, is currently in the hospital, because two days ago she was sitting at the dining table at her retirement home when she had what we now know was a minor stroke. And today, I spent the entire morning rushing—rushing around the house, rushing in the car, rushing to the yogurt aisle—all so Eddie and I could get to Babcia to spend time with her. I don't even want to acknowledge to myself that maybe I'm rushing even more than usual because I'm trying to make the most of the time we have left with her. In the background to all of this hurriedness, I'm increasingly aware that her time is running out.

Eddie has virtually no expressive language—basically he can't speak. He can *hear* just fine, but his receptive language skills are weak too, so to warn him that today instead of going to the train station to watch trains as we usually do on a Thursday, I had to come up with a visual symbol he'd understand. I got up at 5:00 a.m. I printed out some photos I took yesterday at the hospital, then trimmed them and I stuck them onto his timetable, right after the symbol for *eat* and the symbol for *Publix* and *yogurt*. I wrote a social script that explained that today we had to go to the hospital and we would see Babcia, but that she would be in bed and she would not be able to talk with us, and that Babcia was okay and Eddie is okay and everything is going to be okay.

I'm aware that much of the reassurance in that script is a lie. I'm not naive—Babcia is ninety-five years old, the chances of her walking out of the hospital this time are slim—she's probably *not* okay at all. But that's what Eddie needed to hear, so that's what I told him. I sat him down with the schedule and the script and I ran through both until Eddie opened his iPad and the communications program he uses—an Augmentative and Alternative Communication app, AAC for short; it's a simple but life-changing concept—each screen displays a series of images that represent the words Eddie can't say. By pressing on those images, Eddie is able to find a voice. This morning, he looked down at the screen for a moment, then he pressed on the *Yes* button, so I knew he understood what he'd read, at least to some degree.

Everything was fine until we arrived here, and the packaging had changed. In the time that's passed since, concerned staff and shoppers have come and gone.

"Can we help, ma'am?" they asked at first, and I shook my head, explained his autism diagnosis and let them go on their merry way. Then the offers of help became more insistent. *"Can we carry him out to your car for you, ma'am?"* So then I explained that he doesn't really like to be touched at the best of times, but if a bunch of strangers touched him, the situation would get worse. I could see from the expression on their faces that they doubted things *could* get any worse, but not so much that they dared risk it.

Then a woman came past with an identically dressed set of perfectly behaved, no doubt neurotypical children sitting up high in her cart. As she navigated her cart around my out-of-control son, I heard one of the children ask her what was wrong with him, and she muttered, "He just needs a good spankin', darlin'."

Sure, I thought. He just needs a spankin'. That'll teach him how to deal with sensory overload and learn to speak. Maybe if I spank him, he'll use the toilet spontaneously and I can ditch the obsessively regimented routine I use to prevent his incontinence. Such an easy solution… Why didn't I think of spanking him seven years ago? But just as my temper started to simmer she glanced at me, and I met her gaze before she looked away. I caught a hint of pity in her eyes, and there was no mistaking the fear. The woman blushed, averted her gaze and that leisurely journey with her children in the cart became a veritable sprint to the next aisle.

People say things like that because it makes them feel better in what is undoubtedly a very awkward situation. I don't blame her—I kind of envy her. I wish I could be that self-righteous, but seven years of parenting Edison Michaels has taught me nothing if not humility. I'm doing the best I can, it's usually not good enough and that's just the way it is.

The manager came by a few minutes ago.

"Ma'am, we have to do something. He's done hundreds of dollars' worth of damage to my stock and now the other shoppers are getting upset."

"I'm all ears," I said, and I shrugged. "What do you propose?"

"Can we call the paramedics? It's a medical crisis, right?"

"What do you think they're going to do? Sedate him?"

His eyes brightened. "Can they do that?"

I scowled at him, and his face fell again. We sat in uncomfortable silence for a moment, then I sighed as if he'd convinced me.

"You call the paramedics, then," I said, but the knowing smile I gave him must have scared him just a bit, because he stepped away from me. "Let's just see how Eddie copes with a paramedic visit. I'm sure the blaring sirens and the uniforms and *more* strangers can't make things much worse." I paused, then I looked at him innocently. *"Right?"*

The manager walked away muttering to himself, but he must have thought twice about the paramedics because I've yet to hear sirens. Instead, there are visibly uncomfortable store assistants standing at either end of the aisle quietly explaining the situation to shoppers and offering to pick out any products they require to save them walking near my noisy, awkward son.

As for me, I'm sitting on the floor beside him now. I want to be stoic and I want to be calm, but I'm sobbing intermittently, because no matter how many times this happens, it's utterly humiliating. I've tried everything I can to defuse this situation and my every attempt has failed. This will only end when Eddie tires himself out.

Really, I should have known better than to risk bringing him into a grocery store today. I don't think he fully understands what this hospital visit means, but he knows *something* is off. Not for the first time, I wish he could handle a full-time school placement, instead of the two-day-a-week schedule we've had to settle for. If only I could have dropped him off at school today and come here alone, or even if I could have convinced my husband, Wade, to stay home from work with Eddie.

Wade had meetings. He always has meetings, especially when *not* having meetings would mean he would have to be alone with Edison.

"Excuse me."

I look up wearily, expecting to find another staff member has come to offer "assistance." Instead, it is an elderly woman—a frail woman, with kind gray eyes and a startling blue hue to her hair. Blue rinse aside, she looks a lot like my Babcia—short and skinny, but purposefully styled. This woman is carrying a flashy handbag and she's dressed from head to toe in explosive floral prints, all the way down to her fabric Mary Janes, which are patterned with gerberas. Babcia would wear those shoes too. Even now, well into her nineties, Babcia is still generally dressed in clothes featuring crazy flowers or outlandish lace. I have a feeling if the two women met, they'd be instant friends. I feel a pinch in my chest at the recognition, and impatience sweeps over me.

Hurry up, Eddie. We have to hurry. Babcia is sick and we need to get to the hospital.

The woman offers me a gentle smile and opens her handbag conspiratorially.

"Do you think something in here could help?" She withdraws from her bag a collection of little trinkets—a red balloon, a blue lollipop, a tiny wooden doll and a small wooden dreidel. The woman crouches beside me, then drops them all onto the floor.

I've already tried distraction so I *know* this isn't going to work, but the kindness in the woman's gaze almost brings me to tears anyway. When I look into her eyes, I see empathy and understanding—but not a hint of pity. It's a beautiful and unfortunately rare thing to have someone understand my situation instead of judging it.

I murmur false appreciation and I glance between the woman and Edison while I try to figure out if this is going to make the situation worse. He *has* at least turned the volume down a little, and out of his puffy, tear-filled eyes, he's watching the woman warily. He does so love Babcia. Perhaps he sees the likeness too.

I nod toward the woman, and she lifts the balloon. Eddie doesn't react. She lifts the doll, and again, his expression remains pinched. Then the lollipop, with the same result. I've completely lost hope when she picks up the dreidel, so I'm surprised when Eddie's wailing falters just a little.

Colorful Hebrew characters are etched into each side, and the woman runs her finger over one of them, then sets the dreidel onto the floor and gives an elegant flick of her wrist. As the dreidel spins, the colors hypnotically blend into a brilliant blur. "My grandson is on the spectrum too," she tells me quietly. "I have at least an inkling of how difficult your situation is. The dreidels are Braden's favorite too…"

Eddie is staring intently at the dreidel as it spins. His wailing has stopped. All that's left behind now are soft, shuddering sobs.

"Do you know what the Hebrew means?" the woman asks me quietly. I shake my head, and she reads softly, "It's an acronym— it stands for *a great miracle happened there*."

I want to tell the woman that I don't believe in miracles any- more, but I'm not sure that's true, because one seems to be un- folding right before me. Eddie is now almost silent but for the occasional sniffle or echoed sob. The dreidel's spin fades until it wobbles, then it topples onto its side. I hear the sharp intake of his breath.

"Darling boy, do you know what this is?" the woman asks quietly.

"He doesn't speak," I try to explain, but Eddie chooses that exact moment to dig deep into his bag of embarrassing autism tricks as he turns his gaze to me and says hoarsely, "I love you, Eddie."

The woman glances at me, and I try to explain,

"That's just...it's called echolalia...he can *say* words, but there's no meaning behind them. He's just parroting what he hears me say to him—he doesn't know what it means. It's kind of his way of saying *Mommy*."

The woman offers me another gentle smile now and she sets the dreidel down right near Eddie, starts it spinning again and waits. He stares in silent wonder, and by the time the dreidel falls onto its side for a second time, he's completely calm. I fumble for his iPad, load the AAC, then hit the *finish* and the *car* buttons before I turn the screen toward Eddie. He sits up, drags himself to his feet and looks at me expectantly.

"That's it, sweetheart," the woman says softly. She bends and picks up the dreidel, and she passes it to Eddie as she murmurs, "What a clever boy, calming yourself down like that. Your mommy must be so proud of you."

"Thank you," I say to the woman.

She nods, and she touches my forearm briefly as she murmurs, "You're doing a good job, Momma. Don't you ever forget that."

Her words feel like platitudes at first. I lead Edison from the store, empty-handed but for the unexpected treasure from the stranger. I clip him into his special-order car seat, a necessity despite his size because he won't sit still enough for a regular seat belt. I slide into my own seat, and I glance at him in the rearview mirror. He's staring at the dreidel, calm and still, but he's a million miles away like he always is, and I'm tired. I'm always tired.

You're doing a good job, Momma. Don't you ever forget that.

I don't cry much over Eddie. I love him. I care for him. I don't ever let myself feel self-pity. I'm like an alcoholic who won't take even a drop of drink. I know once I open the floodgates to feeling sorry for myself, I'll get a taste for it and it will destroy me.

But today my grandmother is in the hospital, and the kind woman with the gerbera shoes felt like an angel visiting me in my hour of need, and what if Babcia sent her, and what if this is my grandmother's last gift to me because she's about to slip away?

It's my turn for a meltdown. Eddie plays with his dreidel, holding it right in front of his face and rotating it very slowly in the air as if he's trying to figure out how it works. I sob. I give myself eight luxurious minutes of weeping, because that brings us to 10:00 a.m., and we're now exactly an hour later than I hoped to be.

When the car clock ticks over the hour, I decide to stop wallowing—and then I do: just like that I turn the pity off. I wipe my nose with a Kleenex, clear my throat and start the car. As soon as I press the ignition, my phone connects to the car and on the touch screen by the steering wheel, the missed messages from my mom appear.

Where are you?

You said you'd be here by 9:00. Are you still coming?

Alice. Call me please, what's going on?

Babcia is awake, but come quickly because I don't know how long it will be until she needs another nap.

And then finally, one from Wade.

Sorry I couldn't take today off, honey. Are you mad?

We haven't even made it to the hospital yet. It's going to be a long day.

CHAPTER 2

Alina

Tomasz Slaski was determined to be a doctor like his father, but I always thought he was born to tell stories. I decided I'd marry him one day as he told me an elaborate tale about rescuing a mermaid princess from the lake while the rest of our town was asleep. I was nine and Tomasz was twelve years old, but we were already good friends, and that day I decided that he was mine. Somewhere in the years that followed, he came to see me as *his* too, and by the time I finished grade seven and my family could no longer afford to send me to school, Tomasz had a well-established habit of calling on me at home.

Like most of the children I knew, I left school and went to work in the fields with my parents—although *unlike* most of the children I knew, I never really worked all that hard. I was the youngest child, and even once puberty had come and gone, I was still fine-boned and only just five feet tall. Everyone else in my family was tall and strong, and despite my twin brothers being only fourteen months older than me, my family had never really stopped treating me like a child. I didn't mind that too much at all as long as it meant the twins did the heavy lifting with the farm work.

Tomasz was from a wealthier family and long destined for university, so he stayed on at high school far longer than most in our district in southern Poland. Even once our paths diverged, he would regularly climb the hill between our homes to spend time with me, and every time he visited, he'd charm my whole family with outrageous tales from his week.

Even as a child and a teenager, Tomasz had a way of speaking that made you think that anything was possible. That's what I loved about him first—he opened up my world to endless possibilities, and in doing so, filled it with magic. But for Tomasz, I'd never even have wondered about the world beyond my village, but once we fell in love, exploring it with him was pretty much all I could think about.

I wished so much that we could be married before he left for medical school so that I could go with him to the city. Mostly I couldn't bear the thought of us parting, but a part of that desperation was rooted in my impatience to leave the family farm. My home was just past the outskirts of the rural township of Trzebinia, where Tomasz's father Aleksy was the doctor, and his mother Julita had been a schoolteacher until she died in childbirth with his little sister. I was certain my life lay beyond the small world we inhabited, but there was no way to escape without marriage, and I was still a little too young for that—only fifteen at the time. The best I could hope for was that one day, Tomasz would come back for me.

The weekend arrived before Tomasz was due to leave, late in the spring of 1938. Time has a way of diluting how we remember things, but there are some memories too pure for even the ravages of the years, and that Sunday is as fresh in my mind as it was when I woke the next morning. Perhaps it's just a side effect of holding the memory so close to myself over the years, replaying it in my mind over and over again as if it was my favorite film. Even now when I struggle to remember where I am sometimes or what day it is, I'm certain I still remember everything from *that* day—every moment, every touch, every scent and every sound. All day, heavy gray clouds had lingered low in the sky. We'd had so much rain in the days before that my boots were coated, and I wasn't sure how much was from the animals and how much was from the mud. For days, the weather had been dreary, but by that Sunday evening, a cruel wind had blown in that made it bitter.

My brothers Filipe and Stanislaw had both worked all day in the cold while I was chatting with Tomasz, so my parents insisted I do one last task to tend to the animals before supper. I resisted fiercely until Tomasz took my hand and led the way.

"You are so spoiled," he laughed softly.

"You sound like my parents," I muttered.

"Well, maybe it's true." He glanced back at me, still pulling me along by my hand, but the adoration in his gaze was undeniable. "Don't worry, Spoiled Alina. I love you anyway."

At that, I felt a flush of pride and pleasure so strong that everything else became irrelevant.

"I love you too," I said, and he dragged me a little farther and a little faster so that I almost crashed into him, and then at the very last second, executed a sneaky kiss.

"You are brave to do that with my father so close." I grinned.

"Perhaps I am brave," he said. "Or perhaps love has made me stupid." At that, he cast a slightly anxious glance toward the house just to make sure my father hadn't seen us, and when I burst out laughing, he kissed me again.

"Enough fun and games," he said. "Let's get this over and done with."

Soon enough we were finished, and it was *finally* time to go inside to escape the awful weather. I moved to make a beeline for the house, but Tomasz caught my elbow and he said lightly, "Let's go up to the hill."

"What!" I gasped as my teeth chattered. He smiled anyway, and I laughed at him. "Tomasz! Maybe I'm a little spoiled, but *you* are definitely crazy."

"Alina, *moje wszystko*," he said—and that got me—it *always* got me, because his pet name for me meant "my everything," and every time he said it I'd go weak at the knees. His gaze grew very serious and he said, "This is our last evening together for a while, and I want a moment with you before we sit with your parents. Please?"

The hill was a wooded peak, the very end of a long, thin thatch of thick forest left untouched simply because the ground was so rocky and the pinnacle so steep it served no useful farming purpose. That hill sheltered my house and the lands of our farm, and provided a barrier between our quiet existence and town life in Trzebinia. From the top of our hill to the building that housed both Tomasz's family and his father's medical practice was a brisk fifteen-minute walk, or at times when he wasn't supposed to be there with me in the first place, an eight-minute sprint.

For as long as I could remember, the hill had always been *our* spot—somewhere we could enjoy both the view and in more recent years, each other. It was a place where we had privacy if we hid in the pockets of clearing between the trees. If we sat near the long, flat boulder at the very top, we had the visibility to catch any family members who might come for us, particularly Tomasz's younger sister, Emilia, who seemed to have an instinct to come looking for us whenever our passion for each other might burn out of control.

We climbed the incline that evening until we reached the peak, and by then, what scant daylight we'd had was gone and the dull lights of the houses in Trzebinia were twinkling below us. As we took our positions on the boulder, Tomasz wrapped his arms around me and pulled me hard against his chest. He was shaking too, and at first, I thought that was because of the cold.

"This is ridiculous," I laughed softly, turning my head toward him. "We're going to catch our death, Tomasz!"

His arms tightened around me, just a little, and then he drew in a deep breath.

"Alina," he said, "your father has given us permission and his blessing for a wedding, but we need to wait a few years...and by then I'll be earning some money to provide for you anyway. We will have time to think of the details later...just know that whatever places you can dream of, I'll find a way to take you there, Alina Dziak. We can have a good life." His voice became rough, and he cleared his throat before he whispered, "I will *give* you a good life."

I was surprised and delighted by the proposal, but also momentarily insecure, so I pulled away from him a little and asked carefully, "But how do you know you'll still want to be with me once you see what life is like in the big city?"

He shifted then, adjusting my position so that we could face each other, and he cupped my face in his hands.

"All I know and all I need to know is that whenever we are apart, I always miss you, and I know you feel the same. *That* is never going to change—it doesn't matter what college brings. You and I were made for each other—so whether you come to be with me or I come home to be with you—we will always find our way back to one another. This is just a little pause now, but you'll see. Time apart will change nothing."

This was just another amazing story Tomasz was telling—only this time, it was the story of our future, and a promise that we would share one after all. I could see it in my mind as if it had already happened—I knew in that moment that we *would* marry, and we would have babies, and then we would grow old together. I was astounded by the love I felt for Tomasz, and that I could see that same desperate love mirrored in his eyes felt like a miracle.

I was the luckiest girl in Poland—the luckiest girl on Earth, to find such a wonderful man and to have him love me back just as deeply as I loved him. He was clever, and so kind, and so handsome—and Tomasz Slaski had the most amazing eyes. They were a startling shade of green, and they always sparkled just a little, as if he was quietly enjoying a mischievous secret. I pulled him close then and I pressed my face into his neck.

"Tomasz," I whispered, through the happiest of tears. "I was always going to wait for you. Even before you asked me to."

Father took me into the town the next morning to say goodbye to Tomasz before he left for Warsaw. We were engaged now and that was a milestone the adults in our life respected, so for the first time ever, we embraced in front of our fathers. Aleksy carried Tomasz's suitcase, and Tomasz held tightly to his train ticket. Despite the noisy sobs Emilia was making, she looked a picture in one of her pretty floral dresses. I fussed over him on the platform, fiddling with the lapel of his coat and straightening the fall of his thick sandy hair.

"I'll write you," Tomasz promised me. "And I'll come home as much as I can."

"I know," I said. His expression was somber but his eyes were dry, and I was determined to be brave too that day until he was out of sight. He kissed me on the cheek, and then he shook my father's hand. After saying goodbye to his father and sister, Tomasz took his suitcase, and walked onto the carriage. When he hung out the window to wave to us, his gaze was fixed on mine. I forced myself to smile until the train dragged him all the way from my sight. Aleksy gave me a brief hug and said gruffly, "You'll make a fine daughter one day, Alina."

"She'll make a fine *sister*, Father," Emilia protested. She gave one last shuddering sob and sniffed dramatically, then she took my hand and pulled me away from Aleksy's embrace. I didn't have much experience with children—but the soft spot I held for Emilia grew exponentially in that moment as she beamed up at me with those shiny green eyes. I kissed the side of her head, then hugged her tightly.

"Don't worry, little one. I'll be your sister even while we wait."

KELLY RIMMER   27

"I know he didn't want to leave you, Alina, and I know this is hard on you too," Aleksy murmured. "But Tomasz has wanted to be a doctor since before he learned to read, and we had to let him go." He fell silent for a moment, then he cleared his throat and asked, "You'll visit with us while Tomasz is away, won't you?"

"Of course I will," I promised him. There was a lingering sadness in Aleksy's gaze, and he and Tomasz looked so alike—the same green eyes, the same sandy hair, even the same build. Seeing Aleksy sad was like seeing Tomasz sad in the distant future, and I hated the very thought of it—so I gave him another gentle hug.

"You are already my family, Aleksy," I said. He smiled down at me, just as Emilia cleared her throat pointedly. "And you too, little Emilia. I promise I'll visit you both as often as I can until Tomasz comes back to us."

My father was solemn on the walk back to the farm, and in her usual stoic style, my mother was impatient with my moping that evening. When I climbed into bed for an early night, she appeared in the doorway between my room and the living space.

"I am being brave, Mama," I lied, wiping at my eyes to avoid her scolding for my tears. She hesitated, then she stepped into my room and extended her hand toward me. Nestled safe within her calloused palm was her wedding ring, a plain but thick gold band that she'd worn for as long as I remembered.

"When the time is right, we will have a wedding at the church in the township, and Tomasz can put this ring on your finger. We don't have much to offer you for your marriage, but this ring was my mother's, and it has seen Father and I through twenty-nine years of marriage. Good times, bad times—the ring has held us steadfast. I give it to you to bring you fortune for your future—but I want you to hold on to it even now so that while you wait, you will remember the life that's ahead of you."

As soon as she finished her speech, she spun on her heel and pulled my door closed behind her, as if she knew I'd cry some more and she couldn't even bear to see it. After that, I kept the ring buried in my clothes drawer, beneath a pile of woolen socks. Every night before I went to sleep, I'd take that little ring in my hand, and I'd go to my window.

I'd stare out toward the hill that had borne witness to so many quiet moments with Tomasz, and I'd clutch that ring tightly against my chest while I prayed to Mother Mary to keep Tomasz safe until he came home to me.

CHAPTER 3

Alice

As we step into the geriatric ward, Eddie spots Babcia, and he immediately breaks out of my grasp and runs into her room.

"Eddie," he calls as he runs. "Eddie darling, do you want something to eat?"

Echolalia is the bane of my existence sometimes. Babcia is constantly offering Edison—and everyone else—food, and so now, when he sees Babcia, he mimics her. It's harmless when we're alone. When we're in public and he piles on that faux Polish accent, it sounds a lot like he's mocking her. The nurse reviewing Babcia's IV setup frowns at him, and I want to explain to her what's going on, but I'm too stricken by the sight of Babcia herself. She's propped up and her eyes are open. This should feel like an improvement on the semiconscious state she was in last night, except that she's clearly still very weak—she's sunk heavily into the pillows.

"Hello, Edison." I hear my mother sigh as I catch up to Eddie and join him in the room. Eddie looks at Mom, then mutters under his breath, "Stop doing that, Eddie."

Mom remains silent but her disapproval is palpable, as it always is when Eddie's echolalia reminds us all that the phrase he most associates with her is a scolding. Now she turns her gaze to me, and she says, "Alice, you are incredibly late."

I feel justified in ignoring my mother's greeting given it is equal parts social nicety and criticism, which is the exact ratio that comprises almost every communication she undertakes. Julita Slaski-Davis is a lot of things; a lifelong marathon runner, a venerated district court judge, a militant civil libertarian, an avid environmentalist; a seventy-six-year old who has *no* intention of retiring from her work anytime soon. People are forever telling me she's an inspiration, and I can see their point, because she's an impressive woman. The one thing she's *not* is a cuddly, maternal grandma—which is exactly why Eddie and I have a much easier relationship with Babcia.

I take the space next to Eddie at my grandmother's bedside and wrap my hand around hers. The weathered skin of her fingers is cold, so I clasp my other hand around it and try to warm her up a little.

"Babcia," I murmur. "How are you feeling?"

Babcia makes a sound that's closer to a grunt than a word and distress registers in her eyes as she searches my gaze. Mom sighs impatiently.

"If you'd been here earlier, you'd already know that she may be awake now, but I don't think she can hear. These *nurses* don't know anything. I'm waiting for the doctor to tell me what the Hell is going on."

The nurse beside Mom raises her eyebrows, but she doesn't look at Mom or even at me. If she did look at me, I'd offer her an apologetic wince, but the nurse is clearly determined to get her job done and get out of the room as quickly as she can. She presses one last button on the IV regulator, then touches my grandmother's arm to get her attention. Babcia turns to face her.

"Okay, Hanna," the nurse says gently. "I'll leave you with your family now. Just buzz if you need me, okay?"

Eddie pushes me out of the way as soon as the nurse goes, and fumbles to take Babcia's hand. When I let him have it, he immediately settles. I glance back to Babcia, and I see the smile she turns on for him. I always thought my relationship with my grandmother was unique. She all but raised me through different phases of my childhood; my mother's career has *always* come first. But as special as it is, our relationship isn't a patch on the bond she has with Eddie. In a world that doesn't understand my son, he's always had Babcia, who doesn't care if she understands him or not—she simply adores him the way he is.

I survey her carefully now, assessing her, as if I can scan her with my gaze and realize the extent of the damage within her mind.

"Can you hear me, Babcia?" I say, and she turns toward me, but frowns fiercely as she concentrates. Her only response is the swell of tears that rise to her eyes. I glance at Mom, who is standing stiffly, her jaw set hard.

"I think she can hear," I say to Mom, who hesitates, then offers, "Well, then…maybe she doesn't recognize us?"

"Eddie," Eddie says. "Eddie darling, do you want something to eat?"

Babcia turns to him and she smiles a tired but brilliant smile that immediately earns a matching smile from my son. He releases Babcia's hand, throws his iPad up onto the bed beside her legs and starts trying to climb the railings.

"Eddie," Mom says impatiently. "Don't do that. Babcia is not well. Alice, you need to stop him. This is *not* a playground."

But Babcia tries to pull herself into a sitting position and opens her arms wide toward Eddie, and even Mom falls silent at that. I pull the bedrail down, and help shift the various cords out of the way as my very solid son climbs all the way onto the bed beside his very fragile great-grandmother. Babcia shifts over, slowly and carefully, purposefully making room for him *right* beside her. He nestles into her side and closes his eyes, and as she sinks back into the pillow, she rests her cheek against Eddie's blond hair. Then Babcia closes her eyes too, and she breathes him in as if he's a newborn baby.

"She certainly seems to recognize Eddie," I say softly.

Mom sighs impatiently and runs her hand through the stiff tufts of her no-nonsense gray hair. I settle onto the chair beside the bed and reach into my bag for my phone. There's another message from Wade on the screen.

Ally, I really am sorry. Please write back and let me know you're okay.

I know I'm not being fair, but I'm still so disappointed that he wouldn't help me today. I scowl and think about turning the phone off, but at the last second, I relent and reply.

Having a very bad day, but I am okay.

It's a long while later that we're approached by a middle-aged woman in a lab coat, who motions toward us to join her at the nurses' desk. Eddie is holding the dreidel up again in front of his face and doesn't react to me at all as I turn from the bed, so I leave him be.

"I'm Doctor Chang, Hanna's physician. I wanted to update you on her condition."

Babcia is stable today, but given the location of the stroke, her doctors think there's damage to the language centers in her brain. She can certainly hear, but she's not reactive to requests or instructions and further testing needs to be done. Behind us, I hear Eddie's iPad as the robotic voice of the AAC app announces, *Dreidel*.

I'm not paying much attention to Eddie, only enough that I'm vaguely surprised he managed to figure out what his new treasure is called. His visual language app lists thousands of images he can use to identify concepts he might need to communicate, but *dreidel* is hardly going to be in the "most commonly used" section of the menu. I enjoy a moment or two of Mommy-pride in among the panic of the seemingly endless bad news from

Doctor Chang. *Could be permanent, more testing required, scans, this situation is not entirely unheard of, unfortunately high chance of further events. End of life plans?*

I like dreidel, Eddie's iPad says. *Your turn.*

I wince and turn back to glance at the bed, where Eddie has turned the iPad toward my grandmother. He's sitting up now, his back against the bedrail. I don't know what I expect to see, but I'm surprised when Babcia lifts her hand slowly and hits the screen.

I...like...

I interrupt the doctor by grabbing her forearm, and she startles and steps away from me.

"Sorry," I blurt. "Just...look."

The doctor and Mom turn just in time to see Babcia hit the next button. Mom draws in a sharp breath.

...dreidel...too. Babcia hits each button slowly and with obvious difficulty, but eventually, she expresses herself just fine.

Babcia hurt? Eddie asks now.

Babcia scared, Babcia types.

Eddie scared, Eddie types.

Eddie...is...okay, Babcia slowly pecks out. *Babcia...is...okay.*

Eddie nods, and sinks back onto the bed to rest his head in Babcia's shoulder again.

"Is he autistic?" the doctor asks.

"He's on the autism spectrum, yes," I correct her. The terminology doesn't matter, not really, but it matters to me because my son is more than a label. To say he *is* autistic is not accurate—autism is not who he is, it is a part of who he is. This is semantics to someone who doesn't live with the disorder every day and the doctor looks at me blankly, as if she can't even hear the distinction. I feel heat on my cheeks. "He's nonverbal. He uses the Augmentative and Alternative Communication app to speak. Babcia is already used to communicating that way, although she's normally much faster—"

"That's the problem with her hand," Mom interrupts me,

and she's glaring at the doctor again. "I told you, she's having trouble moving her right side."

"I remember, and we're looking into it," the doctor says, then she pauses a moment and admits, "We don't tend to use technology with elderly patients in this situation—most of them don't have a clue where to start. So as difficult as this is, at least she has the advantage of her familiarity with the concept. I'll talk to a speech pathologist. This is good."

"This isn't *good*," Mom says impatiently. "*Good* isn't my mother having to speak through a damned iPad app, it's frustrating enough that we have to use the rotten thing for Eddie. How long will this last for? How are you going to fix it?"

"Julita, in these—"

"It's *Judge* Slaski-Davis." My mother corrects her, and I sigh a little as I turn back toward the bed. Babcia catches my eye and nods toward the iPad, so I quietly leave the doctor to deal with my nightmare of a mother. Babcia hits the *your turn* button, and I take the iPad from her hands.

Are you hurt? I ask her. She takes the iPad and flicks through the screens until she can find the right images. Then slowly and carefully, she speaks.

Babcia okay. Want help.

She hands me the iPad immediately, obviously keen to see my reply, but I have no idea what to say to her or even how to ask her for more information about what she needs. I look from the iPad screen then back to her face and her blue eyes quickly shift from pleading to impatient. She motions for me to pass her the iPad again and so I do, and then she scrolls through screens and screens. She finds the magnifying glass icon and hits it, and the iPad says *find,* but then she goes back to scrolling. Her gaze narrows. Her lips tighten. Beads of sweat break out on her lined forehead, and more time passes as a flush gradually rises in her cheeks. She hits the *find* button again and again, and then she growls and pushes the iPad toward me.

Her frustration is palpable, but I don't know what to do. Mom and the doctor are still squabbling, and Eddie is still curled up beside Babcia, rolling the dreidel along the sheet now as if it is a toy train. I look at Babcia helplessly, and she raises her hands as if to say *I don't know, either.* For a moment, I swipe through the screens of Eddie's most commonly used icons, pausing each time so she can check to see if what she needs is there. After a minute or so of this, a new thought strikes me. I open the app to the *new icon* page, and as soon as I do, Babcia snatches the device back eagerly. She finds a picture of a young man, then starts to type, slowly and carefully. She's not using her forefinger—she's using the side of her pinkie and her ring finger. It's awkward, and it takes her a few goes to form the word correctly, but then she does, and she clicks the save button and shows me proudly.

Tomasz.

"How is she?" Mom asks me from the doorway. I look up to her and find the doctor has gone, possibly to find a stiff drink.

"It's slow, but she's using the device. She's just asked me for—"

It occurs to me what Babcia *is actually* asking, and my heart sinks.

"Oh no, Babcia," I whisper, but the words are pointless— if the stroke has damaged her receptive language, then she's in much the same boat as Eddie; spoken words have no meaning for her right now. I meet her gaze again, and tears glimmer in her eyes. I look from her to the iPad, but I have absolutely no idea how to tell her that her husband died just over twelve months ago. Pa was a brilliant pediatric surgeon until his seventies, then he taught at the University of Florida until his eighties—but as soon as he retired, dementia took hold and after a long, miserable decline, he died last year. "Babcia...he's...he...um..."

She shakes her head fiercely and she hits the buttons again.

Find Tomasz.

More scrolling, then:

Need help.

Emergency.

Find Tomasz.

Then, while I'm still struggling to figure out how to deal with this, she selects another series of icons and the device reads a nonsensical message to me:

Babcia fire Tomasz.

Her hands are shaking. Her face is set in a fierce frown, but there's determination in her gaze. I put my hand gently on her forearm and when she looks up at me, I shake my head slowly, but her eyes register only confusion and frustration.

I'm confused and frustrated too—and I'm suddenly angry, because it is brutally unfair to see this proud woman so confused. "Babcia..." I whisper, and she sighs impatiently and shakes my hand off her arm. My grandmother has an unlimited depth of empathy and she loves relentlessly—but she's the toughest woman I know, and she seems completely undeterred by my inability to communicate with her. She goes back to scrolling through the pages of icons on the screen of the iPad, until I see her expression brighten. Again and again, she repeats this process, painstakingly forming a sentence. Over the next few minutes, Mom goes to find a coffee, and I watch as Babcia tries to wrangle this clumsy communication method into submission. It's easier for her now that all of the icons are on the "recently used" page, and soon she's just hitting the same buttons over and over again now.

Need help. Find...box...go home. Want home.

I swallow my sigh, take the iPad and tell her *Babcia in hospital now. Then go home later.*

This is the language pattern I have to use with my son, and it's one that's automatic for me—*now* this, *then* something else—explaining sequences of events and time to him because he has *no* concept of it without the guidelines of instructions and schedules. Communicating via the AAC is so damned restrictive. With Eddie, I'm used to the limitations because it's all we've ever had—and it is *vastly* better than nothing. Until he learned to read and use the AAC, our whole life was a series of meltdowns inspired by his overwhelming frustration at being locked inside himself, unable to communicate.

The problem now is that with Babcia, I'm used to the endless freedom of spoken communication, and having to revert to this AAC app suddenly does seem an impossibly poor substitute.

Babcia snatches the iPad back and resumes her demands.

Need help.

Find Tomasz.

Home.

Box.

Now.

Help.

Box.

Camera.

Paper.

Babcia fire Tomasz.

Mom steps all the way into the room. She hands me a coffee, then returns to stand at the foot of the bed.

"What's this about?" she asks me.

"I don't know," I admit. Babcia gives us both an impatient glare now and repeats the commands, and when we still don't react, she turns the sound *all the way up* and hits the repeat button again. This is a trick she's learned from my son, who does the exact same thing when he's not getting his own way.

Help.

Find Tomasz.

Box.

Camera. Paper. Box.

Now. Now. Emergency. Now.

Find Tomasz. Now.

Babcia fire Tomasz.

"Christ. She's really forgotten Pa passed," Mom whispers,

and I glance at her. Mom is not known for vulnerability, but right now her expression is pinched and I think I see tears in her eyes. I shake my head slowly. Babcia seems quite determined that she doesn't need me to remind her that Pa has passed, so I just don't think that's it.

Find Tomasz.

Find box.

Box. Find. Now. Need help.

"Oh!" Mom gasps suddenly. "She has that box of mementos. I haven't seen it in years—not since we moved them into the retirement home after Pa got sick. It's either in storage or at her unit there. Maybe that's what she wants, maybe she wants a *photo* of Pa? That makes sense, doesn't it?"

"Ah, yes," I say. A wave of relief relaxes muscles I didn't even know I'd tensed. "Good thinking, Mom."

"I can go try to find it if you'll stay with her?"

"Please, yes," I say, and I take the iPad. I hit the photograph of Mom, and the iPad reads *Nanna,* so I wince and start to edit the label on the photo—but Babcia waves my hand away impatiently. Our gazes lock, and she gives me a wry smile, as if she's telling me *I'm broken, kiddo, but not stupid.* I'm so relieved by that smile that I bend to kiss her forehead, and then I hit some more buttons.

Nanna find box now.

Babcia sighs with happiness and hits the *yes* button, then rests her hand on my forearm and squeezes. She can't speak at the moment, but she's been a guiding light for my entire life, so I hear her voice in my head anyway.

Good girl, Alice. Thank you.

CHAPTER 4

Alina

Information was not so easy to come by in those days, so what I knew of the lead-up to war was scattered at best, but Trzebinia was quite close to the German border, and my town was not immune to the ideology that was gaining traction within that nearby nation. Hatred was like some otherworldly beast, seeded in small acts of violence and oppression against our Jewish citizens, growing in strength as the power-hungry fed it with rhetoric and propaganda.

It's only when I look back now with the wisdom of age that I can see that warning signs were scattered throughout our simple life even then. I remember the first few times I heard that Jewish friends in Trzebinia had been robbed or assaulted or had their properties vandalized. My parents were appalled by this turn of events, and by then, my father had well and truly indoctrinated us children with his opinions on relationships between Trzebinia's Jewish and Catholic communities. *A Polish man is a Polish man*, he'd often say to us, because to my father, a man's heritage and religion were irrelevant—Father was interested only in character and work ethic. But this was not a perspective that our whole community shared, and those ugly strains of anti-Semitism enraged my otherwise mild-mannered father.

In the summer of 1939, Father and I took a trip into the town. Mama had baked an extra loaf of poppy seed bread, and I'd arranged it in a basket with some eggs for Aleksy and Emilia. This had become a regular part of my routine—I visited them for lunch once a week, and in return, Mama was always telling me to take them some food. This felt an odd arrangement to me, given Aleksy was wealthy and we were poor, but my mama was a traditionalist and she had always seemed completely bewildered that a *man* could manage to arrange food for himself and his daughter.

That day, Father and I rode the cart into town to the supplies store. He went inside to conduct his business, and I walked the three blocks to the medical clinic to deliver the basket of goods to Aleksy's secretary. I knew Father would be a while, so I meandered my way back to the store.

As I walked, I daydreamed about Tomasz. In the year he'd been in Warsaw, we'd fallen into a solid routine of taking turns writing letters, and he'd been home for two delicious weeks during his midyear break. That particular day, it was my turn to write a letter, and I was thinking about what I might say, so lost in thought that I was startled when I finally approached the store and heard my father shouting inside. I peered through the doors somewhat anxiously and discovered he was in a heated discussion with Jan Golaszewski, our neighbor to the northeast, the father of Filipe's girlfriend, Justyna. Just then, Justyna rushed out of the store. She gave me a wide-eyed look, then embraced me.

"What's *this* about?" I asked her, but the words escaped as a sigh because I already suspected the answer.

"Oh, my father is blaming the Jews for everything, and your father is defending them." Justyna's weary sigh matched my own, then she shrugged. "Same old argument they always have, just more heated today because of the buildup."

"The buildup?" I repeated, confused. Justyna assessed me with her gaze, then she grabbed my elbow and pulled me close.

"The buildup at the border," she whispered, as if we were

sharing a scandalous piece of gossip. "Surely you know? It's why everyone is stocking up."

"I don't know what you're talking about," I admitted, and in hurried whispers before my father returned, Justyna told me: Hitler's army was coming for us; an invasion now seemed inevitable.

"I can't believe your parents haven't warned you," she whispered.

"They treat me like I am a baby," I groaned, shaking my head. "They think they need to protect their fragile little flower from things that might upset me."

I knew enough about the situation with the Nazi regime that I was nervous, but I was also quite confused by this news from Justyna. Coming for *us*? What could they possibly want from us? Justyna suggested an answer before I even asked the question.

"My father says it's the Jews. He says that if we didn't have so many Jews in this country, Hitler would leave us alone. You know how he is, Alina. Father blames the Jews for *everything*. And you know how your father is…"

"A Polish man is a Polish man," I whispered numbly, repeating the words automatically before I refocused on my friend. "But Justyna, are you sure? Are we really about to go to war?"

"Oh, don't worry," Justyna told me, flashing me a confident smile. "Everyone is saying that the Nazis have barely any ammunition and the Polish army will defeat them quickly. Father is quite certain it will all be over within a few weeks."

From there though, I saw everything differently—for the first time, I understood the recently frenetic activity of my parents and brothers, and I finally understood their bewildering insistence on preserving perfectly good food before it was even necessary to do so. Even as my father drove the cart back toward our house, I realized the unusually busy roads were not a sign of townsfolk making the most of the warm weather—rather, people were shifting. Everyone was operating in a different mode—everyone was rushing somewhere. Some were heading into Warsaw or to Krakow, as if a larger city would provide them shelter. Some were preparing their homes for relatives who were coming from Warsaw or Krakow, because plenty of city folk had decided the country would offer a refuge. No one seemed to know *what* to do, but it was not in our national nature to stay still and await catastrophe, so instead—people kept active. Through enlightened eyes, it seemed to me that the people of my town were scurrying like ants before a storm.

"Is it true? About an invasion?"

"You don't need to worry about that," Father said gruffly. "When you need to worry, Mama and I will let you know."

I sat down that evening and I wrote a very different letter to Tomasz than the one I'd been planning. In the entire page of text, I simply pleaded with him to come home.

> Don't try to be brave, Tomasz. Don't wait for danger. Just come home and be safe.

I'm not really sure now why I ever thought that "home" would be a safe place for any of us given our proximity to the border, but in any case, Tomasz did not come home. In fact, things disintegrated so rapidly that if he sent me a reply to that letter, it never arrived. It felt like the life I'd known disappeared overnight.

On September 1, 1939, I was roused from the depths of sleep by the sound of my bedroom window rattling in its frame. I didn't recognize the sound of approaching planes at first. I didn't even realize we were in danger until I heard my father shouting from the room beside me.

"Wake up! We must get to the barn," Father shouted, his voice thick with sleep.

"What is happening?" I called, as I threw my covers back and slipped from my bed. I had just opened my bedroom door when the first of many explosions sounded in the distance, and the windows rattled again, this time violently. It was dark in our tiny home, but when Mama threw the front door open, moonlight flooded in and I saw my brothers running toward her. I knew I needed to run but my feet wouldn't move—perhaps I was still half-asleep, or perhaps it was because the moment felt so much like a terrible nightmare that I couldn't convince my body to *act*. Filipe got as far as the front door when he noticed me, and he crossed the small living room to take my hand.

"What is happening?" I asked, as he dragged me toward the barn.

"The Nazis are dropping bombs from planes," Filipe told me grimly. "We are ready and we have a plan, Alina. Just do as Father says and we will be fine."

He pushed me into the barn after Stanislaw, Father and Mama, and as soon as we were inside, Father pulled the heavy door closed behind us. Blood thundered around my body at the sudden darkness—but then I heard the creak of hinges as the latch in the floor was opened.

"Not the cellar," I protested. "Please, Mama…"

Filipe's arm descended on my shoulders and he pushed me toward the opening, then Mama grabbed my wrist and tugged me downward. Her fingers bit into the skin of my arm, and I pulled away frantically, trying to step back.

"No," I protested. "Mama, Filipe, you know I can't go down there—"

"Alina," Filipe said urgently. "What is scarier? The darkness or a bomb falling on your head?"

I let them drag me down into the suffocating blackness. As I sank into the cramped space, the sound of my heartbeat seemed unnaturally loud. I scrambled across the dirt floor to find a corner, and then I wrapped my arms around my knees. When the next round of echoing *booms* began to sound, I shrieked involuntarily with each one. Soon enough, I was in a fetal position against the dirt floor, my hands over my ears. A particularly loud explosion rocked the whole cellar, and as dust rained down on us, I found myself sobbing in fear.

"Was that our house?" I choked, in a moment of silence.

"No," Father said, his tone gently scolding. "We will know it if the house goes. It is Trzebinia, they are probably taking out the rail line...maybe the industrial buildings. There is no reason for them to destroy our homes. We are likely safe, but we will hide in here until it stops, just to be sure."

Filipe and Stanislaw shifted to sit on either side of me, and then the cellar was again filled with a stifling silence as we all waited for the next explosion. Instead, we were surprised by a more welcome sound.

"Hello?" a distant, muffled voice called. "Mama? Father?"

Mama cried out in delight and opened the hatch, then climbed up to help my sister, Truda, and her husband, Mateusz, into the cellar. To my immense relief, Father turned an oil lamp on to help them see their way. Once we were all safely inside the cellar again, Mama and Truda embraced.

"What do we do now?" I asked breathlessly. Everyone turned to look at me.

"We wait," Mama murmured. "And we pray."

We spent much of that first day huddled together, hidden in the cellar beneath the barn. The planes came and went and came back again. Later, we would learn that several hundred bombs were dropped across our region during those long hours we spent hiding. The bombing was sporadic, unpredictable and fierce. From my position in the cellar, the explosions near and far and all around us sounded like the end of the world was happening just outside of our barn.

Most people have no idea what prolonged terror really feels like. I certainly didn't until that day. In that terrifying darkness, I sweated through hours and hours and hours of being certain that *any second*, a bomb would fall on us—that *any second*, the cellar would cave in—that *any second*, a man with a gun would appear in the doorway to take away my life. I had not been comfortable with confined spaces even at the best of times, but that day I felt a depth of fear that I'd never even realized was possible. I lived my death that day, over and over and over again in my mind. Extreme anxiety like that doesn't obey the normal laws of emotion; it doesn't get tired, it doesn't fade, you never grow used to it. I was every bit as petrified eight hours into those air strikes as I was when they began, until I was entirely convinced that the only end for the fear would be the end of life itself.

There was an extended break in the bombing early in the afternoon. We didn't dare breathe a sigh of relief at first, because there had been breaks earlier in the day but they hadn't lasted long. This time, long minutes went past, and after a while, even the sound of plane engines faded away to blessed silence.

Filipe was desperate to run next door to check on Justyna and her family. It was only a few hundred feet—he assured us he'd hide in the tree line along the woods and he'd be back in less than half an hour. Mama and Father grumbled, but eventually allowed him to go, and predictably, as soon as permission had been granted, Stanislaw decided he was going too.

The rest of us climbed into the doorway of the barn for some fresh air, and with the skies still clear, we remained there until the twins returned. Father and Mateusz sat in the doorway; Mama, Truda and I sat in a line behind them. Truda and Mama talked quietly as we waited, but I sat silent, my mouth too dry for small talk.

As promised, my brothers were gone for less than half an hour, but they returned visibly shaken, and at first I thought they'd discovered the worst. They joined us in the barn, sitting against the doorposts on either side of Father and Mateusz. There was some good news—the Golaszewski family were fine, and like us were physically unscathed. But Jan had made a trip into

Trzebinia during the last brief bombing break. He had seen locals walking the streets weeping the loss of their families, children with injuries so bad Filipe couldn't bear to repeat the details, and dozens of homes alight.

During my hours in the cellar, I had been so consumed with anxiety that my own safety had monopolized my thoughts, but as my brother relayed Jan's findings, another fear broke through. I was rapidly processing the implications of what a severely damaged Trzebinia could mean and the risk to Aleksy and Emilia. The medical clinic was just off the town square—right where the homes were densest. And if they were dead—that would mean that one day soon, Tomasz would return and there'd be *no* family waiting for him. Suddenly, all roads led to the impact of this potential development on Tomasz.

"Aleksy," I croaked. Everyone shifted to stare at me, and I saw the sadness in their eyes. "Aleksy and Emilia have to be okay. They *have* to be."

"If Aleksy is okay, he will be tending to the injured…" Mama murmured. I could imagine that—Aleksy hiding during the bombing, then emerging to help the wounded, but if that was true, who was comforting and protecting Emilia? I had been riding out the bombing raids surrounded by my whole family—and it was still the most terrifying experience of my life. She was seven years old, and with Tomasz away, she only had her father, so if he was busy or even injured himself…

"We have to get Emilia!" I blurted, and Filipe sighed impatiently.

"*How?* Who knows when the planes will return?"

"But if Aleksy is busy helping people, who will be with her? She might be alone! Please, Father. Please, Mama, we have to do something!"

"There is nothing we can do, Alina," Father said softly. "I am sorry. What will be will be."

"We will pray," Mama announced. "It is all we can do."

"No," I said, and I shook my head fiercely. "You must go get her, Father. You *must*. She is a baby—all alone in the world. She is my family too! *Please*."

"Alina!" Truda groaned. "You are asking for the impossible. It's not safe for anyone to go into the town."

I couldn't let the matter drop, not even when my parents' pleas for silence became sharp demands for me to drop the matter. When I started to cry and threatened to make the journey myself, Filipe pulled himself up from the dirt and dusted his trousers off. Mama groaned.

"Don't be foolish, Filipe! You have tempted fate once already—"

"Alina is right, Mama. Aren't we worse than the Nazis if we leave that little girl to fend for herself while her father works to save lives?"

"If she's even *alive*, Filipe. You may get to the town and find they are already gone," Father said under his breath.

"Father! Don't *say* such a thing!" I gasped.

"I'll go too," Stani sighed.

"I think I should go, too," Mateusz said quietly. It was Truda's turn for an outraged gasp, until he added gently, "I will check on our home while we are on our way to the clinic. The boys and I will move fast and we'll be careful. We can come straight back if we hear the planes returning—you know yourself it only took us ten minutes to get here yesterday."

Mama cursed furiously and threw her hands in the air.

"You are trying to kill me, boys! You have tempted fate once already and survived. Now you are just trying to make my heart stop beating from the fear!"

"Mama, we are just doing what you raised us to do," Filipe said stiffly. "We are *trying* to do the right thing."

"But what if the bombing starts again—"

"Faustina," Mateusz said more firmly now. "You have heard the explosions, just as I have. They are coming from every direction, even to the west where there is nothing but farmhouses—the planes are *not* just targeting the town. We are no safer here than we will be in the town."

There was no arguing with that, and they left soon after—although my father instructed them to run up to the hill and to hide in the woods for a few minutes to be sure there were no more planes on the horizon before they exposed themselves in the clearing on the other side. As soon as the younger men had left, my sister and my parents fixed accusing gazes on me, and I felt myself flushing.

It suddenly, belatedly occurred to me that I had convinced my own brothers and my brother-in-law to risk their lives, all in the hope that I could save *Tomasz* from grief. But I loved Emilia and Aleksy, and I was genuinely afraid for their safety. I didn't regret convincing my brothers to go check on them—I was just deathly afraid that I'd just manipulated my way into an unimaginable loss. I tried to explain myself to my remaining family members.

"I just..."

"It is better that you do not speak until they return," Truda interrupted me flatly. "You sit there, Alina Dziak, and you focus your energies on praying that you have not just killed our brothers and my husband."

That's exactly what I did. The first time my brothers left the cellar, the minutes dragged by, but this was a whole new level of torture. In the end, the silence was punctuated by a different sound—the sound of a child wailing. We all ran out of the barn and found the twins walking side by side down from the hill, Mateusz following closely behind with Emilia high in his arms. She was sobbing, loudly and inconsolably.

"Oh, *babisu!*" my sister cried, and she ran from the barn to her husband's side. He gently passed Emilia to Truda's waiting arms, and Truda immediately began to console the little girl. "Shhh, it is okay, little one. You will be okay now." Once they were within the coverage of the barn, my mother walked to Truda's side and ran a gentle hand down Emilia's cheek, then she raised her gaze to mine. Mama was clearly very sad, but also thoughtful as she stared at me.

I was quickly distracted from Mama's gaze by Emilia's continuing sobs. I turned my attention to my brothers and Filipe shook his head hastily.

"Aleksy is fine. The clinic is fine too, other than some broken windows."

"But there are injured people in Aleksy's home...and worse... a line of people waiting for help all along the street." Mateusz approached me and spoke very carefully, his voice low and soft. "Emilia saw one of her school friends hurt...she ran off and hid in a cupboard. Aleksy said the wounded have been coming to the house since the bombing started and he didn't have time to comfort her. He was very grateful—he asked if we could keep her until things are safer. It might be some days."

"Of course we can," Mama murmured quietly. She took Emilia from Truda and held her for a moment, then passed the little girl to me. Truda and Mateusz embraced, and my mother began to kiss my brothers all over their faces. "You are too brave for your own good."

Emilia wrapped her arms around my neck. She pressed her tearstained face against my shoulder. Her entire body was shaking and she was breathing noisily between her sobs.

"Alina, the noise was so loud...there was a bomb on Mr. Erikson's shop and our house rattled and the glass all broke..."

"I know..."

"And Maja from school was asleep and her mother was shouting and Father couldn't wake her up and I don't understand why there was so much blood on her face. *Why* was there so much blood?"

"Hush now," Mama murmured. Truda approached me, her concerned gaze fixed on Emilia. She slid her arm around my shoulders and gently pulled me to the ground, curling up beside me. I settled Emilia across our laps, and as I stroked Emilia's back, Truda began to sing. Mama sat opposite us, watching closely.

"Just rest, little one," Mama said softly. "You are safe now."

"But what about Tomasz?" she croaked, her little voice weak and uneven still. "He is all alone in Warsaw. What will happen to my brother?"

No one said anything, and I tensed, then rushed to comfort her. Or maybe I was trying to comfort myself.

"Warsaw is *so* far away," I said firmly. "Planes probably can't even fly that far. It is better that he isn't here, Emilia. He will surely be safer there."

Over the days that followed, we took turns crowding around Father's wireless to listen to the news updates. His set was a crystal unit the twins had constructed a few years earlier, and that meant only one person at a time could listen on the tinny headsets. I jostled for my turn like everyone else, but I always regretted those moments I spent at the wireless, because the news was never comforting. Entire cities were being destroyed, but the small stories hurt the most. We heard endless tales of farmers shot in their fields from machine guns on planes and even one horrific story about a grandfather who was harvesting the last of his vegetables when a pilot dropped a bomb right on him. That story spoke volumes to me about the might of the invaders and the way our country was outgunned—we were simply peasants standing in dirt, totally defenseless against massive explosives dropped from airborne war machines by unfathomably hate-filled pilots.

There were Nazi troops in our district within days of the bombing because the local army defenses were quickly overcome. After that, the bombing stopped but there were still more planes, only now they flew over us, but they didn't fly back, and somehow, that was even worse. Soon, the trucks started coming, rumbling through the town, not yet stopping but promising just by their presence that one day soon, everything left intact after the bombing was going to be broken anyway. The men from my family made another trip into town, and again returned sullen.

"There are notices hung everywhere," Father murmured.

"There is a town meeting tomorrow at noon, and we all must attend." Mateusz flicked his gaze to Truda. "We must go home tonight, my love. Perhaps if we are at the house, we can protect it."

"Protect it from the Nazis?" she asked, somewhat incredulously. "With what? Our bare hands?"

"An empty house in the town is vulnerable, Truda," he said. "Besides, the Nazis have breached the national *border*. Do you think that little hill is going to contain them? Now that the bombing has stopped, we are no safer here than we will be there."

"Did you see my father?" Emilia asked. Her voice was very small. She seemed to be shrinking by the hour, despite close attention from my sister, my mother and myself. Mateusz and Father both shook their heads.

"Your father is still very busy helping people, but he is fine," Mama said abruptly. "Alina, entertain the child. Let the adults talk."

We retreated into my bedroom and sat on my sofa, and I tried to play one of the counting games Emilia was so fond of, while simultaneously straining to eavesdrop on the conversation in the main part of the house.

"Everything is going to be okay, isn't it, Alina?" Emilia asked me suddenly. She looked terrified, her huge green eyes wide within the frame of her pale face.

I forced myself to smile.

"Of course, little sister. Everything is going to be just fine."

After a sleepless night, we made our way into the town square on foot. We walked along the road instead of up through the woods and over the hill—the road meant a longer journey, but it seemed that none of us were in a hurry to get to our destination.

By the time we arrived, a crowd was already assembled at the square, waiting in a stiff, eerie silence. As we joined the group, I wedged myself between my parents as if they could shield me from the gravity of it all. Stanislaw left us to stand with Irene, the girl he was courting. Filipe had gone to seek out Justyna. Truda and Mateusz were there too, but to my surprise, had opted to stand with the mayor's wife and her children. I scanned my way around the assembled crowd identifying each of the couples, and I felt dual pangs of jealousy and fear. I so wished that Tomasz was there with me. I was sure everything would feel less bewildering if only my hand was in his. Instead, I held his little sister's hand, and I scanned the crowd for Aleksy. He was tall, like Tomasz, so I was sure I'd find him sooner or later, and then I could point him out to comfort Emilia.

I felt disconnected from it all—at a place I knew so well on a sunny day that should have been beautiful, only nothing *seemed* beautiful—nothing even seemed familiar anymore. There were strangers among us, and they were somehow now in charge; and that very fact entirely warped the landscape that I had known as my home. Those men looked like statues in their stiff, impeccably pressed uniforms, with the impossible splash of red around the armband, the swastika they wore with pride. It occurred to me that the Nazi uniform removed their humanity somehow, drained them of their uniqueness—and left them a unified force of solidarity, like a solid wall encroaching upon our space. These were not even men—they were individual components of a machine that had come to destroy.

The commander shouted around the square at us, entirely in German. At first, I listened only to the tone of his voice—the disdain, the aggression, the authority—but each word tightened the viselike grip of fear in my heart. I just couldn't stand not knowing what he was saying, or even understanding why he didn't even have the simple *courtesy* to speak to us in our native language. After a while, I turned toward Mama and I whispered, "What is he saying?"

My mother's response was only an impatient command to hush, but soon enough, I saw her eyes widen, and for the first time I saw fear cross her face. I followed her gaze to the corner of the square, where still more soldiers pushed two "prisoners" forward into the center of us all, their hands tied behind their backs. I scanned their faces and felt a punch of shock as I recognized them—our mayor was at the back, but right at the front, staring out into the crowd without fear or hesitation, was Aleksy.

Looking back now, I suspect a brilliant man like Aleksy might have understood what his fate was, but he walked into the town square with his head held high. After scanning the crowd, his gaze landed on Emilia, and he smiled at her as if to reassure her. I tugged her to stand in front of me and wrapped my arms around her from behind. She was stiff within my arms, surely as confused as I was. *Why is Aleksy in trouble? He's never done a wrong thing in his entire life.* Aleksy lifted his smile to me, and when our eyes met, he nodded once. He seemed calm, almost serene. That's why I thought for a moment or two that everything would be okay, because Aleksy was the wisest man in the town, so if he wasn't worried, why should I be?

But then the commander grabbed Aleksy's upper arm and he pushed him hard and to the ground—and Aleksy's arms were tied behind his back, so his face slammed unguarded into the granite cobblestone that lined the square. Before he could even recover, another soldier slid his hand into Aleksy's hair and pulled him up until he was on his knees. Aleksy could not contain a cry of pain at that, and it was all I could do not to shout out in protest too.

Mama grabbed my upper arm, and when I turned to her, her gaze was locked on Emilia.

"Cover her eyes," she said flatly.

"But why are they—" I said, even as my hands rose toward Emilia's face. I heard the *click* of the handgun being cocked, and I looked up.

Aleksy's death was somehow too *simple* and quick to be real, one single shot to the back of his head, and then he was gone. I wanted to protest—surely a life so big couldn't end like *that*, without dignity or purpose or honor? But the soldiers tossed his body to the side as if it was nothing much at all, then they shot the mayor in the same way. I felt dizzy with the shock of it all, it was just too much to process on the fly. My own eyes had to be lying to me because what I was seeing was entirely illogical.

Aleksy Slaski was a good man, but the very things that made him so central to our township—his intelligence, his training, his natural ability to lead—also made him an immediate target. To destabilize a group of people is not at all difficult, not if you are willing to be cruel enough. You simply knock out the foundations, and a natural consequence is that the rest begins to tumble. The Nazis knew this—and that's why one of their very first tactics in Poland was to execute or imprison those likely to lead in any uprising against them. Aleksy and our mayor were among the first of almost one hundred thousand Polish leaders and academics who would be executed under the *Intelligenzaktion* program during the early days of the invasion.

The shock wore off too soon for Emilia and she began shrieking at the top of her lungs. A soldier near to us turned his gun toward her, and I did the bravest and stupidest thing I'd ever done in my life, at least to that point. I pushed in front of her, and I begged the guard, "Please sir, please. My sister is distressed. Please, I will comfort her."

And I immediately turned—not even waiting for his response. I tensed, expecting the searing pain of a bullet in my own back, but even as I did so—I locked eyes with Emilia and I pressed the palm of my hand *hard* over her mouth. Her eyes were wild with shock and grief, but I pressed so hard that she was struggling to breathe through her now-blocked nose. The tears poured down her little face, and when I realized I was *not* about to be shot myself and she was finally quiet, I bent low and I whispered to her, "Can you be silent, little sister? It is so very important."

Her little green eyes were still glazed over. She nodded, a barely perceptible movement that I noticed, but didn't entirely trust. Still, I loosened the seal of my hand over her mouth and she sucked in air but she didn't shriek. The crowd began to disperse, but Emilia was catatonic—her eyes fixed on her father's body, crumpled alone against the stone on the other side of the square. I slid my arm around her shoulders and I forced her to turn to my parents.

"We cannot take her, not permanently," my mother whispered to me fiercely. "We are too old and too poor and you are too young and on your own. The occupation will be hard and we just don't know how..." Her voice broke, and Mama's gaze flicked to Emilia's face, and then she looked back at me, for a moment visibly stricken. But she raised her chin, and she hardened her gaze as she said, "I am sorry, Alina. But you simply *must* find someone else."

"I know," I said heavily.

"Then come straight home. This is no time to be wandering the town alone, do you hear me?"

Frankly, I couldn't *believe* they would leave me alone in the town at all after what we'd just seen, so I gave a shocked protest. "But Mama, surely you or Father will stay and help—"

"We have work that needs doing at home. It *cannot* wait," she said. I didn't dare protest further, because she was clearly determined. I looked around for my brothers, but both had already left with their girlfriends—and then Mama walked off too, dragging a visibly reluctant Father behind her.

I stared into the dispersing crowd as I learned for the first time the way it felt to force someone else's welfare to a higher priority than your own instinct for safety. I wanted to crumble and sob, or better still, run after my parents like the frightened child they knew me to be. Instead, I wrapped my arm around Emilia's shoulders, and together, we started to walk.

"Alina," Emilia said thickly, when we were some distance from the square.

"Yes, little sister?"

"My father," she said, then her teeth started to chatter. "My father is gone. The man put the gun on his head and—"

"He is gone, but you, my darling girl, you are still here," I interrupted her. "But you mustn't be afraid, Emilia. Because I am going to find a way to keep you safe until Tomasz returns."

CHAPTER 5

Alina

As Emilia and I walked from the square, I realized with a heavy heart that if Mama wasn't willing to take the little girl on, there was only one other option. There were other families in the town who might accommodate her—but none I trusted enough to care for her the way she deserved.

Truda was much like Mama—kind if somewhat abrupt at times—but Mateusz was gentler, quite jolly and jovial, and he had inherited a textiles factory from his father, so he provided my sister a very comfortable life in the town. They lived in a large house on the best street in town and even had electric lights in their home, something I was very jealous of because we still managed with oil lamps at home. I knew Truda and Mateusz wanted to have children, but even after years of marriage, she was yet to fall pregnant.

They had the resources and space to provide Emilia with a ready-made family, but I was nervous to ask it of them. Truda was eight years older than me, and we were hardly close.

There was just no alternative no matter how hard I racked my brain, so I walked the handful of blocks from the square to Truda's house with a weeping Emilia in tow. We turned into her beautiful street—a narrow cobblestoned laneway lined with mature sweet chestnut trees. This neighborhood was flush with two-story homes, and flower patches were in bloom all along the sidewalk. Many of the homes in her street had cars—still a novelty to me then—and it had been the very first street in the town to get electricity. Perhaps, with such big homes and such a small roadway, that street might have felt cramped, except that the narrow street spilled into a huge parkland at the end. The park was a paradise of soft green grass and still more chestnut trees, a space centered by an immense square pond where ducks swam and children played in the summer.

I thought my sister would come quickly from the town square, but time began to pass and I started to worry that she'd returned to my parents' home after all. Emilia and I sat on the steps at Truda's house and watched as a crowd began to file into a house across the road. That's when I realized why Truda and Mateusz were standing with the mayor's wife at the square—they were neighbors. My sister would surely be there at that house—comforting the grieving widow and her large brood of children. I wouldn't dare to go there myself—so all I could do was to sit with Emilia and wait. She cried endlessly, and sometimes she shook so hard I had to press her against my chest to hold her still.

"Be brave, Emilia," I said at first, because that's what I imagined my Mama or Truda would have said if they were there, but it felt like such a cruel request. After that, I didn't say anything; instead, I cried with her until the sleeves of my dress were soaked with both of our tears.

When Truda finally came along the sidewalk, she stopped dead in her tracks and surveyed the spectacle before her. I drew in a deep breath and prepared to blurt out the sales pitch I had been planning in my mind, but Truda quickly resumed her path toward the stoop. Her steps were falling faster now and her chin was high, her gaze determined. For a moment, I feared she was going to turn us away, especially when she stepped all the way around us and opened the front door.

"Come on then, little one," she said from the doorway. "Let's get your bed organized."

"You'll take her?" I choked.

"Of course we will take her," Truda said stiffly. "Emilia is our daughter now. Is she not, Mateusz?"

Mateusz simply bent down, scooped Emilia up and cradled her in his arms like she was a baby, just as he'd done when he rescued her from the town two days earlier. She was far too old and too large to be carried in that way, but she nestled into his large frame anyway.

"Do you need me to take you home, Alina?" he asked. "I can, but you'll need to wait until we get Emilia settled. Or you can leave now, and you will be home before dark."

Emilia pressed her face into Mateusz's shoulder now and wrapped her arms around his neck, and suddenly I felt like an intruder in the early moments of this brand-new family I had somehow helped to create. I shook my head and looked once more to my sister.

"Thank you," I whispered, but I was completely overcome with gratitude and relief. A sob broke from my lips and I said it again. "Thank you."

Truda was, typically, embarrassed by my overt display of emotion. She waved my thanks away impatiently, but her eyes greedily soaked in the sight of Emilia in her husband's arms.

"Go home," Truda said quietly. "And be careful, please, Alina. This is the last time I want to see you wandering around the township on your own. It's not safe anymore."

I ran the entire way home, up the path through the woods to the hill and straight back down to the house. By the time I arrived dusk was falling and I was completely exhausted. My brothers were bringing the animals into the barn, and we shared a glance as I came through the gate. Filipe's eyes were red, as if he'd been crying all afternoon.

When I threw open the door to our home, Mama and Father were both standing at the dining room table, their hands looped beneath it as if they had been shifting it. That made no sense at all—our furniture had always been in the exact same place for as long as I could remember. I shook myself, as if I was hallucinating one more nonsensical happening in a day that had been the very worst kind of surreal, but the image didn't fade.

"What are you doing?" I blurted. Mama's gaze narrowed at me.

"None of your business, child. Where did you take her?" Her tone was stiff, but her gaze concerned.

"Truda," I said, and Mama nodded, satisfied, and she stepped away from the table back toward the potbellied stove, where a pot of soup was simmering.

"I should have told you to do that... I was too panicked... I didn't think. Good girl."

"What did the commander say today?" I asked her, and the softness disappeared from her gaze altogether as she flung a scowl back toward me.

"He is not a *commander*," she said flatly. "Don't ever name those animals as if they are human. Don't give them the power or the prestige of honored titles. The pigs are invaders, nothing more."

"What did...what did the *invader* say?" I asked weakly, and Mama avoided my gaze.

"You need soup. You must eat and stay strong. These months will be hard until we find a way to defeat them."

"Mama," I pleaded with her. "I need to know."

"All you need to know is what you saw today, Alina." Father said, his voice stiff. "They did not say much more than a whole lot of posturing and warning us that they will be taking the produce...eventually they plan to take the farms for German settlers. This is nothing your mother and I did not expect. We are a tough people—we will ride this out and hope for the best."

"Take the *farm*?" I gasped.

"Their plans are immense...unpractical. This displacement will not happen overnight, and as long as the farm remains productive, perhaps we will be spared."

"But what will happen to us if they take the farm?" I choked. Mama clucked her tongue and waved toward the table and chairs.

"Enough, Alina. We can't know what's coming, or even when. All we can do is to try our best to keep our heads down."

I didn't want soup. I didn't want the hot tea Mama made me. I *really* didn't want the vodka Father pressed into my hands and eventually forced me to drink. I wanted to feel safe again—but our home had been violated, and Aleksy had died in cold blood *right in front of my eyes* and every time I closed my eyes, I saw it happen all over again.

That night, I lay in my bed and I stared at the window. Scattered clouds hung low above our house, and I watched the slight curve of the moon when it appeared in the gaps between them. I'd taken the vodka so reluctantly, but once the burning in my throat passed, I felt it loosen my limbs and my mind, and I finally stopped shaking and relaxed into my bed. At last, I let my mind turn to Tomasz, and I wondered how he would hear about Aleksy's fate. Did the mail still work? Could I send him a letter? *Should* I send him a letter?

And then, finally, from the fog of shock in my mind the most terrifying thought of all gradually rose and grew louder, until it consumed my thoughts entirely.

Tomasz was in Warsaw, studying at university to become a doctor, just like his father before him.

Aleksy had just been killed *because* he was a doctor.

What if Tomasz was already dead too?

My heart began to race and the trembling started all over again. I sat up and opened my top drawer, then fished around to find the ring at the bottom. I squeezed it tightly in my palm— so tightly that it left a deep impression in my skin—which was exactly what I wanted.

I needed my hopes to mark me and for my dreams to become a part of my body, something tangible that could not be lost or taken.

★ ★ ★

After the generalized brutality of the early days of the occupation, the Nazi attention soon took on a narrower focus.
There was a thriving Jewish community in Trzebinia, and as
weeks turned into months, it was the Jewish folk who bore the
brunt of the violence. There was widespread violence and theft
against the Jews; both by Nazis and then, to my father's horror,
by gangs of opportunistic locals who operated openly in the
daylight—their mission was at least in part to express solidarity
with the occupying forces.

Once we learned that Jan Golaszewski had participated in
such a gang, Father told Filipe and I that we were no longer
allowed to see Justyna. I was too scared to disobey, but Filipe
began sneaking out at night to meet with her in the fields. A
curfew had been set by the Nazi forces and we weren't supposed
to leave the house after dark, so when Filipe refused to stop his
midnight trips to see his love, Father was forced to relent.

"Justyna may visit here during the daylight hours, or you
may meet her at the boundaries between the farms. It is not her
fault that her father is who he is, but I won't allow my children
to step inside that bastard's home."

The situation in Trzebinia continued to deteriorate. Jewish
businesses and then homes were confiscated altogether—then
whole families were forced to shift into a "Jewish area," and sent
to work for the invaders. There were restrictions on travel and
marriage, and then we heard the very first rumors of friends
from within the town being shot, sometimes for attempting to
flee, but often for no real reason at all. The oppression came in
waves, each one more determined than the last—setting a new
baseline of "normal" for the stunned Jews in town and those of
us watching nearby.

My Roman Catholic family had lived side by side with the
Jews in Trzebinia forever—we'd been to school with their children, sold them our produce and relied on goods from their

stores. So as the noose around the neck of "our" Jewish community began to wind tighter, the sheer helplessness the rest of us felt affected everyone in different ways. Mama and Father would curse the invaders, but reacted almost violently to any suggestion that we were anything other than helpless bystanders to the tragedy unfolding before us. They were determined that if we kept our heads down, we could stay under the radar and remain safe ourselves. But Stanislaw and Filipe were eighteen-year-old boys—right on the edge of manhood, flooded with testosterone and an optimistic belief that *justice* was achievable. They'd wait until Mama and Father were out of earshot, then have intense discussions about growing rumors of a resistance. The twins traded hints of hope, spurring one another on, until I was absolutely terrified one or both of them would disappear into the night and get themselves killed.

"Don't do anything rash," I pleaded with Filipe at every chance I got. He was the more sensitive of the twins—Mama sometimes said that Stanislaw had been born a hardened old man. But Filipe was softer, vastly less arrogant and I knew if I could convince him to remain cautious, Stanislaw would likely follow.

"Mama and Father think that if we keep our heads down, the Nazis will leave us alone," Filipe said to me one morning, as we collected eggs together in the chicken yard.

"Is that so foolish?" I asked him, and he laughed bitterly.

"Life doesn't work that way, Alina. Hatred spreads—it doesn't burn out with time. Someone needs to stand up and stop it. You watch, sister—when they're done with the Jews, it will be our turn again. Besides, even if we could ride out the war with our heads down, and we sat back while the Nazis worked all of our Jewish friends to death, what kind of Poland could be rebuilt once they were gone? Those people are as important to this country as we are. We're better off dying with honor than sitting back to watch our countrymen suffer," he said.

"The father of your girlfriend would disagree with everything you just said," I muttered, and Filipe sighed heavily.

"Jan is a bigoted pig, Alina. It is hard enough to be civil to that man even on my good days—I can only force myself to be polite to him because if I wasn't, I'd lose Justyna, and I love her. But don't you see? It is because of men like Jan that *we* must find a way to rise up—we owe it to our sisters and brothers."

Filipe's rage only intensified once we had our first direct encounter with Nazi harassment. A group of SS officers stopped Truda and Emilia on the street outside of their home when they were walking to the factory to see Mateusz one day.

"I didn't understand what was happening," Truda whispered to Mama and me as we watched Emilia sit sullenly in the corner. Filipe and Stani were trying to make her laugh, but she was too shocked to even react to their antics. "One of the officers measured her height and said she is tall for her age and her eyes are green, so she is close enough to Aryan and they should take her."

"Take her *where*?" I asked hesitantly.

"I don't know," Truda admitted with a shrug. "But clever Emilia was calling me *Mama*, and my hair is so dark. They looked at me and said her hair would get darker as she got older, and then they told us to go."

"Yesterday, they took Nadia Nowak's daughter," Filipe murmured from his position on the floor. He looked up at us, rage simmering in his eyes. Nadia was Justyna's aunt, the sister of her mother Ola, and I'd met Nadia's daughter, Paulina. She was a tiny slip of a thing, only three or four years old, with a halo of blond curls and bright blue eyes. "It's called the *Lebensborn* program. The SS are assessing each child in the township for their suitability to be taken from their families and 'Germanized.' The soldiers told Nadia that Paulina will be placed with a German foster family and given a new name so she has a chance of growing up to be *racially pure*. Nadia refused to let Paulina go, so the soldiers tore her from Nadia's arms. Ola and Justyna are there today comforting her. Nadia is distraught."

"Oh, that poor thing," Mama gasped, clasping her hands in front of her chest. "Her husband was killed in the bombings too. She has suffered so much already."

"I told you, didn't I?" Filipe said, looking right at me. His nostrils had flared and his shoulders were locked hard. "I told you it was only a matter of time before they came for us too. This is our punishment because we lay down and let them torture our Jewish brothers and sisters, Alina. Now they steal our *children*, and God only knows what will happen to that little one now that she's away from her family."

Emilia was listening to all of this, her eyes growing wider, her jaw going slack.

"Filipe," I whispered, glancing at her anxiously. "*Please*, not now."

Stanislaw broke the tension—he leaped playfully at Filipe, who cried out in surprise. Just as he went to throw Stani away, Filipe looked at Emilia. A startled smile had broken on her face, and so Filipe went limp. Stani had clearly been expecting a wrestling match and didn't seem to know *what* to do with Filipe now that he'd pinned him, so I quickly skipped across the room to join the tangle of bodies on the floor. I grinned at Emilia and locked my hands into claws, then tickled my strapping young brothers. They both looked at me blankly, but then when Emilia howled with laughter, they played along too.

When the time came for Truda and Emilia to leave, Filipe and Stani insisted on chaperoning them. As we watched the foursome walk up into the woods to cross the hill into town, Mama shook her head.

"That boy worries me," she murmured.

I knew exactly *which* boy she meant.

After that day, I became Filipe's shadow. The occupation was months old by then, and I'd heard nothing at all of Tomasz, so

I had little to fill my thoughts but fears for him and terror that my brother was about to get himself killed—and only one of those things could I control. I kept myself busy by following Filipe around the farm waiting for any opportunity to convince him to *stay safe*.

I really thought the biggest risk to Filipe's safety was the temptation to join the resistance, but he never even got the chance to go seeking danger, because soon enough it came to us. I was blindsided by the sound of a truck rumbling on the road beside our property one morning when I was in the field with Mama, harvesting potatoes. The soldier in the passenger's seat stared right at us as they passed, and a sound escaped my mouth that was almost a shriek.

"Mama…"

"Stay calm," Mama said quietly. "Whatever you do, Alina, do not panic."

The blood was pounding through my body—echoing in my ears—my hands were shaking so hard I had to rest them against the soil to hold them still. In the end, I sat on my heels and I stared in horror as the truck came to a stop right at the gate to our farm. Four soldiers stepped from the truck and approached the barn where Father was working.

I couldn't hear them speaking—we were just too far away. It was a very quick visit—the soldiers handed Father a piece of paper and left, so I told myself everything was fine. I watched the truck as it continued along the road, toward the Golaszewski house. Mama suddenly stood and began to run to the house, and I set my basket aside to follow her. When we reached Father, we found him reading the notice, leaning heavily against the door frame of the barn.

Father seemed stupefied. He was blinking slowly, and the color had drained entirely from his face.

"What is it?" Mama demanded, and she snatched the paper

from his hand. As she read it, she made a little noise in the back of her throat.

"Mama, Father..." I croaked. "What is wrong?"

"Go fetch your brothers from the other field," Father said dully. "We need to have a talk."

We sat around the table and each of us took our turn to hold the paper. It was a summons—all families in our district who had children over the age of twelve would be required to send them for labor assignment. I was too upset to read the whole thing, in fact, every time I tried, my vision clouded with tears. Still, I was simply determined to keep a grip on some kind of optimism—or better still, to find a loophole.

"There has to be a way around it," I told my family. My brothers shared an impatient glance, but I ignored them and pressed harder to find a way out of the mess. "They can't make us leave our family and our home. They can't—"

"Alina," Filipe cut me off sharply. "These are the same people who shot Aleksy and the mayor in front of the entire town. These are the same soldiers who are making the Jewish children in the town work from sunup to sundown—the same pigs who think nothing of beating women and children to death if they disobey. The same men who *took* little Paulina Nowak just because her hair is blond. Do you really think they are going to hesitate to take a bunch of teenagers away in case we get *homesick*?"

I went to bed early that night, and I closed the door between my bed and the rest of the house, and I looked around my little room—my little world. My parents had split our tiny house into three rooms—although by today's standards, two of those rooms would be laughably small, no more than closets. We were farmers—peasants, in the local vernacular—people who made only just enough from our land to support ourselves and during dry years, not a single shaft of wheat we didn't desperately need.

So many times since Tomasz left, I'd been so desperate to

flee that house to run to Warsaw to be with him. But that was when I thought I was walking away from my family into Tomasz's waiting arms, an entirely different scenario to this one—where I was being *torn* away and sent to hostile strangers in a hostile land. I was existing here at the farm in a broken world, propelled out of bed each day only by the fact that every sunrise at least had the potential to bring news of Tomasz's safety. If the Nazis took me away, how would he *ever* find me? How would I ever know what had become of him? The months that had passed since his last letter had felt close to unbearable. How could I survive if the *not knowing* became a permanent state?

I lay on my bed and I wrapped my arms around myself and I tried so hard to be brave, but I just kept picturing myself so far away from my family, isolated in a place where I didn't speak the language and where I would no longer be the beloved and somewhat-sheltered youngest child, but instead a vulnerable young woman on her own. Eventually I closed my eyes, and I fell into an exhausted sleep, but I awoke sometime later to hushed whispers from my parents in the living area. I couldn't quite make out what they were saying, so slipped out of bed to stand at the door.

But Stanislaw is the strongest. We must keep him—we cannot run the farm without him. At the very least we keep Filipe—he has no common sense and he will run his mouth off if we let him go—

No! Alina is tiny and she's weak and too pretty. She is but a child! If we send Alina, she will never survive. We must keep her here.

But if we keep her, the farm will never survive!

I opened the door, and my parents both jumped in their chairs. My father looked away, but Mama turned to me and said impatiently, "Back to bed."

"What are you talking about?" I asked her.

"Nothing. It is none of your concern."

Hope blossomed in my chest. This was such an enticing sensation that I had to press a little harder, even though I knew I'd likely be shouted at for doing so.

"Did you find a way for us to stay?"

"Back to bed!" Mama said, and as I'd expected, her tone left no room for argument. There was no sleeping after that, and later, when I heard my parents pull out the sofa that served as their bed, I waited a while until they fell silent, then I sneaked past their bed to the boys' tiny room at the other end of the house. My brothers were wide-awake, lying top-to-tail on the sofa they shared. When I entered the room, Filipe sat up and opened his arms to me.

"What is going on? Can we stay after all?"

He pulled away from me to stare at me in disbelief.

"Didn't you *read* the notice?"

"I read most of it…" I lied, and he sighed heavily.

"*One* of us will be given a permit to stay here and help them run the farm. Mama and Father have to choose," Filipe told me softly. He brushed my hair back from my face, then added, "But to ask them to choose between their children is a cruelty that we will not tolerate. Stani and I will go. You will have to work hard, Alina—and you are lazy, so it won't be easy. But it is safer for you to stay here."

"But I'm going to marry Tomasz soon, and then I'll move to Warsaw," I said stubbornly.

"Alina," Stanislaw whispered impatiently. "There *is* no university left at Warsaw. I heard that the professors have all been imprisoned or executed, and most of the students joined the *Wehrmacht*. Tomasz is either in prison or working with those monsters, but it doesn't even matter which—you're *not* moving away."

I was indignant at the very idea that Tomasz would ever align himself with the Nazi troops.

"How *dare* you—"

"Hush, Alina," Filipe said tiredly. "No one knows where Tomasz is, not for sure, so don't get upset." Then he glanced at me, and he added slowly, "But if you stay here, he has a chance of finding you if he manages to get out of the city to come home."

I'd thought the same thing myself. For just a moment, I clung to the idea greedily, but then I remembered what the trade-off was. I tried to imagine my life without the twins, but the very thought of it filled me with loneliness.

"But I don't want you to go to away," I whispered tearfully, and Stanislaw sighed.

"So, Alina, instead—will you go to the work farm for us then? Miles away from Mama and Father—all on your own?"

In the end, the boys would not be deterred. When the day came for them to leave, Mama, Father and I walked them into Trzebinia to the train station. Mateusz, Truda and Emilia met us there, and when Emilia saw me, she skipped to my side and smiled sadly.

"This is just like when we said goodbye to Tomasz," she whispered.

I nodded, but I was distracted, absorbing the shocking scene before me. It was an overcast day, just like Tomasz's departure, and we were at the train station again—but Emilia was very wrong, because I was immediately aware that *this* moment was something altogether new.

This time, no one was waiting on the platform to send their loved ones on to some exciting adventure. None of these children were leaving Trzebinia to learn or to explore—they were being stolen from us. To the invaders, they were nothing more than a resource to be exploited, but those of us left behind knew that a part of the soul of our district was being torn away. Even Nadia Nowak, who had already lost her husband in the bombings then had her precious Paulina taken for Germanization, stood on that platform and wailed loudly as she said goodbye to her three oldest teenagers. Nadia joined a sea of other mothers who sobbed with equal grief and terror, and a crowd of fathers who cleared their throats compulsively, and dabbed frantically at their eyes to hide any hint of moisture.

The young people stood woodenly for the most part. Some of the very young ones cried, but it wasn't the unrestrained emotion we saw in their mothers—these were tears of shock and disbelief. I got the sense that even once the train arrived at the work farms, those young people would take weeks to accept the reality of their situations.

And that would have been me, but for my brothers.

I'd been relieved since the decision was made that I would stay, but as I faced the consequences of my easy acceptance of my brother's nobility, I was swamped in a wave of grief that threatened to knock me to my knees.

Emilia tugged my hand suddenly, and I looked down at her to find she was staring at me intently.

"Do you think Tomasz is still alive?" she asked me. I blinked at her, surprised both at the question and the resigned tone with which she asked it. I shook myself mentally and forced myself to focus, because there was something not at all right about such a grown-up, pessimistic tone coming from sweet little Emilia. I ruffled her hair and I said firmly, "Of course he is. He's alive and he's well and he's doing everything he can to get back to us."

"How can you be so sure?"

"He promised me, silly. And Tomasz would *never* lie to me."

Her sharp green gaze didn't waver from mine, and it took every bit of strength I had not to look away. I wouldn't break the stare, because I feared if I did, she'd see right through me. Was I as sure as all that? Not at all. But for all of the desperation in our lives that day, I wanted to save Emilia the one small trauma of doubting her beloved big brother.

She nodded suddenly, abruptly, and went back to staring at the assembled crowd around us. All too soon, announcements came that it was time for the young people to make their way to the train. Filipe stepped toward me and enveloped me in a bear hug.

"Look after Mama and Father, Alina. Work hard."

"I wish you could stay," I whispered. My guilt was so palpable in that moment I couldn't even make myself look him in the eye.

"I *couldn't* stay. Not when the alternative was for you to go," he said gently. Then he kissed my forehead and whispered against my hair, "Be *brave,* little sister. You are so much more than you know."

Stani approached me as the tears filled my eyes. He kissed my cheek too, but he was silent, even as he embraced our parents. Father stood frozen, his muscles locked, his teeth set hard. Mama silently cried. Truda was clutching Mateusz's arm so tightly her fingers were white, but her expression was solemn.

The boys gave a simultaneous nod, and they walked away to join the line to fill the train. They kept their chins high, and they both managed a smile and a wave back toward us just before they disappeared from our view.

I was awed by their courage and bewildered that even *that* moment didn't seem to faze them one little bit. Of course, they must have been terrified—they were only boys, and all of the things that had scared me about the forced labor arrangement would have been equally overwhelming to them too. Neither one spoke much German, neither one had ever lived out of home before.

I knew the very act of hiding their fear was one of sacrifice, just like the decision to go in my place. They were good people—the best people.

I still think about my big brothers. I sometimes wonder if I would have done anything different that day, if only I'd known that within a year they'd both be dead—and that those quiet moments by the train station would be the very last time I ever saw them.

CHAPTER 6

Alice

Mom has turned Babcia's retirement home unit upside down but she can't find the box. Now she's headed back to her house; she has some of Babcia and Pa's things in storage. It's been a few hours and she'll be a while yet, but Eddie is pressing the *lunch* button on his iPad dozens of times a minute, and it's driving me, Babcia and the nurses insane. I turned the sound down, but Eddie turned it straight back up—just like Babcia did earlier. One of the nurses quite gently asked if I could take the iPad off him, but it's his voice and his ears, so I refused.

We're actually lucky because now that it's lunchtime, he'll eat soup *or* yogurt—but also supremely unlucky, because given the fiasco in the store this morning, I have neither on hand. Eddie simply needs a can of soup, or better still, some tubes of Go-Gurt if we can find some with the right label. I have to call Wade. I have to convince him to come from work via a store, and to bring something Eddie can eat, or better still, to come and take Eddie home. The reason I don't want to do it is that I already know how this conversation is going to go.

It's an emergency, I'll say. *I wouldn't have asked if I had an alternative, but I can't leave Babcia alone—she's distressed enough as it is. And I don't know how much longer Mom is going to be, but Eddie desperately needs to eat.*

Wade will make all the right noises, and then there'll be some impressive reason why he can't help. He did say he had meetings, so I imagine he'll refer back to that premade excuse again.

I think about just putting up with the endless robotic demands for *lunch, lunch, lunch* and waiting, but Eddie looks so frustrated—like he's about to explode, actually—and now that I think about it, it's a bonafide miracle we've made it this far today with only *one* meltdown. I sigh and dial Wade.

"Honey," he answers on the first ring. "I've been so worried. How are things going?"

"Things are terrible," I admit. "Babcia can't speak and I don't think she can understand us. She's been using Eddie's iPad and she's told us she needs a box of photos from home, but Mom can't find it. And Eddie didn't get his yogurt this morning because there's new packaging on the Go-Gurt at the Publix and he had this meltdown and now he's starving so another one is coming and I can't do this by myself today. I *need* your help. I know you said you were busy…"

"I'm so sorry, honey. I have these meetings…"

"There is *no one else I can call*, Wade."

I've raised my voice, and Eddie and Babcia both look at me in surprise. Even if they don't understand the words, the volume apparently speaks for itself. I wince as I offer them an apologetic shrug, then take a deep breath to calm myself a little.

"I can't take him home, Alice," my husband says, a little stiffly. "I just have too much—"

"Don't worry, Wade. I'm not asking for anything *unrealistic* like you spending an afternoon alone with your son," I say, then I hear his sharp intake of breath, and I realize we're about to argue. Again. Probably because he's being an ass, and that comment I just made fell somewhere on the spectrum between "mean" and "bitchy" so it's guaranteed to get a defensive rise out of him. I close my eyes and aim for a much more conciliatory tone as I say, "I'm only asking you to go pick up some tins of soup or some Go-Gurt if you can find the old packaging. Bring them to me here at the hospital. I'll handle *everything* else." My tone shifts, and now I'm begging him. "*Please*, Wade. *Please*."

He sighs, and in my mind, I can see him in his office on the phone. He'll be sitting stiffly because I'm irritating him, and he'll have instantly mussed up his hair because he's upset at how I just spoke to him. Even now, in the awful silence as I wait for him to speak, I know he'll be repeatedly running his hand over his hair, and when the exasperation gets too much, he'll rest his hand against the back of his neck and slump.

But just as I can picture this with perfect clarity after so many years with Wade, I also know he's going to do what I asked, because if he wasn't, he'd have snapped right back at me and we'd have wound up this call with one or both of us hanging up in anger.

"I'll come now."

"If you go to the store near your office, they might have stock of the Go-Gurt with the old labels." I hesitate, then ask cautiously, "You know what that looked like, right? I'll text you the image. Same for the soup. You have to get the *right* soup."

"I'm not an idiot, Alice," he says impatiently, and I hear the sounds of movement at his end. "I'm leaving right now."

Wade is an excellent father, although if you viewed his behavior only through the lens of his interactions with Eddie, you'd suspect the opposite. He rarely engages with Eddie, he's constantly resistant to the therapies that help our son to survive in the world, he's dismissive and impatient and he's unsupportive.

But with our daughter, Pascale—or Callie, as we usually call her, Wade is a model parent. He's genuinely busy with his job, but he finds a way to be at all of the key events in her life—debate club meets, ballet recitals, parent-teacher interviews, doctor's appointments. Callie and Wade usually do her homework together, though she rarely needs his help. They are twelve chapters into the last Harry Potter book because they have read alternate pages aloud to each other every night without fail over the past three years. She had her first crush last year, and she told Wade about little Tyler Wilson before she even told me.

I can't even remember the last time Wade and Eddie were alone together.

Wade would say we had a perfectly normal son until Eddie was eighteen months old and I took him to a doctor, who put a label on our boy, and that label tainted everything. Wade would say I was so convinced that something was wrong with Eddie that it became a kind of self-fulfilling prophecy, then I spent so much time trying to "fix" him that I actually made him broken.

And he's kind of right about the paranoia, because from the moment I realized I was pregnant, I knew that *something* was different. Even I don't understand how I knew, so I can appreciate that to Wade it might seem that I made all of this happen somehow—at least at first. Maybe that theory could have been valid, right up until Eddie was two, and the developmental pediatrician said the words *Autism Spectrum Disorder.* We didn't yet understand how *bad* it was going to be, but surely that diagnosis was a clear sign that this situation was way out of my control.

It is beyond me how my brilliant husband, a man with a PhD and an entire research program under his guidance, can fail to understand how *utterly helpless* I am when it comes to our son. I am a puppet controlled by medical professionals and therapists. They tell me all the things I need to do to engage with Eddie. Some of those things, like the AAC on the iPad, help me to reach him, but most of their therapies don't reach him at all—they simply enable us to survive. None of those therapies made him different—Eddie just *is* different. That's where my opinion and Wade's diverge.

Wade would say all of my efforts enable a spoiled little boy who *could* be closer to typical if we just pushed him more instead of pandering to him. Wade speaks to Eddie, because he can't accept that Eddie's language is really as restricted as I *know* it is. Wade views Eddie's echolalia as a game—a way to insult and taunt us—and of proof that Eddie could use verbal language to communicate if he wanted to. It doesn't help that when Eddie sees Wade, he often echoes the words *not now, Edison*, although I'm not even sure why that one has even persisted because Eddie no longer makes much of an attempt to engage with his father at all.

What Wade loves to forget is that, initially, he was quite supportive of medical intervention. He seemed to have this idea that Eddie's diagnosis automatically meant our son would be a savant, and Wade was kind of okay with the whole situation right up until the psychologist told us that Eddie's IQ was a little under average, so he was unlikely to possess any quirky but genius abilities. My husband is a quirky genius himself—he could handle having a brilliant but odd child; in fact, we have one of those already in Callie, and he's her best friend in the world. It was the "below average" designation that Wade couldn't deal with, the autism itself was just the straw that broke the camel's back.

That's when the blame game started—but I don't judge Wade for that, because I play it too. My husband and more importantly, his sperm, have spent an awful lot of time around intense industrial chemicals over the years, and he's been exposed to radiation at work more than once. And heavens, left to his own devices? Wade's diet is appalling. We blame each other for Eddie's struggles—the only difference is Wade occasionally has the courage to voice his thoughts on the matter aloud. Maybe that makes him a better person, because at least he's honest. I carry my resentment of Wade around like a millstone around my neck and some days I just know that sooner or later, something is going to snap.

He arrives twenty-two minutes after our call, and just as I expected, he's frazzled. Wade wears a suit to work because he's an executive manager these days. When he leaves home in the morning, his tie is always impressively straight. Right now, it's at a somewhat-crazy angle, and his blond hair is sticking up all over the place. He looks sheepish as he enters the hospital room, his hands caught through the straining handles of two over-loaded hessian bags.

"Hi, guys," he says pointlessly to Babcia and Eddie on the bed, then he nods at me and raises the bag in his left hand. "I got a whole carton of soup—it's in the car. Then they had plenty of stock of the old yogurt labels so I bought it all—here's half of it." He lifts the other bag a little higher and nods toward it. "And I got heaps with the new label too..." At my blank stare, he says hesitantly, "Well...you know, so he can get used to it."

Eddie won't *get used* to the label. I don't know how we're going to manage that yet, but the fact that Wade thinks it's that easy is a blatant reminder of how little he understands.

"Thanks."

I expect Wade to pass me the bags, kiss me politely and spin on his heel, but instead, he sets the bags on the floor and pulls me into an embrace. I'm surprised by this, and even more sur-prised when he places a gentle kiss on the side of my hair.

"Sorry, Ally. Honestly, I'm really sorry. I know you're under a lot of pressure at the moment and I'm not much help."

I sigh and lean into him, then wind my arms around his torso and accept comfort from the warmth of his embrace. *Thank you. Thank you. Thank you.* Rare glimpses of the man I *know* my hus-band to be have sustained our marriage. In these sporadic mo-ments, I catch a hint of hope on the horizon. All I need to keep working and fighting and trying is a glimmer of that, just every now and again. This one comes right when I need it.

"I'm kind of on a short fuse emotionally," I whisper. "I'm re-ally sorry too...about before."

"Would it help if I stay this afternoon?"

He doesn't offer to take Eddie home, but this is as close as I'm going to get and I appreciate the offer.

"Actually," I say, "Callie has ballet at four. If you could go pick her up from school, take her to ballet, then go home and cook some dinner…"

"Absolutely," Wade says, with enthusiasm, or maybe it's relief. "Absolutely, I can do that. Anything you need." He brushes his lips against mine, then glances at the bed again. "How are you doing, Babcia?"

"She can't understand you," I remind him. "She's been using the AAC—if you want to talk to her you'll have to use that."

Wade stiffens, then waves vaguely at the bed and glances at his watch.

"I might head back to the office and tell them I'm going to take off early. I'll see you at home tonight. Let me know if you need anything else?"

"Okay," I say.

Lunch, Eddie's iPad says, then, *Lunch lunch lunch lunch lunch lunch…*

"Okay, okay," I sigh, and I bend and fetch a pack of yogurt. He's so excited that he sits up and his hands start flapping all over the place.

Six tubes of yogurt later, Eddie is settled on the bed watching YouTube videos of trains again. But then Mom flies back into the room with an archive box in her hand, and Babcia brightens until *she's* the one impatiently flapping her hands.

CHAPTER 7

Alice

Mom slides the box onto the tray table while I shift Eddie to the chair beside the bed. Babcia grows impatient and she pushes herself into a sitting position without our assistance, so then we have to hasten to adjust the angle of her bed and fix her pillows. She waves us away and reaches for the box, her hands trembling. There's reverence in her gaze, and every now and then she flicks a glance toward Mom that's brimming with gratitude and relief. I have to help Babcia to lift the lid off the box when it becomes apparent she can't coordinate her right hand to do so, but once I do, she pulls the lid against herself and hugs it awkwardly with her forearms.

"Where was it?" I ask Mom quietly.

"Under her bed at the retirement unit, I missed it the first time I went there," Mom mutters as she shakes her head. "I didn't realize how close she keeps it, but I probably should have. She's always been so sentimental." She makes that last statement as though this is an utterly bewildering character trait—which momentarily amuses me.

"So are you, Mom," I laugh softly, and she frowns at me. "You forget I helped you and Dad move last time. I *know* your attic is basically the Museum of The Slaski-Davis Family." She's kept artworks and school reports for me right from preschool, and ticket stubs from her early dates with Dad, and, because she is a *stickler* for the letter of the law, she's kept sentimental paperwork from her journey to the bench but she's self-redacted identifying details where that might be problematic from a confidentiality point of view. I tried to thin the boxes of mementos out a little when they were moving, but Mom stubbornly held on to every last piece of our history, and when I pointed out how *pointless* those redacted files seem to be—she told me that each and every page triggers a memory of a case that meant something to her. I suspect that my Mom is scared that one day she'll get dementia like Pa did. Maybe those bits and pieces from our past are important in case they one day need to act as a map to guide her back to the memories she cherishes.

In the meantime, it's kind of hilarious that above my mother's industrial minimalist-styled house is an attic brimming with boxes of macaroni art, letters and unsorted photographs. Mom sighs now, but she gives me a rueful smile.

"I suppose she taught me that some things just can't be replaced," Mom murmurs, and we both look back to Babcia, who's awkwardly wiping tears from her face as she stares into the box. "She never said so," Mom adds, "but I always assumed these little things came to mean so much more to her because she had to uproot herself from her whole life back there in Poland."

Babcia motions impatiently toward Eddie's iPad, and he's partway through a train video so I fully expect him to resist and maybe even grunt like a toddler as he pulls the device against himself. Instead, he looks up at her, blinks, then swipes to the AAC and hands it to her. Babcia smiles at him, then she taps the *thank you* icon and shows it to Mom, who nods as she sinks into the chair on the opposite side of the bed. As soon as Babcia's attention shifts, Mom rubs her forehead and for the briefest of moments, closes her eyes. She looks exhausted—maybe more tired than I've ever seen her, and I was waiting at the finish line for every one of her eight marathons.

"Mom," I say softly. "Are you okay?"

"I need this hospital to get it together and figure out what's going on with her. I can't keep taking time off—I have a decision pending and it's just…" She stops speaking abruptly, then raises her gaze to me and frowns. "It's just all too much, Alice. You just couldn't possibly understand."

Any rare glimpse of vulnerability from Mom is always followed up by a reminder of how vitally *important* she is, and often, a little jab like that one—a reminder of how *unimportant* my role is by comparison. I do speak with my mom almost every day and by the standards of most of my friends, we're particularly close—but it's a difficult closeness, because "close" to Julita Slaski-Davis is a difficult place to stay. Almost every day, we end up raising our voices at one another. It's just the dynamic of our family—she doesn't understand this life of mine that revolves around my kids; I don't understand her life that revolves around the law, but we love each other fiercely anyway. Mom was determined that I'd follow in her footsteps and at the very least become a lawyer, and until my late teens, I never even questioned that was to be my path. It was only the year before college that it occurred to me I didn't *have* to go into law, but when I instead decided to "waste my life" and study journalism, my relationship with Mom changed forever.

It changed again the day I told her I was pregnant, two weeks before I was due to graduate, and then the final nail in the coffin was when I didn't even bother looking for a graduate job. There didn't seem any point, since I had no intention of working for several years after my baby's birth, but to Mom—*this* was unforgivable. Didn't I understand how hard my foremothers fought in the first and second waves of feminism for my right to a career? How could I betray them by accepting a life where I was dependent on a *man*?

Even ten years later, I still don't have the guts to tell Mom that Callie's conception wasn't an accident, but rather the result of a carefully considered decision that Wade and I took that I would *not* follow in my mother's footsteps, even in my approach to motherhood. Mom studied, built a career, and then at forty-three went into a panic and thought she'd probably better have a child after all. I *do* so love and admire my mother, but I've spent a lifetime coming second to her work, and I was determined that I would never let my children feel like an afterthought. Wade and I had our kids first, because we were both absolutely sure that I'd find my way into some kind of career once they were at preschool.

Then Eddie came along.

Life has a way of reminding you that you are at the mercy of chance, and that even well-thought-out plans can turn to chaos in an instant. That's why now, when I might be tempted to condemn my mother for her desperation to return to her job during Babcia's medical crisis, I instead force myself to be patient with her. Mom has been here for two days straight, on her own except for the limited time I've spent with her. She has no siblings; I'm her only kid. Dad is retired, but he's on a golfing trip in Hawaii with his old academia buddies and she is far too proud to ask him to come home. My mom has the weight of the world on her shoulders right now. If she needs to retreat for a little while into her work for some emotional respite, so be it.

"Okay, Mom," I say softly. "Eddie has school tomorrow… I can come straight to the hospital after I drop him off and sit with her if you want to go to chambers and catch up a little."

"Good," she says, snapping her chin upward. "Thank you, Alice. Yes, please."

Babcia reaches for my hand and leads it to the box. I lift out a stack of photos and papers and then push the tray table away so I can rest it all on her lap. Her hands move slowly and clumsily as she sorts through this first stack of photos. They are a tumbled confusion of printing technology and eras—photos of Pa and Mom and me and my kids and Babcia herself over the decades, and a few scant photos of beloved dogs from the days when Babcia and Pa lived in their big house in Oviedo. But just a few layers into the stack, Babcia freezes on a single photo that

I've never seen before—it's a sepia print on thick, aged paper. The gloss over the photo is cracked, but the image is still clear.

It's a young man, sitting casually on a boulder against the background of a forest. He's wearing damaged boots, so well-worn that a tattered sock is visible at the toe of the left one. His clothes are equally tired, but he's smiling broadly at the camera. He's incredibly thin—but, despite the gaunt cheeks beneath his sparse beard, still handsome. There's something striking about his eyes—he looks like he's holding back a chuckle.

Babcia's hands shake as she lifts the photo, and she sighs as she brings it to her cheek, cradling it against her skin. She closes her eyes for a moment and rests her head toward the image, then she turns to offer it to me.

I can tell this is precious to my grandmother, and so I try to take it from her with appropriate reverence. I stare down at the photo in my hands, and it strikes me that this young man is both a stranger and, somehow, familiar.

After a moment, Babcia reaches up toward the photo and turns it over. On the back, I see a scrawled message in faded ink—the tiny handwriting is tightly compressed.

Photograph by Henry Adamcwiz, Trzebinia Hill, 1 July 1941

I read it aloud to Mom, and then I pass the photo back to Babcia.

"Poor Babcia. She's really missing Pa," I say, and Mom frowns and stares at the photo again.

"I'm sure she is," Mom says. "But *that* is not Pa."

"How do you know?"

"Pa's hair was dark before he went gray. That man has lighter hair, unless the shades on the print are deceptive," Mom says, then she shrugs. "Plus… I don't know. That guy just doesn't look like Pa. His eyes are all wrong…the shape of his lips. Although, there is definitely something familiar about some of his features. He looks a lot like *you*, actually. Mama had twin brothers. This must be one of them."

"I wonder who Henry Adamcwiz was?" I frown. "And 1941—was that after the war?"

"No, the war didn't end until 1945," Mom murmurs, and then we all stare at the photo, as if it can explain itself. Babcia wipes a tear from her cheek, then reaches for the iPad again.

Tomasz, it says. *Find Tomasz. Please find Tomasz.*

"Are you sure this isn't Pa?" I ask Mom, and she takes the photo from me and stares at it hard, then she shakes her head.

"I'm quite sure."

Babcia looks so frustrated now that if she *could* speak, I'm pretty sure she'd be yelling at us both. I frown and look at Mom, who frowns right back at me. Helplessness and frustration leave my mother looking much more vulnerable than I'm used to—much more human. I feel another alien pang of sympathy for her.

"She's so confused," Mom mutters, then she looks to the door and the frustration gives rise to anger. "Why won't the staff listen to me? They should be reassessing her cognitive state. Clearly there's more than language damaged here."

Babcia hits the replay button on the iPad.

Please find Tomasz. Your turn.

I swallow and take the iPad. Mom is staring at the ceiling now, blinking rapidly—so I guess it's up to me to remind my Babcia that her husband is gone. Rising dread swamps me, and I am shaking a little as I swipe through the screens, then I groan in frustration and try making my own icon.

Pa is d-e-a-d, I type, but Babcia grabs my wrist, shakes her head fiercely and snatches the iPad from me with surprising strength. She flicks back to the AAC and finds an icon we haven't needed to use in twelve months—*Pa*. The sight of his image makes the ache in my chest intensify.

No Pa. Find Tomasz.

Then, she flicks to the "new icon" screen and with painstaking effort, starts to type. She makes a new icon of her own now. It's a picture of houses, a suburban street. She painstakingly adds a label: *Trzebinia*. The AAC makes an attempt at reading the word aloud, but I'm pretty sure it's not accurate.

"That word is on the photo too. Is it a mountain in Poland?" I ask Mom. She stands, then frowns as she reads the icon.

"That's where she grew up. See? She *is* confused. I told you."

I take the iPad and give another fruitless search for a "dead" symbol—but the best I can do is: *No Pa. I am sorry.*

Again, Babcia shakes her head, her expression twisting now with frustration, and she takes the iPad and she jabs her finger at the screen. She points at me, then at the photo.

Not Pa. Trzebinia.

She glances up, sees my confusion, then scrolls through all of the screens until she finds a page of national flags. She selects a red and white one, then adds it to her sentence.

Not Pa. Trzebinia. Poland. Tomasz.

Eddie is watching all of this with an almost-wondrous focus, and he reaches eagerly for the iPad, which Babcia automatically hands to him. He swipes out of the AAC program and loads Google maps, then quickly types in *Poland*. The map zooms in on Europe, then centers on Poland, and Babcia points to the lower half of the screen and looks at me as if this should explain everything.

It's my turn to take the iPad. I swipe back to the AAC, copy the town name, and then paste it into Google maps. Eddie squeals with delight as the screen refocuses on the town, then he claps his hands. I didn't know he knew how to use Google maps. I make a mental note to mention it to his teacher, because he sure does seem excited about it.

Babcia beams at him, then at me. I smile back at her, and for a moment, we're all just sitting there grinning like fools.

"Is that all she wanted, do you think?" I ask Mom, who shrugs.

"To see a *map*?" Mom surmises, almost wryly.

Babcia looks from Mom to me, waits a bit, then when she realizes we still don't understand her, her face twists into a grimace. She has our full attention, but we're helpless and soon she's distressed all over again. I'm not sure what to try next, but again, it's Eddie who saves us. He swipes the screen and flips it back to the AAC, then he hands it to Babcia and he rests his hand against her forearm.

Every time I see a movie where a character has autism and their single defining feature is a lack of empathy, I have an almost-overwhelming urge to smash my television. Eddie is, at times, challenging, even maddening—but his heart is immense. He might never speak or live independently, but what no one ever tells you is that a well-placed hug from the little boy who hates hugs can entirely change your day. Edison Michaels understands frustration better than anyone I know. He recognizes even its most subtle calling cards, because *frustration* defines every aspect of his life.

Babcia types, then plays the words just to make sure we all hear them.

Find Tomasz. Please Mommy. Find Tomasz. Trzebinia. Poland.

This time, when Babcia looks up at me, I stop and I really focus on her. Her eyes are bright and clear. She looks determined and frustrated, and not the least bit bewildered. I still have no idea what she wants, but I am inexplicably certain that *she* knows.

"Mom," I say slowly, "I don't think she's confused."

"Alice, she seems to be telling us that her dead husband is in Poland," Mom sighs. "Of *course* she's confused. Pa is in an urn in her retirement unit, for God's sake."

For the next several minutes, Babcia repeats herself via the AAC, over and over again.

Find Tomasz. Please Mommy. Find Tomasz. Trzebinia. Poland.

Mom shakes her head and huffs out a breath, then turns away from the bed.

"*Now* she wants to talk about Poland," she mutters. "Now that she *can't* talk. You know as well as I do how closed she and Pa were to talking about their life back in Poland. You and I both went through phases as teens where we all but interrogated the woman about the war and she'd always shut the conversation down."

Find Tomasz. Mommy, find Tomasz.

I look at Mom again, and she throws her hands into the air.

"She's calling you *Mommy*, for God's sake!" Mom says in exasperation, but I reach down and edit the label on my photo, then press the icon pointedly.

Alice.

"Better?" I say to Mom, and she sighs impatiently. Babcia reaches for the iPad again.

Find Tomasz, Alice. Please find Tomasz. Your turn.

I take the iPad, and I stare down at her message, then I draw in a deep breath and I type a promise I'm not sure I can actually fulfill.

Yes, Babcia. Alice find Tomasz.

She reads the message, then she looks at me and tears swim in her eyes. I kiss her weathered cheek and sigh.

"I suppose we may as well tell her what she wants to hear," Mom says stiffly.

I can understand why Mom said that, but that's not what I'm doing at all. This is no false promise of assistance to my grandmother to bring her comfort.

This was the woman who picked me up from school most days and who *always* had a batch of fresh cookies waiting for me at home. This was the woman who made it to all of my school assemblies and recitals because Mom never could. *This* woman taught me to deal with heartbreak as a teen and helped me to do my college applications and get my driver's license.

But somehow, most importantly, *this* woman taught me how to be my own kind of woman and wife and mother. I'm the person I am today because of Hanna Slaski, and now that she needs me, I will not let her down. I fully intend to do whatever I can to help her find whatever it is she's looking for.

CHAPTER 8

Alina

Even in the worst of times, life takes on a rhythm and the days blur into one another. The first year of the occupation was no exception to that rule. Every day ran on routine, and that routine began and ended with thoughts of Tomasz. Most of the time, I didn't even let myself consider the possibility that I was pining for a dead man.

There was just so much more to worry about.

From the day my brothers left, my existence was caged. My parents told me I wasn't to leave the farm, although they would permit the occasional visit with Justyna at the boundary between our properties. I argued against this, and at first, I was sure I'd find a way to change their minds. I had friends in the town— Emilia and Truda and Mateusz were in the town, and besides, the farm was surely no safer than the township. We often saw Nazi trucks rumbling past on the road at the front of our home. Since the occupation began, even the newspapers had ceased to operate, other than Nazi propaganda publications, which Father refused to read. Wireless too was now banned—Father destroyed his precious radio unit after the decree that any Pole found owning such a device would be executed.

If I couldn't leave the farm, I'd be cut off from the world altogether.

I was desperate for any news at all, but I particularly hoped for news of the work farms or of Warsaw, where I could only assume Tomasz remained. When Father made his trips into the town, I'd beg him to let me join him, but nothing I said would sway him. He promised me he was asking after the twins and Tomasz, but for the longest time there was no news at all, and with my adolescent arrogance, I was *certain* that I could do better.

"You have heard about the *lapanka*, of course," Father told me casually one day.

"The game?" I asked, frowning. "Yes, of course, we played it as children…" *Lapanka* was much like the English game "tag." Father shrugged.

"The Nazis play *lapanka* too, Alina. They block off the ends of a street in the township and they round up everyone inside and cart them off to a camp or prison for even the slightest reason."

"I wouldn't give them a reason," I said stiffly.

"Can I see your identity card?"

I blinked at him, confused by what I thought was an abrupt change of subject. We'd recently been ordered to carry our identity cards with us at all times, but I was still getting into the habit of carrying mine, and besides, we were in the dining room so I knew I was safe enough.

"It's in my room, Father."

"Well, there is your *reason*, Alina," Father said flatly. "If a soldier happened by you and caught you without your identity card, they would take you or maybe shoot you on the spot. Do you understand that? You tell me you want to go into the township, but even here at home, you cannot remember the basic requirements to keep yourself safe."

After that, Mama sewed pockets into all of my skirts for my identity paperwork, and I stewed in my anger toward Father. I was certain that he was being unfair, that I was perfectly capable of remembering the rules if he gave me the chance to prove myself. The problem with rage is that it takes a lot of energy to maintain, and the very nature of our situation with the twins gone was that all of my energy had to be reserved for farmwork.

Whether or not I was allowed to leave the farm to visit with people in the township became a moot point because most days, I didn't even have the energy to walk to the field boundary for a chat with Justyna. And whether or not I had a pocket in my skirt remained equally irrelevant, because most mornings I still forgot to put the identity card inside. We hadn't yet had any spot checks from soldiers checking our ID cards on the farm, and while Father's story of the *lapanka* roundups in town had frightened me a little, I didn't yet appreciate how close the danger was.

Monday to Saturday I toiled with Mama on the land, sometimes working in the fields from before the sun rose until after it had set again. I'd take the animals to graze before the sun rose, let the chickens out to roam the house yard, and then I'd join my parents in the fields. Almost everything that needed to be done had to be done by hand, an endlessly laborious cycle of plowing and planting and weeding and harvesting, then ploughing again. Mama, Father and my two strapping brothers had struggled to keep up even with my halfhearted help, but now the twins were gone, and with Father's rheumatism worsening whenever the cold came in, Mama and I had to struggle to maintain the usual workload, effectively on our own. The blisters on my hands grew until they joined and then popped, and the raw skin gradually morphed into a thick, dirt-stained callus that covered each palm. I spent so much of the daytime bending over in the fields that by nighttime, I'd have to lie in a fetal position because my back would spasm if I tried to lie straight.

I fretted for my brothers and for Tomasz, but during the daytime, the mere act of surviving took so much energy that thoughts of those missing were just background noise beneath the constant terror. We had to make the land work harder because our very survival depended on it. I had no capacity during the long days to think about anything other than work and the dread that would leave me frozen every time we saw a Nazi vehicle anywhere near our gate.

It was only when the frantic activity stopped at bedtime that I'd let myself focus on Filipe, Stanislaw and Tomasz. I'd pray for my brothers with whatever energy I had left, and then I'd open my drawer, fumble for Mama's ring and fix my mind for one pure moment on Tomasz.

Sometimes I relived a memory, sometimes I imagined a reunion, often I thought about our wedding day, planning that victorious moment in irrational detail, right down to the number of ruby-red poppies I'd carry in my bouquet. I could still see him so clearly in my mind—the laughing green eyes, the lopsided smile, the way his hair flopped forward onto his forehead and he'd push it back out of habit, only for it to fall forward again immediately.

The problem was that once thoughts of Tomasz filled my mind, desperate longing was never far behind. In the quiet seconds before sleep overtook me, I was sometimes overcome with despair at my helplessness, and I'd wake with gritty eyes from having sobbed myself to sleep.

I had no power to change my lot. All I had was the breath in my lungs and a tiny fragment of hope that if I kept moving forward, I could survive until someone else changed my world.

The quotas for our produce increased and increased. Eventually Father had to load the cart with *all* of our produce, and he'd take it all into town to hand over to the soldiers. In return, they would give him our allotment of ration stamps. The first time he returned with food, I thought I'd somehow misunderstood the arrangement.

"You have to go collect the food every day?"

"No, Alina," Father said impatiently. "This must last us the week."

The rations were not simply scant, they were untenable. Father had returned with a bag of flour, small blocks of butter and cheese, a half dozen eggs and some tinned meat.

"How will we live off this?" I asked my parents. "We have so much work to do—how can we run the farm with just the three of us when they are only feeding us scraps?"

"There are plenty who have it worse than us," Mama said.

"Worse?" It seemed unfathomable. Mama's gaze grew impatient, but this time, it was Father who spoke.

"This is nearly seven hundred calories per day, for each of us. The Jews are only allotted two hundred calories each per day. And, child, you think our farmwork is hard? Come into the town with me next time and see the way the Jewish work crews are being treated."

"I want to go into the town," I said, lifting my chin. "You won't let me."

"It is not safe for you there, Alina! Do you know what kinds of things those monsters have done to some of the girls in the township? Do you know what might—"

"We will get by," Mama interrupted him suddenly, and we all fell quiet. It seemed to me that we had a choice: break the rules and survive, or follow the rules and starve, and I was terrified my parents were going to choose the second option. I cleared my throat, and I suggested, "We could just keep some of our food...just a little? We can just take a few eggs or some of the vegetables—"

"The invaders say that our farms belong to the Reich now," Father said. "Withholding our produce would see us imprisoned, or worse. Do not suggest such a thing again, Alina."

"But—"

"Leave it, Alina," Mama said flatly. I looked at her in frustration, but then I noticed her determined stance. Her body language told me what her words did not: Mama had a plan, but she had no intention of sharing it with me. "Just do your jobs and stop asking so many questions. When you need to worry, Father and I will tell you to worry."

"I am not a baby, Mama," I cried in frustration. "You treat me like a child!"

"You are a child!" Father said. His voice shook with passion and frustration. We stared at each other, and I saw the shine of tears in my father's eyes. I was so shocked by this that I didn't quite know what to do—the urge to push and argue with them drained in an instant. Father blinked rapidly, then he drew in a deep breath, and he said unevenly, "You are our child, and you are the only thing we have left to fight for. We will do what we must to protect you, Alina, and you should think twice before you question us." His nostrils flared suddenly, and he pointed to the door as the tears in his eyes began to swell. "Go and do your damned jobs!"

I wanted to push, and I would have, except for those shocking tears in Father's eyes.

After that day, I put my head down, and I continued in the rhythm where work consumed my life.

On an unseasonably warm day in late fall I was working the berry patch, which was just beside the house at the place where the slope first steepened. An early wind had settled and the sun was now out in full force, so I was tanning myself. At lunchtime, I'd changed into my favorite dress—a lightweight, floral sundress I'd inherited from Truda. It certainly wasn't an immodest outfit—I didn't *own* any immodest outfits—but I had chosen that dress because the cut of the neckline meant I could enjoy the warmth of the sun on my arms and upper chest. I was crouched on the ground harvesting ripe berries and resting them in a wicker basket, periodically plucking weeds as I found them and throwing them into a pile beside the patch. Father was having an unusually bad day—he was in such pain from his hips that Mama had opted to stay inside with him to care for him.

I heard the truck approach, then slow. I held my breath as I always did when I heard vehicles rumbling past our house, but then released it in a rush when I saw the truck pull into *our* drive. Just as the roar of the truck engine stopped, there came the sound of the front door opening.

That's when I remembered my ID card. I'd remembered to put it in the pocket of the heavier skirt I'd been wearing that morning, and when I'd changed at lunchtime, I'd left that skirt on my bed and my papers were still inside.

I prayed that they'd leave without approaching me, but I stood even as I did so because I had little expectation that my prayer would be answered, and I didn't want to be crouching in the dirt alone when they came. There were only two of them this time. One was middle-aged, balding and so fat that it made me angry to think about how much food he must eat to maintain his build. His companion was startlingly young—probably the same age as my brothers. I wondered about that young soldier—whether he was scared to be away from his family, as my brothers surely were. For a moment, I felt a pang of empathy—but it disappeared almost immediately when I saw the look on the boy's face. Like his older companion, his expression was set in a scornful mask as he surveyed our small home. Even given the slight distance between us, there was no mistaking the disdainful curl of his lip and the flare in his nostrils. With the locked set of his shoulders and the way his hand hovered over the leather holster at his hip housing his gun, it was clear that this boy was simply looking for an excuse to release his aggression.

And I was standing in a field in a sundress without my ID card, a red flag waving in the wind before an angry bull.

The older man approached the house, but that young man just stood and stared all around. His gaze traced the tree line at the woods on the hill above and behind me, then shifted ever closer to the place where I stood. I wished and wished and wished that I had *some* way to make myself invisible, as the young man shifted back to face Mama and Father, his gaze skimming past me.

I thought for a second he hadn't noticed me or didn't care to pay me even a hint of attention, but just as the relief started to rise and I exhaled the breath I was holding, the young soldier frowned, and then tilted his head almost curiously. It was as if he'd missed me at first and had only belatedly registered that I was there. He once again raised his eyes, only this time, his gaze locked onto mine. There was palpable disgust in his eyes, but it was mixed with an intense, unsettling *greed*. My stomach lurched and I looked away from him as fast as I could, but I still felt his eyes on me, searing me somehow, until I fought to suppress an overwhelming urge to cross my arms over my body.

I knew I couldn't stand there, frozen. To do so would draw more attention to myself, and that would only increase the chance of them approaching me, and if they did—I was done for. I knew they wouldn't let me go into the house to get my papers—that would be an act of kindness, and kindness was not something the Nazis felt the Poles deserved. They considered us to be *Untermensch*, or subhuman—only slightly above the Jews on their perverted racial scale of worth. I had to act busy—I had to be busy—wasn't that how we were to save ourselves? Be productive, keep the farm working, produce at any cost—this had been our mantra since the invasion. I tried to convince myself that strategy would save me now too, even in the face of such direct intensity from this soldier. The trickle of adrenaline in my system turned to a flood, and I felt sweat running down my spine right along with it. I started to move, but my movements were jerky and my palms were so damp, and when I bent to pick up my wicker basket, it slipped straight back into the dirt. The hundreds of berries I'd picked all tumbled out, and I looked back up in a panic to see the soldier laughing scornfully, mocking me without a single word.

I dropped to my knees and began to scoop the berries up.

My hands were shaking so hard that I couldn't coordinate the movements and each time I lifted a handful of berries toward the basket, I'd drop as many as I rescued. I didn't need to look up to know his eyes were still on me. I could feel the intensity of his attention as if he could somehow stare all the way through my clothes. If I ran, they would shoot me, and I was too terrified to think clearly enough to find some work I could legitimately do that might take me away from his view. I was stuck naked under his stare, exposed to his gaze in the light summer dress I had chosen with such innocent optimism and the hopes of a pleasant afternoon in the sun.

At the house, I could hear the older soldier and Father attempting a conversation in German, but it was stilted and awkward because Father knew only a little more German than I did. There was a quiet discussion, then Father said something about Oświęcim, a town not far from ours.

And all the while, the young soldier stared at me.

The older soldier barked at Father, and then spun on his heel in the dust and turned back toward his car. That's when the younger soldier spoke for the first time. He turned lazily toward Father, cast a disdainful look toward my parents, and then looked right at me again as he spoke just loud enough for me to hear a rapid-fire sentence that I couldn't translate. The older soldier called to him, and the two piled into the car, and then they left.

I collapsed into the dirt, confused by how tense that moment had been, and confused as to why even now that they were gone, my stomach was still rolling violently. I pressed my hands to my belly, so focused on the discomfort within my body that I barely noticed Mama approaching.

"You are okay," she said abruptly. "We are okay."

"I didn't have my papers on me," I choked. Mama groaned impatiently.

"Alina, if they had checked…"

"I know," I said, my voice breaking. "I know, Mama. I keep forgetting but... I'll try to be more careful next time."

"No," Mama snapped, shaking her head. "You forget *all the damned time*, Alina. We won't risk it again. I'll hold your papers for you, and we'll make sure if you are outside in the field, I am close beside you."

The cage around me was shrinking, but after the five minutes that had just passed, I didn't mind that one bit.

"What did they want?" I asked Mama.

"They were lost—they needed directions to the barracks. Father thinks they were looking for Oświęcim," she said, then she looked toward the hill, her gaze distant for a moment. When she looked at me again, her eyebrows knit. "I...you must wear a scarf in the fields, or one of Father's hats. You should...always now you must hide your hair. And you must..." She looked down at my body, and she ran her hand through her own hair. "Perhaps you must wear your brothers' clothes..." She trailed off again, then gave me a searching, somewhat-helpless look. "Do you understand what I am telling you, Alina?"

"Did I do something wrong, Mama? What did that soldier say to me?"

"He was speaking to Father," Mama said, then she sighed. "He told Father that he has a pretty daughter." She met my gaze, and she raised her eyebrows. "We must do everything we can to ensure that the next passing soldier does not see a *pretty daughter*. We cannot hide you away altogether, so you must try to hide yourself in other ways. Yes?"

I never, ever wanted to feel so exposed ever again. I wanted to burn that summer dress and wear a coat everywhere I went for the rest of my life. I'd never really thought about my appearance too much before—but that day, I hated the way I looked. I hated my thick, chestnut hair and my wide blue eyes and I *loathed* the curve of my breasts and hips. If there had been a way to make myself invisible, I'd happily have taken it. I was tempted to rush inside and change into my brothers' large, boring clothes right that second.

Mama dropped to her knees beside me and helped me collect the last of the berries I'd dropped.

"If they ever approach you," she said suddenly, "do not struggle. Do you understand me, Alina? You let them do what they…" It was so rare for her to search for words. I squeezed my eyes shut, and she reached across and gripped my forearm until I opened them again. "There is no need for them to kill you if they can get what they want from you. Just remember that."

I shook my head, and Mama's grip on my arm became painfully tight.

"Rape is a weapon, Alina," she said. "Just as killing our leaders was a weapon, and taking our boys was a weapon, and starving us half to death is a weapon. They see you are strong in the face of all of their other tactics so they will try to control you in other ways—they will try to take your strength from the inside. If they come for you, be smart and brave enough to overcome the instinct to try to flee or resist. Then, even if they hurt your body, you will survive."

I sobbed once, but she held my gaze until I nodded through my tears. Only then did her gaze soften.

"Alina," she sighed. "Now do you understand why we do not want you to go into the town? We are all vulnerable. We are all powerless. But you, my daughter…you are naive and you are beautiful…that leaves you at risk in ways you are only beginning to understand."

"Yes, Mama," I choked. Frankly, I never wanted to leave the house again, let alone the farm. Any thought of visiting the town was forgotten for a long while after that day.

It wasn't the only time the soldiers came to our gate—spot checks for our papers and random visits to unnerve us soon became a way of life. Those moments were always terrifying, but never again did I feel so exposed, because that was the last time a soldier came to our gate and found me working alone in a field. Mama was always near me after that day, with our identity papers nestled safely in the pockets of her undergarments. That day was also the very last time a soldier visited to find me wearing my own clothes, and the last time anyone ever came to our gate and found me with my long hair down around my shoulders.

That fall day, a young Nazi soldier had taken my innocence without ever coming within a hundred feet of me.

On Sunday, Truda and Mateusz would walk Emilia up the hill on the town side, and then down the hill to our house to join us for lunch. We'd see them coming down from the hill— Emilia was inevitably hand in hand with my sister, a scrap of paper or a little bunch of wildflowers held tightly in her other hand. Mateusz always walked close behind them, and I understood that this was a protective gesture, but I also knew it was ultimately a pointless one. If a soldier wished to do any of us harm, there was nothing to be done about it, not even for my tall, strong brother-in-law.

Emilia had adjusted quickly to life with her new family, and Truda and Mateusz clearly adored Emilia in return. That little girl loved two things in life most—talking at a million miles an hour, and flowers of every kind. In preparation for that weekly visit, she'd collect a little posy from the park at the end of their street, or she'd draw Mama and I flowers of some sort with some crayons that Truda had procured for her. Most weeks, the flowers were brightly colored, clumsy and cartoonish and the end result was generally a cheery piece of artwork that warmed my heart to see. Other weeks, she drew with heavy strokes and used only a black crayon. It didn't matter what she drew—I always reacted with surprise and delight to her gift, and in return, I'd be rewarded with her smile. Most Sundays, Emilia's radiant smile was the highlight of my week.

Every week, she'd hand me her little gift, then ask me breathlessly if I'd heard news about Tomasz. Every week, I'd pretend I was still sure he was fine, and it was only a matter of time before he came home.

"Of course he is. He's alive and he's well and he's doing everything he can to get back to us."

"How can you be so sure?"

"He promised me, silly. And Tomasz would never lie to me."

"Thank you, big sister," she'd sigh, and she'd hug me tightly.

Life on the farm was hard, but for the most part in the first few years, it was quiet. Mama's theory seemed correct—we kept our heads down and we worked hard, and other than those sporadic spot checks, the occupation raged on around us. We were starved of food and missing our boys, but life was *almost* tolerable.

On Sunday, I was always reminded that life in the town was not nearly so simple. At those Sunday lunches, Truda and Mateusz were stoic, but Emilia was still far too young to hide her trauma. It would spill out of her without prelude or warning, randomly disturbing sentences that none of us really knew how to react to.

"And then the Jews were fixing the building but the soldier said 'filthy Jew' and he hit the old man in the face with the shovel and…"

"Enough of that talk at lunch, Emilia." Truda always spoke to her with the perfect blend of *firm* and *soft*. Emilia would glance around the table, clear her throat and then go back to eating her food in silence. Another week, we were having a quiet conversation about the chickens when Emilia looked at me and said without preamble, "The woman was dead in the pond at the park, Alina. She was floating with her face in the water and her skin was all puffy and the water turned pink."

"Emilia!" Truda winced, but she was flustered. "I told you—I told you not to look at that—I told you—"

Emilia looked between us all, her brow creasing.

"Have some more lunch, child," Mama said hastily, and she

scooped Emilia's plate up to slide an extra potato pancake onto it. "Don't think about such things."

After lunch, the adults would sip at watered-down coffee, and I'd often take Emilia to sit on the steps beside the barn so that she could talk freely for a few minutes. I hated that this sweet, innocent child was surrounded by death and ugliness, but I could also see that she *needed* to talk about those things, even if the rest of our family couldn't bear to hear it.

"I like Truda and Mateusz, but I miss Tomasz and my father," she told me one Sunday.

"I miss them too."

"I don't like the mean soldiers in our town. And I don't like dead people everywhere. And I don't like it when the guns shoot in the night and I don't know if the bullet is coming for me."

"I know."

"Everything scares me too much and I want it to stop now," she said.

"Me too."

"No one ever wants to talk about it. Everyone is so angry with me when I talk about it. Why do they want to pretend it's not happening? Why can't we talk about it?"

"It's just our way, Emilia." I smiled at her sadly, then pulled her close for a hug. "Sometimes, talking about things makes them seem more real. Do you understand that?"

Emilia sighed heavily as she nodded.

"I do. But I feel better when I talk about it. I want to understand."

"You can talk to me. I don't understand, either, but I'll always listen to you."

"I know, big sister," she said, and then at last, her little smile returned.

CHAPTER 9

Alina

We owned an unusually large allotment of chickens for a family in our region, because in the dry years when the crops did not perform well in our poor soil, our family had always survived on a steady diet of eggs. Now those eggs had to be carefully collected and counted, and I didn't dare drop a single one because the Nazis had set us a quota of exactly twenty eggs per day.

Sometimes the chickens laid only eighteen or nineteen eggs. The first few times we were short, I was in a cold-blooded panic as I searched for the others. and then sick to my stomach when I finally conceded defeat and gave my parents the news. The next day, there was always an extra egg or two—and given Father only took the eggs into town twice a week, it always equalized before the soldiers even knew we were short.

We *always* met the quota. Very occasionally, we produced an egg or two above, but never a single egg less. For a while I thought Mother Mary was hearing my prayers and we were being blessed, but over time, I became a little more cynical.

Another summer harvest came and went, and I assumed we'd handed over every single morsel of produce as we'd been instructed to. This was usually a busy period for Mama and me, because after the harvest we would preserve as much as we could to cover the winter months, but now there was no excess to preserve, and our evenings were instead free. It felt strange to me, and I was surprised to find I missed the endless hours of pickling and preserving with Mama that we'd always shared in previous years.

But then I woke up late one night and was confused by the heavy sugar scent in the air. I stared up at the ceiling for a long while, wondering if I was imagining things or perhaps even dreaming, but the smell persisted and I became increasingly confused. I slipped out of bed to open my door, and found Mama standing over the stove. The smell of sugar and strawberries was unmistakably strong in the living area. The oil light was off— the room was illuminated only by the dull flicker of the fire through the grill on the stove. Mama was staring into the pot, her gaze distant and thoughtful.

"What are you doing?" I asked. She startled out of her daze and looked at me sharply.

"Cleaning the pot," she said abruptly. "Back to bed!"

"I... Mama," I said, my throat suddenly dry. I stared down at the pot over the fire, breathed in the heavy scent again and forced myself to state the obvious. "That's jam, Mama. I can *see* you're making jam."

Mama looked back to the pot for a moment. She stirred some more, and then she turned back to me, a challenge in her gaze.

"Of course it's not jam," she said. She lifted the spoon so I could see the syrup dripping off it. A drop formed then fell, and then another, but Mama remained completely silent even as long moments dragged past us while I watched the spoon, and she watched me. My sleepiness cleared, and I swallowed a sudden lump in my throat, then forced my eyes back to Mama. The look in her eyes was so intense that it became very hard to look at her, so I flicked my gaze between Mama and the spoon. In the semidark room, the thick red jam looked exactly like blood. It was quite hot in the house because of the fire, but a shiver ran through me from my head to my toes.

Mama lowered the spoon back down into the mix and resumed her stirring, and she stared into the pot as she murmured, "If it was jam, I'd be withholding produce, and if I was caught doing that, I'd be executed. They'd shoot me or hang me or beat me to death." She left another long pause, and for me, that silence was loaded with the sheer terror of the truth of her statement. "Now, would I *ever* take such a foolish risk?"

There was an open challenge in her eyes, as if Mama was daring me to say otherwise, and as if me stating the blatantly obvious would be the thing that caused her death. I was shaking now—confronted with the reality of our circumstances in a way that I had easily avoided until that moment.

I dropped my chin and shook my head.

"No, Mama. Of course you wouldn't," I croaked out.

"Good. Go back to bed."

I did. I turned quickly and ran into my room and even though it was uncomfortably warm, I climbed under my blankets and I pulled them up over my head. Eventually, I fell into a fitful sleep, but when I woke the next morning to watch the sunrise through my window, there was no way I could avoid facing the truth.

My mother was hiding food from the Nazis. And now that I knew for sure, I wanted to know exactly how extensive her deceit was.

The chickens were hard to count when they were outside during the day—especially because our flock had free rein of the house yard and the large barn during the day. But at night I would chase them into the barn and lock them away to keep them safe from foxes. The next night, I decided to confirm my suspicions. I locked the chickens in the barn, left them to settle, and then went back to count them once they were still.

"We have twenty-three chickens, plus the roosters," I said to Mama when I went inside. She looked at me, then frowned.

"No. Exactly twenty, plus the three roosters," she said abruptly.

"Maybe we have some strays then, because I just counted—"

"We have *exactly twenty*, Alina," Father said flatly. The words bounced around the walls of our small house, and then I knew.

"We have twenty chickens," I echoed dully.

Jam, eggs... Where did it end? I started watching the supplies Father would return with when he went to get our rations, and I compared it to the food we were eating. We were hardly living a lavish lifestyle—but we all ate eggs most days, despite Father only bringing a half-dozen back from the town each week. We'd always had jam with our bread, and I had assumed it was left over from the season before the war, but now I looked closely at the jar we were eating from.

That very same jar had lasted for months. The jam never seemed to go down.

I wondered what my diet would look like if it wasn't for the contraband jam and the extra eggs. I wondered what else my parents were doing that they didn't want me to know about. Soon, I'd stare at the strawberry jam on my biscuit and feel somehow equally panicked that my mother had risked her life to give it to me, and that perhaps it might be the last serving.

One morning, when Mama and I were collecting the eggs, I waited until she'd rounded the corner of the barn to check the house yard. I ran back inside for the oil lamp, then I forced myself to go down into the dark cavity of the cellar. It had been hard enough to force myself into that space with my whole family around me, even when the threat of bombing was looming. My heart was racing as I climbed inside, but it nearly stopped altogether when I found only a single, dusty jar of jam and two bolted potatoes.

That's when I realized that even worse than the thought of Mama keeping a secret supply of food was the possibility that we'd already exhausted what she had. I clambered out of the cellar and back toward Mama.

"Mama," I choked. "We have run out of food, haven't we?"

"No," she said, and she continued her work as if I hadn't spoken. I stared at her in disbelief, then grabbed her upper arm to force her to look at me.

"But I went into the cellar."

She silenced me with a single, incredulous look, and then she barked a laugh.

"Alina," she said, "since when do *you* go into the cellar?"

"I was just so worried…"

"When you need to be concerned, I will tell you. Until then, work hard and don't ask so many questions."

"But, Mama," I said uneasily, "I *need* to understand."

"Sometimes, *not* understanding something is the wise thing to do," Mama sighed, and she glanced up at me. "We are nothing to the invaders, Alina. We were already poor, so there is not much more for them to take from us and if they think they are getting all of our produce, they leave us alone…for the most part. But if they suddenly start paying attention, *then* you and I will discuss this matter. Until that day, you have to trust Father and I to take care of you."

The jam kept coming long after it should have run out, and the potato cakes kept coming on Sundays, and most mornings Mama would silently serve me a heaping mound of eggs with my ration portion of oatmeal. I saw her slipping potatoes and eggs and sometimes even a small bag of grain or sugar into Truda's coat after lunch every Sunday. I saw that all of us looked drawn and too slim, but Emilia somehow kept color in the apples on her cheeks. I saw the large sacks of wheat and sugar my Father uncovered in the back of the cart after a "spontaneous" trip to the town to "visit with Truda."

We were surviving only because my parents were covertly skimming from our harvests and making the occasional dip into the black market. It was thriving in those days, because every single Polish citizen was in exactly the same position.

I didn't question Mama again after that morning. I wanted to protest more, and I always planned to—I just didn't know how

I'd survive once the food dried up. Even with those scant added calories, every now and again I'd find myself light-headed in a field, or so exhausted I'd have to sit and rest midtask. Without that little bit of extra sustenance, I knew I could never keep up with the work my parents needed me to manage in order to keep the farm going.

So instead of digging for the truth from my parents, I quietly added yet another stream of terror to the river of it that ran beneath each hour of my life.

Sometimes, when I was planting or weeding or harvesting in the vegetable field, I'd stand to stretch my aching back, and when I looked to the sky, I'd notice a rising tower of black smoke. At first, this barely caught my attention because there had been smoke on the horizon all the time when the occupation first began. But I gradually noticed that this was different from the smoke that rose when the Nazis destroyed our buildings with fire—because *that* came and went and moved around, and *this* odd smoke was always in the exact same place.

It was initially an occasional landmark, but as one year under Nazi rule became two, the smoke became visible almost every day. Gradually, I made the reluctant connection between that odd tower of smoke and an awful smell that hung heavily in the air some days, like a sickly blanket across the whole district. When the smoke was billowing and there was no wind, that god-awful stench was never far behind. This was a scent unlike any other—not something I could identify, but something that made me feel physically ill and sometimes inexplicably scared. Soon, I didn't want to so much as look at the black line of smoke against the deep blue of our skies, as if the very sight of the smoke was a threat to me.

On cloudless days, I could sometimes trick myself into believing that we had gone back in time, back to the years before Tomasz left Trzebinia. One such day, I'd been working with my hands but my thoughts had strayed elsewhere. I'd imagined that Tomasz might wander down the hill, whistling, to join us for lunch and make my father laugh with some outrageous tale from his high school life, or that Filipe might bound in from the far field to beg Mama to let him go to Justyna's for a visit. I stared up at the sky and ignored for a moment the way that I'd been tired for so long, I'd forgotten what "refreshed" felt like.

Mama and I had been weeding in the morning, but when we emerged from the house after lunch, my hopeful, wistful mood deflated in an instant when I saw that the smoke had started. By afternoon, as we planted on the other side of the vegetable field, the black-gray line had risen so high that it seemed to stretch all the way across the sky.

"Stop looking," Mama snapped at me suddenly. "Looking at it won't make it go away."

I flushed, then glanced at her and saw the scowl on her face. I could tell she didn't like its presence any more than I did, so I dared to ask for the first time, "What do you think it is?"

"I know what it is. It's from a work camp for prisoners," Mama said abruptly. "Just a furnace."

"A furnace?" I repeated, glancing at the tower of smoke again and frowning. "That must be a very big furnace."

"It's to heat the water," she told me. "There are many prisoners in the camp—mostly prisoners of war. They are just warming water for the showers and the laundry."

This seemed to make sense—so I told myself there was nothing at all to fear in that tower of smoke, that my visceral reaction to it was in fact an *over*reaction; that I had been right in trying to ignore it altogether.

But when I saw it again the next day, and the day after that, and then soon it was there day and night, some deep part of me knew that my mother was wrong.

I still didn't know what the smoke represented, but I was increasingly certain that it was yet another sign that the noose around the neck of my nation was being tightened.

We heard of Filipe's death only by chance. The twins had been placed together on an immense work farm hundreds of miles away from us, working with young people from all over Poland, one of which was assigned to camp administration. This man was later "promoted" by the Nazis to a more senior post in Krakow. On his way to the new position, he came through Trzebinia and sought us out.

Just a few months after they arrived at the camp, Filipe had been outraged by some happening in the camp and had tried to intervene—unsuccessfully, because of course the camp was heavily guarded and several soldiers turned their weapons on him in an instant. His death didn't feel at all like an inevitability to me, although in hindsight, maybe it should have.

There was nothing to bury, no body to conduct a service over. Instead, we heard that he was gone, and that was that. There was no verification, no official notification—just silence where there had been silence for many months anyway. Nothing had changed, except that nothing was the same anymore, because once I had two brothers, and now I had one.

This was what the occupation did to families; it shattered them into pieces without closure or explanation. Occasionally, as with Emilia and Truda, random pieces got stuck back together in a whole new way. But mostly? Our oppression was loss without reason, and pain without a purpose.

My parents seemed to retreat into themselves after this, and we all just lived and worked in that tiny little house without ever directly discussing the agony of it all, each of us carrying the burden of our grief alone. I kept moving forward only because I clung to a thread of optimism that just wouldn't die. Perhaps the resistance would make an impact. Perhaps Stanislaw would come home. Perhaps Tomasz would find his way home. Every time Father went into the town, I'd wait breathlessly by the door.

"Any news of Tomasz or Stani?" I'd ask, and he'd shake his head and often give me a soft kiss against my head or a hug.

"Sorry, Alina. Not today."

"Did you ask?"

"Everyone I could, child. I promise."

And then just when the worst of my grief for Filipe was easing, Father came home from a trip to pick up our rations. It was winter by then, and there was snow all around, so I'd finished tending the animals by midmorning and was hiding inside by the fire, darning socks with Mama. I heard the creak of the gate opening and I ran to the door to greet Father as I always did—but the slump of his shoulders and his red-rimmed eyes said it all.

"Tomasz or Stani?" I asked numbly. I saw Father look beyond me into the house and I followed his gaze. Mama had risen from her seat and the color was gone in an instant from her face, and then I knew that she'd read the truth in Father's eyes, communicating with him without a word in that way they had perfected after thirty years of marriage. She let out a wail as she sank to her knees and covered her face with her hands. I looked back to Father and shook my head.

"No," I whispered. He gave a heavy, shuddering sigh.

"Stani," he choked, as his eyes filled with tears. "Dysentery."

Almost overnight, it was as if my brothers had never existed at all. It was one thing for the Nazis to have the power of life or death over us, but this preternatural ability to entirely erase two young men who had meant so much to us? Just like that, my parents had gone from a family of four children to a family of two daughters. Any parent would struggle with the loss—but for a long time, Father was caught in an overwhelming depression. I'd catch him standing in the fields, staring into space, and Mama sometimes had to force him to eat his sparse ration. When Truda, Mateusz and Emilia visited with us on Sunday,

Father would sit apart from the rest of the family, staring into space. It was as if he'd given up. I feared that war had taken his sons and his name would no longer continue after he was gone, so he no longer saw the point of carrying on at all. Mama herself was courageous during the day, but I'd wake sometimes at night to hear the quiet sobs she could no longer contain.

All I had left to hope for was Tomasz. I'd always thought of him as my whole world, but when everything else around me became ugliness and grief, I pined for him with an intensity that frightened me. I was furious with God that He had let these things happen to my country, and often during the day I'd promise myself that I would never pray again. I didn't want to be a Catholic anymore—I didn't want to be a person of faith anymore—if God would let such terrible things happen, I wanted nothing more to do with Him.

But every night I relented, and every night I made a silent truce, at least with Mother Mary. Just for a moment or two, I put my anger and my confusion aside, so I could plead with her to intercede for me and to keep Tomasz safe.

But I no longer asked my father to ask after Tomasz in the town, and I no longer prayed for news of him. Every *other* piece of news in those past months had changed things, and never for the better, so I told myself that even deafening silence was preferable to noise if the noise always ended in grief.

CHAPTER 10

Alice

I convince Mom to go back to her house a second time to bring her own iPad in for Babcia. Eddie needs his so we can't leave it behind, but it doesn't feel right to leave Babcia without a voice. Mom gets the iPad, then I search for the AAC app in the App store. It's an insanely expensive app—almost three hundred dollars. Mom grumbles when she sees the price, but she puts her password in and buys it anyway. Once Babcia realizes what I'm doing, she hits the *thank you* button again and again.

Finally it's time to go home. All I can think about is getting Eddie settled and pouring myself a nice glass of wine, but Callie greets me at the door, blustering with fury.

"You are not going to believe what happened to me today. It's an outrage!"

Eddie *looks* like my child—the same green eyes, the same muddy blond hair, the same essential features. Until his pediatrician put him on risperidone to try to help with his repetitive movements, Eddie even had my slight frame—although he's thirty pounds heavier now and so that "slight frame" is somewhat hidden these days. But Callie is all Wade and she always has been—she's tall and broad, and she has the same shade of hair and cool blue eyes. She also inherited his intellect, and his black-and-white perspective on life.

"What is it, Callie?" I ask her with a sigh. She plants her

hands on her hips and her chin rises defiantly. I recognize the signs of indignation in my daughter, and I mentally brace myself. What is it today? Did someone dare to suggest she might be *wrong* about something again? Or maybe a teacher paired her with one of the slightly less gifted students for an assignment? Right on cue, Callie delivers an outrage.

"There was a substitute teacher and she made me do *regular* class work. Like I was a *normal* kid! It's a human rights abuse!"

Eddie drops onto his beanbag in the front room. He rests the dreidel on his lap, and I realize that he's been carrying that thing all day now. I wish I had asked for that woman's name from the store, so I could send her a note to thank her. The remote is waiting right where he left it this morning on the right-hand side of the beanbag, so he loads the YouTube app on the television, then navigates to a *Thomas the Tank Engine* video. He won't watch those in public anymore and lately at school he's been reacting violently if the teacher tries to put one on for him. She thinks he's socially aware enough to understand that he's probably a bit old to watch them, but he doesn't have the language to talk to us about that, so he only wants to watch them in private. That nearly breaks my heart. I'm glad he still binges on them at home, just as I'm glad I can leave him be now. He'll probably watch a half dozen episodes of the show before dinner. I think it's the Eddie-equivalent of that glass of wine I so desperately need right now.

I look from my son who can't communicate, to my daughter who can't *help* but communicate, and I sigh and grasp for patience. These moments of surreal disparity in my parenting obligations happen periodically and I always manage to navigate them, but I feel my tolerance for *this* moment slipping through my fingers, and I grapple to get a handle on it. My reserve of patience becomes a life rope I just can't grasp, and I say the right words but they come out too short, so that I fire the full force of my adult-grade sarcasm at my ten-year-old daughter.

"I doubt it was 'regular class work,' Callie. I don't think they do 'regular class work' at an academic magnet school."

"It *was* regular work. It wasn't *my* advanced program, so it may as well have been finger-painting to someone like me."

It's the determined arrogance that gets me. It's the wide stance of her feet, the hands pinching into her hips, the jutted chin, the way her gaze keeps flicking to Eddie like she's trying to ram home the point. *I'm your highly gifted child, not your special needs child. I deserve better than this because I'm bright, not challenged.*

I'm raising a monster, and that sudden realization makes me very angry. I mirror her stance and I say flatly, "One day of being treated like everyone else won't hurt you, Callie."

"I *knew* you wouldn't understand. *Dad* understands. Dad knows how frustrating it is to have unlimited intellectual potential and to be forced to do coloring-in sheets like a…like a…" She pauses, then she looks at Eddie once more, but this time she lets her gaze linger before she says bitterly, "Like a *retard*."

I hate that word so much. It's the connotations of uselessness that gets me, the imagery it inspires of padded cell institutions and children left behind. The very sound of it makes me see red.

"Pascale!" I snap. "Go to your room, *now*."

Her nostrils flare as she stares at me, and then she bursts into tears and runs off up the stairs to her room. Wade appears in the doorway to the kitchen. He's wearing my apron; a white and neon pink number he got me for Mother's Day last year. Wade is so tall that the apron barely reaches the tops of his thighs. He's wearing it over his business shirt and trousers, and he looks completely ridiculous.

But for the fact that I'm seething, I'd probably have burst out laughing at the sight of him. Instead, I stare at him, and I hope he's going to say something—anything—to display even just a little empathy.

"It's days like these," he says, starting *exactly* as I need him to, but finishing the sentence with an utterly disappointing focus on Callie, "I think we should think about streaming her into a class with older gifted kids who are operating at the same level as she is. She's not some regular gifted kid—she's highly gifted, so it's frustrating for her to have to—"

"No," I say, far too sharply. He falls silent, and I drag in a steadying breath, then try to soften my tone. This is a well-worn argument—because I'm determined that Callie has some age-appropriate friends as well as academic challenge, and Wade seems to think friends are somewhat overrated and just wants her to work at the limit of her potential. "I'm sorry. I just can't have this conversation again, not today. Please—tomorrow?"

He hesitates, then nods, and he belatedly asks, "Okay. How did it go with Babcia?"

"I'll tell you about it once I eat," I sigh. "What are you cooking? Something smells good."

"It's just some chicken steaks and vegetables."

He leads the way into the kitchen and I see the chaos—pots and pans all over the benches, open packets of ingredients on every conceivable surface, even offcuts from vegetables on the floor. This man literally understands how to create and manipulate nanoparticles to do all kinds of semimagical medical and industrial things, but he cannot get his head around the rule that if you *drop something, you pick it up*. But I can't yell at him about the kitchen being messy, because technically he's helping me right now, even though I know he will serve up the meal, eat it, and then retire to his study to catch up on the work he missed this afternoon, and I'll be left with the disaster zone of a kitchen.

That's a problem for later. He's in the kitchen now, and so for now, it's *his* problem, and I'm going to snatch some time for myself while I can. I walk straight to the cupboard, withdraw a bottle of merlot and pour myself a glass.

"Wade," I say. He looks at me expectantly, as if I'm about to praise him or thank him. He's visibly disappointed when I instead ask, "Can you bring me a plate of dinner when it's ready?"

"Going to eat in the bath tonight?"

The man has some redeeming qualities—at least he knows me every bit as well as I know him.

"I most definitely am. Do you have a problem with that?"

Wade smirks, then shakes his head.

"Honey, we've been married a long time, so I'm very aware that there's not much you *won't* do in a bathtub."

I drink half the wine in one long gulp, then top the glass off before I take a few steps toward the door. An afterthought hits me, so I turn back to the cupboard, withdraw a can of soup and pass it to Wade.

"Eddie needs to eat too. See you soon. Thanks, and...don't skimp on the potato?"

I soak in the bath until my skin has wrinkled. It's my only refuge sometimes, and Wade is right—there's not much I *can't* accomplish as the relaxed, bathtub version of myself. I do hours of reading whenever we encounter a new challenge with Eddie, and most of the time I do that on the iPad or my Kindle here in the bath. Wade used to worry that I'd electrocute myself one day, so he installed a spring-loaded cable to the ceiling. Now, if I drop my device, it bounces up instead of falling into the water.

This place—the gleaming white tiles, the soothing weightlessness of the water, the magnificent, restorative silence—*this* is where my thoughts flow uninterrupted. Callie knows not to disturb me in the bath, and although Eddie will eventually seek me out if he needs me, most of the time he'll just sit in whatever problem he's gotten himself into until I come find him. That's an issue most of the time. It's a blessing when it comes to my bath time.

I luxuriate in the bath. I am *still* in the bath—completely motionless, but for the gentle movements of my arms as I read. In every other sphere of my life, I constantly feel like I'm rushing—

but not here. This is the only treat I give myself, but I take it greedily—during stressful periods, I take a bath every single day. And yes, on days like today, I'm not above a glass of wine or two here—or even dinner. I can't say chicken steak is a particularly bath-friendly meal, but I make it work. Then, when the water has cooled for the second time, I sigh and return to the real world.

Next, I convince Eddie to take his melatonin—the only way he'll sleep more than a few hours. Then, I convince Eddie to half clean his teeth, a task he still hates, even though I've tried every special needs toothbrush, toothpaste flavor and technique known to humankind. Then I convince Eddie to climb into bed, and once he's settled, I call past my daughter's room. She's reading—she's always reading—so much so that it's a challenge to find texts that are complex enough to engage her but don't cover themes that are just too mature for her emotionally. Tonight, she's engrossed in *The Hitchhiker's Guide to the Galaxy* for the umpteenth time, and when I kiss her good-night, she barely looks up from the page.

Not ready to apologize yet, then. I know it'll come, so I tell her I love her and leave her be.

There's no more prolonging the inevitable—that kitchen needs attention, so I head there next. It takes over an hour to undo the damage Wade did cooking tonight, and just as I suspected, he's nowhere to be seen. I try *not* to resent that, because he did help me out today, and in doing so, he significantly exceeded my expectations. Still, my thoughts wander back to Babcia as I clean, and I think about how much easier this whole situation would be if Wade was different—Wade, not Eddie. I can't let myself wish Eddie was different. Even letting that thought linger in my mind would feel like a betrayal to my son.

When I finally wander into the bedroom Wade and I share, I'm surprised to find he's in the bedroom too—I assumed he was in his study working, but he's had a shower and he's pulling on his pajamas. I sit on the bed and watch him dress.

"Want to talk about it?" he asks softly.

The offer is surprising, but it's most definitely welcome. I lean back into the pillows and tuck my legs up, then wrap my arms around them, pulling myself smaller as if that will make me stronger.

"Babcia keeps asking for Pa."

"Poor Babcia," Wade sighs. "Has she…forgotten?"

"I don't think so. Mom thinks she's confused, but… I'm starting to think she wants something else. Maybe she wants some information about Pa, but she doesn't know how to ask."

"That sounds pretty frustrating."

"It is," I sigh, and now dressed in his pajamas, Wade approaches the bed and sits up beside me. He turns me slightly, and I shift to give him access to rub my shoulders. The pressure and the kneading feel amazing, but just as I start to relax, he drops a gentle but lingering kiss against my neck.

There's a subtext in that kiss—an offer and a request, and it irritates me to my very bones. *Seriously? He thinks I'm in the mood for sex after the day I've had?*

I try to maneuver subtly out of his way and keep talking as if I didn't notice the kiss.

"I honestly don't know what we would have done if it wasn't for Eddie's AAC app. Her right hand doesn't seem to be working the way it should—I don't think she can write."

"Uh-uh."

"The thing is, what could she possibly want *me* to find out? She lived an entire life with Pa, what question did she never think to ask him? After seventy-plus years with someone, how can they still have secrets from you?"

There's a moment of silence as my husband ponders this, then he says cautiously, "You have secrets from me and we've been together for well over a decade."

"I don't have secrets from you," I say stiffly. Wade sighs and drops back to sink into his pillows. I turn around and frown at him. "I *don't*."

"You're angry at me all of the time, and most of the time I have no idea why."

"Seriously, Wade? You have *no idea why?*"

He raises his eyebrows at me.

"Go on," he says, taunting me. "Get it off your chest. You're obviously wanting to vent. What is it today? I'm a shit father? I'm a shit husband? I work too much? I don't understand how hard your life is? I don't get what it's like to sacrifice your career?"

I glare at him, then I stand, pick up my pillow and head for the door.

"Go on, Alice," he calls after me, his tone flat. "Run away and feel sorry for yourself because Big Bad Wade tried to make you have an adult conversation."

"You *asshole*," I say, and I turn back to him from the doorway and scowl at him through my tears. "She's going to *die*, Wade. Babcia is going to die and I don't know how to help her and you pick *today* to try to address the problems in our marriage?"

I see the brief flash of remorse cross his face as I slam the door and walk to Eddie's room. My son is curled up in the corner of his bed, but the duvet is on the floor beside him. It's weighted and to me, uncomfortably heavy, but the pressure helps keep Eddie calm, although it also tends to slip off the bed when he's restless. I lift the duvet over his body and tuck him in, then reach under the bed and withdraw the trundle mattress.

It's already made up, because I end up in here pretty often. Usually I come in here to help Eddie sleep, but tonight, it's for me. Maybe Wade is right. Maybe I am running away, but all I know is, I *need* comfort from him tonight and not demands, and if I can't get those things, I'll settle for space instead.

CHAPTER 11

Alina

Since the invasion, the Nazis had been executing any citizen who provided Jews with material assistance—but when this failed to deter some people, they broadened the decree. Now they would execute the family of such a person—women and children included. For a crime as innocent as handing a Jewish person a glass of water, an entire family would now be slaughtered.

We learned about this new ruling the same way we learned about many of the struggles in Trzebinia, from Truda and Mateusz at Sunday lunch. It was snowing that day, and Emilia was wearing a black coat that was several sizes too big for her, inherited from one of the other children in their street. Her gifts of posies had stalled when the cold came, but Emilia still brought me a drawing each week, often on the back of propaganda pamphlets, because paper was increasingly difficult for Mateusz and Truda to come by.

That week, she'd given me an artwork in charcoal, a shadowy image of a rose missing many of its petals. I had a pile of such pictures in my room now, the motifs increasingly dark as the world around us was drained of light. Now Emilia drew in charcoal all the time, and she drew flowers in various states of death and, occasionally, sharp, bewildering abstracts. I still accepted each gift with a surprised smile, and she always looked so happy to have pleased me. The moodiness of her pictures concerned me, but I kept them all—I had a neat pile in the drawer with my precious ring.

That day, the conversation at lunch was focused all around that new punishment for assisting Jews. Truda was sullen in her sadness, but Mateusz was visibly shaking in frustration.

"It's just hopeless," Truda said miserably. "Every time I think it can't get any worse, they find new depths of cruelty."

"This will go a long way to discouraging those who are in the business of helping the Jews in hiding," Father murmured, and his gaze flicked briefly to me. "People are noble, but when you threaten someone's children...the very idea can make even the bravest man rethink heroic efforts."

"Why do the Nazis hate the Jews so much?" Emilia blurted in her usual fashion. Everyone stared at her, searching for a way to respond, until she slumped a little. "Why do they hate *us* so much? What did we ever do to them?"

She was growing up before my eyes, each week a little less innocent than the last. She was a little shy of nine years old, but Emilia sometimes seemed more grown-up than I felt.

"Hitler wants land and power, and it is much easier to convince an army to die for you when you have an enemy to fight," Father said, quite gently. "And the Jews make for an easy enemy, because people will always hate what is different."

"Some people will help the Jews regardless," Mama said suddenly. I felt as though she was trying to reassure us somehow. "Some will be undeterred by any punishment. Some will help them no matter *what* those pigs threaten us with."

"And some are making so much gold from hiding Jews that even the threat of death to their families will not deter them," Mateusz sighed. This was the first I'd heard of such an arrangement, and I was shocked.

"Who would *do* such a thing?"

"They are the worst of our countrymen, Alina, those who

profit from the suffering of the innocent," Mateusz said, suddenly scowling. "*They* are little more than pigs, just as the Nazis are."

"Evil is closer to home than you think," Mama murmured under her breath as she rose to clear her plate. "That's why we trust no one outside of this family."

There was no mistaking the undertone as she said it—my mother was implying something. I waited for someone to elaborate, but instead, my father shot my mother an exasperated glare.

"We mustn't engage in rumors, Faustina. Gossip gets people killed in times like these." Father's tone was dismissive, but I frowned at them.

"Who are you talking about? Do we *know* someone who would do this?"

"Please leave it, Alina," Truda said, nodding pointedly toward Emilia. I glanced at my "little sister." She was watching me closely, and I suddenly felt embarrassed to be dismissed in front of her, yet again.

"I am so tired of you all treating me like a child!" I exclaimed. "You want me to pretend I am a fool, that I don't even have eyes in my head. Does no one in this family trust me at all?"

"We trust you," my mother said stiffly. "It is *everyone else* we don't trust. And Alina—you are only seventeen years old. You have to accept that there are *reasons* for the secrets we keep from you. I spoke out of turn. Please forgive me for that."

"I don't keep secrets from you, big sister," Emilia said hesitantly. Everyone looked at her, and she raised her chin. "I tell Alina *everything* because *she* lets me talk to her."

"I know you do, *babisu*," I said softly, and I reached across the table and squeezed her hand. "And you know I love talking to you." Emilia nodded, then she frowned at the rest of the adults at the table, as if they'd let us both down somehow. Truda changed the subject then and the conversation moved on, but long after our guests had left, I was still thinking about Mama's comment. I'd turned it over and over in my mind during the night—thinking of all of the people we knew in the town and the surrounding farms. Some were easy to dismiss—people like Justyna's father, Jan, who had made his hatred for the Jews clear. But beyond that? *Everyone* was desperate for food—almost everyone was desperately poor too—and gold could buy food on the black market. Despite Mateusz's disgust, I could imagine virtually anyone we knew agreeing to hide Jews if there was good money to be made.

I followed Mama out to the well the next morning when she went to fetch water, and as soon as we were alone, I asked her directly.

"Who were you talking about last night? When you said people we knew were hiding Jews for money?"

"I knew you would ask me today," Mama murmured.

"Well, I..." I paused, then I said in frustration, "Mama, you have to let me grow up. Even Emilia is growing up, but you and Father keep me locked away like an infant."

"One day, when this war is over, you'll look back and with the passing of time, these things that right now feel like unfair deceptions will seem like mercies," Mama said, and her gaze grew distant. "It might not be much, but all we can offer you is to protect you when we can, and sometimes that means to relieve you of the heavy burden of secrets. One day you'll be grateful that we kept you busy and kept your focus on survival. One day, daughter, all of this suffering will be contained in your memories, and you'll be free."

That seemed a dream too unlikely for me to waste energy hoping for it. I slumped even as she said it, and tears filled my eyes. I blinked them away, then whispered, "Do you really believe that?"

She sighed sadly.

"Alina, if I *didn't* believe that, I couldn't drag myself out of bed in the morning."

Spring came again, but it was difficult to find any joy in the blooming of the wildflowers in the grasses around our fields.

Mama and I again resumed our frantic schedule to prepare the new season's crops, but one day when we were working in the field together, I saw Justyna approaching the boundary of her property. She waved to me hesitantly.

"I think your friend would like a chat," Mama murmured.

"Can I go?" I asked. Mama nodded, and I scrambled to my feet and ran to greet her.

"Hello!" I said, excited at the prospect of a conversation with someone *other* than my family. "How have you been? I haven't seen you in months."

"I know," she said, dropping her gaze. "Father has kept me busy. I am sure it is the same for you."

"It is," I sighed, but then I noticed the purse of her lips. "Justyna, are you okay?"

"My aunt...my mother..." she started to say, then she inhaled and said in a rush, "I don't *exactly* know what's going on, but I think my aunt Nadia might know something about your Tomasz."

My stomach dropped to my toes because I immediately assumed the worst.

"Oh no, Justyna...is it *bad* news?"

Justyna shook her head hastily, but then she shrugged.

"I don't actually know. I just heard Father and Mama whispering. They were arguing—Father wants us to stay, but Mama wants to take me to go to her other sisters in Krakow. She said it's too dangerous in the country these days. Father said something about Nadia, and then Mama *definitely* said 'Tomasz Slaski.' I didn't hear much, but I heard that bit clear as a bell."

"Did you ask them what they were talking about?" I whispered, through suddenly numb lips. Justyna nodded, then her gaze saddened.

"They wouldn't tell me. Father got so angry when I asked, and Mama is very upset about something—she was crying so much last night. But you know my aunt Nadia, Alina. She is *so* kind…and she has suffered so much loss herself, I am sure she would be sympathetic to your situation. If you found a way to see her, I *know* she would tell you what she knows."

Nadia's house was just a few streets into Trzebinia, right on our side of town. I could run there, talk to her and still be home in under half an hour.

I turned back to look at the house and saw Mama's eyes inevitably fixed on me.

"I wasn't sure if I should tell you. I know your parents will never let you go to her," Justyna said, her eyes following mine. I swallowed as I nodded. "I couldn't *not* tell you, though. If Filipe…back before…well, if someone had news. Any news. I would want to know."

Could I ask Truda to visit Nadia for me? I dismissed the idea immediately. She would never court danger, not in a million years, but even if I could convince her to do it, I'd never forgive myself if Nadia was tangled up in something dangerous and there were consequences for my sister and her family. Whatever news Nadia had of my Tomasz, I doubted she'd come across it without some risk.

"What are you going to do?" Justyna asked me.

I raised my chin, just a little.

"The only thing I can do."

It was an unseasonably cool night, and I'd left my window open so my parents wouldn't hear the squeal of the wooden frame moving when it came time for me to climb outside. I sat on my bed, fully dressed but hiding in a nest of blankets, dreading the coming moment when I'd have to leave the warmth. There was a full moon, but patches of clouds were floating past. As I stared out the window and waited, I watched the moonlight come and go.

How many stories had I heard over the months since the war began where someone had left home and simply never returned?

Sometimes their families learned their fates, but often they were just lost. I couldn't ask Mama for my ID papers, and my parents would surely catch me if I tried to find them myself, so I'd have to make this run without my documentation, and it was *well* past curfew. If a soldier so much as saw me, I was done for.

How would this story end for my family? Would my parents wake up tomorrow and find me missing, and never know what became of me? They simply wouldn't survive without me, not now that the boys were gone. The farm would fall to ruin, and the soldiers would take them away too.

Or would I climb out the window, run quickly up the hill and down the other side, knock on Nadia's door without incident, and beg her to tell me what she knew. If it was bad news, at least I would *know*. I pictured myself making the return journey sobbing and felt my muscles tense. It was a real possibility that this trip was going to be an ending, not a beginning.

I had long since convinced myself that *no news* was better than bad news, but that was when I had no chance of accessing any. Now that I knew there was potentially an update about Tomasz waiting just on the other side of the hill, there was no way I could remain passive. I'd have walked through gunfire for that news. I just hoped and prayed I wouldn't have to.

I had to take the chance, because this risk I was taking could change *everything* for me. If I knew where Tomasz was, I could try to figure out how to get to him.

And on that thought, I climbed carefully out through my window. The air was so cool my breath escaped as mist. I swallowed my fear, looked toward the hill, and then I forced myself to run.

I was slow and quite clumsy on any ordinary day, but adrenaline was on my side and I moved as quickly as I could. I wouldn't take the path everyone else took—because it wasn't the fastest route and I suspected that if I was going to be caught by some unexpected Nazi patrol crew, it would be on the established path.

I'd never seen soldiers in the woods, but if they were going to be there, they'd never know that territory like *I* did. I'd climbed the hill a hundred times at every point it could be climbed. The very best moments of my life had been spent at its summit, and I knew that space like I knew my own body.

So I climbed the steepest part of the slope, the most direct route to town but also the toughest ascent. I found myself completely out of breath before I'd even reached the top, but I forced myself to keep going, even as my lungs felt like they might burst and my heart was pounding so hard against my chest that I was scared people some miles away would hear it.

It was as I neared the summit that a prickling feeling rose across the back of my neck and just as I identified it as the sensation of being watched, there came the sound of a twig snapping somewhere behind me. I told myself it was my imagination, but the sense that I wasn't alone did not abate even as I moved faster, and soon I was certain I could hear soft footsteps on the ground behind me. But was it imagination or paranoia, or was someone really there? I couldn't risk stopping to check. I told myself it was probably Justyna—perhaps she was coming to join me? Then I told myself it was Mama or Father, hot on my heels. For just an instant that seemed like the worst-case scenario. Being caught by them would be terrible—their disappointment and anger would be difficult to face.

Rationality quickly corrected *that* notion, because of course, being caught sneaking out by my parents was far from the worst outcome in that moment, and with those footfalls drawing nearer, I actually started to pray that my parents were indeed about to catch me, because I was sure now that *someone* was. Someone was most definitely chasing me through the forest. Someone who wasn't willing to call out to identify themselves. Mama or Father would call out. So would Justyna.

I no longer cared if I made it to Nadia's house—in fact, now I wasn't even sure I *should* go to Nadia's house, even if, by some miracle, I made it to the top of the hill then down the other side in one piece. Because if it was a soldier pursuing me, what possible innocent explanation could I give for my midnight run through the woods to her house?

Suddenly, I wasn't running to a place—instead, I was running for my life. I had been afraid so many times over the course of the war, but in that moment what I felt was deeper than mere fear. It was some instinctual, whole-body flight away from the danger—I was operating on the certainty that death was about to catch me, and I felt the terror of that knowledge in every cell in my body.

When I neared the clearing, I heard my name. It wasn't a shout or even a call, it was quite a desperate whisper and when the sound registered in my brain, panic, disbelief and relief merged so suddenly that all of my thoughts went a little haywire. I was running too fast to stop suddenly, but I tried to do so anyway, at the same time as I tried to turn to see if I'd correctly identified the owner of the voice. Perhaps unsurprisingly, I ended up on my backside in the dirt, my head spinning as I watched my pursuer finally catch up to me and sink to the ground near me.

"When I catch my breath, and when you catch yours, you're going to explain yourself, Alina Dziak," Tomasz panted. He sounded exhausted but there was a vein of good-natured humor in his whisper. "How did you even know I was out here? I've been so careful. It was the eggs, wasn't it? I knew I'd taken too many. Are you angry that I stole from your family? I only did so because you have so many chickens… I didn't think they'd be missed."

I rubbed my head, feeling for the shape of a bump. Had I knocked myself out? I must have dreamed the last long minutes of being chased, and now I was hallucinating my deepest desire. But my fingers could find no bump—my bottom was throbbing, but the rest of me seemed unharmed. Except if I wasn't hurt, why was I suddenly seeing Tomasz? Had I lost my mind?

"I…" I tried to talk, but the words stuck in my mouth. I was too confused to be hopeful. A shaft of filtered moonlight suddenly fell across his face and I squinted at him, trying to make sense of what I was seeing. It was Tomasz's hair, overgrown but familiar, and Tomasz's beautiful eyes, shadowed because of the darkness, and Tomasz's face, even if it was hidden under an unruly beard. Even before hope could dawn, I was inexorably drawn to him. I found myself crawling automatically across the ground, tears streaming from my eyes. I was still scared, but now I was simply scared to believe my own eyes. "I…"

"Are you hurt?" he asked, and he scrambled the remaining distance to meet me. I reached up to touch his face incredulously, tentatively, just with the pads of my fingers in case I made contact too sharply and he disappeared. But Tomasz was not so hesitant—he cradled my face in his hands and he peered down at me, urgently scanning my expression in the semidarkness. "Alina, *God*, Alina, please tell me you aren't hurt. I couldn't bear it. I'm sorry I chased you—I was trying to get your attention without shouting, but I didn't know what else to do. They can't find me here." I continued to stare at him in disbelief, and he suddenly dropped his hands to my shoulders and he shook me gently. "Alina, my love, you're scaring me. Please tell me you're okay."

I did the only rational thing, given the circumstances—I thumped him. My hands were still in fists, and I beat the sides of them against his chest again and again as I sobbed.

"Tomasz! I'm scaring *you*? You scared me half to death!"

He pushed my fists aside, but rather than pushing me away, he scooped me onto his lap and pressed my face into his shoulder as he whispered, "Shhh… I'm sorry, my love, I'm so sorry."

I pulled away from him to clasp the collar of his coat in both of my fists, then *I* shook *him*, hard. In the recesses of my mind, it registered how dirty he was. Beneath my fingers, I felt the roughness of dried mud in the wool of his collar.

"What are you *doing here*?"

"Hiding?" he offered, giving me a slightly wry grin. I shook him furiously.

"Tomasz! How long have you been hiding in the woods!"

"Shh!" His hushing was a little more urgent now, because I was shouting in my bewilderment and my shock. "Just a few weeks... I..." He peered at me, confused. "Wait—you didn't know I was here? How *did* you find me?"

"Weeks?" I gasped, then I glared at him. "You have been here for weeks and you didn't come to let me know you were okay? Do you have any idea how scared I've been?"

"Alina," he whispered, gently scolding me. "Surely you knew I'd come back for you."

"I *did* know that!" I protested, but then I started to cry all over again. "But I was scared. I was so worried that you were hurt... or maybe that you'd found another life somewhere."

He brushed my hair back from my face. "I told you that last night before I left. We are meant to be together. I was always coming back for you, and I always, always will."

We both paused at that, and we just stared at each other, soft smiles on our faces. I wiped the tears from my face and made a resolution to myself to *stop crying immediately*, because there was plenty to cry about in those days—but from where I found myself that night, things instantly looked much brighter. I decided there would be enough time for recriminations later, so I cupped his scruff-covered cheeks in my hands and I brought his face hard against mine so that I could kiss him. Oh, it was heaven to be with him again—heaven to press my lips against his and to breathe him in, *all* of him, the scent of the woods in his wildly overgrown hair and his clothes and even the scent of his sweat—just because it was *all* Tomasz, and it all made his return so much more real. By the time we parted, both of our faces were wet with tears.

There are some moments in life that are distorted by anticipation. It has a way of warping our expectations—inflating them somehow. This was not one of those moments. Every single thing about the minute Tomasz and I were reunited was just as delicious as I'd hoped, and sinking back into his arms was just as wonderful as all of the hours I'd spent dreaming had promised it would be.

"Where have you been?" I breathed.

"In Warsaw at first," he said, then he sighed and said it again as he shook his head. "Then these last few months, I've been making my way back here to you. It wasn't easy to get back."

He was only twenty-one, but his entire demeanor suddenly shifted. His shoulders were slumped, and now that I was sitting on his lap and close enough to see his face in the darkness, I could see that his cheeks were gaunt beneath his beard, and the sparkle had faded somewhat in those beautiful green eyes. Still, I loved him with a ferocity that almost frightened me. Dirty, starved, miserable and weary—none of that even registered beyond a passing acknowledgment. I loved him so deeply that all I really saw was that he was mine again. Everything else in the world might have gone to Hell, but that one fact was incontrovertible.

"It will be okay," I promised him. "We're together again now—that's all that matters."

"I know, my love. But you must understand, no one can know that I'm here, not even your parents. I'm in some trouble," he admitted. But before I could even think about what that might mean, it only occurred to me then that he probably had no idea about Aleksy's fate, or how difficult life in the region had become for us all.

"I have to tell you some things," I whispered, staring right into his eyes. For just a moment, I could barely recognize the boy I loved. He suddenly seemed like an old man—weary and worn down by war and sadness.

"If it is about my father, I have already heard," he whispered.

I exhaled, relieved that I didn't need to break the news to

him, but the sadness in his gaze was so heavy that I had to look away. Tomasz would have none of that. He slid his hands up over my shoulders and into my hair, then he cupped my cheek and he turned me to face him again. Our eyes met, and butterflies began to dance in my belly at the intensity of the love in his gaze.

"I know what your family has done for my sister, Alina, and how you saved her that day. I loved you before...you *know* I've always loved you, since before I even knew what that meant. But the way you have cared for her..." His voice broke a little, and he stopped, inhaled sharply, then continued unevenly, "If we weren't already engaged, I'd propose to you right this moment."

"And I'd say 'yes' again," I whispered. I brushed my lips against his, but as he moved to kiss me properly again, I sat back a little. "Wait, Tomasz. Tell me about this 'trouble.' Who is after you? Is it the invaders?"

He sighed, but wouldn't allow distance to grow between us—in fact, he leaned forward and rested his forehead against mine, then he closed his eyes. I closed mine too, and for a moment, we sat together in the silence.

"Everyone, Alina. I wish I didn't have to tell you this, but I am in trouble with *everyone*," he whispered hesitantly. "The Poles...the Nazis...it feels like I have managed to anger the whole world."

I wrapped my arms around his neck, wanting to hold him closer, but I opened my eyes to stare at him.

"What on earth did you do?" I asked him hesitantly.

"I made some mistakes in Warsaw," he admitted. "I've been trying to make up for them ever since. I'm still trying." I waited for him to tell me, but after a moment, he opened his eyes and turned away, exhaled shakily, then glanced back to me, his gaze pleading. "I don't want to talk about that now, Alina—please don't ask me to. There will be time for those discussions later. I just want to hold you, and for five minutes in this godforsaken war, feel like life is worth living again."

I could see the desperation in his gaze, and it broke my heart a little.

"Why stare when you could kiss me?" I asked him. He brought his lips back to mine then, and it was everything I'd missed and everything I'd needed over his absence. *Home*, I kept thinking, *I'm home*, which made no sense at all since I'd been stuck within my home for what felt like *forever* by that stage. But Tomasz's arms were a different kind of home—and I'd been homesick for that embrace for so long. When we broke apart some minutes later, he cupped my face in his hands again to stare into my eyes.

"Alina, you know I'll always find you? Promise me you know that. I don't know what's ahead of us—but when we're apart, there's only one thing on my mind, and that's getting back to my girl."

"I know. I feel the same," I promised him, and he kissed me once more.

"Now, you *really* need to tell me how you found me. Have I been careless?"

"I *didn't* find you. I was going to Nadia Nowak's house," I said. He stiffened immediately and pulled away from me just a little.

"Why were you going there?"

"Justyna heard her parents arguing, and they said something about Nadia…something about you…" I said, warily. Tomasz exhaled, then shifted away from me just a little. He was obviously troubled by this news, and I touched the back of my hand to his cheek gently.

"Alina," he said, glancing at me warily. "What do you know of Nadia Nowak?"

"What do you mean? Of course I know her. She's Ola's sister and… I know her husband has died and her children are mostly taken…" He was still staring at me, warily, but I shook my head. "Tomasz, I don't understand? What do you *mean*?"

"That is all you know?" he pressed, and I frowned.

"What else *is* there?"

"I have to ask you to stay away from Nadia's place, please. And you *must* stay well away from Jan Golaszewski."

"I was only going to Nadia's to ask after you, Tomasz. I have been so desperate for news, and this was the first hint of any I'd had in all of this time, so I *had* to try. And Father has long forbidden me from visiting Justyna at home and he keeps me so busy I barely even talk to her in the fields, so you have no concerns there, either," I told him softly. He nodded, then he pulled me close again and he pressed his face into my hair. "Tell me...tell me *everything*. Please, Tomasz. Where *are* you hiding?"

He hesitated only a moment before he admitted, "Just in the woods for now. I wanted so much to let you know I was okay and that I was here, but... I was scared doing so would endanger you. I thought if I waited here, I could keep an eye on your family and do what I could to be sure you were safe. And I have seen Emilia walking past on Sundays, so this...it is a very good spot for me. I am close and safe, but not endangering any of you by my presence."

"Tomasz, it's the *woods*!" I said, shocked. "There is nowhere to hide here, no protection from the weather. You can't possibly stay here!"

"I have a few spots where I can make myself invisible. The woods are too small for anyone else to bother hiding here, so it's not like the Nazis are sweeping the place every day. For the time being, it's fine."

"How do you sleep?"

He offered me a fond look at the concern in my tone.

"I manage, Alina."

"And food, how do you—" I was thinking through the logistics of his situation, and the more it sank in, the more scared I was.

"*Please* don't worry about me. There are so many who are far worse off than I am."

"Mama always says the same," I said, suddenly frustrated. "But Tomasz, just because our suffering isn't the *worst*, that doesn't mean it doesn't count." I kissed him once more, hard and fast. "Promise me you'll be safe."

"I will," he said, but he said it too lightly, and I gripped his collar tight again.

"You don't understand, Tomasz. I just couldn't bear it if anything happened to you. Promise me and mean it."

"I *do* understand," he assured me patiently. There was the sudden glimmer of tears in his eyes and his arms around me tightened. "The first night I came back here, I came to your window. I couldn't make myself look inside. I was too scared to look because I wasn't sure you would be there and…when I finally saw you sleeping, Alina, peaceful and healthy and…safe…and you were *so damned beautiful* I…couldn't even… I can't even…" His voice broke, and he clutched my upper arms tightly in his grip. A tear fell from his eye and ran down his cheek, and I started to cry too. I *understood* the moment he was describing because I was living it myself, even as he described it. "I don't even have enough words to tell you about that relief, *moje wszystko*. Suffice to say that I was so relieved I *wept* that night. I promise you, I will only take the risks I have to, because I truly understand how much it matters to you that I'm safe."

We sat like that for a long time, basked in a contented silence. For long minutes, I had everything I needed in the world again and I was happier than I could ever remember being. The shadow of reality loomed too soon, because as desperately as I wanted to, I couldn't stay with him like that forever.

"I don't know how I can leave you, but I can't stay out much longer," I whispered eventually. "If my parents notice me missing they will pay more attention tomorrow and I won't be able to come see you again."

"*Don't* come see me again," he said. I gasped and moved to argue, but he shook his head and pressed his finger against my lips. "It is too risky, Alina, it is a miracle that I even saw you tonight. But… God help me, I can't stay away from you now. I will wait until it's very late, and assuming it's safe, I'll come to your window instead, okay?"

"You will?"

"I will," he promised, then he sighed. "I should *not*, but I will."

I swallowed the lump in my throat at the reminder of the danger he was in, but he kissed me, and then gently disentangled our limbs. Then he rose and helped me to my feet, and we walked in silence back to the edge of the woods.

"I love you, Alina," he murmured.

"I love you too. So very much," I whispered.

We shared one last kiss in the moonlight before he gently propelled me toward the house. As I took my first few steps, he caught my hand and I turned back to stare at him. We slipped through time then, back through the hard years to the night of our proposal. For a heartbeat, I was that same spoiled girl I'd been before the war, and he was the muscular, cocky boy who had proposed to me. Somewhere in time, that was who we'd always be, and I felt the certainty of that in my bones.

"I can't help but think that this is a miracle, Alina," Tomasz whispered, his gaze scanning my face. "I can't help but think that you finding me tonight was a gift from God. Maybe He can forgive me after all."

The darkness was returning to his eyes. We had so much more to say to one another, and no time to even start the conversation.

"We will talk tomorrow, Tomasz," I whispered. "Yes?"

He reluctantly released my hand, and his gaze darted to the field beyond me for a moment, then he whispered, "Sleep well, *moje wszystko.*"

"Be safe, Tomasz."

The house was still silent when I climbed in my window. I

pulled off my coat and shoes and climbed under the blankets, but even once I closed my eyes I resisted sleep.

Instead, I basked in the warm glow of something most remarkable—something almost miraculous. I was excited about his return, of course—but equally, I was relieved to welcome a glimpse of happiness and a glimmer of hope in my life again.

CHAPTER 12

Alice

I get up at 5:00 a.m. out of habit and not necessity on school days. I plan out Eddie's visual calendar, lay out his clothing and then pack his school bag—the dreidel, which he's still taking with him everywhere he goes, his stuffed Thomas the Tank Engine toy just in case he wants it, six Go-Gurts, one can of soup and six pairs of spare underpants, each with a matching ziplock bag for the inevitable accidents.

By the time I've prepared Eddie's gear, it's 6:00 a.m. and the house is still silent. I pour myself a cup of coffee and wander into the living room, where I turn the television on to a news channel, and then promptly zone out into the background noise. I look around the room, the endless books on the shelves and the dust on the windowsill I probably should address at some point.

This is my favorite room, and this house feels more like home to me than any other house I've ever lived in. We bought this place six years ago, when Wade got the first in a series of promotions. It's not that we're extravagantly wealthy—but he earns well above an average salary these days, and I can't really get my head around how his bonus scheme works but it seems to bring in a lot of money. Something about performance indicators for the teams he manages and every few months he has a win at work, then there's another large deposit into the account and Wade wants to drink champagne and I listen to him as he tries to explain it. I nod and smile, but I never really grasp it because I just don't have a frame of reference for his world.

I've never had a job with performance indicators. The last job I had was tutoring freshman English majors at college. Even then, I just did it because everyone else I knew had a job, and I mostly spent the money on eating out or clothes. Mom and Dad were borderline obsessed with my education—and I guess that makes sense, with Mom's career being the most important part of her life and Dad himself being an academic at the time. They were more than happy to support me financially throughout my college years.

I had a much easier time relying on my parents for money than I do my husband. I'm a confused mix of grateful, guilty and frustrated about the circumstances of my family every single day. But for *our* decision to have a family young and *our* decision that I should stay home long term once we realized that Eddie was not going to be your run-of-the-mill kid, I'd have a career too and things would be different.

But things aren't different, and they have never seemed equal.

It's not anything Wade does or says that makes me feel that way. Sometimes I wonder if I'd feel this uncomfortable about our situation if I'd set out to be a stay-at-home mom. Instead, that life just kind of happened to me, and now there are some days when this beautiful home is a little like a gilded cage.

"Mommy."

I startle and look up to find Callie is standing in the doorway. She is pale this morning, her honey-blond hair a bedraggled mess around her shoulders, her big blue eyes swimming with tears.

"Honey bear," I gasp, falling back automatically into the nickname Wade and I gave her as a baby. "What is it?" I push the coffee cup onto the table and open my arms to her. She runs across the room and launches herself at me.

"I'm sorry I called Eddie a *retard*."

"Oh, Callie. I know you are. Yesterday was a bad day all round, wasn't it?"

"But maybe you don't know the origin of that word, Mommy. It is a *terrible* word. It once was a legitimate medical term, but it's been used to denigrate disabled people for decades now. I looked it up on etymologyonline.com. I committed a *hate crime* against my baby brother. And he doesn't even know it, which makes it even worse, because only you and me and Daddy know what a terrible person I am. How can you ever forgive me?"

I tuck her in closer to me and hide a smile as I run my hand over her hair.

"You're not perfect, Callie Michaels. You're allowed to make mistakes."

"A *hate crime* is a little more than a mistake," she says, and she's full-on sobbing now.

"Now that you understand why I got so angry with you about that word, will you ever use it again?"

"Are you *kidding* me?" she gasps, pulling away from me to stare at me in horror. Her face is awash with tears, and I wonder how much sleep she's had. A pang of guilt hits me, because I didn't even check that she went to sleep last night. That's what happens in our house sometimes. My default position is checking on Eddie. Callie has learned to fend for herself, but it's not okay. "Of *course* I won't use that word again. I couldn't bear it now that I know what it means."

"Well, that's all that matters. Say sorry to Eddie later and let's drop it."

"But it's unforgivable—"

"Baby. You're overthinking this now," I say softly, and she pauses.

"Oh," she says, and then she gives a miserable little sniff. "Okay."

"Watch a train video with Eddie tonight to make it up to him. All will be forgiven."

"Okay, Mommy."

I cuddle her close again, and rest my head against hers.

"I'm sorry you were frustrated at school yesterday, Callie."

"I'm sorry I acted like a spoiled brat about it, Mommy."

I forget sometimes that she has challenges too. I forget that the world is just as mystifying for Callie, who sees too much of it, as for Eddie, who understands so little. Just as Eddie needs me to make a way in this world for him, Callie needs me to help her navigate her own way.

"Should we wake the boys up and get this day started?" I ask her.

"Can we wait five more minutes?" she whispers, and she snuggles closer into me. "I like it sometimes when it's just you and me."

"Me too, honey bear," I whisper back. "Me too."

I'm at the hospital by 9:00 a.m.—right on schedule today. Babcia is dozing lightly when I step into her room, so I take a seat quietly beside her bed.

The iPad is within her reach, sitting on the tray table. Right behind it is a collection of what I suspect are the most precious things in my grandmother's world. On the very top of the pile, there's a handmade leather shoe, the size a very new baby might wear. The shoe is clearly very old, and not particularly well made—the stitching is coarse and uneven, and it's made up of several shades of aged leather. I wonder if it belonged to my mother, and why Babcia kept it—why she's showing it to me now.

Beneath the shoe there are two letters—the top one is in a fairly modern envelope with my name on it in Babcia's careful handwriting. The envelope has faded a little so I know it's not *new*, but even without that clue I'd have been sure she wrote it almost a decade ago, because the address on the front is in Connecticut. She must have written this letter when I was still at college, because a few months after I graduated, Wade and I decided to move back here to Florida.

Just then, she opens her eyes and raises her left hand to my wrist. We share a smile, then she nods toward the letter, so I tear it open and unfold the paper inside.

Dearest Alice,

How are you, my beautiful granddaughter? I hope you are enjoying your last semester at college. I am so very proud of you for earning your degree. Did you know—your mother was the first person ever in my family to do so? I am so happy that we are here in America where you have so many opportunities.

Darling, I need a favor. It is an immense one, and I hesitate to ask it, but I feel that time might be running out and I am becoming desperate. With Pa's illness, I am going to be needed here more and more, so this might be my last chance to get away.

There are ends left untied from my life in Poland—things left unspoken, and more importantly, questions left unanswered. I am sure that you know by now I find it so difficult to speak about the war and our life back home, but there are things I simply must know before I can finish out my days in peace. But I am 85 years old now, darling Alice, and it has been 65-odd years since I left Poland in such a hurry. I am sure it is a whole new world to the life I once knew. I would like to invite you to join me for a brief holiday there. I will pay your way—I simply need help to plan the trip and then someone to accompany me. You are so smart, my darling, and so clever at finding things out from all of your studies and your writing—perhaps you could think of this as a graduate project on your own family history.

I asked Julita a while ago and thought for some time that she might join me, but she is so busy with her new job now, and besides, now I will need her to look after Pa if I am to go away.

If you can spare me the time, perhaps we could take two

weeks to visit the home of my ancestors and to try to find some information for me. It would mean the world, Alice, truly. We could go as soon as you graduate, and perhaps we could take a trip to Paris or Rome so you can see some more of Europe as an expression of my gratitude to you.
Love always,
Babcia

I'm cast immediately back into the timing of this letter—the most tumultuous time of my life. Pa had just been diagnosed with dementia—just a few weeks after Mom was appointed to the district court. Dad was still working as an economics professor at the University of Florida but talking about retiring so he could travel—without Mom, given he'd finally accepted she was serious when she said she was hoping to work until her brain or body gave out. Wade was finishing his second graduate degree and working in his first full-time job.

And then when my final results came in, there was a marked decline in my academic performance in the final semester of my degree, because I was spending most of my waking hours obsessing about how to tell my family that instead of taking an internship the following school year, I'd be becoming a mom.

I look up from the letter now, and my vision is blurred as I drag myself back to the here and now. Babcia is looking at me expectantly, and I feel a crushing sense of grief for the missed opportunity. If she'd sent the letter, I'd have gone with her anyway—pregnant or not. Even so, I'm not surprised that she didn't ask once she knew I was about to become a mom. Babcia has always respected this singular focus I want to have for my family.

Now Babcia awkwardly picks up the other letter with her left hand, and she drops it near to me on the tray table. I open it very carefully—*this* is clearly *much* older than the first letter. Even unfolding the rough, aged paper, I fear it's going to fall to pieces. It feels like something I should handle while wearing cotton gloves, while standing in a museum.

Most of the ink has faded, and only the bottom few lines of the letter are still vivid. It's in Polish, although it's so light I'm not sure even someone who *did* read the language could make much sense of it. I can barely make out the first few lines—but I can see the name at the bottom. *Tomasz.*

I look at her blankly, but she's silently crying now, and she reaches across to very gently take the older letter from my hands. She folds it again, then rests it on the tray table. Tears flow freely down her cheeks, but she wipes her face with the back of her hands and reaches with some determination for the iPad. She has all of the icons she needs saved into her *favorites* screen, so it takes only a moment for her to start our conversation.

Alice.

Find Tomasz.

Alice plane Poland. Alice plane Trzebinia.

Babcia fire Tomasz.

She looks at me expectantly, then hits the *your turn* button. My heart sinks all over again as I take the iPad. My hands tremble a little as I peck out my response.

Babcia no plane—

She impatiently snatches the iPad from me.

Yes. She types, and I think we're in an awkward argument, until she spends the next several minutes correcting me as she accesses the icons from the recently used screen.

Babcia sick.

Babcia old.

Babcia no plane.

Alice plane.

Alice plane Trzebinia.

Find Tomasz.

Babcia fire Tomasz.

"But… *I* can't go to Poland, Babcia," I protest aloud, forgetting for a moment that it's pointless to do so. She hits the repeat button on the iPad, then looks at me, and when I simply stare at her as I try to figure out how to explain to her how insane this is, she presses *repeat* again, and then again.

Then she puts the iPad down, crosses her arms over her chest and stares at me stubbornly. Her chin is raised. Her jaw is set. Babcia looks exactly like my daughter did last night when I walked through my front door.

"But..." I protest weakly. I couldn't leave Callie and I couldn't leave Wade—and I definitely couldn't leave Eddie. I can't even begin to imagine how I could make *that* work. Wade would never take time off; Eddie would never adjust to my absence; Callie would act up too—God, it would be a nightmare for all of them. Besides, I'm still not sure what *question* Babcia wants me to answer. Who are these people? What the Hell is *Babcia fire Tomasz* supposed to mean? Say I flew all the way across the world for her, what would I even *do* when I got there?

Babcia can either read my mind, or she's thinking the same thing. She swipes back to the home screen on the iPad and finds the FaceTime button, then she points to the icon, and then looks at me again. When I look at her blankly, she swipes over to the *camera* button, then she jabs at it, and she opens the photo roll. It's empty because this is Mom's iPad and she's not really the Grandma-paparazzi sort, but I get the message anyway.

My grandmother wants to see her homeland one last time.

Babcia passes me the iPad now, and I open the AAC and swipe vaguely through the icons, wondering how I'm supposed to use this limited language to say "there's no way in Hell I can arrange to fly to Poland and take some photos for you, especially not on short notice, and we have no idea how long you have left so I'd have to go straightaway anyway."

How do I tell the woman who offered me endless love and acceptance for my entire life that the first favor she's ever asked of me is one I have to decline? How do I tell a person who's given me *everything* that the *one* thing she wants from me is too much? The answer comes swiftly.

I can't. When the family matriarch tells you to do something, you damn well do it.

But she's asking something of me that I'm not even sure I can physically arrange in the timeline we have. But there is no icon for "maybe" on the AAC—the concept is too vague for children like Eddie, and that's who the program was designed for. Instead, I swipe to the Notes screen to type the word *maybe*, but I'm startled to find there are already notes there.

Trzebinia

Ul. Świętojańska 4, Trzebinia

Ul. Polerechka 9B, Trzebinia

Ul. Dworczyk 38, Trzebinia

Alina Dziak

Emilia Slaska

Mateusz and Truda Rabinek

Saul Eva Tikva Weiss

Proszę zrozum. Tomasz.

I look at up her, confused. Those notes are in Polish, which she knows all too well that I don't understand. I lift the iPad so she can't see the screen, then swipe to Google, load Google Translate, and type in the words *Can you understand me?* I hit the speaker icon, and words that mean nothing to me fill the air, but Babcia's eyes widen and she nods enthusiastically. We share a grin, and then I flick back to the Notes section on the iPad, and my heart sinks again.

I can feel my grandmother's eyes on me, sharp and questioning and desperate and hopeful. I swallow, hard, then I raise my gaze to her. We stare at each other in the silence, until she nods, just once, and then she seems satisfied. She sinks back into her pillows and closes her eyes again, the echo of a smile lingering on her lips.

I have no idea what she thought she saw on my face just now. But I spend the rest of the day at her bedside, trying to figure out if there's a way to make this work.

CHAPTER 13

Alina

Tomasz and I immediately fell into a pattern of nightly visits where we'd share a few innocent kisses and an awkward cuddle through the window frame, but it was impossible for us to speak much, because my parents were always asleep on just the other side of the wall. I had a million or more questions I needed to ask him—so many things I wanted to tell him or to hear him say—but it all had to tumble out in fragments of conversation because he never dared stay more than a few minutes at a time.

"Let me come to the woods," I would plead with him. "It is too hard for us to talk here the way we need to."

"I don't think that's a good idea, Alina," he would whisper back. "If your parents catch you leaving the house, it will be impossible for you to explain."

"But if they catch us talking here—"

"If they catch us talking here, I *promise* you I will disappear so fast you will think I've turned invisible."

There was the cocky boy I'd fallen in love with, arrogant in the confidence he had that he could protect me. He seemed to think he had transferred the risk of our meeting from me to himself by coming to the house, but I wasn't so sure. The problem was that it was impossible to argue with him—not least in part because we had to talk in whispers. I wanted explanations, but my desperation to meet him in the woods ran even deeper than that. I wanted to hold him and kiss him and to talk with him openly. I quite desperately missed Tomasz's stories. I missed the fairy tales and the exaggerations and even the possibly out-landish facts about far-flung lands and biology and science—but there was no time for extended conversations like that when we were whispering through my window. Those visits each night were a fleeting luxury, one that felt increasingly too short, but I didn't dare feel disappointed, because at least he was *back* and I was well aware how lucky I was to have even that.

It was only a few days after Tomasz's return that Mama and I walked to tend the field near the Golaszewski property and found Jan on his hands and knees, weeding. I was walking in front, and soon found I was near enough that I felt it only po-lite to greet him.

"Hello, Jan," I said, as politely as I could manage. "How are you today?"

Jan's bushy gray eyebrows dipped low and his forehead creased as he peered up at me.

"Ola has taken Justyna away. I thought you would like to know."

"Jan," Mama greeted him abruptly as she approached.

"Faustina," Jan said, his tone just as short.

"Where has Justyna gone?" I asked hesitantly. "To...to the city?"

"Yes, to the city," Jan confirmed, but his face was reddening and his nostrils had flared, and I knew that he was not pleased with this turn of events. "In any case, she is gone, and that is that."

He nodded curtly once more at Mama, then he dumped his tools into the dirt, then turned and walked away, across the field to their home. Jan had always seemed so imposing to me, but that day, he seemed smaller somehow, perhaps because it was evident to me that for all of his bluster and energy, he was ac-tually just a man, and now a very lonely one at that.

"I am sorry your friend is gone, Alina," Mama murmured, as we returned to our own home.

"Thank you, Mama."

I so rarely saw Justyna, I knew I'd barely miss her. Still, I was a little sad, but perhaps not nearly as sad as I would have been had it happened a few weeks earlier.

On nights when the moon was full and I could really see Tomasz well, there was no mistaking that the hollows of his cheeks grew with every passing day. I decided I would find a way to get him some food.

I was aware that I would be stealing food from my mother—who was likely stealing food from the Nazis—but I was far more terrified of Mama than I was of the invaders, and that was saying something. The first time I passed Tomasz a cup of scraps from my dinner, the flare of sheer hunger in his gaze was worth the terror I'd felt squirreling the food away.

"How did you get this?"

"From my dinner," I said. He hesitated, and I waved toward the food. "Please, Tomasz. Go ahead—I had plenty."

He laughed incredulously.

"Alina Dziak. There has not been *plenty* in this country since the occupation began. Don't lie to me. You're skin and bones."

"Please, eat it. I get two or even three meals a day most of the time—it's not luxurious, but I'm surviving. But you…" I wasn't sure how to draw attention to his rapidly fading physique without being cruel, so after a pause, I simply took his hand in mine, and I whispered, "Tomasz, I'm scared for you. You can't keep going like this. I don't know what you're doing, and you clearly don't want to tell me. But surely it involves a lot of sneaking around, and a lot of trying to keep your wits about you. Let me at least give you the scraps from the scraps they give us."

He picked up a chunk of bread and sniffed it, almost suspiciously. Then he tossed it into his mouth and his eyes widened.

"I am *fairly* sure the Nazis aren't giving you strawberry jam with your bread," he said cautiously, and I shrugged.

"You aren't the only person in this district undertaking covert activities. Mama seems to have a mysterious hidden store some-where."

"I'll do you a deal, darling Alina," Tomasz said thoughtfully as he took some potato from the cup. "If you can spare me some food, I'll eat half of it, and pass the rest on to my friends. Is that okay?"

"But there's barely any food here, even for you," I whispered desperately. "Please, can you just eat this, and tomorrow, I'll try to get more food for your friends."

"Well, if there's a way for you to do that without endanger-ing your sneaky mama or yourself, then—"

My bedroom door flew open just then, and Father was there in my doorway—bleary-eyed and frowning.

"Alina," he said flatly. "Who on earth are you talking to?"

I looked frantically to the window, but Tomasz was gone. In-stead, I looked up to the sky and as I started to desperately pray for a convincing lie, I realized I already had one.

"I was praying," I said.

"Praying," my father repeated, without any attempt to hide his suspicion.

"Yes. Praying. For Tomasz."

Father frowned a little harder.

"Go to sleep," he said. "We have a lot of work to do tomor-row." He took a step back toward the open area, then hesitated. "Leave the door open."

I climbed quickly into bed, my heart racing, my gaze on the window. Tomasz didn't come back—but in the morning, the empty cup had been nestled back through the window and tucked into my bedding.

The night after my father caught us talking, Tomasz came to the window as he had been doing, but he was wearing a heavy frown. I knew before he spoke that he was coming to say goodbye.

"I'm so sorry," he whispered. "It was risky—we knew it was risky. I…"

"No, I'm sorry," I whispered back. "I was careless—I was too loud. I promise I'll be more careful."

He sighed, then pinched the bridge of his nose. Anxiety was radiating off him, and when I reached through the window to rest my hand against his shoulder, I felt his tension in my own body. Tomasz leaned toward me and kissed my cheek.

"Alina, this isn't smart anymore," he whispered miserably. "We can't keep doing this."

I bit my lip.

"But how else can I see you? Perhaps we could just tell Mama and Father—"

"No!" he interrupted me, his voice a desperate whisper. "No, they can't know, Alina. They can't— It's bad enough that you know I'm here. This isn't safe. You *know* that, don't you?"

"How can I know that? I don't even understand what you did."

He sighed and shot me a pleading look.

"If we tell your parents, I don't think they'll allow us to see each other anymore."

"Of course they will!"

"Alina…" he said, very gently. "Please trust me, *moje wszystko*. Your parents love you and they will want to keep you safe. And there is *nothing* safe about you meeting with me."

"But…"

"Even if I am wrong, and they are supportive of us still seeing each other, it is just too risky to let anyone else in on our secret. If *anyone* finds out I'm visiting with you…" He raised his chin, then looked right into my eyes. "I don't care what happens to me. I really don't. But if anything happens to *you* because of me? I couldn't…" He trailed off then, his eyes on my bedroom door.

"I'll find a way to come see you during the day. Would that be better? If I met you in the woods instead?"

"In the *daylight*?" he said this as if the suggestion was absurd, but I shrugged.

"Perhaps before the war, people walked on that hill sometimes. But now? You are the only person I've seen there in years, other than Truda and Mateusz and your sister when they visit for Sunday lunch. It is as safe a meeting place as we are ever going to find." He still stared at me skeptically, so I gave him a pointed look. "You've been there for weeks and not been noticed, Tomasz. Has anyone even come close to finding you? Who exactly do you think is going to catch us there together?"

"Your parents would surely notice if you came to the woods every day."

"I know. I would ask them permission to visit the woods, but not tell them why I wanted to."

He sighed heavily.

"What possible reason could you have to come to the woods *every day*, Alina?"

"You're not the only one in this relationship who can be resourceful," I whispered, but I forced a teasing, lighthearted tone into my voice, and he gave me a reluctant laugh.

"Okay, Alina Dziak. Let's see what you can do."

At breakfast, I delivered the speech I'd sat up half the night preparing.

"Mama," I said, "I have decided that I will undertake a spiritual commitment to pray the rosary for our country each day. I'm going to get up earlier in the morning and spend an hour alone in prayer at the hill."

Mama set her coffee down on the table and raised an eyebrow at me. She and Father shared a glance. Finally, she focused her gaze back on me, and she nodded curtly.

"By all means, go to the hill to pray, but not for an hour—

this isn't a convent. You can take twenty minutes, and you'll stay near the edge of the woods. I might call you at *any* time, so don't get too distracted with your *prayer*."

It was almost impossible to hide my grin as I said, "I'll start tomorrow."

Mama shrugged.

"Maybe *your* prayers will be the ones that inspire God to end this nightmare, so you should get started as soon as possible. Start today."

I could not believe my luck—I was actually going to get *twenty minutes* alone with Tomasz every day—free to talk and to embrace and to see him in the daylight. I ate the rest of my biscuit far too quickly, and then as if things weren't wonderful enough, Mama caught my elbow as I moved to run from the house and pressed something into my hand. I looked down at it, then gasped. She'd given me a surprisingly hefty chunk of bread.

"Mama!"

"To sustain you," she said quietly. "For your *time of prayer*."

There was an undertone in those last three words but I was too excited to really let myself think about that and all of the dangers it might represent. Instead, I smiled at her as innocently as I could manage and I packed up the breakfast dishes, and then went to collect my rosary beads from my room. I made an exaggerated show of holding the beads in my open hands, just to be sure Mama saw them. Even once I left the house, I walked slowly through the field because I wasn't sure my parents weren't watching me—I couldn't seem too eager to commence my "time of prayer." I *knew* my story was flimsy, but it was the best I could come up with, even after racking my brain half the night.

The woods were thick, a curious mixture of dark green fir branches up high and bright green birch trees nestled below. Most of the rest of the land surrounding the hill had been completely cleared for farmland, but this little patch of woods was so rocky and steep it had been left dense and wild. I half expected to see Tomasz sitting on the long, flat boulder in the big clearing at the top as he'd always done in the prewar days, but as I neared it, I realized that was far too exposed now that he was in hiding. I almost called out to him, but then it occurred to me how foolish that idea was.

If he was deep within the woods, I'd never find him—and that was the point, wasn't it? He wasn't even expecting me today—when we made this plan at night, we expected it would take me some time to convince my parents I should come. I walked just inside the thickest part of the woods and found a log to sit on. I was disappointed and dejected, but I couldn't go home so soon, not without arousing suspicion, and I wasn't about to blow this amazing arrangement *on the first day.*

"Alina," a soft voice called, and I spun around—but still, couldn't see him.

"Tomasz?"

"Look up, *moje wszystko,*" he said, his voice lilting with amusement.

He was sitting in the fork of a tree, far too high for my comfort, especially with his legs swinging on either side of a branch that looked barely strong enough to hold even his meager weight. He grinned, then slipped easily from the tree and walked a few steps toward me.

"*That* is not a safe place to hide," I protested, as I rose from the log and jogged toward him.

He shrugged easily and said, "Nothing is safe anymore, Alina." He said the words as a joke, but there was a heaviness in his voice too. I was reminded that we had so much left to talk about now that we could finally *talk.*

"Tell me. Tell me now about this trouble," I demanded, but he hopped over a few boulders to reach me, then he wrapped his arms around me.

"It is so wonderful to hold you again in the daylight," he whispered against my hair. I pressed my face into his neck and closed my eyes, breathing him in. Soon, I lifted my face toward him and simply stared up at him in the daylight for the first time since his return. He stared right back at me, and spontaneously, we shared a contented smile. Even deathly thin, even with a smear of dirt on his cheek, even with a scruffy beard and unkempt hair, he was still handsome to me. The world seemed utterly perfect in that moment—the morning light peeking through the canopy overhead, the smell of dew on the ground, the birds in the distance, and best of all, Tomasz's arms around my waist. He tucked a wayward lock of my hair behind my ear, then he bent to kiss me gently and sweetly.

"One day, I will take you away from here," he whispered, "One day, we will go someplace safe—someplace peaceful. One day, when you're my wife, we will have the nicest house in the nicest street and the cutest children in the town and everyone will say, 'Look at Tomasz and Alina, childhood sweethearts, now growing old together.' You're going to be one of those women who ages well. I can see it now—even when you're an old *babcia* you'll be breathtaking and I won't be able to keep my eyes or my hands off you."

"You've always been such a dreamer," I sighed, but I was happily distracted. I was relieved to see a glimpse of the old Tomasz, relieved that this lighter side of my love had survived whatever had kept him away from me for so long. In those disjointed nights at my window, I'd caught glimpses of a man who wore guilt and sadness like a mask. It was every bit as much a relief to see this sweeter side of him reemerge as it was to hold him close to me.

"So, how did you convince your parents?" he asked me.

"I told them I wanted to retreat to pray the rosary," I told him, and I lifted the beads from my pocket to show him. He burst out laughing.

"And your parents actually believed that you were taking

meditative prayer walks in the woods?" he asked me incredulously. I giggled as I nodded, and he kissed my hair again.

"You need to trust me," I scolded him gently. "I can keep your secrets, Tomasz."

"I have no doubt about that," he said quietly. "But I have a responsibility to keep you safe—above everything else. It's risky enough for us to meet just now."

"Have you joined the resistance?" I asked him. The Polish underground army had been chipping away at the Nazis for some time—more of an irritant to the occupying forces than a matched opponent—but Truda occasionally brought whispers of a secret newspaper and supplies shipments delayed or destroyed by organized attacks. I was scared for Tomasz—but I was also proud to think he might be involved in those efforts. I had a feeling our liberation was only a matter of time if heroes like Tomasz Slaski were on the job.

"I am fighting back the only way I know how," he whispered. "Do you trust me?"

I pulled away to look up at him a little incredulously.

"How can you even ask me that. Do *you* trust me?"

"With my life, Alina," he said.

The intensity in his gaze was breathtaking, but I wasn't distracted this time. I gave him a pointed look and said, "Then you must tell me everything."

"I will," he promised. "I will tell you every excruciating detail, just as soon as I can. But today...let's sit somewhere here and pretend it's an ordinary day and the world isn't going to Hell around us."

I sighed and let him take me away with chatter about this glorious postwar life we were going to share once all of the ugliness and the fighting died down. I gave him the bread, and he pocketed it, but promised to eat at least half himself. I wanted to believe him, but somehow, I knew that his "friends" in the resistance would benefit from the spoils of Mama's generosity much more than Tomasz himself would.

We kissed goodbye, and although it wasn't even 9:00 a.m., we said good-night because he wouldn't risk a visit to me at the window anymore. I ran back down the field to the farmhouse, and I was surprised to find Mama weeding right at the edge of the woods—much closer to Tomasz's hiding spot than I'd anticipated. She was close enough that if we'd spoken at normal volume, she'd likely have heard us, so I was suddenly very glad that we'd kept our voices at a whisper. When she saw me approaching, Mama asked me wryly, "Has your soul been comforted?"

"Oh yes, Mama," I called back, and I threw myself into my chores that day with gusto.

CHAPTER 14

Alice

When Mom arrives from the chambers that afternoon, Babcia is resting peacefully.

"How has she been?" Mom asks me.

"So, it turns out she can understand at least some Polish spoken words," I tell her. "How much Polish do you remember?"

"None, unfortunately," Mom says. "I spoke some when I was a kid, but when Pa was studying to recertify as a doctor here he had to learn English very quickly, and Babcia was trying to pick it up at the same time. They banned Polish in our house when I was maybe four or five so that we'd all have to use English at home, and I haven't used my Polish since."

I show her the AAC message history and Babcia's notes on the iPad, and she pauses and runs her finger over one line.

"Alina," she reads, frowning. "Hmm..."

"Do you know her?"

"No, but..." Mom's brows knit, then she looks at me thoughtfully. "Remember? She wanted me to name *you* Alina."

I look at her blankly.

"I didn't know that."

"Sure you did."

"I definitely didn't, Mom."

Mom suddenly looks a little wistful.

"She said it was a family name. I grew up with an unusual

name, at least unusual for here, and I didn't want that for you. Your father suggested we use an American variation and 'Alice' was as close as we could get."

"Why did she call you 'Julita' if Alina is the family name?"

"Well, this almost proves the point. I'm sure she told me at one point that Julita was from Pa's side, so I guess that means Alina was from Mom's side."

"You've *never* told me this, Mom," I laugh softly.

Mom frowns.

"But I *must* have told you—because you put your own spin on it with Pascale."

I looked at her in disbelief.

"Mom, adjusting the name 'Alina' to 'Alice' is a stretch enough already. How on earth do you think *Pascale* relates to this?"

"Alina—Alice. Ally—Callie," Mom says, then she pauses, and says incredulously, "Are you telling me that was an *accident*? What other reason could you possibly have for giving your daughter a name that shortens to almost *exactly* the same nickname as yours?"

"Mom, we named Callie after Blaise Pascal, just like Eddie is named for Thomas Edison—it was Wade's dream to name his kids after famous scientists, and I just so happened to like those names. I didn't even *notice* the nickname thing until you just pointed it out."

"Huh," Mom says, and we both laugh softly.

I sober quickly though, and I say, "Do you think Alina was Babcia's mother?"

"I don't even know. She just said it was a family name…" Mom frowns, then she looks at the iPad again. "*Dziak* isn't familiar at all, though. Babcia's maiden name was Wiśniewski."

Next, Mom picks up the letter Babcia wrote me, and then she scans the older letter—the one we can't quite read. Finally, I show her the tiny shoe, and recognition and surprise flicker across her face. "I forgot all about that shoe," she murmurs. "I haven't seen that thing in decades." She picks it up and cradles it in her palm with utmost care.

"Was it yours?" I ask her. She shrugs.

"I have no idea. It was probably Pa's most precious possession, other than his US medical board registration once that came. He kept this in a padded box in the top of his wardrobe, and when I was really young, he'd bring it out sometimes and just sit in his armchair to stare at it. Actually, I remember asking him over and over again what it was from, because he would always answer me with silly jokes... One time he told me it was a time machine, another he said it was portal to another world...things like that," she laughs weakly, then sets the shoe back on the table. "Maybe he got sick of me asking because eventually he stopped bringing it out, at least when I was around. I know you've never understood this, Alice, because we tried to be open with you about everything we could right from when you were tiny. Sex, death, Santa Claus...you know how I liked to tell you the truth, as much as you could handle at every stage of your life."

That approach had been uncomfortable at times—like the time I walked in on my parents at a *very* awkward moment, and the next morning they sat me down and talked to me in excruciating depth about love and sex and intimacy and why there was nothing shameful or embarrassing about the whole incident. Somewhat ironically, the single *most* embarrassing moment of my life was not so much seeing my parents' naked bodies in flagrante, but the long postmortem the next day. That conversation aside, I've always appreciated their openness. There was never any time when I'd ask my mom about something and she'd shut the conversation down—that just wasn't how she parented.

"Well, you know Pa and Babcia had a very different approach in life to all that," Mom says now. "There were things we talked about when I was a kid, sure, but...there were also plenty of things that we *did not* talk about. My parents had a whole set of memories they just could not bear to face. *Everything* to do with the war was off-limits. Mama would talk about her childhood a lot, but Pa couldn't even manage that." Mom hesitates suddenly, then she sets the shoe down onto the tray table and she glances at Babcia's sleeping form. "Maybe it's a crazy theory, but sometimes, I wondered if Pa was actually Jewish."

I look at her in surprise.

"But he always came to Mass with us at Christmas and Easter."

"Yes, but the Catholic church was definitely Mama's passion—Pa never once went without her. And even when he did go, he never took communion, and once they moved into the care home, I *think* Mama was taking him to a synagogue. I asked her about it a few times, even directly once, but she dismissed the question and just said they were spending some time with friends who happened to be Jewish. I mean—that retirement home has a great Jewish community, so that did make some sense. But…" She hesitates, then shrugs. "They left Poland bang in the middle of the Holocaust, and I do remember Mama telling me they were petrified when they arrived here and realized that America wasn't the multicultural paradise they assumed it would be. Mind you, I have no idea what actually happened to them in Poland, but if Pa really was Jewish? Well, you don't need to be a historian to know it would have been Hell on earth."

I look down at Babcia, my chest constricting as, just for a moment, I try to picture my sweet, compassionate grandparents surviving in Nazi-occupied Poland. Pa was the kind of person you only meet a few times in a lifetime—whip-smart and determined, but also humble and generous to a fault. As for Babcia, she's tough as nails, but she's always been so optimistic and sometimes too quick to believe in the goodness of people.

I can't even begin to understand the kind of resilience my grandparents must have possessed to survive that war, and remain gentle in spirit the way they did.

"Did they ask you to take them back to Poland?" I ask Mom quietly.

"Yes and no," Mom says. "Pa was adamant he would *never* go back. I think that's why Mama didn't even entertain the idea until he got sick. Then she asked me right after I took the district court posting and there was just no way I could take the vacation time. In fact, the timing could not have been worse for any of us. And frankly, I was a little annoyed she waited so long, just like I'm annoyed about this photo nonsense now. You know as well as I do, Alice—your father and I went to Europe several times when you were a kid—long before Pa got sick. Why didn't she ask me then? I'd have gladly added a stop in Poland if all she wanted was some photos."

"And there's no one back there we can contact?" I ask. "No one at all?"

"She used to send letters to her sister, every week for years and *years*." Mom glances at the iPad again, then reaches for it and unlocks it. "Well, I thought it was her sister, but... I remember her saying she was trying to write to 'Amelia.' But look—she's written *Emilia Slaksa*. I wonder if that's who she was writing to? Slaksa... Slaski...maybe it's a typo... I wonder if it was a relative on Pa's side?"

"Did they fall out of contact?" I ask, and Mom looks up at me.

"Oh no. Emilia or Amelia or whatever her name is *never* responded. Eventually I think Babcia had to accept that she'd died. I'm sure you know Polish history about as well as I do—even once the war ended, the country was occupied by the communists for decades and things were still really rough there. Who knows where this sister of hers ended up, if she was even alive after the war ended. You know, I was well into adulthood before Babcia gave up with those letters. She must have sent hundreds over the years..." Mom pauses, then adds softly, "Actually, maybe it was thousands."

"Poor Babcia," I whisper, my throat tightening. "I can't even imagine what it would be like to leave everything like that and not know what became of the people you'd left behind."

We stand in silence for a long moment, then Mom asks, "So, did she understand when you told her you can't go?"

"I…" I swallow, hard. "I didn't tell her I can't go. Not yet. It's hard to say with the AAC. I need to explain to her all of the reasons why it's impossible. I'll have to think about how to word it tonight."

"Surely she understands this is just asking too much of you."

"I don't know," I say. It's too hard to explain to Mom why I'm so tempted to try to find a way through the difficulties of my home life to actually fulfil this crazy quest, because so many of my motivations start with *when Mom was too busy working to give me what I needed, Babcia filled the gap*.

"Who knows what's going on in her mind? She's probably confused." Mom sighs. "Maybe she'll forget she even asked this tomorrow."

"Maybe," I agree weakly, but then I glance at the time. "I have to go pick the kids up. I'll bring them by a bit later so they can see her."

"Fine," Mom sighs, but then her weary gaze brightens just a little. "You're bringing Callie too this time?"

"Yes, Mom." I match her sigh with my own. "Callie too."

I'm back at Babcia's bedside within an hour, this time with both kids in tow. Eddie climbs up to snuggle into Babcia's side. He pulls the tray table over their legs and he tries to make the precious dreidel spin. After a few attempts, Callie gets impatient, snatches it from his hand and sets it going. Eddie sucks in a delighted breath, then he squeals and claps his hands.

Callie greets Babcia, but quickly falls into a conversation with Mom about her school day. Babcia's eyes follow me as I move around the room. I keep my body busy just to expend the frenetic energy generated by my racing thoughts. I toss out some old flowers in a vase from earlier in the week and adjust and readjust the blinds as the afternoon sunlight grows too bright. I'm vaguely aware of Babcia using the iPad, but I'm startled when it speaks for her.

Alice home now. I turn back to Babcia in surprise. She looks pointedly at me, then she turns back to the iPad. *Alice home now. Later, Alice plane Poland.*

"What's she talking about?" Callie frowns.

"She's very ill," Mom tells her sadly. "She's not making much sense at the moment, darling. You needn't worry."

But Babcia *is* making sense to me. And it's becoming increasingly apparent that she's not going to let this drop.

CHAPTER 15

Alina

Each day over the next few weeks, Tomasz and I would sit in the woods holding hands or embracing—happy enough just to be together. On the very best days, he'd spin a tale for me— usually a tale about us escaping, moving far away from the war and the occupation and the sadness and the hunger. One day, I was sitting on a log, leaning up against a tree trunk, and he was resting on the ground, his head on my lap as I played idly with his hair. I'd trimmed his hair and beard a few times since his return—sneaking scissors under my coat to help tidy him up. I did a woefully bad job of it, but I took an immense amount of pleasure from being able to do that one small thing for him.

"Where should we go today?" he asked me. I pondered this for a moment, running through the very limited list of countries I knew about, but I settled on his favorite fantasy.

"America," I said.

"Ah, America is a very rich country, you know. We would surely live in a mansion," Tomasz said, and a big grin covered his face as he glanced up at me.

"I'd settle for a house," I sighed, because at least that day, I wanted the fantasy to be a little realistic. But then I paused, thinking of my parents' tiny place and how much larger the home Tomasz and Aleksy and Emilia had once shared. "House" could mean so many different things, even in Poland. I couldn't fathom what homes would look like in a wealthy country like America. "A big house, mind you."

"Well, we'd need a big house," he agreed, and when I looked down at him, his eyes crinkled. "For our eleven children, of course."

"Eleven!" I gasped, then I laughed. "This is my fantasy, Tomasz, so I get to pick the number of children we have. We'll have a small family—just four." I paused, then added, "Okay, maybe five, but certainly no more than six."

"And I'll be a doctor, of course."

"Of course."

"Can I be a specialist doctor in this fantasy?"

"A specialist?" I said, then I looked at him in surprise. "What kind of specialist?"

"A children's doctor," he smiled.

"Do children have their *own* doctors?" That seemed as unlikely as the idea of us living in a mansion.

"In Warsaw they do," Tomasz told me. "I am sure it would be the same in wealthy countries like America. Pediatricians, they are called."

"I didn't know you wanted to do that kind of medicine." I gave him a confused smile, and he drew in a sharp breath, then exhaled it slowly.

"At college in Warsaw, I studied under all kinds of specialists in the hospitals. For example, at the Jewish hospital, I met a surgeon." A look of sadness and regret crossed his face. "His name is Saul. He inspired me so much—he made me think that maybe there's something to that more focused path. But surgery is not for me. I like talking to people...putting them at ease. I like the idea that if we ever find a way out of Poland and I can study again, I'd dedicate my life to children."

"We don't need to leave Poland for you to study again," I laughed softly. Tomasz turned his gaze back to me and sadness sparked in his gaze.

"Perhaps we do."

"But...when the Nazis leave, the universities will reopen. You can go back to Warsaw. And trust me, Tomasz, *no one* is going stop me from coming with you this time."

"Alina," Tomasz said abruptly, and he shifted on the ground, then sat up so that he was facing me. He reached up for my hands and held both of them between his, resting them on my lap. I could tell from the intense expression on his face that he was about to say something I didn't want to hear. I resisted an odd urge to cover my ears like a child. "Even when the war ends, we can't stay here. It will be years before the universities run as they should, and I will never be able to rebuild a life in Warsaw or even in Krakow. We will *need* a fresh beginning."

"But... *I* can't leave Poland," I said uneasily. I flicked my gaze toward him. "My parents...even... Truda and Emilia are here. We *need* to stay here for Emilia."

A sudden tension had arisen between us, and I didn't like it one bit—especially when Tomasz tried to deflect away from that statement with another of his silly fairy tales.

"Maybe I'll build you a gingerbread house," he told me suddenly, his tone too light. "Then, if you're ever hungry again, you can eat the house."

"Maybe I'll build you a church," I told him, and he raised his eyebrows at the flatness of my tone.

"I thought the morning prayer was just a cover for us to meet. Don't tell me you're thinking of taking vows?"

He was still teasing me, but I was deadly serious now. I pulled my hands away from his and stood as I muttered, "You can't lie in a church, Tomasz. If I build you a church, you'll have to tell me the truth about all of the things that I don't understand."

He fell silent then, reaching only to pick up a twig from the dirt and twirling it through his fingers. His expression was somber, his gaze distant.

"I'm scared to tell you," he admitted unevenly, then he looked right at me, and there was such breathtaking pain in his gaze that I forgot I was angry with him and took my place on the log again, just so I could reach down and take his hand. I saw shadows in his gaze, like he was staring off into a nightmare. But then he shook himself, looked at our hands and admitted, "I made terrible mistakes. I'm trying to undo them, so I can be a man of honor. All I want in this world is to be a man worthy of a woman like *you*. I'll tell you in time, I promise. But now? You do know what's at stake in this war, even though I am sure your parents still shelter you and treat you like a child sometimes."

"They *do*!" I exclaimed in frustration. "They really do. And that's why I can't bear it when you do the same."

"That is not what I'm doing," he pleaded with me.

"That is *exactly* what you are doing," I said flatly.

I could hear Mama calling me from the field, exasperation in her tone, so I disentangled myself from Tomasz, but I was reluctant to leave him after the surprisingly tense conversation we'd just had. I brushed my lips against his once more.

"Tomasz," I said softly. "Tell me again. About us."

A smile released the tension in his features.

"We are meant to be together," he whispered, trailing his finger down the side of my face. "We were *made* for each other, and everything else in the world will just have to figure itself out, because we are going to be together. I love you."

"I love you too." I pressed one last kiss against his lips, then forced myself to stand. "Good night, Tomasz. I'll see you in the morning?"

He stayed on the ground then, but he gave me a sad smile as he reluctantly released my fingers.

"Every minute till then, I'll be thinking of you."

I turned to walk away from him, but then I paused and glanced back over my shoulder.

"Tomasz?"

"Yes, Alina?"

"It is time, my love. It is time you told me the truth about your situation." He swallowed, hard, but then he nodded. "I am strong, and our love is strong. Whatever it is you have to tell me, it will change nothing."

"You can't promise me that, *moje wszystko*," he whispered.

"I can," I said, raising my chin. "And I do. Tomorrow?"

He closed his eyes as he inhaled, but then when he opened them again, he nodded, and I knew that the next time I saw him, he would tell me the truth.

I just hoped I really was ready to hear it.

I found Tomasz sitting in the clearing the next day, out in the open for the first time since our reunion. When he saw me coming, he looked away, regret and guilt written on his face.

I walked silently to sit beside him, but he didn't move to touch me.

"I watch Emilia come with her new family on Sundays," he murmured absentmindedly. We sat for a little while, listening to the quiet sounds of the woods. "I sit in a tree near the path on Sundays just so I can watch her. She is always holding Truda's hand."

"Yes," I whispered.

"Mateusz is always right behind them. He scans for danger as he walks. I can tell he is a good father to her too."

"He is."

"I have watched you also, sitting on the steps with her after your lunch," he said, then he smiled softly. "I see that my sister still talks a lot."

"She does."

"What is the paper she always carries with her when she visits?"

"Drawings," I murmured. "She draws for me and for Mama. Flowers, mostly." I didn't tell him how dark those pictures had become. He seemed to have plenty to worry about without that knowledge. "They are very good—she is quite the artist."

"Clever girl. She is sad, and she is scared, but she is loved," he added, then he looked right at me. "Most of the Jewish children in Trzebinia are gone now, Alina."

I frowned at the abrupt shift in the direction of our conversation.

"Well, yes… I know."

"Most have starved to death or been taken to a camp or worked to death or executed."

I squinted at him, confused.

"I do *know* this, Tomasz. It is awful and it's sad but I *know*."

"Perhaps, but do you know what the difference is between Emilia and those Jewish children?"

I struggled to find an answer to that, and in the end, could only offer a somewhat helpless, "I… I don't know?"

"They are both children of God, but also children of our great country. They are both our hope and our future as a nation and as a species…and…that is all that should matter." He shifted on the rock, then rose and took my hand. "Let's walk as we talk today. I know you can't go far from the field, but I can't bring myself to look at you while I tell you this."

And so we walked in silence, off the path, along the rocky outcrops where the slope was steep. After a moment or two, he squeezed my hand and he said softly, "If Emilia was a Jewish child in Warsaw, she would be in a ghetto today. I know food is scarce here, but the children in the ghetto have been eating sawdust and rocks to fill their empty little stomachs because after a while, hunger and pain feel the same and they just need relief. And I know people have been getting sick here, but the children in the ghetto have been dying at such a rate that the authorities can't keep up with all of the bodies. And I know that Emilia is scared here, but she still smiles. The children in the ghetto do not smile, because there are no longer any glimpses of joy in that life. There is only fear and pain and hunger. And…" He drew in a shuddering breath, then he said miserably, "Alina, if Emilia was a Jewish child in Warsaw, she would be in that ghetto. And maybe she would be there because of *me*."

I stopped dead in my tracks. I had tried to prepare myself for something shameful, but I was so horrified at that statement that I couldn't hide my reaction to it.

"*What?*" I croaked. I could feel the blood draining from my face. Tomasz too looked much paler even than usual. He exhaled a heavy breath and began to rub the back of his neck. He kept glancing at me, like he was trying to figure out if there was a way to avoid honesty with me even in that moment, or perhaps he was sizing me up to see if I could handle the truth after all. The silence was stretching too long, and I couldn't stand another second of it. I hardened my gaze and crossed my arms over my chest.

"Explain yourself," I whispered fiercely. He closed his eyes and I raised my voice. "*Explain yourself,* Tomasz!"

His eyes dulled, and then his shoulders slumped forward.

"Do you remember when I told you that I want to become a pediatrician?" he whispered.

"Of course," I said, stiffly.

"I...there was...the surgeon. Remember I told you about the surgeon?"

I softened then—just a little, because I recognized the struggle in Tomasz's voice and I realized that I was about to hear a new kind of story from him—a story he didn't know *how* to tell. I stared at him, and in that moment, I had to force myself to focus on the knowledge that I had known this man for our entire lives. He was a good man. This might not be a good story, but the man telling it to me was essentially *good*. If what he had said just now was true, there would be a rationale for it, even if in that moment, I couldn't even begin to imagine what it was.

But I did trust him, at least enough to give him the chance to explain. I reached for his hand and he looked at me in surprise.

"It's okay, Tomasz," I said gently. "Just tell me. I'm not going anywhere."

I started to walk again, his hand tightly in mine. He fell into step beside me, drew in a deep breath, and then he released it in a rush with a tumble of words.

"I fought with the Polish army in Warsaw until they had overpowered us. We put up a Hell of a fight but we were no match for them, not in the end. The Nazis captured me and a group of my friends from the college, and we were given a choice—join the *Wehrmacht*, or they'd kill our families and put us into prison. They said they had intelligence on us all and they knew where our families were—and I thought if I did what they asked, I could save my father and Emilia and maybe even you, darling Alina, because what if they already knew we were engaged? I felt I had no choice. I didn't know what else to do, so I joined the *Wehrmacht*." He spat the word out bitterly. "I wore the filthy uniform and I did everything I was instructed to."

I remembered my brothers telling me that students from Warsaw had been conscripted to the *Wehrmacht*, and how I'd scoffed at them—because I'd been so certain that Tomasz would never comply with such an order. But one thing I knew all too well about Tomasz was how deep the love he had for his family was—how deep his love for *me* was. They had found the only leverage that would have convinced him to betray his country.

"Did you kill people?" I asked unevenly.

"There are worse things than murder, Alina," he whispered. "I betrayed our countrymen, and one day...one day when Poland is whole, you can bet there will be an accounting for cowards like me. *Especially* me. I went to Warsaw to learn to heal, and instead, I enforced their ideology. They liked me because I spoke some German from summers on vacation. They liked me because I was strong and fast—and because..." He broke off altogether now, and I heard the sob he tried to muffle. "The commander said I had a way about me that put people at ease.

They assigned my unit to moving families to the Jewish area. The little children were so scared, and their mothers were so frightened, but I told them it was going to be okay. They just had to do what we told them to do and they'd be okay. But it wasn't okay, not even in the early days, because there wasn't enough room or food and it was just a way to corral them all into one place to make it easier to hurt them. They built a wall around that ghetto. It is Hell on earth and there is no escaping it, and I marched those children in there and I promised them that they'd be okay."

He could no longer muffle the sobs, and I could no longer stand to hear this story without holding him. I stopped, turned to him and threw my arms around his waist. I pressed my face against his chest and I listened to the beat of his heart, the thumps coming faster and harder as the memories and his shame surfaced. I struggled in that moment—horror and revulsion at his actions, but also, growing understanding.

Because it finally made sense—the darkness I glimpsed in him from time to time. It was rooted in mortification and regret of the deepest kind; he had made decisions that betrayed the very values that made Tomasz Slaski the man he was.

He sank to the ground at one point, but I followed him, and then pushed him until he was resting against a tree trunk. Tomasz still couldn't look at me, so I straddled his lap and I cupped his face in my hands.

"Tell me everything, my love," I whispered. The tears rolled down his face into his beard, and he raised his eyes to the forest canopy above us.

"Your father would kill me if he knew what I'd done."

"Perhaps not if he knew *why*, Tomasz."

"Your father is a good man. *He* would have resisted."

"He won't judge you, Tomasz, and neither do I."

"The Poles will kill me one day, if the Nazis don't get me

first. Good men like your father will find me and kill me for what I've done."

I shook my head fiercely, then I kissed him, hard—the best thing I could think to do to stop such talk. He swallowed, then met my gaze again.

"Tomasz," I said firmly. "Tell me the rest."

He drew in a shuddering breath, then sighed.

"One day, I was patrolling the ghetto, and I saw him. Saul Weiss."

"Your surgeon friend?"

"Yes. He and his wife, Eva, had been taken there too. They'd been dragged from a nice apartment near the hospital to a pathetic room in the ghetto they had to share with two other families. I pretended I didn't recognize him at first, because I was so ashamed to be a part of what was happening to him. I looked away from him, and I walked some more, and then I glanced back, and do you know what he did? He smiled at me. *Kindly*, Alina. He smiled at me." I could barely understand the words leaving Tomasz's mouth because he was weeping again. I started to cry too, and I bent and kissed the tears away from his cheeks, then nuzzled my nose against his.

"I'm still here, my love," I whispered. "Keep talking to me."

"But he *should* have hated me, only he refused to debase himself with hatred. We had a shared history—a friendship—and even in those circumstances he extended warmth to me. Saul Weiss had lost everything because of people like *me*; people who didn't have the courage to take a stand, and still? He chose to smile. That was the day that I broke inside and I *knew* I couldn't take it anymore."

"How did you get out of Warsaw?"

"The sewers," he said, then he pressed his forehead against mine and paused for a moment, collecting himself. "We waded through the sewer. Me, Saul and his wife, Eva."

"You let them escape with you?"

"No," he laughed bitterly, then sadness crept over him. "You still think I am the hero of this story, Alina, but I am *trying* to tell you that I'm the villain. They let me escape with them. I went back to apologize to Saul. I dragged him into an empty shop front because I had to play the part, but once we were alone—it was *me* who wept, and a few days later when it was time to go, he trusted me enough to invite me to come with them. They had used the last of their money to pay a guide to lead them through the sewers. Honestly, I thought it was a suicide mission—that's actually why I agreed to go. I had no thoughts of what I'd do if we made it, because it didn't even seem a possibility, and death seemed far better than staying there in that uniform and dying of the rot inside. No one was more surprised than me when we climbed into daylight in the outskirts of Warsaw. Saul and Eva had no plan from there, so we started on foot—we lived under bridges and in barns for months on the way back here."

"But...how? Did you come the *whole* way on foot? It is *hundreds* of miles, Tomasz. It's..."

"Close to impossible, right?" he said sadly. "You see my point, then. We had so many close calls I kept thinking that anytime soon it would all be over...but luck or God or fate was on our side, because we eventually encountered a sympathetic farmer who connected us to the Zegota network—it is an underground council to help the Jews, supported by the government in exile. We would never have been able to cross over from the General Government area without their help."

We fell into a bruised silence for a while. Eventually, I shifted onto the ground beside him, and wrapped my arms around his waist, then rested my head against his chest. I let my mind conjure images of all that he'd told me—even the parts that I didn't want to imagine, because they were a part of Tomasz now, and I wanted to know and understand all of him.

After a while, he cleared his throat.

"You need to understand, Alina. Saul and Eva saved my life,

and I have made it my mission to help them. They are hidden nearby and until I can repay them, I will do whatever I can to help them hide."

"You steal food for them?"

"Yes, if I can find it. I capture birds sometimes, sometimes squirrels. I steal from farmers when I can—only because I know the Nazis take it all anyway so I'm really stealing from them. I've taken eggs from your own hen yard, but only because you have so many chickens I thought they wouldn't be missed…only when I was truly desperate."

I felt like I had to say the words aloud—just to put a name to it all. It took me another few minutes to find the courage to say the words, and even then, I whispered them.

"You are aiding Jews in hiding. Yes?"

"I have three groups of friends in hiding in the miles around your farm, including Saul and Eva. Many others are hidden in houses in the township and from time to time I help them too—but others working with Zegota usually bring them food. Sneaking round in the town is incredibly dangerous."

"*Everything* you have just said is incredibly dangerous!" I exclaimed, drawing away from him. "Don't you understand? The Nazis have made a decree that if you assist a Jewish person with so much as a glass of water, they will kill you *and* your whole family! How could you not even tell me about this? I am your family, Tomasz—but so is Emilia. You could have just gone into hiding alone without them and that would have been so much less dangerous—"

"Saul and Eva have a newborn," Tomasz interrupted me, his expression suddenly hard. I blinked at him.

"A *baby*?"

"Yes. Eva gave birth a few weeks ago, just after we arrived back here. Tikva can't eat anything but her mother's milk, and Eva can't make milk unless I bring her food. Am I to let the newborn starve, Alina?" He held my gaze, the bite of sheer frustration shortening his words. "Saul is a good man, a far better man than me. But he's Jewish, so the invaders would have him starve like an animal, or worse, lock him up in a camp and work him to death. And that baby is the most beautiful little doll you have ever seen. Oh, but she was born to Jewish parents, so I suppose she deserves to die too? Would *you* pull the trigger at her temple, then?"

"Don't *say* these things," I protested fiercely. I was crying, overwhelmed and scared, but Tomasz was undeterred by my tears.

"But that is what *you* are saying when you tell me I should have left them behind." A crippling sadness crossed his face, and his gaze pleaded with me for understanding. "This is why I wasn't going to let you know I was here. I was going to stay in hiding and find ways to help you, but I was never going to show my face to you. I know that would have been cruel, but it would have been safer *for you.* I would choose our love over *anything* else—but I won't choose you over what is right, not this time. I wouldn't be the man *you* deserve if I didn't help these people." He stopped abruptly, and ran his hand through his hair, frustration etched on his face. "Monsters shouldn't feel a great love like we have, should they? I have to *prove* that I'm not a monster. Please don't ask me to stop. *Please.*"

The risks Tomasz was taking were unacceptable—but everything about life in those days was unacceptable, because every time we accepted our lot, things always became even worse. I had a sudden, startling burst of clarity. We had to fight—even if not with guns and weapons, with the sheer strength of our spirit, and for every single one of us, *resistance* meant something different. For me, *resistance* would mean doing whatever it was Tomasz needed me to do, even if it meant certain death for us both. I stared that thought down bravely, confused by my own courage. If anything, Tomasz's revelation made me wonder, not if he was the person I thought he was, but if *I* was the person I thought I was. Even knowing for sure that my relationship with him was in essence a death sentence, I wasn't deterred at all.

I had come to see myself over the years exactly as others expected me to be; tiny in stature, pretty and delicate, too *feminine* to be of much use around the farm—spoiled and lazy and immature and maybe even just a little foolish.

Certainly not brave. Certainly *not* heroic or noble myself.

If I really *was* that girl, the thought of risking my life for Tomasz would have petrified me. I'd have run a million miles in the other direction. But in that moment all I wanted to do was to find a way to make him safe, a way to give him peace, a way to help his friends. The love I felt for him was so big that it eclipsed my fears and it shouldered his burdens as my own. Our love was now a mirror, and within it I could see myself clearly for the very first time. I didn't see a spoiled, foolish girl with a crush on her school friend. I saw a woman who was feeling a very selfless, very adult kind of love.

"I won't ask you to stop," I said, and he raised his eyes to me. "In fact, I am going to find a way to help you."

He shook his head immediately.

"Not a chance, Alina—"

"Don't," I said, firmly but softly. "Don't you dare tell me it's too dangerous. *Loving* you is dangerous now, and I couldn't stop that even if I tried. Your calling is my calling. We do this together, because what do you *always* say to me?"

"We are meant to be together," he whispered, but his gaze was serious. "Even so, I can't let you take any more risk than you already are, Alina."

"You don't *let* me do anything, Tomasz," I said gently, and he gave me a sad, reluctant smile. "I don't know how much help I can be, but I have to try. Even if I can just get a little more food for this mother and her precious newborn. But now..." I drew in a deep breath and glanced back toward the fields. I hadn't heard Mama calling, but surely she had been, and she was probably about to come looking for me. "I've been gone far too long, and I have to go."

I brushed my lips against his. Tomasz Slaski was exhausted—physically and emotionally wrecked. But there was a new depth of honesty between us—an intimacy unlike anything we'd experienced before, born in the deepest kind of vulnerability.

He'd let me see him, every part of him—even his shame. And in return, I could offer only understanding and acceptance. It would be years before I'd appreciate how profound that moment was; what a relief it must have been to him. At the time, I was doing only what the love I had for him compelled me to do. I was acting purely on instinct.

"I love you," he said. I kissed him one last time and closed my eyes to breathe him in.

"I love you too, Tomasz. And you are *no* monster, not to me," I said, then I looked up at him and the tears surged again. "You are a hero, my love. I know you don't feel like one yet. But one day, you'll see."

When I came down from the hill that day, Mama looked at me, frowning.

"You have been crying," she said.

"What?" I feigned ignorance. "No, perhaps I am getting a cold."

"A cold," she repeated, sighing, then, almost to herself, "Alina thinks she's getting a cold."

I knew she didn't believe me, but I didn't have time to worry about that.

I was already thinking about dinner, and how much of it I could hide for Tomasz and his friends.

CHAPTER 16

Alina

The summer of 1941 was fading toward fall, and by then that sporadic tower of smoke that I'd so feared in the earlier days of the war was becoming a permanent landmark. The acrid scent that had so disturbed me when it first appeared became as familiar as the scent of chicken dung in the fields. Flecks of odd gray ash appeared on my clothing and in my hair and settled on the fields like a fine snow when there was no wind. I learned to ignore it. I had to ignore it, because there was simply no escaping it.

Tomasz was still living in the woods without shelter, and he had very little bulk to his clothing—so much so that I was trying to figure out if I could covertly sneak some of my brothers' clothes to him before the weather cooled further.

I knew he was already cold—some mornings I'd go to greet him only to find he was dozing in a hollow trunk because he needed to curl up in the night now, and his lips would be blue and his whole body trembling.

"You are friends with Nadia Nowak, right?" I asked him one day. He stiffened.

"I know Nadia, yes."

"Can you not stay with her now that it's a bit cooler? Or even hide with some of your Jewish friends?"

"No, I can't stay with Nadia…it is far too risky to even attempt it. And as for my friends, it is too hard to get in and out of their hiding places. I need to be able to leave each night so I can get more food for us all."

I believed him when he said he would find a way, but I worried about how far he was going to take this quest to help his friends. I now understood that the guilt he bore from his decisions in Warsaw drove his every thought, and I was scared how far that would take him. He'd already taken on one suicide mission and survived; how long would it be before he did so again?

I was thinking about that one morning as I walked to meet with him, so lost in thought that I was carelessly unaware of my surroundings. I heard movement ahead of me and raised my gaze. I was looking straight into the eyes of a soldier who was standing just a few feet away. I was so startled, I screamed without a single thought. The high-pitched, piercing sound echoed all through the woods and the soldier swung his rifle from his shoulder to raise it toward my face.

"Please," I croaked, shaking my head. "Please, no."

He flung rapid-fire German at me, but I couldn't make sense of it, and I stared at him blankly. I raised my hands over my head in case that's what he'd asked, but he gave me an impatient look and, to my surprise, said in Polish, "What are you doing here?"

"Alina," Mama called from behind me, sounding oddly exasperated. "Would you slow down, child?"

"Mama…" I croaked. I tried to turn to face her to warn her not to approach but I couldn't tear my eyes away from the soldier, and in the end it didn't matter—it was far too late to warn her anyway. I felt her draw near to me and she greeted the soldier.

"Good morning," she said. Her tone was casual and warm, as if there was nothing at all out of the ordinary about the scene she'd just come across. I shot her an incredulous glance.

"What are you doing in these woods, old lady?" the soldier demanded, swinging the rifle from me, to Mama, then back.

"We are walking the path, going to visit my daughter's home

in the town," Mama said easily, then she added with convinc-ing concern, "Are you looking for someone?"

From farther up the hill, I saw another soldier approaching, and behind him, another. As I scanned the hill around me, I saw six of them, arranged in formation, all eyes fixed on me and Mama in that moment. My stomach dropped into my toes, and it took everything within me to stop myself from looking up. What if Tomasz was right above us? What if he'd fallen asleep in the open again? I had to assume he was without identifica-tion, and besides, they would take one look at him and know he was hiding from *something*. He was nothing more than a bag of skin and bones, held together by rags.

"There are Jews hiding in this district," the soldier announced. "We are sweeping the woods looking for fugitives."

"Here?" Mama said, sounding slightly incredulous. She laughed, freely and quite loudly. "Who would hide in this tiny patch of woods? You'll find them in a heartbeat if there's any-one here." She pointed back, vaguely toward our house. "We live just a few hundred feet away. Trust me when I say there is no one in these woods. I would *know* if there was."

"Documents?" the soldier demanded, and just when I thought I'd die from the fear, Mama calmly reached into her shirt, then stepped forward and handed him our identity papers. He scanned these, then nodded curtly, tossed the papers vaguely back in Mama's direction and motioned with his rifle that we should continue along the path.

Mama returned the paperwork to her undershirt, slipped her hand through my elbow, and led me past the soldiers toward the top of the hill. I tried to turn my head back toward them to see what was happening, but she shook me, hard, and muttered a fierce, "Eyes forward, Alina."

Several Nazi trucks were parked at the bottom of the hill on the Trzebinia side, in the space where the grass grew long but the trees had been cleared to make way for houses. Mama and

I walked right past those empty trucks, my arm still caught in the death grip of her elbow. We walked the remaining blocks to Truda's house in a stiff and horrible silence. When Truda swung the door open, I finally burst into tears.

"Get her some tea," Mama sighed, then she pinned me with a stare. "Alina, my girl, I have been more than patient with you but it's high time you told me the truth."

Emilia came bounding down the hallway, delight in her voice as she called, "Alina! You have come to *my* house for a change—" Her little face fell as she saw my tears. "Oh no... what is it?"

"Everything is fine," I told her. I tried to fix a smile on my face but I couldn't hold back the sobs, and Truda glared at me and hastily sent Emilia outside to play.

Mama and I sat side by side at Truda's kitchen table. Truda made us tea, then went outside to Emilia and, all the while, I sobbed and avoided my Mama's gaze. I was in such a panic I couldn't untangle my thoughts. If I'd gone to the hill two minutes earlier, we might have been sitting together when the soldiers came, and I knew we could never risk such encounters again, even if the soldiers *hadn't* found Tomasz in their sweep. After a minute or two, when my sobs weren't even beginning to slow down, Mama sighed heavily.

"Stop fussing, Alina. There is no need for such drama."

"It was the fright..." I said, unconvincingly. Mama rolled her eyes at me.

"I have figured out your secret," she said.

Her announcement made an already-awful situation unexpectedly complicated. Because did she *really* know my secret, or did she just *think* she knew? What if she thought my "secret" was something else? I also didn't want to anger her, because my mother was a formidable woman, and not someone I wanted to cross. I pondered all of this as quickly as I could, and then I looked back to my tea.

"I don't know what you mean, Mama," I whispered, as in-nocently as I could manage given adrenaline had once again flooded my system and my heart was thundering all over again, but then she smacked me on the back of the head and muttered something under her breath that sounded suspiciously like *I'm not an idiot.*

"When did he come back?" she asked flatly.

My heart was thumping so hard against my chest that I was sure she could hear it.

"I—"

"Alina, Tomasz is back, and he's in hiding. Am I right? *Prayer for the country at war,*" she scoffed. I stared at her in shock, but then she chuckled. "Even if we hadn't already suspected, we'd have soon figured it out when you insisted on going to the hill when it was raining." Her gaze softened just a little, and she murmured, "I was eighteen and in love too, once upon a time."

"Why didn't you tell me you knew?"

"Well, to be honest, I was scared to. I wasn't sure why you or he would ever think it was a good idea to hide him from us, so I was waiting for you to tell me what was going on. In the meantime, I decided I would stay close by in the field in case I heard signs of trouble…and it is fortunate for you that I did, given what happened today."

I felt nauseous then, and as I lifted the tea to my mouth, my hands shook a little. Mama and I waited in silence for a while, then she asked me, "You must tell me now, Alina. Why is he hiding?"

I looked at her in alarm.

"I don't know," I lied. She raised her eyebrows at me, and saw all the way through me with one of her stares. I felt my face flush, and I started to sweat. "I don't!"

"Is it the resistance?" she asked, and she leaned back in her chair and added casually, "Or has he tried to help some of those in hiding?"

I didn't say a word, but she must have read the truth on my face. She grunted, and it sounded a lot like approval. I looked at her in surprise.

"Mama?"

"What?"

"If… I'm not saying he is, but…*if* he was hiding some Jewish friends…"

"I would still be confused as to why you didn't tell me this earlier."

"But maybe he was trying to protect me…"

"Then he is not nearly as smart as I thought he was, because if he was, he would know that any contact with you means danger for us all, but that Father and I would understand."

Hope, warm and surprising, blossomed in my chest.

"You understand?" I choked.

"Do you remember when Filipe wanted to join the resistance?" Mama asked me. She so rarely talked about her lost sons, and I was a little taken aback.

"I do…"

"And we all discouraged him. We all thought it was safer for him to just put his head down. Remember?"

"Yes, Mama."

"Well, we were *wrong*, Alina. He is dead anyway, and maybe if we had stood up and fought—" Her voice broke, and she cleared her throat, then exhaled. "We have tried so hard to keep you all safe. We have done everything we could to protect you. But that wasn't nearly enough, and now I am so sorry we didn't instead find *some* way to resist. Perhaps we could have made a difference—if not for Filipe, then for someone else. Our passivity makes us guilty, Alina. Father and I have been talking for some time about how we might rectify that, but the right opportunity had not presented itself. Do his friends have shelter?"

"His friends do…but *he* doesn't…"

"Then what will he do when the winter comes?" I looked at

her, and she raised her eyebrows at me. "It is not far off, Alina. He cannot live in the woods once the snow comes. Tell me you have a plan."

"He hides in the trees, sometimes he hides behind logs. But he's been falling asleep during the day and..." I choked on another sob. "He says he will cope, but I'm so scared."

"Do you understand how much trouble he is in?"

"I do."

"I need to know that you understand how much trouble *you* are in, Alina. You are helping him. By half measures, perhaps, if all you are doing is kissing in the woods and sneaking him some crumbs, but it's still helping him. If he is aiding Jews in hiding, then so are you, and that is punishable by your death." Her gaze was sharp and focused right on my face. I grabbed her forearm and squeezed—hard. She had to understand. She just had to know how much I loved him. She just *had* to know that I would take any risk to help him.

"Mama. It's *Tomasz*. He's all alone in the world except for me. Even if it's dangerous, I could never abandon him." I wiped at my eyes with my spare hand, and then I said firmly, "Besides, Mama, he is helping a family—a new baby will die if we don't help. How can I choose *my* life over that infant?"

Mama stared at me. She surveyed my face and the tears on my cheeks, then she nodded, as if she was satisfied.

"You can't," Mama said. "And neither can I. Let me help."

There was no sign of the soldiers' trucks when we returned to climb the hill, and the woods were still and quiet again. I scanned the treetops desperately but found no sign of Tomasz, either. I tried to convince myself that he'd stayed in the trees or hidden in a hollow log and survived the sweep, but I had *no* way of knowing what had happened.

"Could I call out for him, do you think?" I asked Mama. She shook her head.

"I have something to show you. Come back to the house for a few hours and you can search for him later."

Father greeted us at the door to the house, concern in his gaze. "Where have you been all of this time?"

Mama pushed past him, then she announced, "Alina needs that help we discussed. Watch the road and the woods—there have been soldiers about."

Father nodded curtly, then positioned himself at the window in the kitchen. Mama walked across the room and pushed our table back, off the heavy rug it rested upon. She lifted the rug and I gasped, because attached to the bottom of the rug was a hatch. As Mama folded the rug over itself, she opened a rough-shod doorway in our floor and revealed the entrance to a space below our house.

"Mama!" I choked.

"Hush," she said impatiently. "It is what it is."

It was a *second* cellar, apparently a smaller storage space than the large one we had beneath the barn. This was a cellar that I'd never known about, in all my years living in that very house. I suppose I'd have noticed some unevenness in the floor if I'd walked over the rug—but I never had, because for as long as I could remember, the table had been in that very spot, right atop it. I walked to the edge to stare down into the space.

There was a ladder, and while I was curious about what could be down there, the darkness seemed utterly suffocating and I had no intention of climbing down to find out. Mama turned back to the kitchen and started the little oil lantern that was kept on the bench there, which she passed to me. I held it silently as she climbed down the ladder, then she reached up, indicating for me to pass it to her.

"Come," she said.

"But…"

She waved the light around herself, to show me the space was larger than it first appeared, and her gaze grew impatient.

"Alina, the darkness still frightens you? Death at the hands of Nazis for helping your outlaw boyfriend barely makes you blink, but climbing down a ladder makes you tremble? What nonsense, child."

So I followed her down the ladder, descending into the darkness. The air down there seemed thick, even with the latch open, even with the lantern on. I wasn't sure I could survive two minutes in that place, but as soon as my feet touched the floor, I saw the food. There were dozens of jars of preserves, and a stockpile of potatoes, plus several sacks of flour and sugar. A basket of eggs rested on the floor.

It was more food than the three of us would eat in months at the rate we'd been dipping into it. Dozens and dozens of morsels hidden for our use—every single one of which would guarantee death to my parents if the Nazis found this space.

"How did you hide this from us?" I asked her breathlessly.

"We started stockpiling long before the war, at the first hint of trouble in the papers. We moved everything we had into this space the day the invaders killed the mayor and Aleksy, and ever since we've been adding to it when we could—just in case things got worse. We only ever come down here in the middle of the night when we're sure you're asleep," she said, then she laughed a little. "This is how we caught you 'praying' through your window all of those months ago. Father was waiting to put some eggs down and to bring up a little more jam. That's when he heard you talking." She tilted her head at me. "You *were* talking to Tomasz that night, yes?"

I nodded, sighing.

"He had only just returned then." I digested this, then looked around again. I glanced at Mama again uncertainly. "Why didn't you ever tell me about this?"

"It is the responsibility of parents to provide for their children, and we happened to have a way to do that," she said simply. "You didn't need to know. It wasn't as though we hid the cellar on purpose—in the early years, we didn't tell you this space was here because we knew you children would make mischief if you knew of it. And we never intended it to be used this way. It was luck, not strategy—simply a hangover from back before your grandfather built the bigger cellar with the new barn." Mama rested her hand on my shoulder very gently. "Perhaps this can be of use to Tomasz. There is no heat, but it never gets as cold down here. We can furnish him with this lantern—we can't spare much oil, mind, but perhaps enough for when it's necessary. And I have been saving the food strictly until it *must* be used, but with the boys gone and it being so hard to get supplies over to Truda and Emilia now, I just don't think we can use it all in time. To see food waste in such hard times is the *real* crime." She paused, then she said with a shrug, "It will please Father and I greatly if Tomasz can distribute this food to his Jewish friends. We have been looking for a way to help."

"Mama," I whispered. "They would kill you if they found this."

"Well, Alina," she said matter-of-factly, "there is a good chance that if they find Tomasz and learn that you have supported him, they will kill you too. We all take the risks we can handle in war."

"What does Father know?" I asked, glancing nervously toward the hatch.

"He knows the same as I do."

"Tomasz served with the *Wehrmacht*," I blurted. "In Warsaw. Does that make any difference to you?"

Mama blinked at me, then she sighed.

"A fine young Polish man like Tomasz Slaski would never work with those bastards unless he had no choice. Am I correct?"

"You are," I whispered.

"Then, no, it will make no difference."

"And Father will let Tomasz hide in here?"

"He lets you visit with him alone in the woods each day, so

this isn't too much different," Mama said wryly. I felt the flush creep up my cheeks, and she laughed softly. "Why do you think I follow you? It is not just the soldiers you could get yourself in trouble with, child."

"When can Tomasz come?"

"Wait another hour or two, then go find him and tell him to come tonight when darkness falls."

CHAPTER 17

Alina

I waited almost two hours, then I walked toward the woods as calmly as I could. My thoughts were racing—I was still trying to wrap my mind around the reality that my parents *knew* and that Tomasz could soon be living under our roof. When I reached the top of the hill, I saw him slip down from a treetop to rush toward me.

"I saw them coming, and I saw you coming, but they were right below me and I couldn't do anything," he choked, pulling me close. "My God, Alina, I'm so sorry— I— We can't do this anymore. It's too risky, it was so *stupid* of me to—"

"My parents know," I blurted, and he braced himself as if he was about to sprint away. "Wait—they know, but they want to help you."

"*Help* me?" he repeated. He seemed incredulous at this, as if I'd suggested something completely absurd, and that broke my heart just a little more.

"I told you they had food somewhere? There is another cellar. The hatch is under the rug beneath the table in our house. They said you can hide there."

Tomasz blinked, then he caught my shoulders in his palms.

"Alina," he said flatly. "This is very kind of your parents and very kind of you, but I can't accept that offer."

"But why not?" I asked desperately. "It's not safe out here, Tomasz. I'm so scared for you."

By the time I'd finished speaking I was sobbing, and he pulled me hard against his torso again.

"They would kill you if they found me there and I can't..." He choked against my hair. "It's selfish enough for me to see you like this, but I thought they'd only link us if they caught us together. But if you hide me in your house..."

"That is not your concern," I said.

"*You* are my concern."

"If that is true then you will grant me one small mercy and let us help you in this way. My parents have been trying to figure out how to get the food to those who need it, so perhaps *you* are the answer to their prayers." When he remained stiff within my arms, I added softly, "Tomasz...can you imagine how much help that food will be to this young family you are caring for?"

"I..."

"And there are others too? Others in hiding? Mama has a whole *sack* of potatoes."

"Can you just give me the food, *moje wszystko*?" he pleaded. "I'll get it to those who need it. I don't *have* to stay in your home where the Nazis might find me. If I were to do as you ask, I'd have to come to and leave your house at least once a day. It is far too dangerous."

I rocked back on my heels and crossed my arms over my chest.

"Remember when you said I was spoiled, Tomasz?"

"I...do..."

"Well, I am accustomed to getting my own way," I said flatly. "And I am not above blackmailing you when I know it's for your own good. So you *will* come stay with us, or I will find another way to get the food to those who need it." He stared at me impassively, so I raised my eyebrows and added slowly, "Maybe I can visit Nadia Nowak? Perhaps she has some ideas how I could distribute this food myself."

His eyes widened.

"Alina Dziak," he said incredulously. "That is…"

"That is the deal." I shrugged. "Take it, or leave it."

"You leave me no choice."

"That's exactly what I was intending," I said. He shook his head at me, clearly frustrated. "I have more tricks up my sleeve, Tomasz. Don't make me use them."

"What are these tricks?" he asked, frowning harder now.

I leaned forward and brushed my lips against his.

"I will save them for the next time you underestimate me," I said softly, then I brushed the hair back from his eyes. He was still frowning at me, so I kissed him again, then turned away to return to the house, calling softly over my shoulder, "Come once it's dark. We'll be ready for you."

CHAPTER 18

Alice

I go through the motions at home. Wade is working late, making up lost time for yesterday—he has some plastics project on that's been causing him grief so I'm not surprised. As soon as the kids are in bed, I pour myself a glass of wine, put some music on and sink into the sofa.

Alice plane Poland.

It's an absurd request. Completely unreasonable. Totally impractical.

I just have no idea how I can ever decline it. If Babcia asked for the moon right now, I'd have to try to find a way to get it for her. And I *think* all she's asking me to do is get on a plane, take some photos and come home. How quickly could I go? How quickly could I come back? I don't even know where Trzebinia is. All I really know about the geography of Poland is that it's in Europe, and Warsaw is the capital.

I could look it all up on Wade's laptop. It's just within my reach, resting on the coffee table in front of me. I don't reach for it. Instead, I listen to the music, and I wait until I hear Wade pulling into the garage.

We haven't spoken a word to each other since the argument last night, but even so, I know he's going to bring flowers home with him tonight and he'll be desperate to earn my forgiveness. Right on cue, he walks into the house carrying a bouquet of long-stemmed red roses and wearing a contrite expression. I set the wineglass next to the laptop as I stand, take the roses and accept the kiss he offers.

"I'm sorry," he whispers.

"Me too," I whisper back.

"How are the kids? How is Babcia? How are *you* doing?" Wade asks.

"Why don't you go get your dinner and I'll fill you in while you eat?"

"...even if I wanted to go, it would be impossible."

Tonight, Wade has been listening in silence while I talk, and it kind of reminds me of our earlier years, when I was the chatty one and he was the calm, scientific one. It used to astound me that someone so brilliant seemed to have endless interest in whatever I had to say—in the early months of our relationship, we talked until the sunrise more than once, and I'd never felt so *important* before. We're a long way from that place these days, but for a moment, it actually feels nice to remember that's the kind of people we used to be together—almost like we've taken a brief vacation back to a special place we used to visit.

Wade's gaze is expressionless as he asks, "Do you want to go?"

"It doesn't matter what I want," I say stiffly. "How could I possibly leave the kids?"

He's back in my good graces well and truly after listening to me prattle on and on about this for the last forty-five minutes, but in one fell swoop, he's right back into my bad books.

"Jesus, Alice," Wade says. His exasperation is immediately on *full* display. "Give me at least a little credit. I have a PhD, for God's sake. I can handle a few days on my own with two kids."

Red rage rushes in at me, so vivid and sudden that I can't actually see past it. I'm a boiling, seething pile of fury and I have no idea what I'm supposed to do with all of this *anger*, so I just stare at him, my jaw hanging loose.

"Really?" I say when my rage fades enough that I can bring myself to speak again. "It's as simple as that, is it?"

"Yes, it is that simple," my husband says flatly. He leans back in the chair and crosses his arms over his chest. "I'm not saying I'd do everything *your* way, but we'd get by."

It's my turn to lean back in my chair, and I *exactly* mirror his stance—crossing my arms over my chest and jutting my chin up a little.

"And what would that look like, Wade? What would you do with Eddie, for example?"

I've broken the unspoken rule of our family life: one does not draw attention to the elephant in the room. Wade's lack of a relationship with Eddie is a ghostly specter we can all see, but we never directly address. The flush on my husband's cheeks suggests he's embarrassed by the question, but the impatience doesn't fade from his glare.

"He'd go to school. Like a *normal* kid."

"He can't handle full-time school, Wade," I say pointedly. "Even his teachers agree."

"Well, he'd deal with it for one week. Maybe it's time we push him a bit more."

"Push him a bit more?" I repeat the words blankly, but I can feel my eyebrows drawing down as my face shifts into a derisive scowl.

"*Yes*, Alice," Wade says impatiently. He pauses, then he says carefully, "It's just that sometimes, maybe, you coddle him a little—"

"*Coddle* him?" I gasp, and that's it—I am *done*. I slam my hands onto the table, ready to stand, but we've been married for ten years—Wade really does know me too well.

"Don't you dare storm off," he groans. "You asked what I'd do, and I'm telling you. You have no right to cut me off just because you don't like my answer."

"Do you have any idea how difficult it would be for Eddie

if you just threw him into full-time school without planning or explanation?"

"Maybe if you give the kid a chance, he could surprise you."

"What is that supposed to mean?"

"It means that you were convinced something was seriously wrong with Eddie from the time he was a baby, and you've never given him a chance to prove you wrong."

"Oh sure, Wade. This is all me, isn't it? The doctors and teachers and therapists are all wrong—"

"I'm not saying he's a typical kid. He's clearly autistic, Alice. I'm not blind. I just think that maybe—" Wade starts out fiercely, but then the sound of that harsh tone echoing all around our kitchen must have bounced back into his ears because he winces and he pauses. When he speaks again, he pulls the aggression right back, until he's speaking almost *too gently*. "I'm scared we underestimate him, honey. That's *all*. I'm just saying that maybe if you spent as much time challenging him as you do protecting him, maybe your life would look different. And if you'd just *loosen* the goddamned reins for just a little bit, then maybe *I* could—"

I stand so fast and so hard that I tip the chair over and it crashes to the tiles. The sound is loud and it echoes all around us. Wade falls silent, but his determination to hold the line is evident. This argument is overdue. Maybe by weeks, maybe by years. Apparently we've both been looking for a reason to dump our cards on the table, and that time has now arrived.

I don't want to fight with him. I *don't* want to hurt him. But I have to make him understand, and the only way I can do that is to be honest.

"You couldn't cope, Wade," I blurt. He raises his eyebrows at me.

"Are you kidding me? I'm responsible for three hundred people at work, Alice. I can deal with our kids for a few days. Christ, it would be a fucking holiday."

There's an odd sensation within my chest—the splintering and shattering of something precious that had been straining under pressure for years. Truths unspoken are falling out all over the place today, and it turns out there *is* a straw that's just too heavy for this old camel to carry.

I spin on my heel and walk toward the family room. I slam the door behind me, and then I return to my armchair. I down the last of my wine in one gulp, then I reach for the laptop. I open the photo I snapped of Babcia's notes, and I start rapid-fire Googling. It takes about two minutes to confirm some of the entries are addresses—and Google maps them easily, so I take that as some kind of cosmic confirmation and it amplifies my determination to help her. Next, I search for the names. I get a lot of pages—mostly social media pages for young people with the same arrangement of names, but then I find a Wikipedia page for Henry Adamcwiz.

Henry Adamcwiz (1890-1944) was an American photographer known for his coverage of Nazi-occupied countries during World War II. He was part of an early but unsuccessful effort to alert American and British governments about increasing Nazi brutality toward the Polish Jewish population, working with the Zegota Council to arrange for couriers to smuggle film and documentation out of occupied Poland. He was executed by Nazi forces during the Warsaw Uprising in 1944…

I Google frantically—looking at maps and Google Translate and the calendar. I learn that I can fly into Krakow and be at Babcia's childhood town within an hour. I need a few days to prepare, and then I need to be back within a week—so I decide to stay for four nights. Last-minute flights are expensive—obscenely so—and at last, that gives me pause. I'm being impulsive, and despite what my mother sometimes implies, I don't do impulsive. The things *she* sees as impulsive in my history reflect my lack of courage, not impulsiveness—all of the times when I didn't dare warn her in advance that I wanted so desperately to take a different path to the one she'd chosen for me.

I can deal with our kids for a few days. Christ, it would be a fucking holiday.

The door flies open and Wade storms in after me.

"What are you doing?" he asks, staring at the computer on my lap.

I look up at him calmly.

"You can handle our kids for a few days, remember? It will be a *holiday*."

"Alice. Come on, I can't take time off quickly. You know that," he says impatiently. Patronizing me. Condescending. As if I am a silly child, instead of the woman who holds his entire world together—*which is exactly what I am.*

"I'll tell Babcia not to die until it suits your work schedule," I say bitterly, and then I select the tickets.

"Alice...what are you doing?" I hear the sudden anxiety in Wade's tone. He can't see the screen but he *can* see the expression on my face, and something there is making him very nervous. Well, so it should.

I let the browser prefill the credit card and then before I lose courage, I jab my finger against the mouse to activate the purchase button.

Please do not press the back button on your browser. This may take up to a minute.

For a split second, I feel triumph, but then it hits me what I've done, and I feel my heart rate zoom *all* the way up until adrenaline floods my system and I can barely force myself to breathe. I look up at Wade in a panic, and for the first time, he panics too.

"Ally..." he says, then he rushes around the coffee table to stare down at the laptop screen. "Honey...what did you do?"

I do the sensible thing then and I think about how much

money I just wasted on flights and how impossible it all is, and I burst into tears. Wade takes the laptop from me just as it gives the *ding* to indicate the purchase has been successful.

He's silent as he reads the payment receipt that's now loaded on my screen. I glance up at him, and I see the tightening in his jaw and the way his nostrils flare. He doesn't look at me, not for the longest time.

"Alice—" he finally starts to say, but I hold up my hand toward him abruptly.

"Don't," I say. "Don't. Just...*don't*."

"I'll give you some time to cool off," he sighs, and he drops the laptop onto the lounge without further ceremony. It bounces against the leather, then comes to a stop near the edge. Neither one of us reaches for it, like we're scared to touch it in case it poisons us. Wade turns and walks toward the door, but just before he leaves the room he throws a final missive over his shoulder. "But we *need* to talk about this tonight."

CHAPTER 19

Alice

Wade retreats to his study, but when I walk past the closed door, I can hear the rhythmic clicking of the keys on his electronic keyboard. When he is stressed or pondering some complex problem, he does one of two things: he runs miles and miles, or he puts his headphones on and he sits at the keyboard and he tries to learn impossibly difficult piano concertos—a habit that's lingered from his childhood when his mother correctly predicted that a boy so enamored with math would enjoy the challenge and symmetry of musicianship. In the weeks after Eddie's diagnosis, Wade worked on Rachmaninoff's Third until he gave himself a nasty case of Repetitive Strain Injury in both hands. He says distracting the conscious part of his brain with some other kind of work helps him to process things.

I've long suspected that Wade suffers from the exact same challenge we have with Callie—his brain runs too fast, and unless he occupies himself with something really intense, he tends to work himself into knots.

And that's kind of the opposite to my coping mechanism, because I'm upset too, so I run a bath. Tonight, I take the time to light several of the candles—the rose-scented ones—because they remind me of Babcia's beautiful rose garden at her old house. I dump the whole bottle of bubble mixture into the water, and the foamy bubbles on top rise until they spill over onto the flat edge of the tiles around the bath, but I don't even care. I sink into the water, and I cry some more because I'm completely confused about what to do next.

This should be simple. I should call the airline and cancel the tickets.

I'm just not sure that's what I actually *want* to do. There's a battle raging inside me; exactly 50 percent of me is cheering and desperate to go on this crazy quest, but the rest of me is every bit as desperate to stay home.

I stay in the bath far too long. The bubbles slowly pop. The water cools. I refill the tub with hot water several times and my skin wrinkles, but I still don't move. When the door opens quietly, it's just after midnight, and I'm still sitting here in the bath, still crying on and off. The candles have burned down, and even though they are long finished now, their scent and the smell of the wax linger too heavily, leaving a sickly sweet smell in the air. Wade enters the room gently, as if he's expecting me to be asleep and he's afraid to wake me, but then he knocks the toilet lid down and he sits heavily upon it.

"You really want to do this," he says. It's a statement not a question, but I seriously wish this were that simple. I look up at him through bleary eyes.

"I don't know. I know it's too much to ask. I know it's going to be too hard for the family but... I feel like I should do it."

"Ally," Wade sighs. "I don't know how we got here. Do you?"

I hate it when I can't keep up with him in a conversation, and this one has only just started, but I already have no idea what he's talking about. I scan around the bathroom, then back to him blankly.

"Here?"

"Remember back at the beginning? We talked about *everything*. Once upon a time you'd call me because you read an article in a newspaper that interested you or you saw something unusual on your way home from the store—and I loved that about you…" A desperate sadness creeps into his expression, and he exhales, then adds, "I loved that about *us*. Now you book tickets to Europe without telling me. We live in the same house, but I have no clue what's going on inside your head. Are you even happy? Do you…" His voice breaks, and he stops for a moment before he asks me in a whisper, "Alice, do you still love me?"

There's a moment of painful silence. We stare at each other—close enough almost to touch, despite the ocean of distance between us.

"Eddie," I say. That single word is rough with years of withheld emotion. Wade swallows and looks away, down to the gleaming white tiles on the floor. "Eddie changed everything."

Just as there's a curtain of chaos between Eddie and the world, there's now a curtain of chaos between Wade and I, because my world revolves around my son, and my husband hasn't found a way to connect with him at all. I hate that even on the best of days, but right now as I stare up at Wade, I wonder for the very first time if *he* hates it too. It's been easy to assume that Wade's failure to connect with Eddie was a purposeful form of sulking—the world hasn't given him the son he wants, so he refuses to acknowledge the son he has. If I force my emotions aside and make myself be completely rational here—that kind of behavior is just not in Wade's nature. It's more comforting to tell myself that Wade is at fault here, because the alternative is that Wade doesn't know *how* to connect with Eddie—or that he's too scared to try.

"I found a tour guide," Wade says, in another abrupt change of subject that leaves me feeling lost all over again. I wave vaguely toward the towels and he hands me one, then watches silently as I step out of the bath. Once the towel is wrapped tightly around me, I glance at him again.

"A guide who can visit those places for Babcia?"

It makes perfect sense. We can cancel the insanely expensive airline tickets, and pay someone who is already in the country to go take some photos for Babcia. I can't quite understand why I feel so disappointed at the solution Wade has found, given it actually solves every single one of my problems.

"No." He frowns, then he gives me that haughty look, the one I hate so much—the one he gets sometimes when he's busy being brilliant and I'm just not keeping up. "Someone who can take *you* to those places, Ally. She's fluent in English and Polish, she has a master's degree in modern history and she's a licensed tour guide. Her name is Zofia. I've just been on the phone with her, and she sounds perfect. She does family history stuff all the time—she said family and war history tours make up most of her business, actually. But she's normally booked out months in advance and she's only free because she had a cancellation next week, so I booked her on the spot. She'll take you to the town and help you see the things Babcia wants to see. She said the three days you've booked should be plenty of time to visit the town and take a good look around—it's a pretty small place."

"You...you *what*? But..."

"The town is Trzebinia, right?"

I stare at him in disbelief.

"How could you even know that?"

"You left the tabs open on the laptop..." He shrugs, then his gaze meets mine again. "You can email her and do some planning, but the gist of it is you fly out Monday night so you'll arrive in Krakow on the Tuesday. She's booking a hotel for you and she'll meet you there Wednesday morning and take it from there."

I panicked when I booked the tickets, but that was a blistering act of rage and it was something I was half intending to undo. This panic is different; it feels a little bit more like fear, because I have a sneaking suspicion I'm about to find myself well and truly out of my depth. I pinch the bridge of my nose and try to take some deep breaths, because I have no idea whether I should yell at Wade for babying me or thank him for helping me. I look up at him suddenly as I try to decide how to react, but my chest constricts when I see how he's sitting.

His shoulders have slumped, and he's staring at the sudsy tiles on the floor, utter misery in his gaze. He feels my eyes on him, though, and he raises his chin to look back at me. As our eyes lock, I feel so many things—*sadness* that things between us feel so broken, *confusion* because I still don't know how to react to his intervention here, and *love.* Love, maybe most of all. The man has broken my heart more times than I can count in the last few years, and he's let me down, and he's let our son down. But at the end of the day, the love I have for him hasn't waned even a little bit, and I am furious with myself that he's ever had cause to think otherwise.

"You know, for months…maybe even years…I've been trying to figure out how to make it all better," he says heavily. Weariness crosses his face, even as he shifts to avoid my gaze again. "I have everything I ever wanted in life. *You.* This house. My job. This family…for the most part. But every day it feels like you slip a little further away from me and you're the key to it all. If I lose you, Alice…the rest of it goes too."

There's a rawness in this declaration that takes my breath away. Wade reaches for my hand, and he holds it against his cheek, then closes his eyes. I stare down at him, sitting there so vulnerable and, well, sitting on our toilet seat, of all of the places in the world we could have had this conversation. It turns out I do have some tears left after all, because as I see my handsome, brilliant husband so desperate at last to *fix us* when for so long I've feared he didn't even care that we were broken, my vision blurs again.

"Babcia means the world to you, and you mean the world to me," he whispers now. "I love her too, of course, but…even though I said stupid things and you were angry, I know you wouldn't have booked those tickets if, on some level, you didn't want to go. So—knowing that—I'm going to do everything in my power to help you to get there."

"I think you're conflating two disparate issues," I say unevenly. He gives me a wry look.

"Am I?"

"Babcia's situation has nothing to do with…"

"Let's do a thought experiment," Wade says. He releases my hand, then leans back against the toilet cistern and raises his eyebrows at me. "Imagine a situation where we had our second child and he happened to be exactly like his very gifted big sister. No…challenges. Tell me what your life would look like by now?"

I can't let myself picture that. I can't let myself want a different son, not for a single second. We got the son we got. I love him just the way he is, and I always will. I stiffen and shake my head.

"You know what it would look like."

"Humor me, Ally. Would you have gone on this trip if we had more typical seven- and ten-year-old children?"

In a heartbeat.

I already hate this game, but it brings startling clarity. I keep telling myself *my family needs me to stay.* But maybe it's not *my family*—not Callie or Wade or the group collectively that hold me back from going away for a few days. It's Eddie, because unlike my brilliant husband and equally brilliant daughter, Eddie *needs* me. Wade stands, and he rests his hands on my shoulders gently. I reluctantly meet his gaze.

"You'd have gone on the trip, Ally," he whispers. "Because you would have trusted me to look after our kids if Edison had been born different."

"I do trust you," I say, but the words are stiff so the lie is unconvincing. Wade sighs, then he tenderly brushes a wet tendril of hair from my shoulder.

"We were always going to go to Europe, weren't we?" he says softly. "Shit, I've been half a dozen times for conferences and you never even blinked an eye while you waited back here at home for me. We were going to be the family who took their kids on overseas holidays, to broaden their horizons and show them the world. I know that's not really possible for us at the moment, but it was something *you* always wanted, even more than I did. You took so many great holidays as a kid with Pete and Julita, didn't you?"

"I don't want to take this trip to go on a *holiday*," I say defensively.

"I know. I'm not even saying that. I'm saying…this *means* something to you, and this is the first time I've seen you reaching for something beyond the kids in years."

"The kids are important. They're…this family is my life's work, in the same way that your job and your research is yours."

"I get that. I really do. The kids *are* important but…" Wade says hesitantly, "so is Babcia, right?" When I nod, he adds softly, "It's okay to want something that doesn't involve me and the kids, you know. We're all important—but damn it, Ally—so are *you*."

I can't remember the last time he said those words to me. It nearly breaks my heart to hear them—and I start to cry again. I nod at Wade through my tears, and he embraces me tightly. We stand like that for a few moments, until the chill in the air starts to get to me and I pull away from him and reach for a Kleenex to wipe my eyes. I open the door to our bedroom and step out to find some pajamas, and Wade follows me, watching silently. Once I'm dressed, he smiles gently.

"So, honey…this is happening?"

I'm reassured. I'm comforted. I feel supported now, but I'm still torn, and honestly, I'm still scared. I shrug a little.

"Can I think about it tonight?"

"Sure," he says, then the corner of his mouth lifts and he flashes me the cheeky grin that was half the reason I fell in love with him in the first place. "I mean, you've already paid for flights and I've just splashed out a small fortune for a private guide for three days, but sure—go ahead and think about it too."

"God," I whisper, then I close my eyes and swallow. "Even aside from the family, I'm kind of nervous. I don't really know what Babcia wants—not exactly. And I don't know how to prepare Eddie for this—or even how to prepare *you* for the—"

"Leave Eddie to me," Wade says.

I open my eyes and stare at him. "What would you even do with him on the days when he's not at school?"

"I've already thought about that. Ideally, he'd go to school full-time, but if you're absolutely sure he can't deal with that—"

"He can't."

"Then I'll take him to the office with me."

Once upon a time I desperately wanted Wade to take Eddie to work for a visit, but Wade was determined all along that it was just too risky—he has a very large, chaotic office full of towering stacks of paperwork and heavy reference books—and it's in an industrial research complex that he insisted was fraught with danger. Callie has visited Wade at work several times. Eddie has not. That was Wade's decision all along.

"But—"

"*I know*, Alice," he interrupts me, abruptly. I fall silent. "I know I said it was a bad idea when you asked me in the past, but I've really thought about it tonight, and we can make it work. I *want* to push him a little this week, to get him out of his comfort zone."

It's late. We're both exhausted. We stare at each other, and I can tell we're *both* desperately trying to stop this from disintegrating into a fight. Even with the tension, this is still a more honest argument than any we've had in recent history, which have always been littered with passive-aggressive taunts and hints.

"Let's view this as a question of science," Wade says, a little lighter now. "My theory is that Eddie and I can get on just fine this week if we bend some of your rules. If the experiment is a failure, we'll dismiss the theory and I'll admit we need to do things your way. Maybe I'll understand a little better why you're so rigid about how his routine works. Okay?"

"I feel like I might not have a choice."

"Well, Ally Michaels," Wade sighs, and he cups my face in his hands to stare down at me tenderly. "One way or another, we *will* all survive. You, me, Callie...and yes, even Edison." He bends and kisses me gently, then rests his forehead against mine. "I love you."

Despite the tension between us, despite the distance in these recent years—I know that Wade loves me, and I know that I love Wade. Sometimes I also kind of hate him, but mostly, I love him. That's marriage sometimes. That's just the way it is; the years can't all be kind, because life isn't always kind. We've been in a rough patch—a *very* rough patch—but I know we're still walking on the same path. I nod slowly, and a smile breaks over his face.

"I love you too," I whisper, then I kiss him hard. "I love you so much Wade, and I always will. No matter what else happens in our life, please don't *ever* doubt it again."

"Come to bed," he whispers, tugging at my hand as he turns away.

Last night, that very same suggestive tone felt like a burden and it made me furious.

Tonight, I can't wait to reconnect with him, and I'm glad to let him lead the way.

CHAPTER 20

Alina

It was completely dark when the hesitant knock came at the door, and I held my breath when Father opened it. Tomasz stood on the stoop, his tattered hat against his chest, his eyes downcast.

Mama pushed Father out of the way, then she grabbed Tomasz by the shoulders and she held him away from her, staring at him in horror.

"Tomasz Slaski!" she gasped. "You are skin and bones. Sit." She clucked her tongue, then pushed him toward the table. "What have you been doing with the bread I've been sending with Alina? Not sharing it *all* with our Jewish brothers and sisters?"

"My friend's wife had a baby…" he said weakly as he sank into one of the chairs. "I have been giving her every mouthful I could spare."

"That stops today." When he didn't react, she rested her hands on his shoulders again, this time to shake him a little. "Do you hear me, young man? You will be no help to them if you do not eat yourself first. From now, you let me fatten you up a little. I'll show you the cellar shortly and you can see the rich bounty we have to share."

Tomasz shot me a glance, and I stifled a giggle at the mixture of joy and bewilderment on his face. Sometime later, once he had a belly full of soup and egg and bread and even a few shots of vodka that my father furnished him, Tomasz climbed down into the cellar to take a look around. I sat at the edge of the dark space. He looked up at me, amused.

"You blackmailed me into coming here, now you won't come down to visit my palace?"

"I will," I admitted, then I shuddered. "But the darkness scares me. I don't know how you will bear it all day."

"Darkness is just like sleep," he shrugged. "And anything has to be better than sleeping in a tree like a squirrel."

"Are you very upset that I forced you to come?" I asked him hesitantly. He sighed, and ran his hands through his hair.

"It is hard for me to answer that right now. I'm compromised because it's warm in here and I'm a little drunk and the mattress is so comfortable and my belly is so full…" he said with a reluctant smile, but the smile quickly cleared and concern took its place. "I am grateful to you and your parents, but I will never forgive myself if this turns out to be a mistake."

"Will you stay in tonight?" Mama called to him, from the other side of the living room where she was making up her own bed. "You could do with one good night's rest."

"It would be better if I didn't," he called back. "Most of my friends would be okay for a day or two—but not Saul and Eva. The farmer hiding them does nothing more than required to collect his gold and Eva so badly needs the food."

"I made a loaf of bread yesterday—you can take everything that is left, and a whole jar of jam from last season, *and* I'll boil you some eggs…but only if you sleep. We will set the alarm, and you can go and be back before the sun comes up."

Tomasz took a few steps up the ladder, until he was standing beside me. He seemed almost overcome with emotion—his eyes wide and his jaw set hard.

"Thank you, Mrs. Dziak," he said roughly, then his gaze shifted to my father, who was warming his back by the fire.

"Thank you, Mr. Dziak. For your courage. Your generosity. Your kindness toward me."

"But for the damned war, you'd be our son by now," Father said stiffly. Tomasz reached for my hand, and he squeezed it.

"One day," he whispered to me, then he smiled and my heart skipped a beat. "One day soon, my love."

"Sleep while you can, Tomasz," I whispered back. "We can talk tomorrow."

We had to maintain a militant schedule now that Tomasz was in the cellar. He'd leave the house just before my parents went to bed—taking with him whatever food Mama offered him, and he'd return in the morning, usually just before dawn. As he came back to the house, he or Mama would wake me, and I'd spend some time talking with him in the cellar. While I was down there, Mama would make breakfast and, because she was there to keep watch, we'd leave the latch open.

Even with the light from the windows in the upstairs, I never got used to the darkness of the cellar. Every single time I climbed down the ladder, I'd feel sick to my stomach at the darkness and the musty, dusty scent. We would sit on the makeshift bed and Tomasz would wrap his arms around me to help me through the panic of it—then we'd leap away from one another guiltily whenever we heard Mama walk near to the opening.

We talked about so many things in those weeks. We talked about the agony of the separation we'd survived, and we daydreamed about our future. Now that there were no secrets between us, Tomasz told me all about the work he was doing and his fears for his friends.

"Some farmers do this only for the money, and I wish we were not so desperate as to use those people," Tomasz told me. "The man hosting Saul's family makes me very nervous indeed. We want to move them from that house as soon as I can, but it's just so difficult to find suitable places."

"And the others you are helping?"

"It is just a handful of people, Alina. I can't travel far because I have to go on foot each night, so I just take food to those on farms I can reach from here. We wouldn't use the empty farmhouses at first because we assumed the farmers had been moved to make way for German settlers, but there has been no sign of that so far in this district and the shelter was too good to waste. It's perplexing, though, why the Nazis would clear the farms and not use the houses."

"Maybe the farmers are fleeing into the cities? I've always wondered if life in the cities is easier."

Tomasz gave a bitter laugh.

"Not from what I saw in Warsaw. Not by a mile."

I had no solutions and no insight, but I loved partnering with him in bearing the burden of the problem.

Sundays had once been the best day of the week for me, but now, they were almost the worst. We had decided that it was too dangerous to tell Emilia or even Truda and Mateusz the truth about Tomasz. The fewer people who knew our secret, Father had sighed, the better our chances of keeping it, and it was too much to ask of an eight-year-old to keep a secret as big as this one.

That meant Tomasz would sit hidden in the cellar beneath his sister while she sat at the dining room table to chat with her new family. I knew this was very difficult for him. I could see the strain on his face on Sunday mornings before they arrived, and the refreshed grief in the evenings after they'd gone.

"This is still better than being so far away from her," he murmured to me one day, when I opened the latch after she'd gone. "But I can't wait for the day when I can hug her again."

"I will hug her for you until that day comes," I promised him. After that day, every time I hugged her at the dining room table I'd tell her, "*This* hug is from Tomasz, little sister," and she'd always grin at me.

"Are you sure he's still okay, Alina?" she'd ask me.

"Of course I am," I said, only this time, I was actually telling the truth.

"How can you be so sure?"

"Because he promised, silly, and he would never break a promise to me."

And that ritual became a part of the rhythm of our life for those weeks. At night, I'd stay up until it was time for Tomasz to leave again, just so we could share a chaste kiss in front of my parents as he left for the night.

"Stay safe," I'd whisper to him, as he slipped out the door to leave. And he'd always turn back to me and offer me the same determined, confident smile before he disappeared into the night, as if the reality that he was *not* safe at all was some minor detail I needn't worry about.

CHAPTER 21

Alice

I'm nervous about telling Callie that I'm leaving, until it occurs to me that I've yet to tell Mom, and I still have to figure out how to tell Eddie—so Callie is actually the *easiest* person I need to talk to today. I'm driving to her Saturday morning ballet class, but I look up in the rearview mirror to find her sitting perfectly still, looking down at the book on her lap. It's a textbook—maybe her French one. Her golden blond hair is in a thick bun right on top of her head, and she looks serene and more focused than any ten-year-old child has a right to be.

"Callie," I say brightly. "Guess what? I'm going on a trip."

"Oh?" she says mildly. Her gaze passes briefly between me and Eddie, who's staring out the window, but she's already looking back to the textbook as she asks, "Where are you guys going?"

"Just me," I clarify. "I'm going to Poland."

Callie slams her book shut and I can feel her eyes boring holes in the back of my head as I watch the road.

"Without *Eddie*?" she says, aghast.

"Daddy is going to look after Eddie for a few days. He'll be fine," I say. I meet Callie's eyes briefly in the rear vision mirror. She blinks at me.

"Mom. Daddy will most certainly *not* be fine with Eddie for a few days. Does Dad know the first thing about Eddie's life? He doesn't even use the AAC. And he can't work the coffee machine, and you know what Dad is like in the mornings if he doesn't get his coffee. And you've seen what he does when he tries to *cook*. Oh—and please, don't even get me started on *my* life—Daddy won't know where to take me or when to pick me up...no. This won't do at all, Mom. I mean, I love Daddy very much but he's hardly equipped for *this*."

I would definitely feel guilty in this moment if Callie's outrage wasn't so damned hilarious. I try to keep my expression mild, but I fail to hide my amusement, and as the smile breaks through, I let myself go and I actually start to laugh.

Callie does not echo my laughter with her own. When I glance in the mirror again, she's an adorable mix of outraged and anxious.

"Callie Michaels," I chuckle. "You will all be fine without me for a few days. You can help Dad with Eddie's routine. You can *teach* Dad how to use the AAC when he finally realizes he needs to—and you know what, honey bear, I'm actually a bit jealous that you'll probably get to see that moment and I won't."

"Mom. Please. That is *not* going to be funny. Dad's been refusing to use the AAC for *years*."

"Exactly. But he's never had to manage Eddie's routine on his own, and you know as well as I do that without the AAC—there is just no way to do that."

Callie falls silent. I glance at her in the mirror again and find she's staring out the window. She looks genuinely scared.

"It will be okay, honey bear," I say softly.

"I don't like this, Mom," she says.

"I need to do this for Babcia and, frankly, having heard that little speech you just gave, I think I need to do it for you too."

"Now I know you've lost your mind. You think you're abandoning your family for *me*?" She's scowling at me now, and I can tell she's preparing to launch a full-throttled pout.

"One day, baby girl, you could have a family of your own, if you want one. And I don't want you to think that becoming a mom means your entire existence has to revolve around your kids and partner. Our circumstances are difficult, but that's not really an excuse. Daddy and I haven't been very good role models for you in having a balanced family life." I draw in a deep breath, then I admit, "Besides, this really matters to me. I'm nervous about leaving you guys, but I need to do it."

Callie sighs impatiently and sinks back into her seat.

"Fine. But I hope you realize—I'll help Dad with the basics, but if he messes things up completely, he's on his own." I start to laugh again, and this time she meets my gaze in the mirror and gives me a resigned smile. "Good for you, Mom. What's in Poland?"

"Some special places from Babcia's childhood."

"She just wants you to visit some places?"

"And take photos. I think there's more but...I'm not really sure what else. You know it's been hard to communicate with her, but it's very clear she wants me to go."

"So—" She ponders this for a moment, then she brightens. "It's like you're going on a quest. You're not completely sure what the quest is but you're going anyway and hoping you figure it out on the way. That's *badass*, Mom."

"Watch your language, Callie."

She smirks and glances back to her book. When we get to the ballet hall, she hops out of the car and scoops her bag up off the backseat, and then for the first time in ages, she actually approaches my window and plants a kiss on my cheek.

"Oh," I say, surprised. "Thank you, honey bear. I love you."

She throws a casual wave over her shoulder as she runs off toward the hall. I smile to myself as I turn toward the hospital, pleased that Callie was, eventually, supportive of this little venture, and then the day seems even better when we get to Babcia's room, because not only does Eddie know the way and leads me there with enthusiasm, but Babcia herself is stronger today. She's already sitting up in bed when we enter her room, and her expression brightens when she sees us. Eddie climbs up onto the bed beside her and cuddles up to her. I take Mom's iPad from the tray table and with shaking hands, I give Babcia my news.

Alice plane Poland.

Babcia reads the symbols on the screen. I watch her eyes track across several times, then she looks up at me and a smile breaks over her weary features. Her eyes fill with tears, and a soft sob breaks from her lips. She doesn't need speech to convey her gratitude. The expression on her face says it all.

And just for a moment, I'm not at all torn about this. I know there's more she wants than photos, and she has no way of telling me what it is, so I'm going to have to hope that I can stumble onto the needle in the haystack. It's insane—but I'm now certain that I'm doing the right thing.

Of course, that certainty evaporates the instant my mother bursts into the room in a cloud of expensive perfume and fluster. She's wearing a stiff black suit despite the fact that it's the weekend. I know she'll go into chambers today—that's pretty typical for her. Weekends have *never* meant much to my mom.

"I've just come from hospital administration," she greets me, and I can see from the set of her jaw that some poor receptionist has probably just copped a dressing-down. "My God. I just wanted to see about getting a Polish interpreter but apparently no one knows how to arrange one on short notice *let alone* a weekend. Honestly, the fees they charge here you'd think that we could—"

"She's doing okay, Mom," I say quietly. "We're managing fine with the AAC." I know Mom is worried sick about Babcia. I just wish that instead of focusing all of her energy on battling and belittling the hospital, she'd admit she's hurting and feeling alone and scared. Maybe she should take the time she just spent throwing her weight around and put it into an honest phone call with Dad, one that ends with a request or demand for him to simply tell his golfing buddies that his mother-in-law is sick and he has to come home.

Then it occurs to me that she doesn't even know she's going to be alone for a few days, because I haven't told her yet. I take a deep breath.

"Mom," I say abruptly. "I'm going to Poland."

She blinks at me.

"What?"

"Monday afternoon. Wade and I decided last night. I've booked flights and there's a guide who's going to take me around—"

"You have *got* to be kidding me, Alice. I don't even know where to start here—this is so *like* you, isn't it?" For a seventy-six-year-old woman with a successful professional career, my mom sure does do an impressive impersonation of a bitchy fourteen-year-old when she's pissed. Her gaze narrows, and she goes for the sucker punch. "This is college all over again. Alice has an impulse, so Alice goes right ahead and acts on it. Feel like rebelling? Ignore a decade of planning and working toward law school and study *journalism* instead. Feeling randy? Get yourself knocked up by your TA—"

"Mom, he wasn't *my* TA—" I groan, although there's no point, because she knows *damn well* that Wade never taught me—what interest would I have had in nanotechnology? Mom isn't looking to be factual—she's looking for dramatic effect.

"Feeling overwhelmed?" she adds now, the snide tone sharpening further. "Drop out of your career *altogether* before you've even given it a shot and stay at home like some 1950s housewife. And now the kicker—feeling pity for a confused old lady on her deathbed? Then jump on a *plane* for God's sake—"

"Mom!" I exclaim. "Just *stop*!"

Mommy hurt, Eddie's iPad says. Mom and I stare at each other in the strained silence, until Babcia's iPad announces, *Alice okay. Julita naughty.*

The voice is robotic, of course, but that doesn't mean it's not accusatory. Mom and I both turn sharply toward the bed. Babcia looks pointedly at us—no words required to communicate her displeasure with our raised voices and Eddie's reaction to them. I glance at my son, and he's staring at me, visibly concerned and confused. I offer him a smile, trying to project a calmness that I don't feel at all. Mom is in fine form today and apparently we're going to dredge up every past disappointment I've ever managed to inflict upon her.

"Mom," I say, drawing in a deep breath. "May I speak to you outside, please?"

Mom grunts her reply, then follows me into the hallway. We stand facing one another like fighters in a ring, our breathing ragged.

This conversation is not new to us, so we both know how it goes now. This is the part where I back down—maybe I go ahead and do what I want later anyway, but at *this* point in the conversation, I usually concede that she's right just so I can end the tension. Even when she's not being downright *mean*, like today, my mother can run rings around me in any argument. She was a prosecutor for forty years—she *knows* how to get her point across. In some ways, it's actually easier to argue with this emotional version of my mother because she's not quite as rational as she ordinarily would be. Maybe that's why, today, I'm going to ignore my automatic inclination to acquiesce.

"She is not confused," I say flatly. "She knows exactly what she wants. I don't know *why* this is so important to her, but it clearly is."

"So you're just going to leave me here to deal with all of *this*?" Mom says. It's hard to stop my eyes from widening in shock, because suddenly I understand what this little spat is really about. Mom doesn't care that I'm *going*; she cares that I'm *leaving*.

The very idea of the formidable Judge Julita Slaski-Davis being afraid of anything—let alone something as pedestrian as *being alone* is jaw-dropping. I love my mom—I admire her—I resent her—I am intimidated by her—I'm so many things about and toward her, but one thing I've not often been is surprised by her, and I'm not sure I've *ever* felt *sorry* for her before.

"Maybe it's time to call Dad—"

"I am *not* asking him to come home."

"He'd understand, Mom. He'd come right away if you asked him to."

"I am not *you*, Alice Slaski–Davis," she hisses at me, predictably resorting to my full name as if I'm a child, also predictably refusing to acknowledge that I took Wade's surname *without so much as a hyphen*! Mom is nothing if not consistent; she was horrified with that decision ten years ago, and apparently it still smarts today. "I do not and will not rely on a *man* to get me through this. It is—"

"Listen," I interrupt her, because I know we're about to start the whole *Alice-is-a-bad-feminist* argument again and it never ends well—or at all, actually. "I don't want to argue with you about Dad." Or Wade. Or my surname. Or my mind-boggling ability to survive without a career. "I just want you to understand why I want to do this for her. She's given me real places, real names…" At least, I seriously hope so. "I'm just going to go to Poland and take some photos for her, maybe FaceTime her once or twice if the time zones line up okay. I don't really understand why this matters so much to her, but clearly it does and God only knows how much time she has left."

"What on earth do you think you're going to achieve? Who travels halfway across the globe to take some *photos*? It's a fool's errand."

"Well," I say quietly, thinking of Callie's comments about Wade in the car this morning. "Let me find that out the hard way."

I pack Eddie up after that and kiss Babcia on the cheek.

Today is Saturday. I tell her, via the iPad. *Alice home tomorrow. Alice plane Poland Monday.* She looks at me, and her brow furrows with confusion.

"See?" Mom says bitterly. She's sitting in the corner with her arms crossed over her chest. "I told you we need a translator."

I look at the iPad, and for a moment or two I can't figure out what's confusing Babcia. She knows the symbols for *today* and *Alice* and *home* and *plane* and she had no trouble at all finding the flag that means *Poland*.

It's the days. The titles are in English, so she can only use the icons she creates herself and the ones she already knows. A sudden thought strikes me and I hit the settings on the iPad.

Polski.

I change languages, and move back to the icon screen. Babcia looks again, and she grins at me and nods. She takes the iPad and I wait as she plays with the device for several minutes. She takes a selfie, grimaces, deletes it and repeats this process several times until she's apparently happy with the result. Finally, the device reads me a string of robotic Polish. I look at the icons, and find she's created a new icon and adorned it with a selfie of herself midsmile, and she's wedged that around grinning clip art faces. I flick the iPad back to English and reread it.

Babcia happy. Babcia proud.

Five minutes later, Mom, the head nurse and Babcia all know how to use the AAC as an inelegant translator. I take Babcia's precious letter and snap a series of photos, trying to catch it in *just* the right light so that Zofia-the-Polish-tour-guide has a chance of translating it.

"Okay, I'm going now," I say, pointing toward the door. Babcia beams. Mom stares at me impassively. "I won't be in tomorrow, I have to get things ready for the kids. But I'll be home in six days, and I'll try to keep in touch via phone and text messages."

Mom is still giving me that expressionless stare. I sigh and kiss Babcia, and then I walk around her bed, and I bend to kiss Mom's cheek too. At the last second, Mom catches my forearm in her hand, then she stands and kisses my cheek in return.

"Good luck," she says stiffly. I thank her, but then bolt out the door before she can add the inevitable *you're going to need it* and spoil the gentle buzz her farewell has given me. Once Eddie and I are in the car, I grit my teeth and dial Dad.

"Ally," he greets me warmly. "How are things? How's your grandmother?"

"Not good, Dad," I admit. "Has Mom told you she can't speak?"

"She did. And your mom seems to think the hospital is dropping the ball."

"Yeah, I know..."

"But *you* think Mom is being a hard-ass, like she always is."

I laugh weakly. I seriously love my Dad, especially the *oh-so-chill* retirement version of him.

"I kind of do. But, Dad—I actually think Mom needs you. I know she doesn't want to ask you to come home, but I think you need to. Babcia has asked me to go to Poland, and I'm going to go, so Mom is going to be alone—"

"Just back up a bit there, love," Dad says patiently. "What's this about you going to *Poland*?"

"It's complicated," I mutter. "Babcia asked me to go and I'm still not sure why, but I'm going anyway."

"Well, that's unexpected. How fun for you."

I laugh at the ease of Dad's acceptance of my crazy quest.

"This is almost exactly the opposite of how the conversation with Mom went when I told her," I tell him. "She's stressed out of her mind—between her work and visiting Babcia at the hospital—I'm a bit worried how she'll cope if anything happens with Babcia while I'm away. Can you come?"

"Of course I can," Dad says, and he sighs heavily. "If she'd asked, I'd have come right home when Babcia got sick. You know that, right?"

"I do, Dad." I sigh too. "I really do."

"Well, when are you shifting gears from stay-at-home mom to international jet-setter?"

"Tomorrow afternoon," I say, then I swallow.

"I guess I won't see you until you get back," Dad says. "Do me a favor, Alice, and bring me back some vodka. Good stuff— as strong as possible. I think I'm going to need it to deal with your mom when Babcia finally goes."

"I can't even think about that yet," I admit.

"Well, my darling daughter, I won the mother-in-law lottery when I met your mother, so I hate to say this—but Babcia is ninety-five years old. Sooner or later, we're all going to have to let her go."

CHAPTER 22

Alina

After a few weeks with Tomasz in our house, I started to entertain fantasies that things might go on that way indefinitely. I should have known it wouldn't last forever. If anything about the war had been consistent, it was that things *always* got worse.

The morning everything changed, I'd just said goodbye to Tomasz, and Mama was about to shut the latch so he could sleep. I walked from the house into the fields, knowing she wasn't far behind me, already thinking about the day's tasks. Father had been in the town delivering the week's produce, but I heard him shouting as he returned through the gates. He leaped from the cart and started running—something my Father *never* did because of his rheumatism.

"Alina!" he shouted, as he ran toward the doorway. "Run, Alina! For God's sake, *run!*"

He disappeared inside and I sprinted to catch up to him.

"What is it?"

The table was shifted and the hatch had been reopened. Mama and Father were crouched beside it, whispering urgently to Tomasz.

"There is no time. Into the hatch. *Now*," Mama said flatly.

"But what is—"

She grabbed my forearm and as she pushed me awkwardly beneath the table, I felt the tremors running through her whole body. That startled me into silence, so I climbed quickly down the ladder, and Tomasz took me into his arms. He pressed his forefinger over my lips and he led me to the mattress, then sat beside me. The cellar was thrown into darkness, then we heard the heavy *thump* of the hatch and the rug, and the dragging sound as the table was pulled into place.

I'd been into that tiny cellar every day for several weeks by then—but never with the latch closed—and even with the door open I'd still panicked every time. Now, my eyes began adjusting to the dim light, but my brain somehow could not adjust to the stuffiness of the air. Every time I drew in a breath, I was convinced it was my last.

Breathe in. Oh! I found some air!

Breathe out. That will be the last of me. Now I will suffocate.

Breathe in. Oh! There is a little more air after all.

I knew I wouldn't stand two minutes in there, let alone two hours, so I had to ask Tomasz what was happening.

"Tomasz," I started to say, but he pressed his hand over my mouth—hard, just as I had done for Emilia once upon a time. I peeled his fingers from my face but sat in silence with him, simmering in my frustration, my confusion and—soon enough—genuine anger.

But I heard the rumble of the truck as it came ever closer—and I knew when it was right at the front door. Until that rumble sounded, I was far more annoyed than I was scared. There was something ominous about that sound from underground—the way it rattled through the earth, as if the cellar would cave in all around us—it reminded me so vividly of those early air strikes and the terror that never seemed to end. I had no idea what the *exact* danger was this time, because our whole lives were danger by then. I just knew that for Mama and Father to hide me, it must be significant indeed.

There were muffled greetings—but not muffled enough to

hide the subtext. I heard the stiffness of the soldiers' voices, the hopeful politeness of Mama's.

"Hübsche tochter?"

I was already confused and on edge and terrified, but at the sound of *those* words, my blood ran cold, because I knew then which soldier was in the house.

Pretty daughter.

It was the young soldier from that day in fall, the last time I wore a dress. He was back, and he was asking about me. I was too terrified to cry out, but equally, I was too terrified to control myself and I couldn't think rationally enough to be sure of *what* I might do next.

But Tomasz's arms tightened around me, and he raised his arm to gently begin to stroke my hair. I closed my eyes and rested against him, and he planted the softest kiss against my temple. I had never understood the phrase "draw strength" from someone until that very moment, because with the entire universe out of my control, the only thing that grounded me into silence then was the strength of his arms around me and the warmth of his body beside me.

"Gone to Warsaw…" I heard my mother say. "…caring for her sick nephew…"

Sick *nephew*? I didn't even *have* a nephew—Mama's lie was outrageous and ridiculous—and what's more, it made no sense at all for her to tell it. In all that we'd survived to that point, she'd never done something so crazy before. I started to tense up again—because surely, she'd be caught out, and surely, we'd all pay the price for that. Had she lost her mind?

Then the soldiers' voices—fiercer now, more determined, and closer, and closer again until…*oh my God, they were in the house.* They were standing right above us, next to the table that sat right over the hatch.

Tomasz held me so tightly in that moment that the pressure around my reed-thin arms was painful, so I focused on the discomfort. I needed the stimulus to ground me, because other than that mild pain, *all I knew* was fear. I heard the soldiers stomping through the house. Heard as they walked into my bedroom—heard the way they mocked our simple life—heard as they walked *right past the table* again on their way to check for me in my brothers' room.

And then I heard the front door close. Everyone was outside now, and the voices faded again, until the truck started up, and then there was silence.

Tomasz and I waited for a very long time. I thought perhaps Mama and Father would go about their business outside and leave us down there for a while, until they were sure it was safe, but time passed and the door didn't open, and their voices did not return. Eventually, Tomasz shifted just a little, and he made a sound with his nose that I didn't initially recognize. I turned to him and waited. I was used to the dark by then, but even so, it took me a moment to realize that his face was shiny.

"Why?" I whispered. I didn't know what question I was asking. Why are you crying? Why are they not coming back inside? Why the war?

"They told your father at the rations station. They told him to go home and pack a suitcase. They told him they were coming for you."

"For *me*? But—"

"No, Alina. The soldiers came for *all* of you."

"But is this because of me? Because I…"

I didn't say it, because I didn't want to make him feel bad—but was this because I'd helped him?

"It is simply for the fields, Alina. This morning when he went into the rations station, they told Bartuk they are creating an *Interessengebiet*—an 'area of interest' around the big work camps, and he was to come home and pack a bag and prepare to leave immediately. At least we know now why most of your neighbors have gone. There are tens of thousands of prisoners in the camps now, an army of free labor—and your rations are scant, but still vastly more than the workers receive."

"So where have my parents gone?"

"Alina, *moje wszystko*...it doesn't matter where your parents are, we *have* to leave now. As soon as we can."

"Leave the house?"

"Leave...the district, at the very least."

"*Leave?* You want to leave *now*? My parents are gone and we have no idea where they are—are you insane? I have to stay! I have to try to help them!"

"This is bigger than your parents, Alina," Tomasz whispered. "Your father heard talk of a *fence* around the whole district. Who knows if this farm will be within that boundary line, but we need to get out in case it is."

"But my parents..."

"They are resilient and resourceful people," he said, but the attempt at reassurance was entirely unconvincing.

Earlier, I had been convinced that I couldn't bear two minutes in the cellar, but we stayed in there for the entire day. We huddled together under the blankets on the mattress and we listened to the clock upstairs chime away the hours. I cried a little, and sometimes, Tomasz did too.

When I finally started to feel sleepy, he helped me upstairs and he fetched some fresh water from the well while I used the outhouse. We weren't able to start the fire or turn on the light, just in case someone was keeping watch on the house from afar, so instead, we stumbled around in the dark. When the time came to climb down the ladder, it occurred to me how difficult it was going to be to replace the table and rug over ourselves without outside assistance, but Tomasz had already made a plan with my parents for a situation like this. He pulled the table over just a little, so that two of the legs no longer rested atop the rug, but the table still covered the hatch. Hopefully, to anyone visiting who had not been before, it would look only like our little table was off center on its rug. It was awkward for him to climb back inside with the table over top, but now, when he pulled the hatch closed, the rug sat flat atop it.

He climbed back under the blankets with me and he held me until I slept for a while, but when the clock upstairs chimed 2:00 a.m., he roused me with a kiss to my forehead.

"I have to go," he told me. I was frantic at the thought of it—and I tried to convince him to stay, but he was insistent. "I need to find out if anyone knows where your parents have been taken, and to take some food for Eva. I'll be gone a few hours because I will need to go into Trzebinia to see Nadia."

"Tell me," I murmured. "Is Nadia your Zegota contact? Is that why you were so determined that I should stay away from her house?"

He nodded silently. "Yes. She is coordinating the efforts for this region."

"And Jan was angry because she was helping Jews?" I guessed. Tomasz shook his head.

"Do you remember the farmer I didn't trust?"

I gaped at him.

"Jan is hiding Jewish people in his house?" I said incredulously. "This...that makes *no* sense, Tomasz."

"He has sealed himself off into the front half of the house because he is too stupid to see through the Nazi propaganda, so he is convinced my friends carry disease," Tomasz said, his disgust evident. "And he allows Saul and Eva to use only the tiniest space at the back of the house, so there is a buffer between them. Make no mistake, Alina. He does this only for the gold. Nadia only approached him because we were desperate. We had to find somewhere safe for Eva to give birth."

"This is why Justyna and Ola left."

"Ola didn't want any part of this. She was furious with Jan *and* Nadia for risking Justyna's life." Tomasz brushed his hand against my cheek.

"Let me come with you tonight," I pleaded.

"No, Alina. Not when I must go into the township. If I was caught breaking the curfew it would be bad, but I would at least have a chance of talking my way out of danger. But *you* are too memorable, my love. You must stay here hidden for now."

"But what if you don't come back?" I whispered. I pressed his hand to my jaw, trying to stop my teeth from chattering.

"Do you think they could stop me coming back, Alina? After all we have survived? After all I have been through to get back here to you?" Tomasz whispered, then he brushed his lips against mine. "Not a chance, *moje wszystko*. But if I don't come back as quickly as I plan to, just hide in here. You have food and water that will last for weeks, and I will make sure Nadia knows to come find you."

He packed his little rucksack with potatoes and a handful of eggs, then he climbed up out of the cellar, replaced the rug and the table, and then went on his way.

CHAPTER 23

Alina

I heard the clock chime one hour, then two, then three. And all the while, I waited, and I rode the waves of panic and fear as they came. I wanted to howl at the injustice of it all—I wanted to be angry with Tomasz for leaving me in the cellar alone on the worst day of my life—I wanted to go back in time and bury my head under the pillow on my bed upstairs and pretend that none of this was happening at all.

It was just past 5:00 a.m. when I heard a sound upstairs. I heard muffled movement above me, then the hatch lifted, and when I recognized Tomasz in the opening, I burst into tears. He waited until he'd set the hatch back in place before he comforted me. He was shaking too, from adrenaline and the cold, I guessed.

"Did you find anything out?"

"Yes."

"Okay. Where have they been taken?"

"To Oświęcim," he said.

"Okay," I said, then I exhaled with relief. "Okay. To the town, then?" That didn't sound so bad at all. Oświęcim was a nice enough place, a place much like Trzebinia with many factories and homes. I imagined for a moment them both taking a job on a factory line for the Nazis—it wasn't ideal, but I felt confident that they could survive it.

"No, Alina. Not in the town. They've been taken to the work

camp," Tomasz said, then he drew in a deep breath. "Although there are two there now, and I couldn't find out which one."

The daydream of my parents on a factory line shattered, and now instead I saw them crammed in like sardines with the tens of thousands of farm workers Tomasz had warned me about. My heart sank all over again.

"It does not matter which camp, does it?" I surmised, suddenly feeling very heavy. "We can't rescue them anyway. Or does Nadia Nowak have the ability to circumvent the entire Nazi army?"

"No. It does not matter which camp," he conceded heavily.

"But they will just wait out the war there. They will work hard and stay out of trouble, just as they always have," I said with some determination, until a thought struck me. I stiffened a little. "Wait—these are the camps with the furnaces?"

"Yes," Tomasz whispered. "They call the smaller camp Auschwitz. The larger camp is called Birkenau." He shifted on the bed, drawing me closer. "There *are* large furnaces at both camps, and—"

"Mama said the furnaces are just to heat the water," I interrupted him, but even to my own ears, I sounded slightly hysterical.

"We don't know for sure. *No one* outside the camps knows for sure," he said, but then he drew in a sharp breath and his tone hardened. "But the Nazis have been seen transporting trucks full of ash to dump in the river, and there is some suspicion that this may be the remains of some of the prisoners. Perhaps your parents will be lucky…or perhaps they will manage to find a way to survive. But thousands of people have gone into the camps, thousands of Jewish people from many nations, thousands of Catholic Poles like your parents and *thousands* of political prisoners…but only recently have the Nazis needed to expand their accommodation. All of those prisoners are going *somewhere*, and whether they are murdered or worked to death—the most likely place they are ending up is in the furnace."

This was the new Tomasz—the man who was broken by hardship and remorse, the realist who had replaced my beautiful dreamer. He was giving me a verbal slap in the face because he believed that I needed a reality check. For just a moment, I hated him for it—until I remembered that *none of this was his fault.* I started to cry then, and he rained kisses down over my face.

"They aren't coming back, Alina."

"But maybe…"

"They *aren't coming back*," he whispered. "If I can find a way out of Poland, we have to take it. Promise me you'll come with me if I can find a way."

"*Out* of Poland?" I repeated through my sobs. "That's not even possible. How would we get *out* of Poland?"

"I don't know exactly. Not yet," he admitted. "I met a photographer a few months ago. He was documenting the work of Zegota and I know he was using couriers to smuggle film out of the country. He asked me then if I would make a journey for him. I was tempted, Alina, I will be honest with you. It was just before we reunited and I nearly went, I thought I would try to flee, and then maybe you could have followed me after, but I couldn't make myself leave you. Now…well, I don't even know if he's still nearby but Nadia is trying to find him. If we can find him and he will help us, *moje wszystko*, there is no other option. Not for us, not now. We have *no choice* but to try to get out."

"But we could stay!" I whispered. "We could live undercover as you've been doing—"

"I don't want that life for you, Alina."

"But we could stay here—"

"The food will eventually run out—and if the fence is built before then, we'd be trapped inside this zone."

"We could try to get into the city—"

"*I do not want this life for us, Alina*," Tomasz repeated—raising his voice, hardening the tone again, until I pulled away from him. "Yes, there may be ways we could survive here—perhaps we could get false identity papers. We could shift into Krakow or Warsaw and try to live in plain sight. Maybe we'd be caught and we'd be killed. Maybe we'd survive and suffer through however many more years of starvation and abuse the war would inflict upon us. But there is no way for us to *live* here. And there is *no* way for us to build the life we'd planned. Not if we stay." He sighed heavily, then pulled me close again. "I *need* for you to be safe."

"But this is home," I said. "Poland is our home. What else *is* there for us?"

"Home is not the country we stand in—it's *us*. Home is the future we have been planning and dreaming of. We can build it anywhere. And yes, you are a tiny waif of a thing—" I grunted in protest, and he laughed softly "—but you are tough, Alina, and I think you know it too now. I can see it in you—a fire to survive—a fire to have a better life. It is the fierce flash of indignation in your eyes when you think you are out of the loop on a secret. It is the strength you showed when you decided to stand by me, knowing that doing so could get you killed. And if we can get out of this place *together*?" His tone softened again, until he was gently pleading with me. "Just imagine it, *moje wszystko*. I could start studying again and finally become a doctor, maybe *you* could study. We could get jobs...a house...have children one day and give *them* a future too. Don't you see? To stay is to accept death at the hands of these monsters, and they have taken enough from us both already. Our only choice is to try to run."

"What if we try and fail?"

"Then..." He paused, and for a moment, fumbled for words, then he whispered, "Well, Alina? At least we will fail together. That's worth something, isn't it?"

I squeezed his hand, drew in a shaky breath, and then closed my eyes. In some ways I felt like I had nothing left to lose—but I *did* have something left to lose, and he was sitting right there with me, begging me to try to run.

I was beyond scared. But if Tomasz was going, I didn't really have a choice, because staying behind wasn't even an option anymore.

"Okay," I whispered. "Okay."

CHAPTER 24

Alice

I spend the next thirty-six hours in a panicked marathon of desperate organizing that amuses my daughter and confuses my son. Eddie watches me silently as I search the web for ways to communicate to him that *Mommy is going away*. In the end, I write a social script that Wade can give him each day to remind Eddie where I am, then create a calendar of days he can count down. I write strict instructions to Wade to mark off a day each morning so Eddie can see how many sleeps are left. I print out a photo of myself and stick it at the end, then color all around it in bright green highlighter for emphasis.

When I'm done, I look into my son's beautiful green eyes and I burst into tears. Eddie ponders this for a moment, then he silently walks away. He returns a few minutes later with his iPad in his hand and asks:

Mommy hurt?

I calm myself down, assure him that I'm okay, set him in front of *Thomas the Tank Engine* and start documenting his routine for Wade. I try to strike a balance between wanting Wade to do *everything* just right, and just giving him the basics so that he can get through each day. The problem is, with Eddie, there's not really such a thing as "just good enough." Everything does have to be just right. I know Wade doesn't get that, so I know he won't respect it. I have no idea what's going to happen with my son while I'm away.

In the seven years since he was born, the whole world has changed for me. I joined a club I never wanted to be a part of—the autism mom's club—and its membership cost was the life I'd planned until then. Someone once told me that having a child with autism was like taking a trip to another country where you don't speak the language, and at the time, I thought that analogy was clever and fitting. But over the last few years as the extent of Eddie's disability really became apparent, I've wondered if instead of being in a whole other country, I'm on a whole new planet.

Now I'm leaving Eddie for six whole nights. I'm traveling through time, back to a phase in my life when I didn't have a son who commanded the vast bulk of my focus. Will I miss him? Will I fret for him? Or the most frightening possibility of all—will I feel relief to be unburdened of the responsibility for his care? I love Eddie—God, I adore him. But so often when I think about the life I have with my son, I feel completely alone and endlessly overwhelmed.

The spiteful part of me hopes that in the next six days, Wade gets a taste of what that's like. That's the part of me that knows all of this documentation I'm doing about Eddie's routine is pointless, because my husband is far too arrogant to bother to follow it.

I have a PhD, Ally. I can handle a few days with two kids.

It's the casual dismissal of the complexity of my role in our family that goads me—rarely spoken so explicitly, but *implicit* in so many of our interactions over the last few years. Even now, when Wade is very much in my good books for how supportive he's being, I know he's underestimating the difficulty of what he's signed up for in this coming week.

And I'm chiefly concerned about Eddie, but Callie factors into this equation too. She's a beautiful little girl, but her giftedness is a challenge of its own sometimes. She's a terror when she's understimulated so her schedule is jam-packed, and her mind runs at a million miles an hour all of the time. That needs care-

ful monitoring, because when it all overwhelms her, she tends
to melt down. Wade's never really had to deal with that side of
her. What would he even do if she was upset?

I draw in a deep breath and promise myself that whatever
happens, they will survive. They will *all* survive. And so will I.

I've organized everything I can organize, I've emailed the
tour guide everything she needed, and I've packed with military
precision—but the minute we step into the airport, the enormity
of what I'm leaving behind settles around me like a heavy fog, and
suddenly, that's all I can think about. I feel only dread and anxiety
and regret—what a stupid, impulsive thing I've done! What if something happens to Eddie or Callie and I'm on the other side of the
planet? It would take me days to get home. And—*my God*—what
if something happens to Babcia? What do I really think I'm going
to find for her, anyway? I don't even know what she's looking for.

"Alice," Wade says suddenly.

I turn to him, and I'm suddenly aware that I'm audibly hyper-
ventilating. He grips my upper arms, and he stares down at me.

"I will not let you down," he says softly. "The kids will be
fine. I promise you."

"This was a mistake," I breathe. "I was impulsive and angry
and I'm upset—"

"No," he interrupts me, but he does so gently, carefully. I'm
struck by the tenderness in his voice, and I trail off my protes-
tations to let him take his time before he explains. He draws
in a deep breath, then he lifts his hand from my upper arm to
cup my face gently between his palms. "In these past few years,
you've lived and breathed our family. You're a wonderful wife.
A brilliant mother. But... Ally..." He draws in another soft
breath, then his gaze grows pleading. "As great as that is, that's
not *all* you wanted to be, honey. I know this trip is for Babcia.
But... I also... I kind of hope it's also for you. A chance for you
to drop some of the heaviness of our family life and for *me* to

catch it, so you can pick up something else too. I've been doing some thinking since we talked the other night. Never for a second of our life together have you asked me to put *my* stuff second. Well, this week I want you to know what that feels like, so you can know that I do appreciate it. Maybe…we can figure all of this out and share the load of it better one day. I don't know what that looks like, or how we do it, but I want to be a better husband for you. A better Dad…for…for Eddie."

That's the first time in years he's called Eddie by his nickname. It's also the closest Wade has ever come to admitting he's failed our son, and in doing so, he's failed me. I should probably be upset at this acknowledgment—that he does, in fact, know exactly what he's done to us in these years of neglect of his emotional obligations.

But I'm not upset.

Because this is not news to me, and it's not news to Wade, and now it's not unspoken. There's something exceptional about having this awful thing out in the open between us, and just like that, I can breathe again. I know it's going to be hard to get on that plane. I can't even imagine how I'm going to sleep tonight, knowing I'm so far away from them, knowing I'm all on my own.

But Wade is right. There's a chance here for me. Somehow it's simultaneously a chance he's giving me and a chance I'm taking greedily all for myself, and that's kind of how a partnership *should* work—we are both making this happen, for Babcia and for me.

I have no idea what waits for me in Poland. I have no idea how I'm going to find answers when I don't even know the questions but the *challenge* of that goal suddenly seems divine.

"Go," Wade says, and he kisses my forehead gently. "I love you. I won't let you down. Go on your trip…and try to have some fun too, okay?"

I have to turn away before the tears overwhelm me, so I do—I spin away from him and I grasp my suitcase tightly in my hand and I march to the check-in counter.

CHAPTER 25

Alice

I've been worried about the language barrier, given the only Polish words I know are *Jen dobry*—hello—and, somehow during my many hours being babysat by Babcia as a toddler, I picked up the phrase *Iść potty*—go potty—neither of which seem likely to be very useful in all of the steps I need to take before I meet with Zofia tomorrow. But as soon as I clear customs, I find the driver from the hotel waiting, holding an iPad that displays the logo of the hotel and my name. He introduces himself in lightly accented English.

"Nice to meet you," he says. "I'm Martyn. Long trip? Let's get you to the hotel."

I settle into the back of the late-model luxury car and stare out the window as the city flies past. Everything is much more modern than I'd expected, with seemingly endless construction work and block after block of modern buildings as we move through the city. The traffic is heavily congested, worse even than the traffic I'm accustomed to when I drive at home. Some single-lane roads manage to house simultaneous modes of transport—cars and buses, a tramway *and* the surprisingly heavy foot and bicycle traffic. At the outskirts of the city, other than the plentiful advertising being in Polish, I could almost be at home. But as we get deeper in, the modernity fades from the facades of the buildings that line the streets—until I am surrounded by stone and brick buildings that wouldn't have looked much different even a hundred years ago.

The hotel lobby is plush, with huge crystal chandeliers hanging from the ceiling and highly polished marble floors, and amongst the other guests mingling in the space, I hear plenty of English—in fact, plenty of English accented just like mine. The driver brings my bag in, and I approach the counter.

"Checking in?" The young receptionist greets me, again in English.

"Yes, thanks. I'm Alice Michaels. I have an early check-in arranged."

"One moment," the receptionist says, and her fingers fly over the keyboard, then she looks up at me and winces. "I'm sorry, Mrs. Michaels, your room isn't quite ready."

"Oh—but my guide said she'd confirmed an early check-in? I'm just getting off an overnight flight and I haven't had any sleep…"

"I'm sorry. It won't be too long, maybe another hour or two? You can leave your bag here. Why don't you go for a walk, find yourself some lunch and come back in the early afternoon."

I blink at her. What I *want* to do is put my head on a pillow and get some sleep. Exploring a foreign city on my own probably wouldn't sound appealing even on a normal day, but when I'm this tired? Hell no.

"But…"

She smiles at me reassuringly and withdraws a map from beneath the desk.

"You're here. Old Town is just here, and the Square is there too. Enjoy!"

I glance at the clock on the wall and see that it's 11:45 a.m. here in Krakow, which means its 5:45 a.m. back home. I can't call yet, even if I do get into my room, and I'm starving.

Looks like I'm going for a walk.

It's busy on the street. The traffic is manic, with endlessly congested cars and trams and buses competing for the narrow street space. The sidewalk is packed with people too, all flowing in the same direction I'm headed, so I slip into the crowd and start to walk. Bicycles push past me on the sidewalk, and a few adults ride on skates and rollerblades. It's now midday on a Tuesday morning, but as I walk with this crowd, I feel a bit like I'm headed to a party or a festival. Soon, the restaurants start— brands I know from home, as well as unfamiliar restaurant names promising "authentic Polish food" and even "authentic American cuisine." I'm struck by the flowers all around me—brightly colored blooms on live plants are featured in pots on tables and in planter boxes along the street, even hanging in pots from balconies, and cut flowers rest in the arms of men and women as they walk. Babcia's love of flowers is starting to make a lot of sense.

I planned to stop at the first appealing place that I came across, but I just keep walking, because everyone *else* is walking and I thought I'd feel alone, but I don't. The sidewalk is paved with a delicate cobblestone comprising slightly uneven square granite bricks. Maybe heels would be impossible to manage on it, but I'm just wearing canvas shoes and even the sidewalk seems charming.

Soon, I arrive at an expansive square, and it's clear that the crowd and I have arrived, because *this* is a place that would draw you. There are immense, ornate churches and restaurants and stores around the edge, and young people holding giant strings of helium balloons and carts for lemonade and pretzels and coffee in the center. One young man is working enormous sticks wound with rope, and he's dunking the rope into a huge bucket of watery bubble mixture, so that when he lifts it into the breeze, giant bubbles float all around the square. Masses of young children squeal and run to pop or try to catch them. Other performers sit on cushions and sing or play accordion or guitar. Several of these have adorable puppies or kittens sitting sedately on cushions beside them, patiently watching their owners work. It's a magnificently sunny day, but the sunshine has no bite to it, and as I step into the square, I close my eyes for just a moment and I breathe it all in—the sunshine, the laughter of the children as they run around the car-free space, the scent of sausage and beer and even cigarette smoke.

I wonder if Babcia ever visited Krakow—if she ever visited this square. I wonder if it looked just like this, seventy-odd years ago—the buildings feel old, so surely it did. I fish into my pocket for my phone and I snap a few quick, casual photographs, then I turn the camera around and take a selfie in the square with the buildings and crowd behind me. I stare at the photo, and then I can't help but grin, because I look *exhausted* but also, I look happy. Proud. Excited.

I send all of the photos to Mom and ask her to show Babcia, and then I march across the square to a restaurant with planter boxes of red and white geraniums all along the outside of the outdoor seating area. The menu on display is entirely in Polish, and I hesitate a moment before I walk toward the waiter.

"Table for one?" he says in English. When I give him a surprised nod, he reaches under a counter and says, "English menu?"

"Yes, please. How did you know I speak English?"

"We assume everyone speaks English until they tell us otherwise." He shrugs. "All young Polish people speak English and so do most of the tourists so...makes sense, no?"

As I settle at my table, I plan to order the safest dish I can find, maybe just a sandwich, perhaps a strong coffee—I mean, perhaps with some caffeine, I *could* stay up until a more sensible bedtime and explore just a little. But then I read the menu—and there are no sandwiches on offer at all. Instead, it's herrings and soups and sausages and odd cuts of pork and something called bigos and stews, and then several pages of varieties of pierogis. And the beverages list is equally decadent—there's vodkas and wines and beers. So many beers.

"Have you made a selection?" the waiter asks me. I close the menu.

"Yes please," I say. "Can I have a beer and some pierogi?"

"Which kind, miss?"

"Surprise me," I suggest, and he laughs as he nods.

The pierogi is a revelation—but the beer goes straight to my head, so I'm a little *too* happy as I wander back to the hotel, and more than ready for a nap by the time I get to my room. It's 7:30 a.m. back home now, so I crawl onto the hotel bed and Skype to Wade.

"Honey," he greets me. As the video feed kicks in, I see he's sitting at the kitchen table. He's clean-shaven and his hair looks damp. He's wearing a neatly pressed business shirt—and I normally do the ironing, but I ran out of time this week, so I know he's had time to iron it himself.

He looks perfectly put together, and not at all flustered. I'm surprised and kind of impressed.

"Hi," I say.

"You made it safely?"

"Yep. I just had lunch in the Old Town Square. It's..."

"It's what?" he prompts when I trail off, and I smile uncertainly.

"You know, it's actually a pretty amazing city."

A broad smile covers Wade's face, and I am struck by how handsome he looks this morning. Familiarity has a way of masking that kind of observation. I guess that right now, I'm basking in all of the benefits of doing something completely out of routine.

"That's great, honey," he says, and he sounds thrilled for me, which makes me even happier.

"And things are good there?"

"Oh sure. Things are fine," he says, and he smiles again. "All under control."

Except that just then, there's the sound of glass breaking, and Wade's easy smile becomes panicked. He stands and I see that he's only wearing his boxers, and then Callie comes flying into the room and she's still in her pajamas and she's screaming at the top of her lungs and Eddie is hot on her heels and he's clutching his stuffed Thomas the Tank Engine and sobbing. The last thing I see before the screen goes black is Eddie's tearstained face as he picks up Wade's phone from the table.

Adrenaline pumps through me as I redial, and Eddie answers on the first ring. He's staring into the iPad, and he looks incredibly distressed.

"Eddie," I whisper, touching the screen with my fingertip.

"Eddie, I love you," he says, and then he drops the phone back onto the table. He's rocking back and forth and still visible just at the edge of the screen. I can see that he's pinching his upper arms.

"It's okay, darling," I say, then I call furiously, "Wade Michaels! What the Hell is going on there?"

"Everything is fine!" Wade calls from somewhere in the background. "It's all under control, Ally, I just—"

"Mom..." Callie snatches the phone from Eddie and her face fills the screen. "It is *not* under control. I told you Dad wasn't up to this. Dad said Eddie didn't need melatonin so Eddie hardly slept and he kept us both awake half the night, and Dad couldn't figure out the iron so he burned a hole in his trousers and we're not sure what Eddie eats at school and he just smashed a glass because Dad wouldn't give him his sippy cup—"

There's another struggle for the phone, then Wade appears again.

"Everything is fine," he says firmly. "It's all under control. But we have to get ready for school and work now so I'm going to have to say goodbye and we'll talk to you later. Okay?"

Everything is clearly *not* fine, and the urge to fix it for him is almost overwhelming. But seeing my generally unflappable husband who was *so sure* this would be a walk in the park in this state of panic is kind of satisfying. So I draw in a deep breath, and then I ask lightly, "Did you give Eddie his visual schedule and the social script I prepared?"

He confirms my worst fears when he says dismissively, "It's fine, Alice. It's all fine."

"Okay then," I say easily, although I actually suspect things are about to get worse for my husband given he clearly *hasn't* read my documentation so he probably has no idea about Callie's after-school routines this week. "Well, I'll talk to you tomorrow morning, about the same time?"

"Sure…sure…"

I hang up, and the memory of Eddie's distressed face flashes before me, and I could *almost* panic—except that the beer still has me feeling so mellow and sleepy that I convince myself that I can maybe just postpone the panic until a bit later. I mean, there's not actually all that much I can do to help them right now… I curl up in a little ball on the bed and fall quickly to sleep, and when I wake, there's a message waiting from Callie.

Mom. I set up messaging on my iPad so we can keep in touch while you're away. I miss you and love you very much.

I sigh and reply.

Callie Michaels, you know you're not allowed to have text messaging. And aren't you at school??

Her reply comes instantly.

I promise I'll only use it with you. Yes I am at school but I explained to Mr. Merrick what I was doing and he thought it was a great technology and geography extension project. So have you seen anything cool? Can you take some photos for me?

I send her the photos from the square, and she replies immediately.

Mommy! That's so cool! We were just talking in class about inspirational figures in our lives and I was going to talk about Grandma but I talked about you instead because it's so amazing that you're doing this. Don't worry about Dad and Eddie. I'd like to say they're fine, but instead, I'll just remind you that a few days from now you'll be back and I'll help you clean up the mess. Haha. Love you Mommy.

I decide to focus on the part of that message that *doesn't* make me want to run home right this very minute. *My daughter actually thinks I'm inspirational.* All I've done is caught a damned plane by myself, and Callie thinks that's amazing. There's something both exciting and depressing about that.

Love you too, honey bear.

I put the iPad down and glance at the window. It's still light outside. I was planning to have an early night in with some room service, but suddenly I'm dying to see what the square looks like of an evening when the city has finished its workday. I pull my shoes on, fix my hair and head out for another walk.

CHAPTER 26

Alina

When the clock struck 10:00 p.m. the next night, Tomasz said, "Come with me."

I was dozing lightly in his arms, but I woke immediately at that.

"Yesterday you said it was too dangerous."

"Yesterday I had to visit four nearby farms, then go into the town to see Nadia. Today I am only going next door to the Golaszewski house, and just for Eva. Tonight's trip is so much less risky, and I would love for you to meet my friends."

The last thing in the world I wanted to do was to remain in that cellar without him for a second night in a row, and so we climbed out of our hiding place together and slipped into the night. The moon was full and the skies were clear, but I still managed to convince myself that every shadow on the horizon was a Nazi soldier. By the time we'd crossed the fields to the Golaszewski house, I was shaking with fear.

"I don't know how you do this every night," I whispered.

"You'll understand when you see the baby," he said quietly.

The Golaszewski house was much larger than my own; their soil was very fertile and their farm was much more profitable than ours ever had been. Jan had added many rooms to the house over the years, and it was now a hodgepodge of materials and building styles. Tomasz avoided the front portion of the house;

instead he led me to the back of the structure. I knew the lay-out of the house, so I was surprised to see where we stopped.

"Knowing how Jan feels about Jews, I can't believe he has given your friends his *own* bedroom," I whispered to Tomasz. Tomasz sighed.

"He has walled them in behind a false wall, my love. Even the exit is blocked—they are trapped unless Jan moves a heavy bookshelf in his room. Besides which, as soon as he moved them in, he locked the doors to that part of the house and shifted into his son's old bedroom at the front to keep a buffer between Eva and Saul and his space. If I didn't visit to pass food through this vent, they'd die in days. Make no mistake, their situation is dire."

A memory sprang to mind of the times I'd been inside the Golaszewski house as a child, before Jan and Father's relationship soured. I remembered being amazed by how much space they had—it amazed me that parents would have their *own* bedroom, given my parents had always slept in our living space. I remem-bered that large bedroom, and I also remembered the tiny little nook at the very back, which had once housed a bookshelf. It would take very little effort to wall in that small nook, but it would leave such a tiny cavity.

"How do you talk to them..." I started to ask, but Tomasz held his finger up over his lips and bent to the ground level. There was a small rock sitting in the dust at the bottom of the wall.

"We devised a system so I'd know if they'd been compro-mised. If the rock is here, it is safe for me to knock on the latch. It opens from the inside," he murmured, then he stood and knocked on one of the wooden panels on the walls. The panel trembled, then it slid down to reveal a gap in the wall at face height. I caught my first glimpse of Eva's wide brown eyes and high cheekbones, and a delicate heart-shaped face that I knew would be strikingly beautiful if she wasn't so deathly thin. Be-hind her, I could see the interior of the false wall—and as I'd feared, the space was so small the two barely had room to move around.

For a moment, though, she didn't seem fazed by her predicament, because all of her attention was on me and her eyes were alight.

"Tomasz! Is this the famous Alina?" she whispered excitedly.

"It is," Tomasz said, and he slid his arm around my shoulders and squeezed. "Alina, meet Eva Weiss."

"Hello," I said, feeling suddenly shy. "It's so nice to meet you."

There was more movement in the window, and then Saul was there, positively beaming at me.

"I'm Saul, and the pleasure is all ours," he assured me, reaching out through the window frame to shake my hand. His fingers were bone thin, but his grip was strong. His facial hair was very dark, which made for a shocking contrast against the ghostly white skin of his face. "We have heard so much about you."

"*So* much," Eva said, flicking a slightly teasing glance at Tomasz. "All of those months traveling and every day it was the same thing—*Alina this, Alina that.* It wasn't enough that he was willing to walk across Poland to get back to you, he had to try to make us fall in love with you too."

I glanced at Tomasz, and then giggled a little at the embarrassment that crossed his face. He looked back at me and gave me a rueful shrug.

"It should be no surprise to you that you were on my mind," he said. I felt heat on my cheeks.

I whispered back, "And you were on mine."

"Thank you for everything your family has done for us, Alina," Saul murmured suddenly.

"It is nothing…" I said hastily, and I meant it. Whatever we had done, it wasn't enough. Not for these people—who immediately struck me as kind and cordial, despite the desperate circumstances they found themselves in. I was embarrassed in that moment that I hadn't found a way to do more—to do *something* real for them beyond letting Tomasz bring them crumbs of food that was probably going to spoil anyway.

"Nonsense," Eva said, eyes widening. "You have risked your lives for us, and the food…the food is probably the only reason…" She cleared her throat suddenly, then held up one bony hand. "Well, let me show you." She bent away from us, and then straightened, bringing a little bundle back with her. "Would you like to hold her?" Eva asked me softly.

"I… I don't really have much experience of babies," I admitted.

"Just hold her gently against your body and support her head—it's still quite weak," she said, as she passed the tiny bundle through the gap in the wall. The few babies I *had* held in the past were pink and perfect, their faces plump with milk fat and their smiles angelic. Tikva Weiss looked different from the first moment I saw her. She was only a few months old, but the skin on her face hung across the hollows of her cheeks and stretched over her cheekbones, as if there was nothing between the two surfaces.

The lightness of the bundle she was wrapped in seemed impossible—I pulled the blanket back a little, just to reassure myself that there was a whole baby inside.

She was so small—too small, but Tomasz had been right. The child was perfect and precious, and well worth every single risk he'd ever taken to help this family.

"What is her name again?" I asked Saul and Eva.

"She is our little Tikva," Saul murmured. I glanced up at him, and he smiled. "Her name is the Hebrew word for *hope*."

I reached down and reached my finger over the soft skin on the baby's face. I brushed the thin thatch of dark hair back from her forehead. I held her a little closer, a little higher in my arms. I realized in that moment that I wasn't just holding a baby—I was holding all the hope that these two had left in the world. My eyes filled with tears, and I blinked them away rapidly. I knew I had to hold myself together. It would do this little family no good at all to have my pity.

Tomasz peered down at the baby in my arms, and then he nudged me gently with his shoulder.

"It will be our turn one day soon," he whispered into my ear. The warmth of his breath against the skin of my ear gave me shivers, the good kind at last. I glanced away from the baby just for a moment, and we shared a gentle smile.

We stayed only for five or ten minutes. Tomasz emptied the chamber pot for Saul and Eva and brought them fresh water to last them several days, then he handed over all of the food. I held the baby for almost the whole time, until she started to wriggle and grizzle and Eva said that she was probably getting hungry again.

When I passed the little bundle back through the window, I wanted to say something—anything. I wanted to apologize and to beg their forgiveness, not for anything I'd done wrong, but for all that I hadn't done. Through the years of the occupation, I'd allowed myself to be sheltered and I'd focused only on my own self-preservation.

I'd felt helpless throughout the war, but that night, I realized with some shock that I had never actually been powerless. At any given time I could have taken a stand—like Tomasz, even like Filipe, or thousands of others I'd heard rumors of, but never dared to reach out a hand to help. I didn't yet understand the horrific depths of the evil of the Nazi agenda—but somehow in the moonlight that night, I *felt* the loss of humanity, a very pause in the heartbeat of our shared existence on this planet.

That baby should have been fat and her cheeks should have been pink and she should have been living in a house, not a mouse hole, and as I handed her back to her mother in that hidden room, I was ashamed of my cowardice, as if it was the very thing that put her there. Had I done something, anything, would

the flap of that butterfly wing have changed some small branch
of the path that led to that family being trapped within that wall?

"We really need to get back," Tomasz said apologetically.

"It was so nice to meet you," Saul said, his tone so warm, it
made my heart hurt.

"And thank you again," Eva added sincerely.

I couldn't speak, I could only force a smile to my face and a
nod, but as Tomasz and I walked away from the house, I started
to cry. Tomasz took my hand and he held it tightly as we walked,
but he didn't stop until we were in the field near my house. He
looked down at me, and he sighed helplessly.

"Alina..."

"It's not right."

"*I know.* All we can do is try to help them. We can't change
the war, and we certainly can't change the world. But we can
do this little bit for them—help them to hide, bring them food,
be their friends. It is so much more than some of our countrymen are doing. You should be proud of that."

"But the baby..." I whispered thickly, and another sob burst
from my lips. "Tomasz, the baby is trapped in there with them,
and they are sitting ducks... All the Nazis have to do is hear
her cry—"

"We have to believe that there is hope," Tomasz said flatly.
"They have made it this far, against so many odds. That counts
for something, my love. In fact...perhaps in times like these, it
counts as everything."

CHAPTER 27

Alina

"Tomasz. Tell me about this photographer friend."

It was very late, but I couldn't sleep. I kept picturing that baby's thin face every time I closed my eyes. Tomasz yawned loudly, then cleared his throat. His voice was rough with sleep when he said, "His name is Henry Adamcwiz. He's an American."

"American?" I repeated. "What is he doing *here*?"

"His parents are Polish, but they emigrated to America and he was born there. He works for a big newspaper in America and now he is covering the occupation. He told me his home is in Florida," Tomasz said. "It's tropical there—there's almost no winter. And from his house, you can *walk* to the beach. Can you imagine it?"

I closed my eyes and let myself dream for a minute. I'd never been to the beach, but I had some idea what it looked like. I imagined sand and water and warmth, and I couldn't help but smile.

"If he can help us, we will have to smuggle some photographs?"

"Film. It's not developed."

"What are the photographs of?"

"Last time it was photos of the camps, some photos of Jews in ghettos, even a photo of me on your hill, believe it or not. He took one when he came to visit with me and asked me to do the courier run."

"I'd like to see that."

"I'm sure I looked devastatingly handsome."

I laughed softly.

"I'm sure you did."

"Henry told me last time that he is forever looking for couriers, and he thought I was resourceful enough that I would make a good one. Last time he was quite desperate—I am just hoping that is still the case. You do happen to be engaged to a brilliant medical student who excelled at his plaster cast studies. I told him I'd plaster the film onto my arm to keep it safe, and he was excited by that idea."

"That's…"

"Genius?" Tomasz proposed. I could hear the grin in his voice, but I only sighed.

"Tell me honestly, Tomasz. How risky is this?"

"Well, the greatest risk at this point is that Henry doesn't need us or doesn't have a route out of the country."

"The last time, when you decided not to go, what was the plan then?"

"Nadia told me that they put the man who went in my place into the back of a supplies truck to smuggle him close to the front, then he went on foot. She knows he made it into Soviet territory, but I don't know if the film made it to its destination."

I'd heard plenty of stories about the Soviets over the years—they had occupied half of Poland at one stage, while the Nazis occupied the other half. The stories that had come across from the Soviet-held territory were no less horrific than those on *our* side. If that was our plan too, I suspected we were about to jump from the frying pan into the fire, and the fragile hope that had budded in my chest started to fade.

"And you decided not to go because of me?"

"I thought perhaps I could talk Henry into letting you come with me…but…" He sighed, brushing his hand up and down my arm. "Well, I would have appeared at your window out of the blue one night and told you I was a wanted man, then asked you to run away with me from *relative* safety, into extreme danger. It didn't seem fair, and I thought if you had any sense you'd have said no anyway."

"I probably would have," I admit. "But not because I didn't want to be with you, just that Mama and Father were relying on me then…" Just the thought of Mama and Father and my throat started to tighten up again. "I can't think about this anymore," I whispered, holding him a little closer. "Tell me a story. Tell me about us." Then, because I knew he'd love it, I added, "Tell me about us living in America like Henry. Near the beach, where there is no winter."

"Okay." He smiled, then he laughed softly. "We'll get ourselves a big house in Florida. We'll have a car, of course."

"Of course."

"And I'll be a pediatrician. And do you want a job?"

"Why yes, thank you," I said, then I pondered this for a moment before I decided, "I think I'll work in a library."

"And our children? What are their names?"

"Hmm. Perhaps our son can be Aleksy, after your father."

"A lovely choice," Tomasz whispered, then he kissed my hair.

"But can we call our daughter Julita? After your Mama?"

"Should we not honor your parents too?"

"Oh, there will be more children, remember? At least three more. We can honor them later."

He laughed softly, and that was how we talked ourselves around from pessimism and fear to a strange kind of happiness that buoyed our spirits. I had been so determined earlier that night to cast off my childish thinking, but a few hours of daydreaming with Tomasz, and I gave myself wholly into the fantasy of a happy ending for us. Even after all I'd seen, when I was with him, I could still believe that life might be a fairy tale.

We slept then, and the next day, we woke in the darkness to endless hours of privacy and peacefulness while we waited for Henry. There seemed nothing left to do but to enjoy those precious hours, and to enjoy each other in all of the ways that we'd never had the time or privacy to really enjoy. We gorged on intimacy in the same way that we gorged on food, sharing a blissful honeymoon of sorts, as if the war wasn't carrying on above us, as if we really were going to live out that happy ending.

And in those too-brief days in the cellar I had once been so terrified of, I proved to myself once and for all—happiness really could be found anywhere, just as long as Tomasz was with me.

CHAPTER 28

Alice

Zofia is much younger than I imagined. She greets me warmly in her lightly accented English, then leads the way to a restaurant so we can get some breakfast. The enthusiastic waitress greets Zofia by name and leads us to a table, then disappears inside to fetch us some coffees.

"What do you recommend eating here?" I ask Zofia. She grins at me.

"That depends how brave you are. Because what I honestly recommend is the *smalec* on fresh rye bread, but I'm not sure whether your American palate will appreciate it. It's basically pork lard. Seasoned, of course. Quite delicious."

I imagine eating thick, gelatinous lard and can't hold back a grimace, but Zofia laughs and suggests, "I'll order a serving—you can taste mine." She reaches to the little stand where a cash register is currently unattended, and helps herself to two menus. She passes both to me, but points to the top one. "In the meantime, perhaps you can have something from this menu—it's American breakfast food."

I settle for bacon and eggs, and while we're waiting for the food, Zofia suggests, "Let's plan this trip to Trzebinia," she says. "It is a very small place but we don't actually know what we want to find out, right?"

"That's about the size of it."

"Well, I did some homework yesterday afternoon with the details you emailed me," Zofia says, and she withdraws from her bag an iPad. She slips it onto the table between us and loads an ancestry mapping application. "Something a lot of tourists who visit here don't realize is that very few of our birth, death and marriage records are digitized or even centralized. I drove up to Trzebinia yesterday afternoon as soon as I got your email, just so I could sort through the records at the municipal council. Some people really like to do it themselves, but you just don't have the time. I did take scans of the relevant records so you're not missing out on anything."

"I don't mind," I assure her. "But I'm curious…what kinds of things were you looking for?"

"I mostly wanted to see if I could figure out who they all were," Zofia says quietly. "The good news is, I managed to identify a few of them. Emilia was your grandfather's younger sister. His parents were Julita and Aleksy Slaski. Now, I couldn't find a death record for Emilia or Aleksy, but Julita died in child-birth with Emilia."

A few presses on the screen later, Zofia shows me a scanned page of Polish words that are initially meaningless to me—until Pa's name jumps out at me.

Tomasz Slaski, 1920.

"His birth record," Zofia tells me, and I take the iPad and stare down at the page. She reaches across and flips it again to show me a scan of a similarly handwritten page. "And this was one of the other names, Alina Dziak. She was born a few years after your grandfather. Your grandmother also gave you the name Truda Rabinek—well, it turns out that was Alina's older sister. She married Mateusz Rabinek in the early 1930s. I couldn't find death records for Truda, Alina or Mateusz."

"Does that mean they are still alive?"

"Alina would be in her nineties, Truda and Mateusz well over one hundred, so it's unlikely. I did check the phone book just in case, but no luck there. Unfortunately, in this case, a missing death record is not a reliable indicator that they are alive. Our records from the war era are patchy at best. The Nazis kept meticulous records within the concentration camps, but many of those were destroyed during the liberation, and deaths in the community were haphazardly recorded around here."

"So these people—Alina and her sister—were they related to Babcia?"

"I have no idea," Zofia tells me. "I couldn't find a record of your grandmother anywhere."

"Oh…" I say, frowning. "She definitely was born here."

"Well, that's actually pretty unlikely, given there's no birth or baptism record for her," Zofia says. She's apologetic, but there's also finality in her tone, and I'm still pondering this when she says, "Now, this other family she mentioned—"

"No, wait," I interrupt her. "Babcia was definitely born here. We don't know much about her life, but I know for sure that she was born and lived in Trzebinia. Her whole family did—she had siblings too, and they were all born in the house they lived in until the war."

Zofia's immaculate eyebrows draw in, then up.

"I don't know what to tell you, Alice," she says, with a careful little shrug. "There's no records for her. In fact I couldn't find any record of the Wiśniewski family locally. My best guess is that she was born elsewhere and moved here as a child, that would probably explain it. The same goes for Saul, Eva and Tikva Weiss. Do you know anything about them at all?"

I'm still thinking about Babcia, because I know so little about her life before she moved, but one thing she *has* been clear on is that her whole world was Trzebinia before she emigrated, and I distinctly remember her telling me she'd been born in the house she grew up in. I force myself to refocus on Zofia.

"No, I'd never heard those names before."

"Eva is reasonably popular with Christians *and* Jews here in

Poland, but particularly in that era the name 'Saul' was popular in Jewish families, and Tikva is *definitely* a Jewish name... I mean, it's a Hebrew word. There was no listing for these people anywhere, either, so I tried to search the Jewish records for births and marriages and deaths in the town. Unfortunately, I found no reference to any of them, so that likely means they were also not locals."

"Disappointing," I murmur. "Is there anywhere else we can check?"

"Unless you know of another locality, then no. I hope the fates of these people is not what Hanna sent you here to discover, because if it is...well, there might not be a way, especially in this short time frame."

"I don't think that's it," I say slowly. "She just seems more interested in Pa, to be honest—as little sense as that makes. It was Pa she's been asking about since we realized she could communicate with us with the iPad."

"What I found most interesting about the list your grandmother gave you was not that Tomasz was listed there—but the Polish words around his name." She runs the tip of her finger along the words *Proszę zrozum. Tomasz.* "This translates loosely to *please understand Tomasz.* Any idea what that might mean?"

"I don't know... I mean, how am *I* supposed to understand a man she lived with for well over seventy years—a man who's now dead?"

"This letter you sent was also interesting. He starts with something about them sitting together while she's reading, but she's laughing at him for questioning that he would make it to where she is. Then he tells her that the war has been chaotic...and life is somewhat risky so he wants her to know his feelings." She looks up and laughs softly. "Your grandfather was a romantic, it seems."

"It seems," I say, then I frown a little, because until Pa was really sick, I can barely remember seeing them so much as touch one another. "Although, that did seem to wear off a little in his old age."

"Many decades of marriage have that effect on a man," Zofia laughs. Then she says, "Now some of these words are illegible, but I think the basic gist is that his love for her was the great driving force in his life—and that he would always find his way back to her if they were separated because they were made for each other. I can't see who it's addressed to because the first few lines are too faint, but given your grandfather wrote it and your grandmother has possession of it, I don't think that's much of a mystery. But these last few lines… I have to guess a little because there are words missing here and there, but I *think* he is saying they were together when he wrote it. Then he talks about a potential separation, and now she's asking us to understand Tomasz… I wonder if perhaps they had lost each other for a period during the war, and she now wants to know what he got up to while they were apart?"

"If that is what she's looking for, that's surely impossible."

"Unless by some miracle one of the people on her list is alive and we can find them and they happen to know—we'd never be able to find out something so specific."

"I know it's crazy to come here with such little info but… even mute, she can be very persuasive."

"Is there *anything* else?"

"A few times she's said *Babcia fire Tomasz*—I just have *no* idea what that's supposed to mean."

"Well, in this letter he does talk about their love being the *fire* that is the driving force in his life, words to that effect anyway. Perhaps she is talking about passion?" Zofia suggests.

"I didn't think of that. There's a symbol on her device for *love* but maybe she couldn't find it?" I say, thinking aloud. "Surely that must be it."

"One mystery solved already." Zofia smiles. "Let's eat, then we'll head into Trzebinia and see what we can find, no?"

The waitress approaches with two plates of food. She sets fresh bread and a bowl of *smalec* in front of Zofia, then slides my eggs and bacon in front of me. Zofia cuts a square of the bread, then spreads a spoonful of the lard onto it and hands it to me.

"Oh," I say, and I clear my throat. "I'm really not sure…"

Zofia's eyes crinkle a little when she smiles.

"It's a delicacy, I promise."

I pop the entire chunk of bread into my mouth, and as I chew, I give her a surprised look. The *smalec* is salty and tasty, and the texture is not nearly as sickly as I'd expected. The whole effect between the delicate *smalec* and the heavy bread grows on me as I chew, until I could very easily imagine myself eating a whole plate of this stuff.

"Well?" Zofia asks, laughing again. "Another day we return for breakfast here and *smalec*?"

I laugh softly and nod.

"Okay, you've convinced me. *Smalec* next time."

CHAPTER 29

Alina

As the clock struck 6:00 p.m. on our third night in the cellar, Tomasz was starting to talk about heading out to collect some of the fresh eggs so they didn't go to waste, and I was trying just as hard to convince him to stay in our little bubble just for one more night. We heard the door upstairs open, and a voice called out quietly, "Tomasz?" and just like that, Henry Adamcwiz had found us.

Tomasz helped him into the cellar, then resealed the hatch, and for the first time in two days, we turned on the little oil light. It gave our little love nest a romantic yellow glow, and I could once again see Tomasz. Our eyes met—and in that gaze, we silently spoke of all of the secrets we'd shared in the darkness. We'd spent two glorious days alone comforting each other and resting together, and I was more than a little sad that those wonderful hours had come to an end.

Henry was far shorter than Tomasz, and much older than I'd expected. His Polish was fluent but heavily accented, and it took me a few minutes of fierce concentration listening to him speak before I could easily understand him.

"It is so lovely to meet you at last, Alina," he said, and he shook my hand. "Truly, Tomasz speaks so highly of you. I knew you must be a special girl when he decided to stay just for you."

"Thank you," I said, flushing.

"Well, maybe that, *and* he was a little suicidal," Henry said with a laugh.

I frowned, but there was no time to fixate on the comment, because Tomasz prompted, "Give us some good news, Henry. You are here, so I am assuming you have some?"

"We think the route we used with our last courier is still going to work, with some adjustment. The Eastern Front has moved significantly in the time since the last boy went through, so it's going to be a longer journey, but we hope to get you out of Poland in much the same way."

"Good," Tomasz nodded. He sat forward, rubbed his hands together, then sat back—as if the excitement was too great for him to sit still. Our gazes met again, and Tomasz flashed me a broad smile. In that moment, I felt the details were irrelevant—Tomasz looked as delighted as if we were already free and safe, so just for a second that's how I felt, despite the reality of our circumstances.

"Before you get too excited, let me tell you what I'm proposing. Jakub has built a large wooden carton. From the outside, it looks like many cartons stacked atop one another. Inside, there *is* room for two, although he says it will be tight and uncomfortable and likely little room for bags—perhaps one small suitcase for food and water. You will be in the deepest part of the truck, so you will have to make the entire journey without a break from the space inside the carton. It will take at least a day—longer if he has to stop for sleep, which he is hoping to avoid but…"

Tomasz and I shared a glance. His broad grin had faded now. He was assessing me—ensuring I understood what this meant. No bathroom breaks. No privacy. No *daylight.* It would be every bit as bad as our current situation in this cellar, where I'd been humiliated to have to use the chamber pot in front of him—but worse still, because at least in the cellar, I could stand and stretch and even pace if the anxiety became too intense.

Could I do it? The very thought made me feel ill, and even

despite the glow of the lamp, the cellar walls were suddenly closing in on me. But I had to be realistic—and I had no choice but
to be brave. I raised my chin and looked right at Henry.

"And after that?"

"Our driver will take you to a place where the Don River is
accessible. There is a local there with a boat—he will take you
across. Stalin has freed the Poles he was holding, so *technically*
you'll be free once you reach the other bank and you're into
Soviet territory."

It took a long moment for that last word to register, and when
I did, I blurted it out incredulously, "Free?"

"*Free...*" Tomasz repeated it too but he said the word slowly—
as if he was savoring its taste on his tongue. Our eyes locked,
and we grinned at each other again.

"Yes, you'd be free, although," Henry said cautiously, "the
journey would not be over, and you'd not be out of the woods
yet. After you cross the river you'll need to walk on foot into
a city called Voronezh—it's not far from the Eastern Front, but
still well under Soviet control. You can board a train there,
which will take you as far as Buzuluk. I just need to be sure
you understand what you're in for, my friends. This will be an
unpleasant journey too—and long, at least a few weeks. The
trains are overcrowded with your fellow Polish citizens recently
released from the gulags and the work camps. They are *all* desperate to get to Buzuluk."

"What's at Buzuluk?" Tomasz asked.

"The Polish Second Division are reforming and they are training
there. But we have heard that conditions there are also difficult—
food is scarce, disease is rife—and some Polish refugees are suffering immensely. But I *need* you to get to Buzuluk, because there
is a shipment of British clothing coming to keep the new Polish
troops warm over the winter. If this works as I hope, the British
officers who are bringing in the clothing shipment will be looking
for you, and when they return to Britain, they will take you both

back with them and deliver you to the US embassy. My brother will take things from there."

"Your brother is…?"

"He is a judge in America. He has contacts in the government… We are hoping if we can show them how bad things are here, they will intervene. Our efforts have not been fruitful yet, but…perhaps this new film will be the thing to motivate them." He sighed heavily and offered me a sad shrug. "We will just keep trying. It is all we can do."

"We too will do whatever we have to, won't we, Alina?" Tomasz said, checking in with me, and I smiled weakly as I nodded.

"We will."

Any excitement I'd felt at the prospect of freedom was now well and truly tamped by Henry's reminders of the difficult road ahead. It still seemed impossible. It still *felt* impossible.

"Here—" Henry retrieved from his backpack a roll of cloth and a small canister, then a tin and several small bottles. He passed these to Tomasz. "I'm sorry—that's all I could find. Will it make a convincing plaster?"

Tomasz read the labels and checked the containers, then winced.

"There's not much to work with here."

"It's so hard to get medical supplies—as you well know."

"Yes," Tomasz murmured, surveying the gear carefully. He shrugged. "But I will make it work."

"Can't we just carry the film?" I asked.

There was a pause, then Tomasz said softly, "If we are caught, it is better that the film is not discovered."

"And once you arrive in Soviet territory, you will find many people who are very desperate—anything that has potential value for sale is at risk of theft. The film *must* be hidden," Henry said quietly. "Now, I purchased these rubles for you—it's not much, but you'll likely need to buy some new clothes and food may be hard to come by there. You might have to be resourceful, but you've more than proven you're capable of doing that. And finally, you'll need your papers to gain access to the camp at Buzuluk—there are so many people trying to join, I understand they are strictly refusing entry except to those who can prove Polish citizenship." He glanced at Tomasz. "You still have your papers?"

"Yes, I've managed to hold onto my prewar passport," Tomasz said, but my stomach had dropped.

"Oh no," I whispered, and I turned to Tomasz in a panic. "Did Mama give you my identity card before they took her away?"

He shook his head, frowning, and I started to shake.

"My...she always held it on herself, because we were never apart and I kept forgetting. I...the ID card was all I had. I don't have a passport."

Henry opened his mouth, then closed it. Tomasz shut his eyes. Hope was draining out of me, despair rushing in to replace it. I felt sick with regret. Mama had only held on to my papers because I'd been foolish early in the occupation—careless and lazy, despite the fact that my very life was at risk. *Stupid, stupid, stupid.*

"We can get to Buzuluk without a passport, right?" Tomasz asked suddenly. Henry nodded cautiously.

"Of course. You'll be hidden in the back of a truck. No one will be checking your paperwork."

"And I will be granted access to the camp? With my passport?"

"As I understand it, yes."

"Then—" Tomasz glanced at me and shrugged "—we get to Buzuluk and hope for the best. Is the worst-case scenario that Alina will just wait outside for me?"

"The camp is *immense*, Tomasz. Tens of thousands of people are already inside. I am concerned that you don't realize how difficult it would be for you both if you were separated there. In fact, knowing you as I do, my friend, I have a sneaking suspicion if you get *all the way to* Buzuluk and Alina is left outside the camp alone, you will refuse to enter too, and that makes this whole mission pointless," Henry said, his voice curt with frustration. He sighed and rubbed his temples. "No, it seems to me that the only way we can proceed here is for me to go back to Nadia and see if we can secure some false papers for Alina. It is our *only* chance at success here." Tomasz squeezed my hand, and I nodded. Henry spread his hands wide. "That would be hard enough at any time, but our problem is that time is short because... If we are doing this—it has to be tomorrow."

"Tomorrow?" I choked, and if I'd felt anxious before, now I was positively sick with it. I blinked rapidly, refusing to allow myself to cry. Henry's gaze was sympathetic.

"I am sorry, Alina. Jakub can't risk this when he has a traveling companion. We got lucky today but it may be months before this happens again."

"No, it's fine," I said, and I raised my chin stubbornly. "I will be fine."

"Nadia knows this? She will know to care for my friends once I'm gone?" Tomasz asked. Henry nodded, and Tomasz exhaled. "Okay, good. Still, I will need to go see them—at least Eva and Saul."

"I'll leave you to it," Henry murmured. He gave us instructions to the meeting point, which was not far from my home— off the main road, at the outskirts to Trzebinia. We saw him upstairs, and then Tomasz and I were alone.

"How long do we have?"

"About eleven hours," Tomasz murmured.

"If Henry can't find me a passport..."

"Then we will go anyway," he said flatly. "We are resourceful people, my love. We will get to the camp and find a way to get inside. I *promise* you."

I exhaled, then nodded.

"There is only one thing I need other than my coat." I took

his hand and took him into my bedroom. I pushed aside Emilia's drawings and exposed Mama's ring.

"Mama gave this to us. For our wedding," I whispered as I lifted it carefully into my hand. I remembered so vividly in that moment the night she'd given it to me, and how Tomasz leaving for college had felt like the worst thing in the world. That naive version of myself felt like a friend I'd long lost contact with. Tomasz kissed me softly on the forehead.

"As soon as we are out of this godforsaken country, Alina, I will make you my wife. The first priest we see…" Tomasz promised me. "I will put this ring on your finger, and everyone will know—I am yours, and you are mine."

"It's *far* too big, I can't wear it until we find a priest *and* a jeweler," I laughed weakly, but the tears rose again. I closed my eyes for a moment, then whispered tightly, "If I can have five minutes with the lamp, I'll sew it into the hem of my coat, so it's not lost on the journey."

"We have some time—there's no need to rush. Take the time to look around this place and say goodbye. I know…" He paused, then whispered, "My love, I know this isn't easy. I know it's all terrifying. If there was any other way…"

I kissed him hard on the lips and drew in a deep breath.

"Mama would tell me to stop sulking and get my work boots on," I said, with determination. "I can sulk and cry in the back of this Nazi truck that may be leading us to our doom."

"Our doom?" Tomasz laughed, then he shook his head. "To *freedom*, Alina. And I'll be there to hold you. I'll hold you for the whole damned journey."

"Then I will survive it well." I smiled at him, and I believed it with all of my heart as I said, "As long as you are with me, I can survive anything."

CHAPTER 30

Alice

As we drive toward Trzebinia, Zofia gives me a history lesson—
a rapid-fire summary of the history of Polish life, right up until
communism was disbanded and the country joined the European
Union. I ask her about the graves and monuments I see scattered
by the side of the road. Some are elaborate—some small enough
to be almost unnoticeable, but for flowers or lanterns sitting on
the ground beside them.

"Some are in honor of saints or the Blessed Mother," she explains, pointing to a stone monument adorned with blue rib-
bons. "This one, for example—it is from a recent festival to
honor the Virgin Mary. Others are graves, or monuments in
memory of those lost. Some are modern, some very, very old—
and plenty are from wartime. There are graves everywhere in
the countryside, but it was worse in Warsaw. I've seen photos
of makeshift graves in the streets—no gravestone, no way to
memorialize the person." She sighs heavily. "Six million Polish
citizens died in that war. The scale of the death and the suffering is unimaginable to our modern-day minds."

We drive in silence for a while after that. Soon, we turn off
the highway and into Trzebinia, and I can tell immediately that
it's an industrial town. The first blocks are lined by large factories and businesses, and today at least, there's visible air pol-
lution even at the street level. As we reach the residential area,

Zofia casually flicks her forefinger toward a dilapidated building on the left.

"That's the only synagogue left standing here after the war," she tells me. "At the start of the war, there were several thousand Jewish people in town—four synagogues, a thriving community. By the end of the war, they were *all* gone. That remaining synagogue is unused and poorly maintained. You can't rebuild a community when there's no one left to do the rebuilding."

I crane my neck to look back at the synagogue as it fades behind us into the distance, and I don't know what to say to that. Of course, I learned about the war during history classes at school, but never in detail, and it never felt entirely real—it seemed too big and too bad and too *alien* to actually have happened in such recent history.

I'm suddenly thinking again about Babcia and Pa's inability to share their stories from their lives here, and wondering about all the things they surely must have seen and experienced that I will never know about now, no matter how well this trip goes. What happens when stories like theirs are lost? What happens when there's no one left to pass your experience on to, or you just can't bring yourself to share it?

Not for the first time, I wish *just once* when I asked my grandmother about the war, instead of her telling me "that was a terrible time, I don't want to talk about it," she'd been able to say something more. *Anything* more. Maybe if she could have shared some of her story, I could have learned from it, I could have taught my children from it—we could have built a better world from the hard lessons she surely learned.

The residential area ends abruptly, the last row of houses backing onto a thick patch of woods sprawled over a small hill. The road curves sharply through the woods around one side of the hill, and quite suddenly, we're surrounded by fields, and the road isn't even sealed. Because the hill shelters the town from these fields, within a few hundred feet it feels like we're in the middle of nowhere—there's not much to see out here at all but farmland. There are a few long, thin patches of crop, but most of the fields on this side of the town look like they've been abandoned—the grass is high and sprinkled with purple and red wildflowers. As the gentle breeze passes through the flowers, they wave to me like a greeting.

"The address she gave you is not far along this road," Zofia murmurs. "We're headed to that house over there on the left. It's quite unusual to see a prewar house in this district...we're lucky it's still there."

"Because it's so old?"

"No—just because farmhouses in this region generally didn't survive the occupation. I'd say what saved that one is the construction material—if it were brick, it would be gone too. The Nazis deconstructed all of the brick structures because they couldn't manufacture bricks fast enough to expand the second part of Auschwitz—the camp they called Birkenau," she says. "That's not far from here, and I'm pretty sure this property would be just within the twenty kilometers they designated for their 'area of interest.' They basically cleared the farms of all residents so they could put up a big fence and make sure no one inadvertently saw what they were doing in the camp. They did it under the guise of making a huge work farm—which was true too, of course, they did farm much of this land but...secrecy was the real goal."

"I can't even imagine living in such a small house," I admit. The house is probably only the size of my living area at home, maybe even smaller.

"It was a different time. People's expectations were different." Zofia pulls up into the drive, then glances at me. "And here we are."

I stare down the drive at the house and the woods on the hill beyond it, and to my surprise, I *recognize* the scene before me. I've never been here before and I know nothing about Babcia's life during the war, but I know *all* about her childhood. I've heard about the woods on the hill behind her home and the township on the other side. She told me she lived in a very small house with a large barn. She told me the land was poor because it was so rocky and most of their fields were steeply sloped.

And that's *exactly* the scene before me.

"Is that hill called Trzebinia Hill?" I ask Zofia. She tilts her head.

"I don't think that hill has a formal name, but the township of Trzebinia *is* on the other side, so I suppose that would make sense."

"Babcia told me so little about her life once the war began, but she always told me stories about her childhood...life with her brothers and her sister and her parents on their tiny little farm," I say to Zofia. "This is everything she described to me, and it is exactly as she described it."

I am totally caught off guard by the swell of intense emotion that rises as I step from the car. There is something unexpectedly profound about being here—in this country that was my grandmother's home and a place I have always understood she once loved very dearly and has *always* missed. I feel Zofia's patient gaze on my face, and I try to blink the tears away, but one escapes and rolls down my cheek.

"Do you need a minute?" she asks softly, and I clear my throat and shake my head.

"It's so silly..." I mutter through my embarrassment. "I can't quite believe I'm here. I've always known her as the other version of herself, you know? And this is like a glimpse into..." I clear my throat, unsure if I am expressing myself adequately. "This is *just* a farm, right? An unimpressive one at that, and we can't even be sure it's the one she told me about. I don't know why I'm so emotional about it."

"You're looking at it all wrong, Alice. This might be 'just' a farm to anyone else—but to you? It's clear just by your willingness to come here that you have a great depth of love for your grandmother. This may be a piece of your own history, and it's a history that was lost to you until now. I've helped people track their ancestors before, and the smallest things are sometimes unexpectedly intense."

I nod, and another tear trickles over onto my cheek.

"I just wish I had come here when she could travel with me," I whisper, then I impatiently swipe the tear from my cheek and clear my throat one more time. "I wish she'd been able to tell me more about her life here. I wish she was just standing here with me, telling me the things she wants me to know."

I stare at the house, set against that odd little hill, framed by the thick green woods behind it and the shock of deep blue sky that stretches above. The scent of dust and grass hangs heavily around me, and the breeze stirs my hair. I breathe in that country air, taking it deep into my lungs, as if I can store the memory of it, as if I can take it home with me.

There's a rusted and low chain-link fence around the yard, with a gate at the front. The lock on the gate seems a little redundant—it would be easy to jump the fence anyway, and I have a feeling that with a little pressure, the hinges would give way. Zofia approaches the gate, then looks back at me expectantly when I hesitate.

"Are we going to trespass…?"

"If trespassing bothers you, perhaps you've just come halfway across the globe for nothing," she laughs. I still hesitate, and she waves her arm around expansively. "Look at the property, Alice. No one is living here. Most likely it's abandoned and has been for decades—that's not at all uncommon. More recent generations either can't or won't make a living from small plots like this one, so sometimes the land just wound up left behind. In this case, perhaps there was no one left here to take the property on after the war."

"There are car tracks in the grass," I point out, and Zofia shrugs.

"It's not *so* recent."

Beyond the gates, I can see what amounts to something of a rough driveway through the grass, leading past the house—but she's right, the grass is bouncing back even along this path—it's hardly in frequent use. Zofia jumps the fence and starts walking along the quasi path. I'm still nervous to trespass, but it doesn't look like I have much choice.

"Are there snakes here?" I call after her, and her soft laughter at the question carries on the wind past me. I decide to take that as a no, and I climb carefully over the fence, then jog a little until I catch up to Zofia. I stare at the tiny house as we walk. The roof is made of corrugated concrete tiles, but it sags in places. The walls still look sturdy enough, but that roof looks like it could cave in the next time a leaf lands on it. I can see two wooden structures beside the house—a tiny outhouse behind, and what I assume is a barn in front of it. The barn roof has indeed caved in, along with one of the narrow walls.

The electricity poles on the road run right past this house, and I have a sneaking suspicion that outhouse might not connect to a sewer. I don't have the best eye for the size of spaces, but Wade's brother has a hobby farm in Vermont. That property is twenty acres—and this feels maybe half that size. And the house feels even smaller now that I'm close. Babcia and Pa's house at Oviedo was at least ten times as big, maybe more. I know they lived elsewhere in America before that big house—Mom remembers living in some very ordinary places as a child while Pa's medical certification was recognized, but even so, to Babcia, it must have been quite the culture shock to shift from this life to the one she landed in once she arrived in the US.

I step gingerly through the long grass until I can snap a photo that includes both the house and the barn, then send it back to Mom.

Please show Babcia. This is the first residential address on her list. We can't find birth records for Babcia here in Trzebinia and the guide thought that might mean she was born elsewhere, but this looks exactly as she described her childhood home to me.

It's 6:00 a.m. back home, so I know Mom will be on her way to the hospital before work but I expect it will still be some time before she replies. Zofia and I wander around the house separately. She heads toward the barn; I walk right up to one of the small windows at the side of the house to peer inside. It's difficult to see through the tattered curtain and dust that clings to the pane of glass in the window, but from what I can see, it appears the building was split into several tiny rooms. As my eyes adjust to the darkness inside, I can see a living room of sorts—there's a potbellied stove, sofa bed and small dining area. The table and one of the chairs are both off center, as if someone has stood up too roughly from dinner and failed to put it all back in place.

I wonder suddenly if this house has been abandoned since the war. If so, I'm looking through a window but seeing back in time almost eighty years. I have no idea how or why Babcia came to leave this place, but it's unexpectedly eerie to think that I might be staring all the way back into that point of her life. Maybe she was sitting at that table when the moment came when her life changed forever, and maybe that journey she began that day ended all the way in America and with our family.

Just as I step away from the window, my mom calls.

"Hi," I smile down the camera lens.

"Alice, hello," Mom says. "I have one very excited grandmother here."

She turns the phone to Babcia, who has tears pouring down her face, and is grinning at me like I've just discovered the holy grail.

"Jen dobry, Babcia," I say, and she gives me a delighted smile and an awkward clap. I flip the camera and walk all around the house—showing her the fields, the decrepit barn and even the long-overgrown yard around the house. As I walk around, I shift

my gaze from the fall of my steps to her reaction on the screen. I watch the dawning joy and sadness and longing on her face, and I *know* we're at the right place.

I can't help but imagine this scene playing out in a very different way if we'd made this trip together ten years ago. I'd have asked her a million or more questions. Maybe she'd have answered some.

"Alice," Mom interrupts me, after a few minutes, and then it's her face filling the screen again. "I need to get to chambers. Is that it, then? She seems…" Mom's eyes flick from the camera, then back to me. She shrugs and smiles, and her sudden approval is quite dazzling. "You know? She suddenly seems incredibly happy."

"Good," I say, and I beam at her. "Good." I pause, thinking again about that missing birth record, then ask, "Mom, did she ever tell you she was born in the house she grew up in?"

"That's right. She and her twin brothers and her sister were all born at home."

I glance at Zofia. She's tilted her head to the side and she's staring at the iPad curiously.

"Huh," Zofia murmurs thoughtfully. She raises her voice a little as she confirms, "Twin brothers, you say?"

"Hello there," Mom says, frowning. "Who is that, Alice?" I adjust the camera so that Mom can see Zofia, and Zofia waves and smiles.

"Mom, meet Zofia, Zofia meet my mom—Judge Julita Slaski-Davis."

"It is so lovely to meet you, Julita," Zofia says. "Tell me, was Hanna the youngest of her family?"

"That's correct. She used to tell me she was the spoiled baby girl, although I don't imagine *spoiled* in her childhood context means the same as it does in ours."

"Do you know her siblings' names?"

Mom looks uncharacteristically uncertain.

"I always thought the sister's name was Amelia, but then we saw the list she wrote for Alice last week and it said *Emilia* so I'm not really sure…"

"*Emilia* was Pa's little sister," I confirm for Mom, and she sighs.

"I'm really not at all sure how it all fits together. I distinctly remember her saying she was writing to *her* sister, but maybe I'm wrong…"

"Perhaps her parents' names…" Zofia prompts. "Do you know what they were?"

"I only remember her mother's name. That was definitely Faustina," Mom gives a little laugh. "The Catholic church can-onized a Saint Faustina…goodness, maybe twenty years ago, and Babcia was excited like a kid in a candy store."

"Ah. Her mother was Faustina, and her father was…" Zofia reaches into her handbag and withdraws her iPad, then says, "Bartuk. Yes?"

I see Mom glance beside herself, and I can hear some kind of movement offscreen. Mom is frowning.

"What is it, Mom? Is everything okay?"

"Hang on a minute, Alice," Mom says, and the camera shows her walking back to the bed. She sets the phone down for a mo-ment, onto the bedside table I think, and all I can see is the ceil-ing in the hospital room. "Mama? Are you okay?"

The camera swings wildly, and for a minute, the camera is blocked by a finger. It shifts, and then I see Babcia's face.

"Hello, Babcia," I murmur, by habit. She looks distressed and frustrated, and I peer helplessly into the screen. "Mom? Could you give her the iPad? I think she wants to tell us something."

"Alice, did you say she still understands spoken Polish?" Zofia asks me softly. I nod, and she extends her hand toward my phone. "Do you mind if I…may I?"

I pass her the phone, and Zofia smiles gently into the camera. She speaks very slowly and carefully for a few minutes in Polish. A single tear rolls down Babcia's cheek, but she's nodding. Zofia looks at me and she grins.

"Well, that's *one* mystery solved."

"It is?"

"Alina Dziak was the youngest child of Faustina and Bartuk Dziak. They had four children...a daughter, Truda, twin sons and then Alina. I only remembered the composition of the family because the twins and Alina were born very close together and I felt so sorry for poor Faustina," Zofia says wryly, but then she sobers. "Alice, I just asked your grandmother if *she* is Alina, and she's nodding yes."

My eyes widen.

"*What?* Mom? Are you listening to this?"

I see Mom hand Babcia the iPad, and she takes her phone back. Her face fills the screen, and she's frowning.

"Her name is Hanna," Mom says stiffly. "She's confused."

"I couldn't find any records at all for Hanna, or a family of origin with that surname in this district," Zofia tells Mom gently. "It makes no sense. If this is her childhood home, and she and her siblings were born here, the Wiśniewski family would have left behind *some* records."

Mom is shaking her head, but then I hear the electronic sound of a camera shutter in the background at the hospital room. Mom looks away from the screen, and then I hear Babcia's iPad say *Alina*, and Mom's eyes widen in disbelief. She silently turns the camera around, and I see Babcia sitting on the bed, the iPad resting awkwardly on her lap, facing toward Mom.

Babcia's face is set in a mask of pure determination, and she's made a label on the iPad screen for *Alina*, complete with a brand-new selfie of herself for the image. After a moment or two, Babcia gives us an impatient look, then she holds her left forefinger up, points to the screen, then stabs her finger against her own chest.

"Holy shit," I say.

"That's pretty definitive confirmation," Zofia says.

"No. I don't believe this," Mom says. She turns the camera around again and she's scowling at the screen. "Alice, I don't *understand* this. It makes no sense at all. She's *lied* to me for my whole life? No. I don't—"

"Mom," I interrupt her carefully. "Remember she wanted you to *name* me Alina? Maybe it does make at least a little sense."

Mom's expression stiffens. We stare at each other for a moment, then the camera picks up the sound of Babcia's iPad speaking again.

Alina fire Tomasz. Babcia fire Tomasz. Alina fire Tomasz.

"Christ, she's getting upset now," Mom mutters. She's visibly frustrated, and she glares into the camera screen. "I'm going to go calm her down. Alice, I'll talk to you later. I need to think about this."

The call disconnects abruptly, and I sigh and glance at Zofia.

"So, my grandmother adopted a false identity eighty-odd years ago. Is that what we're assuming here?"

"I think that's fair to deduce, yes."

"Any ideas *why*?"

"There are an infinite number of possible explanations. Identity forgery was a thriving industry in occupied Poland." Zofia shrugs. "Perhaps she ran afoul of the Nazis at some point and needed to go into hiding. There's not really any way for us to know, unless she finds a way to tell us."

I look around the farm again. There's not really that much here, but I find I'm not at all ready to leave, so I make an excuse to stay. "I think I'll take some more photos... I'd like to send some back to my husband and my kids."

"Take as much time as you like, Alice." Zofia smiles, and then she steps away from me and says, "I'll give you some space, hey? I'll wait for you at the car."

When I've photographed every feature I can find around Babcia's old house, Zofia and I drive back into the town. The next address is only about a mile away from the farmhouse, nestled deep within a narrow laneway. As Zofia turns the car into the little street, I survey the towering trees along the sidewalk.

"Sweet chestnut trees," Zofia explains. "They are all through that huge park at the end of the street too. What a beautiful spot. I'm guessing this must have been quite a prestigious address in your grandmother's time."

There are some *very* old, very large houses here and when we first enter the street, I fully expect that we're headed toward one of them. I'm disappointed, though—because the number my grandmother has guided us toward happens to be one of the recently modernized homes in the street.

"I guess we got lucky with the farmhouse, but whatever she was expecting to find here seems to be long gone," Zofia says.

"There doesn't seem much I can do except take some photos to show her what it looks like now," I say with a sigh. We knock on the door anyway and discover that the owners now are a young professional couple, and the house has sold at least twice in the last twenty years, so the woman who answers the door has no idea why my grandmother might have wanted a photo of it. Still, she's warm and friendly—and once we explain why we're there, she's kind enough to offer to show us through the house in case it's of importance. As we enter the ultramodern lobby, it's clear that whatever Babcia wanted us to find here is long gone.

We leave empty-handed—and I knew this might happen, but it's disappointing after the high of seeing the farmhouse and discovering Babcia's real name. It's now well past lunchtime, and my stomach is starting to growl. Zofia suggests we take a break, so we head back to the town square for a break.

"Let's see what this afternoon brings." She winks, as we sit down to lunch.

After we eat, I leave Zofia to the second coffee she "desperately needs," and I walk to a nearby laneway to find some privacy to call back to my family.

"Where are you, Mommy?" Callie asks, as soon as I call. The connection is not great here, so the video feed of her face isn't quite as clear as it was yesterday in the city, but even so—the sight of her is enough to make me feel a pang of homesickness for the first time. I push that away and keep my tone light.

"We're at a small town called Trzebinia, which is where Babcia and Pa were born," I tell her. "How's things back there?"

"Oh, you *know*," she says. "Don't worry, I'm helping Dad more now—he's almost got the basics down pat. Almost." I try to laugh, but it comes out with a wince, and Callie's expression grows a little sadder. "Mommy. When Daddy goes away for work, we miss him a lot, but this is so different. I just *really* miss you."

"I miss you too, honey bear," I say sadly. Callie's big eyes fill with tears, and she blinks rapidly.

"Anyway," she says, and for just a second she sounds *so* much older than her ten years that my heart aches a little more. She exhales, then asks me brightly, "Have you found anything else cool today?"

I fill her in about the farmhouse, and then promise to send her some photos. When Wade takes the phone, the homesickness returns. I spend a lot of time at home worrying about the things that seem broken in my marriage. It's only now, when I'm on the other side of the world, that it's crystal clear to me that *some* things are still whole. The connection between us feels less vibrant than it once was, but Wade is still my best friend, and I'm still deeply, hopelessly drawn to him.

"Hey," I say softly.

"Hello, lovely wife," he says with a smile. "How's things in glamorous Europe?"

"Oh, glamorous," I joke, turning the camera around to show him a view of the laneway. When I switch the camera back, he's laughing. "We visited Babcia's childhood home, and we called back to Mom while we were there so Babcia got to see it. That was pretty amazing, actually—such a special moment, I'm so glad I got to do that for her. And guess what? Babcia's *real* name is Alina."

"No way."

"It's true. Mom told me the other day that she'd tried to convince Mom to give me that name, but we had no idea where it came from," I say.

"That's incredible. Any idea why she used another name once she moved here?"

"We don't know yet. Oh—and Zofia is lovely, by the way—an excellent driver, and very knowledgeable. Well done."

"Thank you." Wade does a fake bow for the camera, and then we both pause. Things seem more peaceful at home today, but I'm nervous to ask how Eddie is.

"He's in his room, watching his videos," Wade says, correctly "hearing" the question I haven't asked, which thrills me. "He's doing okay, Alice. I took him into the office yesterday and he made friends with some of my team."

My eyes widen at that.

"Really?"

"Sure," Wade says, and he shrugs. "Well, when you think about it, my office is kind of Eddie's ideal place. I mean, there are rules upon rules upon rules, and *everything* is written down. I just gave him the visitor's safety manual, he read through it and then he sat quietly in my office all day and played with his iPad. Oh, then he came with me to a meeting and he just sat and played with that dreidel thing for a while. It probably helps that none of my lab rats are particularly chatty—Eddie was right at home, in a way." Wade pauses, then clears his throat and admits with obvious difficulty, "Made me wonder why I haven't done it before."

I feel a sudden rush of confusion, because I'm somehow delighted and relieved at this admission, but I'm also instantly resentful. In these last few years I've given up trying to convince Wade to try to connect with Eddie, but before that? In the early years?

Back then, I tried all the damned time.

Be the bigger person, Alice. Don't say it.

Do. Not. Say. It.

"I *told* you years ago you should take him to the office with you one day. I told you he'd love it. I told you that your team would understand but you said it would be too dangerous but I... I *told* you," I blurt.

Wade's jaw tightens.

"I know you did," he says stiffly. I have to redirect this conversation before it spirals into an argument, but I need some more information about my son, so I try to brighten my tone as I ask, "And did he sleep last night? Has he eaten?"

Wade is staring at the camera a little warily now.

"I gave him the melatonin last night, and yes, he slept pretty well. He's been asking for you on the iPad sometimes—Pascale has been pointing him back to that calendar you made him." His gaze softens, and so does his tone, as he provides me with reassurance I desperately need. "It's nothing we can't handle though, honey. Everything is okay."

All I can think about for a second is my poor son, bewildered by my absence, asking again and again but with no way to really understand why I disappeared while he was at school one day. Just as the tension starts winding through my body, I force myself to think about how bad this all *could* have been—how bad I expected it to be, and the positive things that have already come out of this trip. If Wade can just take Eddie to work with him on the *very rare* occasion when I'm sick or I can't juggle Eddie and Callie's schedules—

My whole life would change.

I'd have a backup plan for the moments when I so desperately need one. I'd have a chance of some respite every now and again.

I'd have someone to pick up the slack when I need a break,

someone to share the ups and downs with. Which is all I ever wanted in the first place.

I open my mouth to say something like this but at the very last second, a stack of out-of-place objects in the background of the video feed catches my eye.

"Wade—what's that on the countertop?"

Wade glances behind himself, then he shrugs.

"Cans of soup."

"Why… Wade, why are there *six* cans of Eddie's soup on the bench?"

"I don't know, Alice. I didn't notice them until now. I guess Eddie is putting them there…" He clears his throat, then adds with audible bewilderment, "…for some reason."

There's only one reason Eddie puts soup on the bench. He does it when he's hungry and I'm running late or busy with something so he wants to hurry me up. If there are six cans of soup there, that probably meant he asked for dinner and didn't get it, so he tried to hurry things along by getting a can out. And when that didn't work, he tried it again, and again…

"What did he eat for dinner the last two nights, Wade?" I demand. My tone has sharpened again—that gratitude I was feeling a moment ago is *gone*. I'm shifting into full Tiger Mother mode, and Wade knows it. Even over the slightly pixelated video feed, I can see the defensiveness in his gaze.

"I gave him some McDonald's the first night like Pascale and I had, and last night we had mac and cheese."

"How much yogurt did he eat yesterday?"

"It's *fine*, Alice," Wade snaps. "He's eating. I'm handling it. An attempt at variety can only be good for him. How healthy do you think it is for him to eat only *two foods* for his entire diet?"

"How healthy do you think McDonald's and mac and cheese are!" I exclaim incredulously. "Just make him the damned soup! I *knew* you'd do this, Wade. He doesn't eat anything that's solid or has lumps in it. He has sensory—"

"Listen, I'll give him the soup." Wade's tone takes on an urgent, conciliatory tone as he apparently realizes that the tension that's been simmering underneath much of this conversation is about to boil over. Even the tone of his voice frustrates me now, because he's not conceding that I'm right—he just doesn't want to get into a screaming match with me when I'm five thousand miles away. "I just didn't notice that he was putting it there, okay? I just *thought* it would do him some good to try different foods—to get used to different textures so his diet wasn't so restrictive. He's not starving, anyway—not in two days, and he's been eating loads of yogurt. I even got him eating the Go-Gurt with the new label—"

"You can't just change his entire routine, Wade!" I interrupt him impatiently. "I've worked his entire life to get him to this point."

"Alice," Wade says. His voice is deadly quiet now. "I'm trying here, okay? We agreed that you'd go on this trip, and I'd handle things at home. We even agreed I'd do this *my* way. I made a mistake with the soup—I'll fix it today."

The rapid de-escalation is every bit as frustrating as the rapid *escalation* was, because I really want to make him understand how important it is that Eddie gets that soup, but just then, I notice Zofia walking around the corner. She's looking at her own phone and doesn't seem to be paying attention to me, but she surely heard at least part of that conversation, and I'm embarrassed. I puff out my cheeks as I exhale, then look away from the phone for a minute as my eyes fill with tears.

"I better go," I say abruptly.

"You don't want to talk to Eddie?" Wade frowns. I shake my head, and a tear spills over. I'm too upset to talk to Eddie, and I *know* Eddie would see through any facade I tried to put up. There's no point upsetting the poor kid more.

"No. Zofia is back and we have things to do, I really—maybe I can call tonight."

"Have a good day, Alice," he says, but his jaw is still set tight.

"You too, Wade," I echo. I missed him when he answered, but by the time I hang up the phone, I feel only relief to be saying goodbye. I'm impossibly frustrated, and it takes me quite a few minutes to realize that I cut my husband off as he tried to tell me something about the new label on the Go-Gurt.

And now that I really think about it, it sounded like he said something about Eddie eating from the tubes with the new labels—something I was 100 percent sure would *never* be possible.

CHAPTER 31

Alina

Tomasz and I were packing food into pails to take across to Saul and Eva when he suddenly stopped and looked at me.

"Maybe Saul and Eva could come here, instead of us taking the food to them. That way they could have it *all*."

"Will Jan let us get them out?" I asked, uncertainly. Tomasz grimaced and shook his head.

"No, he'd be furious if we woke him."

"Well, they won't fit through the latch?"

"Tikva will be easy. And maybe we can very quietly pull away just a few more of the boards on the wall around the latch. We wouldn't need much more space to be able to pull Saul and Eva through too. Jan wouldn't be happy, but if we're careful enough not to wake him, he won't find it until morning and we'll all be long gone by the time he even knows. I know it's only a short-term fix, but it would be so much more comfortable for them here, even if it's just for a few nights." He paused, then he nodded, apparently having made up his mind. "Alina, I think I can make this work."

"My parents won't mind," I said unthinkingly. Tomasz looked at me sadly, and I cleared my throat. "I mean, if they manage to come home…"

We decided to at least try—we still had some time to spare, and so we left to make that fraught trek through the fields to the back of the house next door. When we were close, Tomasz pressed his fingers to his lips, just as he'd done the previous night. He bent to check for the rock, then Tomasz stood, frowning. He gave me a hand signal to *wait here*, and then he inched around the corner and along the wall toward the front of the house. I remained at the back corner, but I stretched my head out from the corner so I could watch him.

When he reached the front corner of the house, his shoulders slumped. As he turned to round that next corner, I caught a glimpse of his face in the moonlight and the pain in his expression was so vivid that it took *my* breath away. Tomasz was no longer trying to hide—instead, he stepped away from the wall, his hand outstretched as if he was reaching for someone.

I knew he'd told me to wait where I was, but I couldn't— not having seen the expression on his face. I repeated that same journey he had just made, with careful footsteps along the wall of the house.

"No, Tomasz." The hoarse words were carried on the otherwise-silent night air. "You can't be here. They *asked* about you. What if they came back for you?"

"If you think I am leaving you alone to deal with this," Tomasz choked in return, "you are sadly mistaken, my brother."

I wanted to stay at the back of the house, but my legs seemed to have other ideas. They propelled me forward automatically after Tomasz, and when I reached the front corner of the house, I took a deep breath and forced myself to peer around it.

I couldn't even make sense of the scene before me at first. Under the glow of the moonlight, Saul sat slumped on the front step, Eva's limp body cradled across his lap. I gasped as I recognized the unseeing face of baby Tikva, her tiny body tucked tightly between her parents' torsos. Saul's face was set in a mask of grief too deep to be understood—his jaw slack, his eyes wide—and now that I was closer, I could see that the *only* movement he made was the sporadic blink of his swollen eye-lids and the rattling *inhale* then *exhale* of his chest.

"Saul," Tomasz whispered. "What *happened*?"

Saul turned toward Tomasz's voice, but his gaze was un-focused. He blinked again, and then he gave a shake of his head, then a convulsion racked his whole body and he pulled Eva and the baby higher against his neck as a series of sobs broke over him.

I stayed at the corner of the front of the house, unable to look away but far too afraid to move closer. Tomasz, however, sat right beside his friend and slid his arm over his shoulders.

"Saul," Tomasz said again, and this time, his own voice broke. "I'm so sorry, my friend. I'm just so sorry."

"The soldiers knew everything—they even knew about you and Nadia." Saul sobbed, and I caught the full force of agony in his expression as he turned to face Tomasz. "Tomasz, they have taken everything from me now. There is nothing left for me to live for. Run for your life, but let me die. Please, let me die."

Tomasz sat on the step with Saul for so long that my legs became numb, and I had to sink down to sit on the ground—although I stayed at the corner of the house. I couldn't bring myself to go near to them—partly out of respect for Saul's right to privacy as he grieved, and partly because I was sickened by the sight of the bodies and the heavy scent of blood in the air.

Every time I closed my eyes, I saw baby Tikva's face in my mind. She had been sleeping when I held her, but now that I had seen her face set in death, I could no longer remember the innocence of that moment when she was safe within my arms. And the worst thing was that I *knew*, from having witnessed Aleksy's and the mayor's deaths, that this image was a part of me now. I would never be the same again having witnessed this moment in time.

After a while, Tomasz stood, and he approached me. His face

and his beard were wet with tears, and as he embraced me, he was shaking.

"Alina," he whispered. "I have to ask something of you. Can you wait with him?"

"*Wait* with him?" I whispered back, my gaze frantically flicking to the man and the bodies just a few feet away. "Where are you going?"

"He is covered in their blood," Tomasz whispered. "He needs fresh clothes—I will have to go back to your house and get something for him to wear."

"Can't we all go? Can't we take him with us?"

"We have to…" Tomasz broke off. His gaze dropped, then returned to mine. "We have to bury them first, my love. It is the very least they deserve."

I squeezed my eyes closed for a minute, then suggested hopefully, "But Jan's clothes will be inside…"

"Jan is entirely responsible for the death of Saul's wife and baby, Alina. I *can't* ask that of him."

I wanted to say no, and the old Alina would have. But I was determined to be an adult now, and to make Tomasz proud of the woman I'd become. Still, it wasn't easy to agree to remain alone with a man and two horrific bodies in a space where Nazis had clearly been in recent hours, particularly given the likelihood that they'd return. I gritted my teeth as I said, "Can we at least move him into shelter?"

"The inside of the house…it is…" Tomasz trailed off, then shook his head. "Don't go in there, love. I saw it through the door. It's a mess." He brushed my hair back from my face, and he whispered, "I really don't think they will come back here tonight. He still can't tell me what happened, but either they purposefully left him alive or he somehow hid from them. And if they *do* come back, it will be in a vehicle, so you'll see the lights or hear the engine long before they near the house—take him to the barn and hide. Okay?"

My breath caught, and I bit my lip hard and I forced myself to nod. My chest felt tight, as if the fear could choke the life right out of me too. Tomasz nodded toward Saul, encouraging me to go to the other man's side, and I whimpered a little as I made myself step closer to the bodies. I told myself not to look at the baby again. I told myself I could sit with him and pretend it wasn't there.

But I couldn't look away, and it was Tikva I stared at as I walked. As I came closer, the stench of blood became overwhelming, and my stomach turned over again and again. I battled to clamp down the urge to retch, but I walked to Saul's side, and I sat right beside him as Tomasz had done.

"Hello, Saul, it's Alina," I said, very gently. "Tomasz is going to get you fresh clothes. I'm going to stay with you. You are not alone. We are here for you."

The man turned to me, and I could see him trying to focus his gaze.

"Thank you for your kindness, Alina," he choked out. I nodded once, and as I went to look away again, he blurted, "I don't know if they caught Jan or if he turned us in. But he must have told them everything—*everything*—where we were hiding, how we were surviving. They wanted us to give Tomasz up, they told Eva they'd let her go if she told them where to find him but she was far too smart for that, my beautiful, brilliant wife. But then they took Tikva from Eva's arms—"

"You don't have to tell me," I whispered hastily, but he didn't seem to hear me.

"—and they put her on the ground and they shot her in the chest because they thought then we'd talk—but didn't they realize? Once they shot *her*, we had nothing left to survive for anyway. And then my wife..."

It occurred to me then that he wasn't speaking for my benefit at all. This was a repeat of those moments with Emilia each Sunday, on my own front steps. Just like little Emilia, Saul just needed to tell *someone* what had happened to his family, and I happened to be the only bystander now that he was ready to talk.

"Eva was hysterical, and the soldier who was holding her— he threw her against the wall and she went quiet and I could see her skull was… I tried but…it was…no… So I was hoping I'd be next and we could travel together to the afterlife but I didn't flinch or try to fight to get away once the others were gone. The sergeant was so angry that I didn't struggle…he said to leave me. He said it was a worse punishment to let me alone to die slowly." Saul's voice broke again. "I begged them to shoot me. I want to be with my family." I didn't know what to say to that, and all I could think was to do as Tomasz had done, and to slide my arm over Saul's thin shoulders. He slumped forward again, utterly broken as he whispered, "How God must hate me…to leave me to suffer like this? Surely…"

"Don't you say that," I said fiercely, and Saul startled, as if he'd only just noticed I was there. I was sorry to speak so harshly to him—but I knew all too well that the only way we'd survive the darkness was to hold on to a vestige of hope. There was nothing else I could do for Saul, except to keep my arm on his shoulder, and point him back to what he still had—and *all* that he had was his faith. "You must believe that if God allowed you to survive this far—there is a purpose to it. You *must* believe that there is work left for you to do on this Earth before you are released to peace. Hold tight to what you have left, Saul Weiss. And if *all you have left* is your faith, then you cling to it with every shred of strength you have left—do you hear me?"

He blinked at me. For a minute, I thought I'd gone too far, and I was shaken by an intense regret. Who was *I* to speak so harshly to this Jewish man about his faith—*in the very moment* when he nursed the cooling bodies of his entire family? Saul's shuddering breaths were coming harder and faster, but then he nodded sharply, and he turned his head toward the fields and he closed his eyes.

The string of words that burst from his lips was a language I didn't know, but our traditions were irrelevant in that moment— the depths of his loss transcended every one of our differences. We weren't Jew and Catholic, we weren't even man and woman— we were simply two human beings, grieving an inhuman act.

I squeezed my eyes tightly closed so I didn't accidentally look down at the face of the baby beside me, and I bowed my head while Saul and I prayed together.

Tomasz was very quiet when he returned, carrying two full pails of supplies, and with a set of clothing for Saul over his shoulders. He emptied the supplies onto the ground, then filled the pails at the well nearby. While I sat some distance away to give them privacy, my wonderful Tomasz helped Saul to clean the bodies, and finally, he helped Saul to bathe and dress himself.

Saul insisted on digging the grave, but he was just too weak and eventually he had to accept help. He would labor with visible difficulty until he had to stop, then Tomasz would work furiously until Saul had rested and was ready to take another turn. There wasn't time for depth or care—instead, they were seeking only to give Eva and baby Tikva the dignity of a resting place.

Saul carried his wife into the grave first. He was almost calm in that moment, as he carefully set her down and spoke to her gently, then he kissed her forehead. The calmness disappeared when Tomasz handed him the body of his infant daughter. Saul began to wail again, loudly and inconsolably. He bent to place the baby on Eva's chest, then he carefully wrapped her arms around their daughter. At the very last minute, Saul bent again and took one of the tiny leather shoes from Tikva's feet. As I watched that man climb reluctantly away from the family he was leaving in the earth, I knew how desperately he wished to be staying with them.

After Tomasz filled the grave, Saul dropped to his knees be-

side it, and he prayed aloud around shuddering sobs, clutching
that tiny shoe against his chest.

Tomasz wiped his eyes and jogged to my side. We embraced,
and he whispered thickly, "We're running out of time."

"I know," I whispered back. "But…we can't leave him here.
Is there anyone else we can take him to?" Tomasz stepped away
from me, and he stared at me then. "No," I said automatically.
"*No*, Tomasz. We can't stay here! You said it yourself, if we
stay—"

"I have no intention of us staying," he interrupted me. "It's
not safe for you—they know your name, they know what you
look like—*you* cannot stay, Alina. There is *no chance* I am going
to sit by and watch while—"

"They know who *you* are too now," I exclaimed. "Did you
not hear what Saul said? This is exactly why we have to leave."

"They know who *I* am, which means it is only a matter of
time before they figure out who Emilia is," Tomasz said abruptly.
I hadn't thought of that, and as he said it, my stomach dropped.
"I have to tell my other friends to flee. I have to warn your sister and get Emilia to safety. But…" He grabbed my upper arms
in his palms and he held me tightly, his gaze hard on mine as
he whispered, "Alina, you *must* go. We can't miss this chance."

"What? No! I can't go alone, Tomasz!" I cried in shock, and
his beautiful green eyes pleaded with me as his voice broke on
a sob.

"I know. I know that is too much to ask, and yet, I am asking even more of you than that."

I stared at him blankly, and then his gaze tracked back to Saul,
still sobbing on his knees by the grave.

"Tomasz…"

"He is weak. He is in shock. You are going to have to carry
him, if not physically, then emotionally. But you'll see, once
he's well. He is qualified—a fully equipped specialist with immense knowledge and skill…he can do so much good. He can

help hundreds, maybe thousands of people. It would be unforgivable for me to go tonight when *he* could go in my place."

"No! Don't ask this of me! I *can't*—"

"Please, *moje wszystko*."

"I can't go without you."

"I'm begging you, Alina," Tomasz said. He was still staring down at me with that same intense expression, but I heard the shift in his tone. He had made up his mind, and nothing I said was going to change it.

"How would this even work? Does he even have identity papers? Won't they be *Jewish* identity papers? Will they even admit him to the camp?"

"We can't risk it," Tomasz murmured. He released me gently, and I opened my eyes to see him reach into the pocket of his trousers. He carefully withdrew a card, which he opened to show me. Illuminated only by the moonlight, I saw his tattered passport. There was a tiny photo of him on the page, but the image was worn and so dark, even I might never have recognized him. "It is from before I even left for college, back when Father used to take me on vacations. Surely the camp will never know the difference. This photo looks nothing like either of us now that we both have beards. And his hair is darker, but the photo is so dark... I am *sure* he can pass. I am sure of it."

"I don't want to do this," I choked.

"It's not forever," Tomasz said, then he stopped to draw in a desperate breath. "As soon as my other friends are safe—as soon as *Emilia* and your sister are safe—I will find a way to come after you. Henry will arrange to get me false papers, and we will meet up in Buzuluk."

By then, we were both sobbing—clutching at each other, each one of us desperate to change the other's mind.

"I'm not strong enough to do this. I'm not brave enough. I'm not clever—"

"You are all of those things, Alina Dziak, and more," Tomasz said fiercely. "You are the fire that keeps my heart beating and the fuel that has powered my dreams even through this war. You are *my everything*. I know you better than anyone else, and that's the very reason I am trusting you and pleading with you to lead this man to safety tonight."

I couldn't say no to him. I *wanted* desperately to—to refuse, to plead weakness, to plant my feet in the soil of my homeland and to cling tightly to Tomasz, even if it meant death.

But I couldn't let him down. I couldn't disappoint him. And even at the time, I understood that *this* was something Tomasz needed to do. Before we could start our life afresh, he simply had to absolve himself of the guilt of his compliance with the *Wehrmacht* in Warsaw. Given the depth of his loss and the impossible circumstances Saul now faced, Tomasz would never be able to resist the opportunity to offer safe passage from Hell to the man who had once done the same for him.

"Please, *moje wszystko*," Tomasz whispered. *"Please."* I caught his head in my hands and I kissed him then, and that kiss said everything there wasn't time to say. "We will always find our way back to each other, Alina," he breathed, when we broke apart. "Our love is bigger than this war—I promise you that."

CHAPTER 32

Alice

Babcia's next address leads us to a medical clinic, situated in a huge historic building at the corner of two quiet streets. The building has been lovingly and lavishly restored—there's a wheelchair ramp built at the front door, and an automatic sliding glass door. Zofia tells me the large sign above the door simply says Trzebinia Medical Clinic, and none of the physicians' names listed on the sign end with "Slaski."

"That would have been a bit too easy," Zofia laughs.

But my eyes have fallen to a bronze plaque beside the front door, because although it's in Polish, one word *does* indeed say Slaski.

"Actually," I say wryly, and I point to the plaque.

Zofia's eyes widen, then she reads quietly, "'In memory of Dr. Aleksy Slaski. An example to all of leadership and courage, 1939.'" Zofia offers me a sad smile. "Hmm. Perhaps we are on the right track after all."

I take some photos of the plaque and the building, then I follow Zofia inside the door and survey the interior. It's mid-afternoon, and there are only two people sitting in the patient chairs—but behind the reception desk, a young woman and man are seated. The young man is talking on the phone, but the woman sets her headset down as we enter the room, and she stares at me with an intensity that makes me quite uncomfortable. I wonder what it is about my appearance that gives away that *I'm* the outsider, not Zofia. As we approach the desk, Zofia greets the receptionists in Polish, then gestures to me and introduces me, but she flicks back to English as she says, "Alice is here from the United States researching her family history. We believe Aleksy Slaski may have been her great-grandfather."

"Actually, that's not possible," the young woman interrupts Zofia, and she gives us a polite but apologetic smile.

"Why do you say that?" Zofia frowns.

"Well, Aleksy Slaski was *my* great-grandfather, and my grandmother was his only child."

At first, I'm not sure whether I should be disappointed or confused, but I quickly settle on confused, and so I decide to clarify.

"Was your grandmother Emilia?"

The woman's eyes widen, then she concedes carefully, "Yes, she *is*…?"

"Well," I say, and my heart starts racing as I realize we've stumbled upon a link to someone who's actually on Babcia's list. And the receptionist said *is*, not *was*, so… Emilia is alive! "That's fantastic—I was really hoping we could track her down—"

"Perhaps we should have a chat in private," the woman murmurs. She rises and motions toward a hallway. "Please, follow me."

She closes the door behind us as we step into a small meeting room. The woman is still offering that same polite smile, but she's crossed her arms over her chest and her gaze has narrowed *just* a little.

"What exactly is it you want from Emilia?" she asks me directly. "Is it money?"

"Oh no," I say, shaking my head. "I don't want anything from her, just to connect with her. Tomasz Slaski was her brother, and he was my grandfather."

Now, the hint of suspicion in the woman's gaze becomes more pronounced.

"I'm really sorry, that's not possible."

I give her a confused smile and start to counter with, "It's definitely—"

"I don't know where you are getting your information from, but Tomasz Slaski died in 1942," she interrupts me gently. I share a confused glance with Zofia. "I'm quite certain about this. I visit his grave with my grandmother sometimes."

"But…" Memories rise to the forefront of my mind. I think about my grandfather's gentle hugs and the way his rare bursts of laughter could light up a room. He was more *alive* than just about anyone I know, purely because of the way he threw his arms around life, as if he was constantly searching for an opportunity to make a difference or to give love. But this young woman doesn't know that, and she's looking at me with overt sympathy now.

"Tomasz is not an uncommon name in Poland, nor is Slaski. I think you have the wrong family."

"But your great-grandmother was Julita, yes?" Zofia prompts.

"Yes, but…"

"I'm not sure what the confusion is, but I *know* we have our facts straight," Zofia says. "I did the family history research myself. Aleksy and Julita Slaski were definitely the parents of Tomasz Slaski, born in 1920, and he *is* Alice's grandfather."

"Well, *I'm* sorry," the woman says, and she's just a little defensive now, "but I'm not mistaken, either—not about this."

I'm getting a little desperate here, so I try a different tack.

"What's your name?"

"I am Lia Truchen."

"It's really nice to meet you, Lia," I say quietly, hoping to get the conversation back onto a warm footing and disperse this odd tension that's starting to rise. "The thing is…my grandmother is ninety-five now and she's quite unwell. She left Poland during the war and wasn't ever able to return. My mother thinks that my grandmother used to send letters to Emilia, maybe even hundreds of letters over the years, trying to get back in touch once the war was ended. We're not sure exactly what she wanted, but it seemed to be very important to her."

"Emilia is also very old, and she's also quite unwell," Lia says quietly. "I'm sure you understand why I don't want to upset her. If she didn't reply to your grandmother's letters, there must be a reason."

Lia is trying very hard not to be rude—if anything, her gaze is pleading with me for understanding. And I *do* understand her wanting to protect her grandmother—probably better than most, but that doesn't mean I can let this go.

"Perhaps they could just talk on the phone—"

"Emilia is very frail..." Lia says, a little firmer now.

"Maybe..." I feel this moment slipping away from me, so I fumble to get Lia back on side. "I don't want to upset your grandmother, either—that would be terrible. But perhaps if you could *tell* her about my grandmother, perhaps she might be interested—"

"*Who* is your grandmother?"

"My grandmother is Hanna Slaski—" I say automatically.

But Zofia says at the same time, "She was Alina Dziak before her marriage."

"Alina or Hanna?" Lia looks at us, her suspicion no longer hidden at all.

"It's complicated," I sigh, then I briefly explain the morning's events. "But the point is, Emilia might know her as Hanna *or* Alina. But she's definitely Slaski. The surname we're sure of, because she took it when she married my Pa."

"Well, she'd be Alina *Slaksa* if she'd married a Polish man," Lia points out. I look at Zofia in confusion, and she nods.

"Well, yes. It is Polish convention to change some suffixes to denote gender—a female *would* generally be 'Slaksa' rather than 'Slaski.' But I see this all the time with American clients—the convention generally does not persist after immigration."

"It doesn't matter anyway—I don't know her by either name. I'm sure my grandmother has never mentioned her." Lia sighs.

"I still think you've got the wrong family, or perhaps the wrong town."

"No, my grandmother definitely said Trzebinia, and we even found her childhood home. Besides, *all* of the other details line up," I say. I look to Zofia, then double-check, "Am I missing something here?"

"Everything lines up," Zofia says, frowning at Lia now. "Alice and I are quite sure of our facts. Are you sure the disconnect isn't at *your* end?"

"Surely you can see how upsetting it would be for me to go to my *eighty-five-year-old* grandmother and tell her that some American woman thinks her beloved big brother was *alive* for seventy-five years longer than he actually was."

Lia isn't *quite* rude, and she doesn't throw us out of the building, not exactly. Regardless, Zofia and I quickly find ourselves back outside in the sunshine.

"The family must be wealthy," Zofia says.

"But we told her we didn't want money," I say helplessly. She shrugs.

"If you're Tomasz's granddaughter, perhaps he was entitled to a share of whatever inheritance Aleksy left behind. And if that was significant, maybe she's nervous about what that would mean for her family." Zofia glances back at the building. "It wouldn't surprise me if she made up the story about the gravesite, just because it gives her an excuse to refuse to engage with us."

"How do we sort this out?"

Zofia pauses thoughtfully, but then she slowly shakes her head.

"Well—the birth records were clear. There *was* only one Tomasz Slaski born in this parish in that period, at least that I could see. As far as I'm concerned, the only thing we can clarify is Lia's story."

"Maybe hers *is* a different family with similar names."

"In a tiny little town like this, what are the odds of there being *two* Aleksy Slaskis who married Julitas and then had children named Emilia and Tomasz?"

"Well..." I ask hesitantly, "How common are those names?"

"Not *that* common," Zofia laughs.

I hesitate, glancing back at the doors. Then I straighten my posture and say, "Wait here? And if she throws me out bodily this time, try to catch me before I hit the cobblestone?"

I walk back to the counter, where Lia and the young man have their heads close together, and they are whispering furiously. They only notice me when I'm close, and I bend down low and I say, "Lia, I understand you wanting to protect your grandmother—I'd probably do the same. But *my* grandmother doesn't have long left, and she's sent me here on this wild-goose chase and she's looking for something. I just can't help but think that your Emilia might be able to shed some light on all of this—and who knows? Perhaps this confusion is part of the puzzle. So, will you at least *think* about talking to her? Just tell her Alina Dziak or Hanna Wiśniewski is trying to get in touch with her, that's all I ask. And—" Lia is glaring at me, but I reach across the desk, help myself to a pen and a sticky note, then scribble down my name and cell phone number. "I'm here for another few days," I say. "Call me anytime."

Lia hesitates, but when I hold her gaze, she eventually nods. I breathe my thanks, then quickly spin on my heel and leave before she can change her mind. I find Zofia leaning against the wall of the clinic. She surveys me warily, then laughs.

"What on earth did you say to her?"

"I felt like she slammed the door in our face," I admit. "So I stuck my shoe in it, and made sure if she changes her mind, she has a way to contact me. That's all I can do, right?"

Later that night, after dinner and a glass of wine at the hotel restaurant downstairs, I pick up the phone and call Mom. She's driving to the hospital when I call, and her greeting seems unusually subdued.

"Hello, Alice."

"Hi, Mom. How was your day?"

"Fine," she says, but she sounds distant.

"Is everything okay with Babcia?"

"Oh, it's fine. I'm just tired...a little confused by this whole *secret identity* thing with her. I don't understand why she wouldn't tell me if she changed her name," Mom sighs.

"I know," I murmur. "I'm sorry, Mom. I don't know what to say."

"I'm just hoping she recovers enough to explain herself. I was thinking that your friend there or a translator could ask her about it, but I can't see the point, because how can she tell us what happened if she can't speak? There's a million reasons she might have changed her name so we're never going to *guess*, and the AAC doesn't exactly have a button for this." Mom trails off, then she clears her throat and asks, "How's the rest of the expedition through Poland going?"

"Good. We found out that Emilia Slaski is still alive. We found her granddaughter today, and her name is *Lia*, which is surely just a shortening of her grandmother's name."

"So, will you get to speak to this Emilia? Maybe she can tell us what happened with Babcia."

"Something weird happened, actually. Lia was adamant that Emilia's brother Tomasz died in 1942, but...well, obviously he didn't."

"So, some mix-up, then?"

"Yes, definitely," I say. "Zofia seemed to think Emilia was assuming I was after her inheritance or something and trying to protect her family but..." I pause, then admit reluctantly, "My gut says that's not it, to be honest."

"Well, sometimes you have to trust your gut," Mom says quietly. "And, Alice, given you're in Poland despite my...subtle disapproval..." I snort, and I hear a smile in her voice when she continues. "I do suspect you already know this but I'm going

to remind you anyway. You must always remember that sometimes knocking on doors just isn't enough."

"What else is there in a case like this?"

"Sometimes, if you want something badly enough, you have
to smash the damn door down."

"If I was going to make a Julita Slaski-Davis motivational
poster, that's exactly what the tagline would be." I smile to myself. Mom laughs.

"Damn straight, daughter. I'm at the hospital so I'm going to
go now. We'll talk tomorrow?"

"Thanks, Mom."

Even after Mom and I say our goodbyes, I'm thinking about her
advice. At home, I automatically apply my mom's level of determination to accessing help and support for Eddie, but when it comes
to connecting with the man I share a bed with, it's a whole other
story. Why *haven't* I forced the tension with Wade to a head in the
last few years? I was definitely raised to address things straight-
on, so I'm not quite sure how I managed to find myself in a situation where so many things remain unspoken in my own home.

I run a bath, buying some time to think before I place a call
back to Wade. When I'm there at home, in the day-to-day grind, I
never have the space and time to try to be an impartial observer of
the dynamics of our family, but now, I start to reflect on the pat-
terns we've fallen into. I think about the resentment I feel toward
Wade—that awful feeling that's muddled up with guilt and confusion because I'm in this role where I'm somehow the domestic
kingpin of our family, but not at all the equal financial provider
I always assumed I'd be—somehow both a reluctant dependent
and the family chief operations officer. I think about the way I've
let that tension fester for so long. I'm not at all a timid woman, so
why haven't I been more assertive at home? Why haven't I forced
the issue of Wade's disconnect with Eddie? Why haven't I *demanded* an equal partner in the parenting that needs to be done?

I'm terrified of what I might lose if I do.

Maybe I cling too tightly to the things I can control—the routine *I* put in place for Eddie—the tasks around the house I like to be done *just so*—because deeper and broader and wider than all of that run the things in my life I can't control. I run myself *ragged* trying to control the world that exists around him, because I can't change him at all.

I can't fix Eddie, because Eddie is not broken. He is simply different, and he is going to be like this forever because this is who he is. This is what my life is always going to look like—probably into old age, because Callie will grow up and leave home, but Eddie will never live independently.

I haven't grieved the life I thought I'd live, and I sure as Hell haven't grieved the son I thought I'd get. I got right on with accepting the son I *did* get, which is exactly the opposing coping mechanism to the one my husband has applied to the situation.

I sink a little deeper into the bath, tears filling my eyes as I'm struck by a wave of longing so intense that it's all I can do to stay where I am. I want to run to the airport and fly home *right now* and take Wade and the kids into my arms and hold them all so close that they can never slip away. Even Wade—maybe especially Wade. He and I actually need *each other* to achieve some kind of balance.

I can't wait to hear Wade's voice and to resolve the lingering tension before I go to bed. It's 10:00 p.m. in Krakow now—that means 4:00 p.m. back home, and because it's Wednesday, he and Eddie should be in the viewing room at ballet, watching Callie's class. I slip quickly out of the bath, pull on the hotel robe and call, but when the call connects, it's immediately obvious to me that they are *not* in the viewing room at ballet.

"Wade?" I call, surprised.

"Eddie, I love you," Eddie echoes, surprise and delight in his tone. The phone shifts a little and his face fills the screen. He stares into the phone, bringing it too close.

Eddie looks blissfully happy—his big green eyes are positively brimming with joy. Eddie looks as if he's just been given some kind of deliriously magical gift. Eddie looks as if my call is icing on an already pretty exceptional cake. As I digest all this, I suddenly recognize the brick wall behind him.

"Hello, baby," I say softly. "Daddy has taken you to the train station, huh?"

"Hello, Alice," Wade says, from offscreen. "Yes, we figured there was not much point watching Pascale at ballet so we went for a walk. Once we got onto the block near the station Eddie went on autopilot and all but dragged me in here, so I'm guessing you do this too sometimes."

I would never take Eddie for a spontaneous walk like that. I'd never risk it. What if we ran into a situation where he had a meltdown? What if he ran off? I plan my outings with Eddie like teachers plan their excursions—I schedule things, I put them onto his visual timetable, I consider the risks, I make contingency plans.

But that also means I don't ever get to see that same, surprised joy on Eddie's face that Wade has managed to achieve right now. There are no surprises in Eddie's life with me. I'm utterly bewildered by the jealousy I feel.

"We go there on Friday morning if he stays at school all day on Thursday, and we park at the same place for ballet, so I guess he knows the way…" I say, my voice trailing off. I fall silent then, watching as Eddie's gaze leaves the phone screen to focus on something in front of him. I suspect from the ever-growing excitement in his eyes that he's looking at an approaching train. "What's the plan tonight?" I ask Wade.

"Soup is the plan tonight," he says. He's still offscreen, but there's no mistaking the edge of bitterness in his tone. "Is that why you called? To check?"

"I called because I had a really emotional and confusing day, and I just wanted to hear your voice," I say. It's *astounding* how I genuinely wanted to connect with him on this call, but less than sixty seconds into it he makes a comment like that and in an instant, I feel defensive, and the bitterness that leaps into my tone instantly matches the level in his. No wonder we're in such a mess. I feel like we're on either side of a very long footbridge and we're both afraid to set out onto it. Each time one of us steps forward, the other steps back in case the bridge can't take our weight. I can't fight with him tonight—I just don't have the emotional reserves. I take a deep breath, and say evenly, "But now isn't really the time for that chat, I guess. I'll talk to you tomorrow."

Eddie's face disappears from the screen, and in his place, I see Wade. There are heavy bags beneath his eyes and for the first time in living memory, he hasn't shaved on a workday.

"Don't hang up, Ally," he murmurs. "I have to say something—and brace yourself, this is going to be shocking."

I can tell he's about to make a joke, and I laugh a little in anticipation.

"I'm braced," I joke in return. "Go ahead."

"Two kids? Significantly more difficult to manage than three hundred lab rats. *This* is no holiday. And I'm really sorry about before—and I'm sorry about the soup," he sighs heavily, then says wryly, "Let it be known that I'm sorry about pretty much everything at this point."

"I'm sorry too," I whisper, and then I touch the screen with my forefinger, feeling again that soul-deep pang of longing. I stare right into his eyes on the screen and my voice is rough with emotion as I choke, "I really miss you, Wade."

"I miss you too." I hear the rumbling of the coming train, and then I see the rush of wind mess with Wade's hair. I want to ask him about the new Go-Gurt labels, and to see Eddie again—to see that Eddie really is okay. But this clearly isn't the time to talk, because Wade has to shout into the phone as the train draws near. "Let's talk properly tomorrow, when I'm not at a train station?"

I laugh and nod, then kiss my finger and press it to the camera.

"I love you," I whisper. He reads my lips, and I see him echo it back to me.

CHAPTER 33

Alina

As we walked back to my family home, Saul tried hard to convince us to leave him behind, but he was too exhausted to make a convincing argument. He eventually gave up on Tomasz, and when he instead tried to convince me, I found myself in the god-awful position of taking Tomasz's side.

"It makes sense for you to join me on the journey," I forced myself to say. "Tomasz is needed here."

It would take at least six hours for the plaster cast to dry, and Tomasz wanted it close to set before we boarded the truck. The original plan would have had us back to my family home with plenty of time for the cast to cure—but now we arrived back at the farmhouse just as the clock struck 3:00 a.m. I'd be boarding the truck with the cast still well and truly soft.

"You will have to be so careful," Tomasz whispered, shaking his head as he wound the bandage onto my forearm. I had been staring up at the floorboards of my childhood home—trying to convince myself that this really was going to be my very last time there—unable to bear to watch as he wound the plaster around the canister onto my wrist. "Be absolutely sure not to bump it until it dries—it simply has to look realistic or someone might become suspicious that there's something valuable in there. And *do not let this cast get wet*. Even once it's cured—the film must stay dry."

"Farther toward the wrist, Tomasz," Saul said. His voice was suddenly strong, as if he hadn't just lost his whole world a few hours earlier. Tomasz adjusted the placement of the soft bandage that would line the cast, shifting it a little farther from my elbow.

"Better?"

"Yes. You are very short on supplies—better to do a short cast and make it thick, to hide the bulk of the canister. Remember you're not actually needing to stabilize the movement of her arm in this case, however if this were a real fracture…well, this would be inadequate. However, in our circumstances, if anyone even knows to question the length of it, Alina can say the fracture was right above the wrist and her physician did the best he could with what he had." I looked down at Saul. He was sitting on the floor against one of the walls of the cellar. His arms were around his legs, his knees drawn up to his body, and he stared up at us on the makeshift bed with flat eyes and a deathly pale face. He met my gaze and his tone softened a little as he suggested, "If someone asks how you got the injury, say you fell and had stretched your hand out before you—the wrist bore the impact. Say the bone was reset by a field surgeon, and it was agonizing—white-hot, searing pain. With such detail, the story is at least realistic."

When I looked back to Tomasz, he gave a pointed nod toward Saul, and I swallowed. Because clearly the medical knowledge was second nature to Saul, spilling out of him even at this point when his mind was full of grief and pain. I could see why Tomasz thought that was important—but it only underlined the decision we'd already made—that Tomasz would stay, and Saul would go. Brilliant surgeon or not—the man was currently sitting on the floor of the cellar, intermittently weeping, and every now and then there were periods when he'd fall completely silent to rock back and forth like a child, holding that tiny leather shoe against his cheek.

The most responsibility I'd ever experienced before was when I had to find Emilia a temporary home—it had been overwhelming and terrifying—and *this* dwarfed *that* by miles. Not only was I now a reluctant courier of Henry's photographs, but I would also be dragging along behind me a man who had *just* suffered unimaginable tragedy and trauma. Instead of following Tomasz, I'd have to lead the way. Tomasz leaned all the way over my arm now, assuming quite an awkward posture and momentarily blocking my view of the cast he was constructing. Unthinkingly, I reached up to touch the thick locks of his hair. He desperately needed a haircut, and it was almost irrational how much I wished we had the time for me to do that for him once more. Such a small thing, but it would have been so lovely to nurture him in that way, as if that could remind him while we were apart how deeply I cared for him. When he sat up, he smiled at me, sadly.

"It's going to be fine, you know. *You* are going to be fine."

"And you'll find me," I said, not for the first time. In fact, I'd been repeating this almost the entire walk back from the Golaszewski farm—checking then double- and triple-checking that I still understood the plan. "You'll get this sorted here, and you'll make the same journey—you'll meet us at Buzuluk."

"That's exactly right."

"And if the camp won't accept that your passport belongs to Saul?"

"Then you will find a way to *make* them accept him."

"And if they catch us before we get to the Soviet border. What do I do then?"

"That won't happen." He dismissed the mere suggestion as if it was entirely impossible, which made me impatient and somewhat furious—given there was *no way* for us to know how safe this plan was. For all we knew, the Nazis intercepting me was the likely outcome, and I knew I had to be prepared.

"Answer me, Tomasz. If we are intercepted before we even leave the district, and Saul has a passport with *your* name on it. What exactly am I to do then?"

"It won't—"

"We both know it's a possibility!" I exclaimed, then I lowered my voice. "They were already looking for you at Warsaw because you deserted the *Wehrmacht*, and now they are looking for you locally because Jan told them about your work for Zegota." Tomasz sighed and nodded. "So tell me—*what do I do if we are caught?*"

Who was this woman, staring bravely into the face of danger? She had been within me all along—I'd seen glimpses of her that day at the square when I saved Emilia, then again when I had decided to support Tomasz despite the danger. I was nearing full flight now, and only a trace remained of the scared little girl I'd once been.

Tomasz stared intently at the bandage as he wound it around and around my forearm, the lump of the long canister slowly disappearing into the bulk. After a while, he whispered, "If...if something happens to you, and the film is lost, there is nothing we can do about that. Henry might have different instructions when we meet with him at the pickup point, but for me?" He finally looked up at me, and his eyes swam in fresh tears. "I simply have to believe you'll make it. I have to believe you're going to be cursing me in a few days' time when you're magnificently free in Soviet territory but the cast is starting to itch and you can't reach beneath the plaster to scratch it. That is the *only way* I can watch you go." I reached up with my left hand and cupped his jaw, and he rested his head against my palm. "I hate it when we're apart, Alina. I *hate* it, but there is just no other way."

"You're sure this is the right thing for us to do," I whispered. He stared right into my eyes and he nodded.

"I have never been more sure of anything in my life."

I exhaled, then sat up a little straighter.

"Okay then, Tomasz. Okay."

My confidence came and went in waves, and I was once again second-guessing the whole plan as we approached the meeting point. Tomasz was no longer marching in strides ahead of me—he was behind me, all but dragging Saul, who was struggling to keep up. Tomasz kept reminding us that we had to hurry—we couldn't afford to miss the truck. Every time he said it, I couldn't help but wonder if we'd all be better off if we did.

Henry was waiting for us, pacing beside the main road. The dawn was near and the darkness was disappearing by the second, and once he saw us, he sprinted toward us. I saw the confusion on his face as it registered that we had a third person in our party.

"They may have Nadia, and they are looking for me," Tomasz called before Henry could ask. "We have to hurry."

Henry stared at us, his gaze lingering on the cast on my arm. "What has happened?"

"Saul is going in my place, and they need to leave *now*."

Henry fell silent for a moment. When the moment began to stretch, Tomasz stepped toward the older man and he dropped his voice, so low that I could barely hear it.

"There is no time, Henry," Tomasz murmured. "They *know* who I am…what I've been doing… Soon enough, they will be looking for me if they aren't already. Jakub needs to get on the road as fast as he can, in case they set up checkpoints. There is just no time for debate."

"Tomasz," Henry said, lips pursed. "Are you sure about this?"

"There is *no* other way."

Henry sighed and ran his hand through his hair, then threw his hands into the air and turned to me.

"You have the film?"

"I do."

"You have the rubles?"

I patted the leather bag I'd slipped across my shoulders, now hidden under my clothes.

"I do."

"And you know the plan?" he said, as he withdrew from the pocket of his coat a small envelope. I nodded, and he held the envelope up right before me. "Here is a new identity card for you, in the name of Hanna Wiśniewski. It's a forgery, and not a particularly convincing one, but it is the best I could do on such short notice, so you will have to make it work."

I took the envelope and moved to put it into the pocket of my coat. Henry shook his head, and said incredulously, "Tuck it into your undergarments, Alina! You must protect this with your life. Do you understand me? No identity papers means no admission to the camp, and the British soldiers will be looking for my film *inside the camp!*"

Tears stung at my eyes, but I blinked them away as I pushed the envelope beneath my clothes, into the leather bag with the rubles. Henry looked from me to Saul, and he gave me a somewhat-desperate look.

"Dear God," he muttered. "This is…"

"Henry. Alina is up to this," Tomasz said flatly. "She will get that film where it needs to go. She is every bit as resourceful and capable as I am. Now *let's go.*"

I grabbed Henry's arm frantically.

"If I…if we happen to get captured? Is there anything I can do?"

He exhaled heavily, then gave me a searching look.

"If you're captured and there's time, destroy the film. Find a way. Otherwise…we must just hope that whatever happens to *your* body, that your captors don't pay any attention to the cast, because if they find that film, it won't be long before they find me and my colleagues too."

We stood by the side of the road discussing the possibility of our executions as if it was nothing much at all—because in the scheme of things it wasn't. In that circumstance, death was simply one of many things that could happen.

"Okay," I said stiffly. "Got it."

Henry led the way down a track, and soon the truck came into view. I hadn't prepared myself for the sight of a man in a

Wehrmacht uniform, leaning against the truck, smoking a cigarette. It was all I could do to stop myself from turning and running in the opposite direction.

"That's Jakub," Henry said quietly. And of course it was—
because who else could drive openly on the roads to the Eastern Front, but a *Wehrmacht* driver, driving a *Wehrmacht* truck?
I just hadn't prepared myself for the sight of it. I hesitated and
once again drew Henry's ire.

"We must hurry, Alina—you know what's at stake here, girl!"

It took more strength than I'd ever realized I possessed to
start my feet walking again and move *toward* the man in that
uniform, then to place my life in his hands.

"I'm Jakub," the driver said as we neared.

"Alina," I said automatically.

"No," Henry corrected me impatiently. "You are *not* Alina.
Who are you?"

I looked at him, but my mind was blank.

"I...can't remember..."

"Hanna Wiśniewski!" Henry said impatiently. "You are *Hanna
Wiśniewski.*"

"You know the plan?" Jakub glanced between us, his brows
drawing. I swallowed hard as I nodded. Jakub frowned toward
Tomasz, who was now jogging toward us—*carrying* Saul in his
arms.

"Who's going? There's *definitely* no room for a third in there."

"Just me and Saul—the man being carried," I said miserably.
Jakub winced. "Are you sure you're up for this, lady?"

"Of course she is," Tomasz said flatly, having finally caught
up to us. Inside the truck, I could see the row of rations boxed
against the deepest wall, behind several barrels and other loose
containers. Jakub helped me to climb up into the tray, and Tomasz did the same for Saul, then leaped up to stand beside me.
Henry was standing at ground level, but he was watching us
and wringing his hands.

"You *must* be sure you are quiet," Jakub said. "Perhaps you can whisper or talk quietly when we're out on the road, but if the truck slows for any reason or it stops, you must assume I'm doing a delivery or picking up, and then be absolutely silent. So much as a cough or a sneeze—and not only are you both dead, but so am I."

"What are you transporting?" I had a sudden terror that we'd be hidden in the back of a truck filled with explosives. Just *one more thing* to be terrified of—death by accidental explosion.

"Just fresh fruit and vegetables grown by the prisoners at Auschwitz," he said, then he added bitterly, "The senior officers on the front line demand fresh produce, all the better if it's drenched in the blood of our people."

Jakub walked to the boxes. He slipped a screwdriver from his pocket, opened a panel, and then helped Saul to climb inside. Tomasz turned to me, and I caught his face between my palms and I searched his gaze desperately, looking for some sign of hesitance that I could exploit to convince him to come with me like we'd planned. He seemed only determined, and when I recognized this, I felt all of my courage slipping away all over again—replaced instead by sheer panic.

"I don't want to do this," I choked, riding on one final wave of hesitance. "I can't..."

"You can," Tomasz simply whispered, smoothing my hair down against my head, peppering my face with soft kisses. "I know you can."

"But...instead, let me *stay*. With you. Until you can go too. Saul can go on his own."

"Alina, you already have the cast on," he said very gently. "Henry has arranged this for us *only* because of that film. There is no other way."

"But we could..." I started to protest, but my voice trailed off. We could... What? There was no more plaster, and no way to get our hands on any more. If we took the cast off, we'd have to think of another way to smuggle the film out—and this one thing had been difficult enough to arrange. Tomasz reached to touch my chin, lifting my gaze back to his.

"Saul *can't* go on his own, Alina." His gaze flicked behind me, then he added softly, "He's broken, my love. He's barely holding himself together."

"But...what if you never find me?"

"Alina," he said, very softly. "Don't you know by now?"

"Don't say it," I choked, and I shook my head fiercely. "Don't you dare say it when you're putting me into this truck and sending me off by myself."

"But, Alina," Tomasz whispered, and he lifted his hand to press the pad of his forefinger against my lips. "It is the only truth I live by. Everything else is gone. We are made for each other...meant to be together. It doesn't matter what happens in this life or the next, Alina. We'll always find our way back to each other."

"But what if you can't find me?" I wept, and he brushed my tears away and he said very quietly, "Just promise me one last thing..." he said now, his eyes flicking briefly to the crate behind me. "Take good care of Saul." Tomasz tucked his forefinger under my chin, prompting me to meet his gaze. "Promise me, Alina. He is a good man—a better man than I am. Think of the people he can help with the skills he has. You must take care of him for as long as he needs you to."

I never could say no to Tomasz, especially not that day. I could tell by the stubborn set of his jaw and the fierce determination in his gaze that these things he was asking of me meant the world to him.

First, I had to walk away from him—and if that wasn't already an impossible ask, then, I had to continue his work in helping Saul to escape.

"Promise, Alina?" Tomasz asked me one last time. I closed my eyes, because I couldn't look at him while I did so, but then I nodded. "Good girl."

He reached forward and kissed me again then. This kiss was different from any other we'd shared. It was a plea, a promise, and a farewell. When we broke apart, he was softly crying, and my heart was threatening to pound its way through the wall of my chest. I wanted to beg him to find *any other way*, but I knew it was pointless to do so—and besides, there was no time left for cowardice.

I crawled into the crate then, and as I'd feared, it was tiny, barely a foot wide and the width of the truck across. The scent of the pine and of dust was overwhelming. There would be enough room for us both to sit, and enough room for us to stand at a crouch so we could turn around if we needed to. I sat behind Saul and closed my eyes. Just then, I felt Tomasz reach inside to press two fingers gently against my lips.

"What is your name?" he asked me. "Your new name."

My mind was blank and I began to panic all over again.

"I don't know, Tomasz. I already don't remember. I can't do—"

"Hanna Wiśniewski," Henry called impatiently. "Repeat in your mind until it sticks, Alina. *Learn it*."

"You learn it too," I said, frantically clutching Tomasz's hand before he could withdraw it. "You'll need to know what name I'm using so you can find me. Right?"

"I have already memorized it, my love. Your name is Hanna Wiśniewski," Tomasz whispered. "Travel safely, Hanna."

"I will," I said, as bravely as I could, given I was only *just* holding the sobs at bay. "I'll see you at Buzuluk."

And then Tomasz and Jakub sealed the door, and Saul and I were trapped alone in the darkness.

"Are you okay?" I whispered to Saul.

"Do you think this is how they feel?" he whispered back. I could hear the rising panic in his voice.

"Who?"

"My family in that grave," he said, his voice a little louder now. "The suffocation…the darkness…it would feel like this, wouldn't it?"

Every muscle in my body tensed. For a minute, his words sent me into such a spiraling panic that I almost convinced myself that *I* was in a grave—but I forced myself to push down the panic and return to the present reality.

One breath at a time, Alina.

Breathe in. Oh! I found some air!

Breathe out. That will be the last of me. Now I will suffocate.

Breathe in. Oh! There is a little more air after all.

"No." I choked out the words he needed, even if I didn't believe them myself at the time. "I don't think this is how they feel. I think they are freed from feelings like this. I think they are waiting for you on the other side, and *they* are safe and at peace."

I felt him relax then, even though his only answer was a muffled sob.

CHAPTER 34

Alice

As Zofia and I begin our second trip toward Trzebinia, she chatters as she drives—falling automatically into tour guide mode. I keep zoning out as she's speaking. All of this information really *is* interesting—but the truth is my mind is elsewhere.

I'm thinking about these wide-open days ahead of me, and the fact that I have absolutely no idea what to do with them. And even more disturbing, Mom's words on the phone last night are swirling around my mind, giving me all sorts of crazy ideas.

Sometimes you have to smash the damn door down.

"What's the plan?" Zofia asks me, when we turn off the highway into the little town. I sigh and lean back in my chair. I'm about to say I don't know, but then it occurs to me that in all of the places we visited yesterday, only *one* revealed a lead.

"To the clinic again, please," I say.

I ask Zofia to stay in the car this time, hoping that Lia will be more open to me if I go in to the clinic alone.

"Cousin to cousin?" Zofia suggests with a grin.

"Something like that," I say. I'm sick with nerves remembering how determined Lia was yesterday that she couldn't help me, but I force myself to march into the clinic. Lia actually groans when she sees me in the reception area, and I hold up my hands as if that will placate her.

"Come with me," she says abruptly, and she swipes the headset from her head to throw it onto the desk.

I wave to her companion and offer a weak, "Hi."

"Hello," he says uncertainly. I follow Lia down the hallway, then turn into the meeting room.

"I told you—" she greets me with audible frustration, and I hold my hands up again and try to make her understand.

"Listen," I say, very quietly. "You're my *only* lead, and I can tell that you love your grandmother just as much as I love mine, so I understand why you don't want to help me. But I hope *you* can understand my position too. The *only* concrete thing I've found since I arrived here is her childhood home—which isn't giving up *any* secrets—and *you*. So—okay, there really does seem to be some confusion around my Pa and your Tomasz Slaski—but if you can spare me a few minutes, perhaps we can resolve that. You said Emilia still visits his grave, right?"

"She does," Lia says. Sadness leaps into her gaze, and in that instant, I *know* she's not lying about this. "Every month. She used to go more often when she was younger. He was her hero."

"Okay," I say, then I suck in a breath and ask hopefully, "So, can you tell me where *the grave* is?" Lia hesitates just a little, and I adjust the strap of my handbag because I'm too nervous to be still while I wait for her answer. The silence stretches some more, and I try to make a joke. "I promise not to camp out there for a month and bully my way into seeing your grandmother. I'd just like to *see* it."

"Fine," Lia sighs. She walks across the room to a cabinet, and withdraws a piece of paper and a pen. She sets both onto the board table in the center of the room, then scrawls down an address. "It's not easy to find—you have to drive out of town. Follow the main road—it curves around behind the hill you can see to the east from pretty much any point in town. There's an old property there—this is the street address. We drive all the way onto the farm, but my grandmother has the only key to the gate, so you'll have to park in the driveway and jump the fence."

I know *exactly* the place she's describing—there's no way it can be anywhere but Babcia's family home. Still, I'm too nervous to get my hopes up, so I interrupt her gently to ask, "Is this Świętojańska, 4?" I say. Predictably, I *totally* muddle the pronunciation on the street name—but not so much that Lia doesn't understand it, because her gaze narrows.

"I don't understand." She scowls. "You already know where it is?"

"That house," I say, but my voice comes out a little husky, so I pause to clear my throat, then I ask, "Why is the grave behind *that* house?"

"The house is abandoned—it has been since the war, not even the communists wanted it," Lia tells me. "But he's not buried there *at* the house, he's buried on the hill behind it. I'm just directing you to the house because it's much easier to get to the grave from that side than from the town side now. There are new houses all along the hill on this side so the path is blocked."

"But *that* particular spot...? Why there at *that* hill?"

Lia passes me the paper and frowns.

"I have no idea. Now tell me—*how* did you know that address?"

"It was my grandmother's childhood home," I tell her, and her eyes widen. There's an awkward pause while she ponders this, then Lia concedes, "Well, that's quite a coincidence."

"Surely that *can't* be a coincidence," I say incredulously.

"This entire area was overrun by Nazis. There are unfortunate souls buried in every conceivable place around here—my great-uncle is lucky he at least has a headstone. But I'll be honest with you—I have no idea *how* he came to be buried there. My grandmother isn't exactly keen to discuss the worst days of her life on a regular basis, you know? She won't talk about the war, and we've given up asking her."

I laugh weakly as I nod.

"I know exactly what that's like."

"That's actually *why* I can't let you talk to her," Lia says softly. "She's like a different woman on the days when we visit his grave. It costs her something to honor his memory, and I won't ask more of her than that. But if it helps you, by all means, visit the grave." She shrugs. "I just don't think there's anything more I can do to help you beyond this one thing, okay?"

"Thank you," I say, then I throw myself at her and hug her. She stiffens, then returns the hug briefly and nods toward the door.

"Good luck."

Half an hour later, Zofia and I stand at a clearing in the woods behind my grandmother's childhood home, staring at the creepiest thing I have ever seen.

Tomasz Slaski. 1920 to 1942

His name is etched into the polished red granite of a tall headstone. The stone is clean; clearly lovingly maintained. A semi-fresh set of mixed flowers is dying on the grass in front of the stone, and it's surrounded by clean candles, the wicks unlit now but black from prior use. There's even a few LED lanterns in various shapes and sizes. Zofia bends and turns one of the lanterns on, and it lights up without delay.

I look back to the stone and stare at the name again. This time, I notice that below the name and dates, a medal has been attached to the headstone. The inscription on the medal is in Hebrew.

Zofia and I stare silently at the grave for a while, like it's a puzzle we can solve if we just stare long enough, but it's not long before I find I just can't *look* at it any longer. I turn away, and exhale shakily.

"Poor Emilia," Zofia murmurs. I glance back at her, and find she's crouching close to the medal. She runs her finger over the characters very gently. "This is the medal awarded to the *Righteous Among The Nations*. It indicates that *this* Tomasz Slaski took great personal risk during the war to aid Jewish people. It means his name is listed on the Wall of Honor in the Garden of the Righteous in Jerusalem." She pauses, then bows her head. "It is a big deal. Truly, a huge honor."

"This is just *awful*," I say, and I stand and frown. I'm feeling suddenly irritable, as if my skin has grown too tight, and I shiver because despite the sweltering day, there's a chill running down my spine as I stare at a grave that *I know* is not my grandfather's, despite the fact that grandfather's name is on it. "It's just so creepy, isn't it?" My hand twitches against the phone in my hand, and I raise it to take a photo, but as soon as I do, I lower the phone in a rush. Zofia stands and offers me a questioning glance.

"I can't show her," I blurt. "It would…it will upset her so much!"

Zofia inclines her head in acknowledgment.

"But this is quite the mystery, no?"

"It's Pa's name and that's the year he was born, but this *obviously* can't be Pa."

"No," Zofia agrees softly, and she stands. "But Emilia Slaski doesn't know that."

"How could this *happen*?" I whisper. "Do you think this is what Babcia sent us for? To tell Pa's sister the truth?"

There's no way to answer that question, and I'm not surprised when Zofia remains silent. We stare at the grave for another few minutes in silence, then she asks me, "How did your grandparents get to the US?"

"I don't even know. All I know is that Mom was born in January '43 and they were already settled there by then."

Zofia frowns.

"That can't be right."

I stand and look at her quizzically.

"No, I'm sure it is."

"They must have left before the war."

"I know they were here when the war began, that's about all I do know, actually."

"But…they left *during* the occupation?"

"They must have."

"That's…difficult to believe." Zofia shakes her head slowly, her eyebrows knitted. "It was all but impossible to get out of Nazi-held territory."

"All I know is that they came on a boat from England. I have no idea how they got from here to England."

Zofia exhales, then she looks at the headstone again.

"I'm just thinking aloud here but—do you think Emilia might have *assumed* her brother died, but he was actually on his way to America? She must have been very young when this happened. Perhaps she or someone else even mistook another body for his? Because if *this* guy died in 1942, and Tomasz fled from Poland in 1942…"

"That might be the only explanation," I say. My throat feels tight with tears that I will probably shed later, because while I don't understand this at all—the only thing I know for sure is that this is utterly tragic for Emilia Slaski. "This *is* a really strange place for a grave, right?"

"Perhaps this was just where he died," Zofia suggests.

"*Behind* my grandmother's house?"

"Plenty of people hid in patches of woods during the war."

"And was it *my* grandfather who was the hero saving Jews? Or this other guy?"

I glance back at the headstone one last time, and a shiver runs down my spine. I remember Pa so well—I just *can't* imagine him letting his sister think he was dead for all of those years. It's much easier to imagine him taking heroic measures to help his countrymen, because he was one of the most giving men I've ever met.

"Zofia?" I ask quietly.

"Yes?"

"Do you have *any* idea how we can untangle this without Emilia's input? Or whether or not we should even tell her, even if we do happen to get access to her?"

Zofia gives me a sad smile.

"I hate to say this, Alice…but I think the only way forward here is via Lia Truchen."

I leave Zofia in the car again when I step into the clinic for a fourth time. I feel like I made better progress this morning, and maybe there were even a few moments there where Lia and I really connected. I find that she's serving a patient when I enter the room, but her companion sees me, and he elbows her gently, then points to me. There's visible frustration in Lia's gaze as she stares at me, but then she fixes a smile to her face, finishes serving her patient and leads the way back to the meeting room.

"Lia…" I take a deep breath, then blurt, "I saw the grave. It's definitely my grandfather's name and year of birth, but it *can't* be him because he only died last year. It seems to me that the only way we're ever going to understand this is if you or even I could talk to Emilia—"

"Listen, Alice," Lia says flatly. "I feel for you. I really do. I've done everything I can to help you—what you're asking for now is simply impossible."

"Maybe you could just *mention* Alina—"

"Every month we take her to visit that grave," Lia says abruptly. "On the very last Sunday of every month she goes to Mass in her very best clothes, then she stops for flowers at the market, and then us grandkids have a roster and we all take turns driving her up there. And do you know *why* we each take turns?" When I shake my head, Lia's gaze grows sharp. "Because Alice, nearly eighty years after he died, my beautiful, brave grandmother still cries sometimes when she sees his grave and it's heartbreaking. Do you even understand what you are *asking* of me?"

"Imagine if Emilia was on her deathbed, and she sent you to America, and you were in *my* position," I plead with her.

"We have one upset elderly lady at the moment, yes?" Lia says. "If we do as you ask, we will have *two* upset elderly ladies, and what do we achieve? *Nothing.* Most likely, my grandmother will be as bewildered by all this as you and I are, and if she never replied to your grandmother's letters, there is almost certainly a reason for that. Please, *please* stop bothering me here—this is my workplace."

I'm about to leave. I'm about to walk out the door and concede defeat. I walk all the way out to the waiting room, and I head toward the door, and then I think about driving away from this place and living the rest of my life without knowing why Babcia sent me here.

It's too late for Babcia to tell me her story. It's too late for me to understand all of the moments big and small that led to the family I have in America now. It's probably even too late for me to explain to Babcia just how important she's been to me, and how deep the love I have for her is.

But it's *not* too late for me to plant my feet hard against this carpet and to give this bewildering mystery absolutely everything I have. Lia is my *only* link to Emilia—my only link to "understanding Tomasz."

Sometimes you have to smash the damn door down.

I can't walk away. I just can't give up this easily. I sit heavily in a visitor's chair by the door and raise my gaze to Lia. She's staring at me incredulously.

"You absolutely cannot stay here," she calls, paying no heed to the confused patients who sit in chairs all around me.

"I'm not going anywhere until you agree to talk to her for me." I shrug. It's uncomfortable for me to be this *difficult*. I mean, once upon a time… Well, this was kind of the life I thought I'd lead. In my idealistic youth, I really thought I'd be the sort of journalist who uncovered deeply buried truths, a woman who made a way to tell the stories that need to be told.

"Fine," Lia says, and she sits back at her desk, slides her phone headset back on, and for the next little while, she does a pretty good job of ignoring me. Zofia texts me after a while.

Are you okay in there?? It's been an hour and I'm getting worried.

I glance up at Lia and catch her staring at me. She avoids my gaze, and I hope that's a sign that I'm wearing her down.

Lia refused to help, so I'm basically holding a sit-in until she changes her mind.

Zofia replies with a shocked emoji, and then a little while later:

Let me know if you need anything. I'm just waiting at the cafe across the road. And...good luck!

Another hour passes, and then another. None of the magazines on the coffee table beside me are in English, but I thumb through them all anyway, trying to look as if I'm not at all fussed about our current standoff.

But on the inside?

I'm melting down like Eddie on his worst day. My thoughts are an absolute muddle—I'm second-guessing this *insane* course of action I've set myself on, and frankly, pretty much every single decision I've made in the last week since I decided to actually come here. Doctors come and collect patients, and every single time, they stare at me. Patients come in, stare at me, go in for a consult, then come out, stare at me some more, then leave.

I feel like I'm on a stage, and the show is something like *Watch Alice Michaels Lose her Dignity in a Foreign Country!*

Lia approaches me around lunchtime, and for a moment or two, I think I've won. Before I can celebrate, she sits heavily in the chair beside me, and she drops her head into her hands.

"You just can't stay there," she says desperately. "You seem like a reasonable person so I'm going to beg you to reconsider this. I have *work* to do, Alice—patients are asking questions and I can't let this go on. You *won't* change my mind."

"I'm not going anywhere until you do," I say simply, and then I raise my chin, hoping I look like Babcia, or even Callie, when they are being overtly stubborn. Lia's gaze narrows and she sits up again, straightening her spine.

"Right, you've left me no choice. I've been patient. I've asked you nicely, several times, and now I'm warning you. This is a workplace, and if you won't respect my request for you to leave, I have no choice but to call the police and have you removed."

Okay, I didn't expect *that*. I frown at her.

"Lia…please…"

"Five minutes, Alice. Then I'm calling the police."

I hear Mom cheering me on inside my brain. *Sometimes you have to smash the damn door down, Alice.* I lean back in my chair and cross my arms over my chest.

"A much easier way to get rid of me would be to agree to speak to your grandmother."

Lia growls and stomps back behind her desk. She's conferring a lot with her colleague, and a few minutes tick down while I busy myself praying with all of my might that the *police* threat was an empty one. I see her pick up the phone, but I pretend I don't notice—because maybe she's bluffing, and obviously I'm getting to her, so maybe if I just hang in here a little longer—

The doors swing open a few minutes later, and two policemen enter the room. They approach the counter, and Lia, wearing a scowl, points to me. The officers approach me.

"You've been asked to leave," the older of the two says abruptly. "We'll give you one last chance to do it voluntarily. After that, we'll be carrying you out—and you'll go straight to our car and then our station so we can charge you with trespassing."

I'm sure they hear my petrified *gulp* as I rise to my feet and nod.

"I'm going," I squeak.

"And madam?" The other officer says, as I pick up my bag, preparing to sprint to the door.

"Yes?"

"If we see you here again, we *will* arrest you."

I shoot one last, pleading look toward Lia, who's watching me with her hands crossed over her chest, and then I bolt out the door and back to Zofia's car. Once I'm inside, I collapse into the chair and try to catch my breath.

"Did you just get arrested?" Zofia gasps.

"Almost," I groan, and I cover my hands with my eyes. "I can't believe I did that."

Zofia starts the car, and drives away at what can only be described as *breakneck-but-legal* speed. We're almost back to the highway when she starts to laugh, and eventually, I join in.

"You're either really, really determined to do this for your grandmother or you're *completely* crazy. I can't really tell which at this point."

"Me, either," I admit, the laughter deflating. "But it was all for nothing."

"We can come back tomorrow?" Zofia offers.

"And do what?" I ask. "Take a free ride to the police station?"

"Well, how would you *like* to spend tomorrow? Do you have any other ideas? Did she give you anything else to go on?"

"No," I admit, and look back to my phone to start flicking through the photos I took of Babcia's notes and her AAC screen. I read each entry aloud.

"Trzebinia. Well, we came here."

"Yes."

"*Ul. Świętojańska 4.*"

"Her childhood home."

"Yes. *Ul. Polerechka9B.*"

"A beautifully renovated historic home in a gorgeous, sweet chestnut–lined laneway. We have no idea why it was important." I sigh heavily.

"*Ul. Dworczyk 38.*"

"The medical clinic where Aleksy Slaski worked."

"Emilia Skalski."

"Your great-aunt."

"Alina Dziak. My grandmother's real name."

"Yes."

"Saul Eva Tikva Weiss."

"We have literally no idea."

"*Proszę zrozum. Tomasz.*"

"Your pronunciation is beyond appalling, but yes, she asks us to please understand Tomasz."

"Which we have no idea how to do."

"And that's *everything*?"

"The only other thing she said was *Babcia fire Tomasz*," I say, then I groan in frustration. "But I know we think that just means love, which is sweet, but it really…"

"Doesn't help us much. Look, there's a saying in my family, Alice, and I think it applies perfectly to today." I glance at her, and she grins. "*Everything* looks better after some vodka."

We try several varieties of local vodka at a restaurant on the square back in Krakow, and try to brainstorm other ways we can approach this mystery.

"Okay, let's think about Lia," Zofia murmurs. "Lia's a receptionist, right?"

"Seems to be."

"But her great-*grandfather* once owned the building. Coincidence, or is there still a family connection?"

"What are you suggesting?"

"Maybe the business is still owned by the family. Maybe Emilia became a doctor too, or maybe one of her children owns it now." Zofia fishes her phone out of her pocket and a quick Google search later, we have a list of the GPs at the clinic. "Agnieszka Truchen is one of the owners. That's *got* to be Lia's mother, or at least a relative…"

We find a few dated and grainy pictures of Agnieszka online, but no social media, and all of her listed contact details point back to the clinic. Zofia is on her phone replicating my search, but I'm staring down at the photos on my own screen. As grainy as those images are, I think I can see a similarity to myself. I turn my phone back to Zofia.

"Do you think she looks like me?" I ask her.

"It's hard to tell because the photos are so poor. But yes, it looks like there's a resemblance there. Did you see *her* at the clinic today?"

"No, there were a few doctors coming out to get patients, but I would have noticed her."

"We could call and ask to speak to her," Zofia suggests, then she looks at her watch. "It's not quite five o'clock…"

"They'll recognize my accent…" I say weakly. Zofia grins.

"They won't recognize mine."

She finds the phone number on the clinic website, then she dials. I hear her speaking in Polish, but the call ends quickly and her shoulders slump.

"Agnieszka still owns the clinic, but other doctors do the patient care," she sighs. "She retired a few years ago."

"Of course she did," I mutter, but then I brighten again. "What about Emilia herself? We could search for her on the phone directory?"

"Well, she had at least one child, so she's almost definitely married, and given her age, I'd say there's virtually no chance she'd have kept her surname," Zofia says apologetically. We search anyway—but unsurprisingly, my eighty-seven-year-old great-aunt doesn't seem to have a Facebook page. After that, we order a second mixed platter of local vodkas, and things get a bit silly.

"Well, if Lia won't *tell* us where Emilia is, maybe we could get a private detective to track her down…"

"We could take out full page ads in the newspapers asking Emilia to contact us…"

"We could break into the medical clinic and see if we can find Agnieszka's address…"

"Maybe I can cancel my return flight and wait in hiding outside the clinic until Agnieszka shows up for a visit and hope she's more helpful…or at least helpful enough to *not* call the police…"

"Maybe we could steal some of Lia's fingernail clippings and get a DNA test done…"

"Or we could offer a million-dollar reward for anyone who solves the mystery!"

At that, Zofia looks at me.

"Do you have a million dollars?" she asks hopefully.

I pause, then slump.

"I'm a stay-at-home mom, so no, not really."

"Ah. That one sounded promising for a second there."

We're laughing a little too loudly when the waiter approaches with the bill, so we go for a walk to clear our heads, then share a delicious meal at yet another restaurant on the square. We chat about everything *but* my mission while we eat—I tell Zofia about my kids and the difficulties of leaving them. I even skim over the difficulties of leaving Wade alone with them, and the surprising realization I'm starting to form that just maybe, I've been holding on to Eddie a little too tightly. Zofia tells me about her work and some of the heartbreaking and hopeful family history searches she's been involved with. I'm totally engrossed in the chat and enjoying the distraction from the awful dead end my search for Babcia has arrived at. Time gets away from us, so I gasp when I see the clock on the wall.

"I better get back and call my family," I say, but despite the silliness of the evening, I'm definitely feeling better than I was. "Thanks for tonight though, Zofia."

"It's no trouble at all. I'll walk you back to the hotel and we'll start again in the morning." She smiles at me gently. "Don't lose heart, Alice. We'll think of something."

I call back to Wade without texting first, because it's now 10:31 p.m. Krakow time and that means 5:31 p.m. Florida time, and I know they'll all be home. Callie answers the phone on the first ring, and she's crying.

"Mommy," she croaks.

"Baby!" I gasp. "What happened?"

"Daddy forgot to get me from French club and they were closing up and they called him but he didn't answer and Mrs. Bernard got cranky and I couldn't remember Grandma's phone number and I didn't know what to do," she says, and then her eyes fill with tears again. A fresh tear slips from her eye and her voice is small as she whispers, "Mommy, can you come home now?"

"Oh, honey bear..." I whisper. The buzz from the vodka is fading rapidly. "But he got you eventually, right?"

"No." She scowls. "Mrs. Bernard drove me to Daddy's work and left me at reception. And the receptionist had to go find him because he was in a *meeting*."

"So where was Eddie in all of this time?" I ask slowly. "Not at school, surely?"

"Oh no," she says, but before I can breathe a sigh of relief, she adds, "He was with Daddy because he got sent home from school today because he had a meltdown in class and he threw a chair at Mr. Bailey. *And* Eddie had five accidents in his pants today but don't worry, I put his dirty clothes into the washing machine already."

"Why are you doing that instead of Daddy?" I ask, although it's difficult to speak, because I am *so* enraged I can barely focus enough to ask the question.

"Daddy's in his office on Skype back to his office. He had to finish his meeting," Callie says. She turns the phone camera around, to show me two open cans of soup waiting on the bench. "Don't worry, Mommy—I'm making Eddie dinner now."

"No, Callie, no—" I gasp. "No, you don't know how to use the cooktop, sweetheart—you'll burn yourself."

"I'm microwaving it," she says defensively, and just then I hear the *ding* of the microwave. Callie is plenty old and mature enough to use the microwave *or* the stove—if she knew how, but I've never shown her, because frankly she's never had to know. I do almost all of the cooking in our house. It's never even occurred to me that perhaps I should be sharing those duties—not for my own sake, but for *theirs*.

"How long did you cook it for, sweetheart?" I ask, my heart pounding in my throat.

"I guessed. I thought ten minutes would be enough," she says innocently, and I grasp the phone a little harder when I see her standing and walking toward the microwave. It sits high on a shelf so Eddie can't reach it. To get that boiling hot soup out, she'll have to reach up over her head.

"Don't touch that!" I say frantically, and Callie frowns into the camera.

"But why?"

"It's going to be *very* hot, honey bear. Just...*no*." I draw in a deep breath and try to stay calm. "Darling, just do me one little favor, okay?"

"Okay, Mommy?"

"I want you to go into Daddy's office, and interrupt his meeting, and—"

"But he said not to—"

"*Callie*, just listen to me," I say urgently. "Walk up to Daddy's office and tell him Mommy is on the phone and it's an emergency."

"Okay," Callie says, then she sighs. "I just don't want to get in trouble, Mom."

"If anyone is getting 'in trouble,'" I say fiercely. "It's *Daddy*."

She's a child of the millennium, that's for sure—Callie automatically walks to Wade's office upstairs with the camera frontward so I can see where she's going, then she opens the door to his office to show me Wade sitting at his big desktop computer. I recognize the lab technician who's on the huge monitor, and I also recognize that the scratch pad they are sharing between screens is full of mathematical formulas. I can tell Wade is engrossed, because when Callie walks into the room, he doesn't even look away from the screen.

"Not now, Eddie—" he says, without turning to see which kid it is.

"Daddy," Callie says hesitantly. "Mommy wants to talk to you."

I see Wade's shoulders lock. He reluctantly farewells his lab rat, and I notice the slight pause before he turns to face the phone. Now that he's facing me, guilt is written *all* over his face. Callie flips the camera lens around and passes him the phone. He looks down at the screen, surveys my expression, then sighs and says softly, "Callie, can you give Mommy and me a few minutes?"

"Don't you dare touch that microwave, Callie Michaels!" I call frantically, and confusion filters over Wade's face.

"But the soup is ready—" Callie protests, and Wade's eyes widen.

"Callie, go downstairs, *do not touch the microwave*. Read a book or something till I finish talking to Mommy," Wade says, and once the door closes, he raises the camera and stares right into my eyes. "Alice, *please* don't overreact."

"Eddie threw a chair and got sent home from school? *You*

forgot to pick Callie up? Callie is washing Eddie's soiled pants and trying to feed him while you tinker with formulas with Jon? I am so furious right now I do not even know where to *start*—"

"Eddie had a bad night, and then he had a bad day. It would have happened even if you were here—there's nothing I could have done to prevent it."

"Are you kidding me right now, Wade?" I scoff. "Of course you could have prevented it. If you had any clue about how to relate to him you'd have known this morning he was having a bad day and you could have *stayed home with him* to ride it out like *I* would have done."

"We've hit a major snag with this plastics project, Alice. I couldn't just *stay home with him*. My team needs me too. I'm trying to juggle a million things this week so *you* can be there—"

"When I called, Callie was just about to get the soup out of the microwave. Soup she'd been cooking in there for *ten minutes*."

"Shit..." Wade groans, then runs his free hand through his hair. "Well, why doesn't she know how to use it?"

That hits a sore spot. She should know how to use it—I'm just in the habit of doing every damned thing myself around that house.

"She has *two* parents, Wade," I say defensively. "You could have taught her just as easily as I could have."

He sighs heavily, then he mutters, "Honestly, Alice—today has just been Hell. The very last thing I need tonight—"

"Callie is ten years old," I say flatly. "Yes, she's gifted—but she's still *ten*. You can't expect her to pick up the slack because you happen to be busy at work." I groan and rub my eyes with my hand. "I *knew* I shouldn't have left you guys."

"It's *one bad day*, Alice," Wade snaps. "I'm allowed to have *one bad day*."

"But I *knew* this would happen," I say. I sound bitchy. I sound like my mother, actually, and I hate that—but I am just so angry I can't stop myself. "I knew you'd let me down—"

"I have *never* let you down," Wade says, and now he's furious too.

"Eddie is seven, Wade," I say blithely. "You tell me one damned time in all of his life when you *haven't* let me down."

It's the vodka talking. It's the disappointment speaking. My trip has come to nothing, and I'm going to have to admit to Callie and Babcia and even Wade that I've failed. Regardless, I've said something I can't take back—something that's just way too far over the line of what's acceptable. Over the screen, I watch as Wade's eyes widen with shock and a deep kind of hurt that I've rarely seen him display. I'm still angry—that doesn't mean I'm not wishing hard that I could pull those words back in. But I can't, and so we both just stare into the lenses of our cameras in stiff, uncomfortable silence. It's Wade's turn to battle to get control of his temper, but in his case, he wins the battle, and he speaks calmly and evenly.

"I'm going to go downstairs," he says. "I'm going to go check on Edison and apologize to Pascale. I'm going to salvage the soup. I'm going to take over the laundry. Then I'm going to start the night routine and try to get ready for the school day tomorrow." He draws in a deep breath, then adds, "What I'm *not* going to do is to get into a screaming match with you over FaceTime. I don't think it's a great idea for you to talk to Eddie tonight, either. He's pretty fragile today and I think it would make things worse."

I hang up on Wade without a farewell, then I bury my face in my pillow, and I give myself over to sobs—but only *then* does it occur to me that I've yet to call Mom to check in on Babcia. So I drink some water, then I make a cup of coffee and I watch TV for a while until I feel like my voice might be back to normal and my emotions have cooled.

I place a voice call to Mom, because I don't want her to see my face. She answers on the first ring.

"I can't talk for long, Alice."

"What's happening?"

"Babcia had some kind of turn a few hours ago and she's been moved to the ICU," Mom says. I hear the frustration in her voice as she mutters, "I'm waiting for the neurologist but he's been next door with another patient for *half a damned hour*. But the nurse said it was another minor stroke. She said it's not uncommon in someone her age but that it's a concern that it keeps happening..."

"Is Babcia okay?"

"She's *not* okay, Alice," Mom says abruptly. "I think it's time we accepted that her days of being *okay* have passed."

I know her time with us is winding down. Why else would I be in Poland on this wild-goose chase? But hearing Mom say those words makes me want to weep.

"Can you text me when you know what's happening?" I croak.

"Alice—" I can hear the apology in Mom's voice, but knowing Mom as I do, there's a good chance it's going to be followed up by some kind of sharpness anyway and I *just can't deal* with that tonight.

"I have to go," I say unevenly. "Just text me, okay?"

And for the second time today, I hang up on someone I love.

Twenty minutes later, I'm still sobbing when a text comes from Mom.

The good news is it was a small bleed today and there's no new damage, but Babcia's condition is no longer considered stable. Dr. Chang is finally organizing that translator for me. She wants to talk to Babcia about whether she's ready to sign a Do Not Resuscitate order.

Then a few minutes later, when I'm trying to craft a reply, another text arrives.

By the way, your father arrived a few minutes ago. I don't suppose you had anything to do with that? Perhaps he's not the only one who should think about coming home early.

"I am thinking about it, Mom," I whisper to my empty hotel room. "In fact, that's pretty much all I can think about."

CHAPTER 35

Alina

I thought I'd be terrified while the rest of the truck was loaded. It was surely the most dangerous moment in a series of dangerous moments. But listening to the laughter and jokes of the Nazi soldiers loading the truck made me furious instead of terrified. I knew we must be at Auschwitz, and that meant my parents were possibly nearby.

Were these the men who took my parents? Were these the men who killed Saul's family?

I was suddenly, overwhelmingly incensed. I had been worn down by the years of occupation—so much so that I'd almost forgotten how to be outraged. But listening to the carefree tinkle of that laughter, a furious, murderous rage surged through me—especially when it occurred to me then that Saul was right behind me, hearing that very same soundtrack, probably wondering the very same things. I reached up behind myself and squeezed Saul's shoulder, hard. After a moment, he set his shaking hand over mine.

Sometime later, we heard the door to the cabin close, and the engine started again.

Time lost all meaning after that. For the most part Saul and I sat in total silence, moving only when numbness or necessity commanded. The suitcase contained preserves jars full of water—and once each was empty, they were awkwardly repurposed for our waste. I'd packed the last of our rations biscuits and some jam, along with the very last of Mama's bread—a veritable bounty by Saul's standards if it only had to last us for a few days. I waited for hunger, but instead, I had to force myself to eat every now and again, and when Saul ignored my offers of food and water, I had to awkwardly shuffle until I could lift the jars and the bread to his mouth. He was a walking skeleton. I knew he simply could not afford to go too long without sustenance, and so, I fed him like a baby.

I was endlessly aware of the fear and the suffocation and grief for my parents and longing for Tomasz and the itch of the cast and of the sting of splinters that came upon any part of my skin that happened to rest against the wooden crate—it was as if the entire world had paused except for my suffering. Sometimes the truck would slow or stop and I'd hear voices and I'd be completely resigned to what felt like an inevitability. *This was so surely the end*. We'd been discovered, we were done for, death had arrived, I had failed. But despite the sheer terror, each and every time the truck then started up again and we'd amble on, until the next stop and the next scare.

When the noise of the truck was loud enough, I'd try to strike up a whispered conversation with Saul—anything to ease the boredom, anything to distract myself from the way my mind raced with all of the horrible possibilities of what lay ahead of us. Sometimes he answered me in grunts, but mostly, he didn't answer me at all.

I got the impression that he was sleeping a lot, or perhaps that he'd lost himself altogether in the memories of that night—in the first tender stages of a lifetime of grief, amplified by the terror of our current situation and the sensory deprivation of the *entirely* dark cavity we were trapped in. Eventually, I accepted that he didn't want to talk, or perhaps he was exhausted to the point that he simply couldn't. Sometimes, he'd cry very quietly, and at first, I hated that, but I soon realized there was something even worse, because other times he'd fall silent and I'd feel a suffocating anxiety that he'd died and I was trapped in what amounted to my *coffin*, still breathing beside an emaciated corpse. I'd hold my own breath for a moment so I could concentrate on feeling the movement of his chest behind me, just to be sure he was breathing, but sometimes it took me hours to work up the courage to do so, because I knew the reality of my situation. Even if Saul *had* died, I was stuck in that cavity with him until we stopped, and there was nothing at all I could do about it. By then, the smell in the cavity of the truck was so thick I felt like I could taste our sweat and waste in the air—a different kind of death, a living prison of our life.

I'd lost track of the stops and starts of the truck's journey, so I was startled when it came to a stop, and then I heard footsteps in the tray and cartons shifting around, but no conversation. Saul and I both tensed as the steps came near to us, neither one of us relaxing even as Jakub called quietly, "Are you two okay in there? We are at the Don River, but we have to hurry—I am running late to the command center to deliver the last of the supplies."

He helped us out onto unsteady feet, then lifted us both onto the ground because our limbs were too stiff to climb down. Finally, Jakub passed us the suitcase, and then he started shifting boxes around. It took me a moment to realize that he was trying to get the crate we'd traveled in out from behind the load of supplies.

"What are you doing?" I gasped.

He glanced at me, confused.

"I need to dispose of the crate and make the last delivery."

"*Dispose* of the crate?"

"I can't take it into the command center with me," he explained quietly. "If someone tries to unload it, they'll soon realize it's not what it looks like. I'd be done for."

"But you used it once before. With the other courier."

"The front was much closer to home back then and a resistance unit hid the crate for me until I made the return journey. We're well into what used to be Soviet territory here—I just don't *know* anyone to hide it for me."

"But…there are so many who need your help. So many who—"

"I'm not much good to them dead, am I?" Jakub interrupted me, but not unkindly. "I built it once, I can build it again. You best be making your way to the river. I don't know what time your boat is coming. Do you have some food left?"

"Some," I whispered, but I was reluctant to drop the issue of the crate so quickly. "Maybe you could leave it here—"

"Take these," Jakub said, and he tossed me a handful of carrots. I didn't catch them—instead, they scattered around my feet, and I scrambled to collect them. "Try to convince your friend to eat some too. He looks like he's going to need the sustenance if you two are going to walk soon."

"But…"

Jakub nodded toward the woods.

"You ready for this?" he asked me quietly. "Things are still going to be tough from here, you know."

We both looked to Saul, who had slumped against a tree. It was dawn again—we'd been inside the crate for an entire day—and my companion looked no more lucid after the long stint inside the truck. He was slight, but so was I—there was simply no way I could physically carry him if he stopped walking, nor would I leave him behind. I'd made Tomasz a promise and I intended to fulfil it.

"I don't know," I admitted.

Jakub's gaze was sympathetic.

"Get moving, girl. And good luck." Jakub waved toward Saul, who raised his hand in return.

"Thank you," I whispered numbly. I picked up the suitcase and walked stiffly across to Saul. Behind me, I heard the sound of the crate crashing to the ground, and then the splintering crashes as Jakub destroyed it. Tears filled my eyes, but I couldn't let myself look back. Instead, I slid my hand into Saul's arm, and led him into the tree line, then helped him to sit on the ground. He slumped forward, elbow on his knee, palm over his eyes.

I hastily threw away the jam jars containing our waste, and then withdrew the last of our biscuits and dried bread, and what little water we had left.

"You need to eat again," I murmured.

Saul opened his eyes. It was as if he'd emerged from a deep, god-awful sleep and was, at last, conscious again.

"Alina," he said suddenly.

"Yes?" I said, startled by the unexpected speech.

He inclined his head toward me, and he said softly, "Thank you."

I'd feared the river crossing would be an ordeal, but we simply boarded a little boat with a gruff old farmer and were rowed across to the other side—no drama, no tension, no struggle. We were some miles to the west of the front, so while we could hear shelling in the distance, it was certainly no threat to us. If anything, the crossing was a moment of pleasant peace after the most stressful twenty-four hours of my life. When the boat stopped at the other side, the farmer nodded toward the riverbank. He didn't speak Polish, and neither Saul nor I knew his language, but we murmured our thanks anyway then moved to climb out of the boat. This seemed to inspire an almost violent reaction in the farmer, who blocked our way with an oar and started pointing to the suitcase.

"I think he wants money," Saul whispered.

I reached deep under my clothes, fumbled with the bag and withdrew some coins, then offered my palm to the farmer, who scooped them all up with a frown and grunted at us. I had no

idea how much I'd given him—nor how much I had left—but
he was no longer waving the oar at us, so we were free to go.

I helped Saul down onto the riverbank, and then I stepped
down myself. As my feet hit Soviet soil, I stopped and drew a
deep breath into my lungs. If Tomasz were with me, I'd have
grabbed him right then and I'd have kissed him full on the lips.
Then I'd have told him all of the thoughts as they raced through
my head—how much sweeter the air tasted here, how amazing
it was to be *alive* and to have made it this far, how much closer
we were to the life we'd dreamed about. Instead, though, I had
Saul—who ambled up to the top of the bank, then glanced
back at me questioningly. All I could do was make a note of my
thoughts. I promised myself that one day I'd tell Tomasz every
single thing about that moment. Until then, I had to carry on.

"Come on, Saul," I murmured, as I climbed up the riverbank to stand beside him. "We're not there yet, but we're much
closer than we were."

"How many miles?" he asked me.

"I don't even know," I admitted. "But I know it's to the east,
and it's not far." I offered him my arm. Saul leaned on me just
for a moment, then he seemed to lift himself to his full height,
and he shook himself.

"Enough," he murmured. "It is time to carry on."

And after that, he walked all the way to the township. We had
to stop a few times so he could rest, but he made it the whole
way without much help at all.

We had to wait a full day for the train that would take us toward
Buzuluk, and there was nowhere for us to go in the meantime,
so we slept on the platform—Saul and I crammed ourselves into
a tiny alcove near some bathrooms and we protected the suitcase
and our meager food with our bodies while we slept. Despite the
hordes of hungry Polish souls around us waiting for the same train,
despite the concrete behind us and the cool breeze that never re-

ally stopped all night, I actually slept so well that when I woke the next morning I thought the entire trip had been a dream.

I left Saul to find a bathroom, and while I was gone happened upon a local woman who was selling dried bread to the refugees. I handed over more coins—again no concept of how much or how little I'd given her—and when I returned to Saul I was carrying not one but two entire loaves hidden beneath my coat. I was worried for a while that I'd purchased too much and it would go to waste—but in the end, that bread likely saved our lives.

The train was a walk in the park for me after the darkness of the truck, despite the fact that Saul and I were sharing a cattle car with several dozen strangers in various states of health and cleanliness. There wasn't even enough room for all of us to sit at the same time, so by silent agreement, we passengers took it in turns, standing on our exhausted feet for hours at a time to free up some space for others to rest.

I thought *I'd* had it tough during the war—but these people had clearly suffered in ways I couldn't even imagine. The woman next to me—sitting all but on *top* of me—was covered in weeping sores and I could see the lice crawling through the matted lengths of her hair. Every now and again she'd start sobbing, and then just as abruptly, she'd stop and close her eyes and lean limply into me, as if she'd passed out. The man traveling with her was every bit as thin as Saul, but his skin had taken on a luminescent yellow tinge. There were children on the train who were too traumatized to even cry—they'd just sit in silence—and some of them were even traveling alone. There was no toilet—so people were relieving themselves through a hole in the floor of the train, and I realized some of the sick people couldn't wait their turn when a suspiciously rank slurry started to roll around the floor.

I had the suitcase with me, and I nursed it most of the time—too afraid to spoil the food by setting it on the floor and having it contaminated with the waste. I was also too scared to open it inside the train in case we were overwhelmed by the hungry crowd. Instead, I'd crack the lid a little, push one hand inside awkwardly, and rummage around inside. By doing this, I sneaked small chunks of bread to Saul when I thought no one was looking. I'd eat myself by pretending to scratch my nose with my cast-wrapped right hand, and sliding my left hand and the food beneath it to my mouth. Within a day of leaving the station, Saul and I had seen enough to know that if we dared to sleep at the same time, *someone* would steal the suitcase. After that, we slept in short shifts—if you could call it sleep, given the almost-impossible physical discomfort we were both in.

But as god-awful as *all* of that was, for me it was still preferable to the cavity of the truck—the cool breezes and light that crept in through the cracks on the cattle car walls made all the difference. Those hints of daylight were actually glimpses of something even more precious—I could see *freedom* through the cracks of the wall of that cattle cart, as ever so slowly, it dawned upon me that I was actually out of occupied Poland. Although I was a long way from safe and a long way from settled, I was finally free from the Nazis.

As that realization started to solidify, a heaviness lifted from my chest. It was the dawning of something I'd been missing for years by that stage; the expectation that I was going to survive. As that train ambled forward, I became quite sure that everything was going to be just fine—because if Saul and *I* could make it that far, then of course Tomasz would. If all that we had left in the world was each other at the end of this journey, that was more than enough for me to look forward to.

To most of the people trapped within that train carriage full of sickness and death and stench, the moment surely would have been a low point in their lives—but to me, I felt like I'd stumbled upon the very beginning of the future I'd dreamed about.

The journey to Buzuluk took two full weeks. The train stopped periodically, but there was rarely food available, and when there was, those poor starved creatures we were traveling with would descend on it like animals. Saul and I managed to make the loaves of bread last for the entire journey—only on the last day did we entirely run out of food. We were lucky. Several people from our cart died, and on those infrequent stops, the train attendants simply dumped their bodies in fields by the side of the tracks.

When the attendant walked past and rolled the doors open and announced that we were at Buzuluk, Saul and I turned to one another and shared a delighted, surprised smile—as if to say, *We're alive. Can you believe it?* He'd grown stronger over the journey, rather than weaker like most of our traveling companions, and as we stepped off the platform at Buzuluk, Saul actually led the way. He was devastated, of course, but becoming strong enough to put one foot in front of the other and move under his own steam.

We stopped in Buzuluk and visited some stores before we made the walk to the camp. Our clothes were disgusting, so we replaced them with the cheapest and warmest we could find. All that I kept was my coat, and I told Saul this was because "it wasn't too smelly," but the truth was, Mama's ring was still in the hem. We bought still more dried bread and some biscuits. We were hopeful that once we arrived at the camp, we'd be fed real food, but we couldn't be sure so we wanted to be prepared.

"Well," he said quietly, as we followed the last stragglers from the crowd on the train toward the army camp. "What do you think is ahead of us next?"

"Hopefully," I said, "a nice bed with a blanket. Somewhere to lie down and actually stretch out. And food—oh, *hot* food. Imagine that!"

We laughed together, optimistic about the camp we expected to be welcomed into. It was only when the crowd's progress began to slow, and then stopped altogether that we realized there was a problem. Soon, soldiers began walking along the line, talking to people, and we saw most of the people ahead of us in the line turning back to walk toward the station, cursing and shaking their heads.

"What is it?" Saul asked the soldier, as he neared us.

"The camp is full," he said. "The Soviets say we only need 30,000 soldiers—we have over 70,000 people already. There's nothing here for you. You will have to return to where you came from."

"But we need to wait at this camp. We are meeting British soldiers here when they bring a shipment of uniforms. We can't go back."

Frankly, the suggestion that anyone return to that train was ludicrous—it was pointing people to their deaths, plain and simple. Aside from the exposure to disease, no one who was lucky enough to have food for the journey would have had enough to survive the return. The soldier shrugged at us and moved to walk on.

"No," I said flatly, and I reached out to take hold of the soldier's arm. "I mean it. We are meeting the British here—we will not go back."

"Alina..." Saul said very quietly, and he touched my arm to console me.

"I have not come this far to be turned away now," I whispered fiercely to Saul. "And neither have *you*."

The soldier looked me up and down—the irritation in his gaze giving way to something I liked even *less*. The sudden flare of interest in his eyes reminded me of how sick I'd felt standing exposed in the strawberry patch that day, right at the start of the war. This time, though, the soldier leering at me was standing right beside me and my hand was on his arm. I dropped my hand hastily and stepped back toward Saul a little, as if he could protect me.

"I could perhaps be persuaded to make an exception for a lovely girl like you," the soldier said, leaning down until his face was very close to mine, and I could smell coffee on his breath. I battled *hard* against the urge to show my revulsion or lean away, and I went weak at the knees with relief when he stood to his full height, until he added firmly, "But just for you. Not your boyfriend."

"No!" I exclaimed, shaking my head frantically. "He has to come with me. He *has* to." The line around us had all but dissolved—even those who were intending to stay and hope for the best had shuffled away from me—scared, no doubt, that the guard was about to shoot me. All that I knew was that my future lay beyond the camp. I had to get inside, and I had promised Tomasz so I *had* to take Saul with me. I started to beg. "He's a doctor. I'm sure you could use doctors in the camp if it's full, especially if the people inside are as sick as everyone here seems to be."

"We have doctors," he said, then he tilted his chin at me. "What else do you have, beautiful?"

"Food?"

"Try again."

I was getting a pretty clear idea what the soldier might want from me, and it was making me physically ill—my empty stomach threatening to try to empty itself even more. We'd used most of our rubles by then, so all I really had to offer the soldier was some coins, and I'd figured out they weren't actually worth very much. I had to think of something, because I wasn't going *anywhere* but through those gates.

"I have some coins," I offered, and I rummaged around in my pocket and withdrew what was left.

"Please," he scoffed. "Don't insult me. That's crumbs."

"Gold," I said heavily. I sighed, then said it again. "I have gold."

"Gold?" he said incredulously, and beside me, I saw Saul raise his eyebrows. I fumbled in the bottom of my coat for the lump, then raised the hem. The soldier continued to stare at me blankly, so I reached for his hand and held it against the lump. "See? It's a ring. Solid gold. If you lend me your pocketknife,

I'll give it to you. Surely that's enough to encourage you to let my friend come in with me."

"Let me cut it," the soldier said abruptly, and then the next thing I knew, he'd taken a knife from his pocket and had sliced the length of the seam. The ring fell out into my waiting hands, and I was trembling as I offered it to him. The soldier snatched it up into his hand and hid it quickly in his pocket. "Do you have Polish identity papers? No one gets in without them, you know. I can't do anything about that."

"We do," I said. "Both of us."

"Real ones?"

"Of course," I said, as if he'd offended me. Then I held my breath, but it escaped as a hiccup when he turned to walk away from us.

"But—" I started to protest, and he gave me a pointed look and motioned with his head for us to follow him.

Saul and I scampered after him—all the way to the gates. The other guards let us in without so much as a second look, and then the soldier pointed toward a ragged tent.

"That's where you register—get your papers ready. And if he's really a doctor, make sure you tell them. They sure could use the help." After he turned to walk away, the soldier glanced back at me and gave me a wink. "Hope I see you round."

Saul slid his arm around my shoulders and turned me toward the registration tent.

"Alina," he said quietly. "That was the bravest thing I've ever seen."

"Tomasz told me to look after you," I said stiffly, but what I was thinking was, *One of these days saving people for Tomasz Slaski is going to get me killed.*

"Where did you get the ring?"

"My mama," I mumbled, and then it hit me what I'd done, and I had to blink *hard* to fight back the tears. "I had saved it. I was keeping it. For my wedding to Tomasz."

Saul's arm across my shoulders tensed a little.

"I'll find a way, Alina. I'll find a way to repay you for this. *All* of it."

"You already saved us. He wouldn't have survived if he hadn't left Warsaw with you, I'm not sure *I* would have survived if he hadn't come back to me." I wanted to weep, but we were in the short line waiting to register, and I knew I had to stay calm. I tried to inject some lightness into my tone. "I think we are even now."

"Not by a long shot, Alina. But I will find a way."

The line moved forward then, and we shuffled up together, and when we got to the front, with shaking hands, I showed the administrator the falsified paperwork Henry had given me.

"Hanna Wiśniewski," he murmured, as he scrawled the name down, but he barely even looked at my paperwork, because his focus was immediately on Saul. He looked closely at Tomasz's passport, then peered up at Saul, then back to the aged passport. For a moment, I expected him to comment on Saul's age—he was five years older than Tomasz, and he *looked* much older still. But war had aged us all beyond our years, and instead, the guard's gaze narrowed on Saul's hair.

"You're not Jewish, are you?" he asked. For a split second, Saul hesitated, so I interjected, "Of course he's not. Why do you ask that?"

"Dark hair, miss. It's a standard question. We enrolled too many Jews in the early days so we can't let any more in. They aren't really cut out for war—they're just too cowardly."

In an instant, I was speechless with rage, but Saul reached down and he took my hand, and he squeezed it—hard. Then he smiled at the officer, as he scooped the passport up quite casually.

"Is that all you need from us?" he asked with a smile.

"All done. Welcome."

"Where do we go next?"

"Head over to the next tent. They'll assign you jobs and sleeping quarters."

We walked toward the second tent, and I glanced at Saul.

"I don't know how you can bear it," I whispered shakily beneath my breath.

"It's just for a few weeks," he whispered back. "We can figure it all out when Tomasz gets here. Besides, if they let me work as a doctor, perhaps they will be more concerned with my skill and less with my heritage by the time I tell them the truth." He exhaled, then he admitted weakly, "Honestly, Alina, I am not yet strong enough to suffer for my faith again. Not yet. God forgive me, but it will be a relief to stay undercover for just a while."

CHAPTER 36

Alice

Zofia texts me and suggests we meet for an earlier breakfast and try to come up with a plan, so by 8:00 a.m., we're seated in the hotel restaurant. I order a double espresso, because I've had almost no sleep—and for the second day in a row, I order *smalec*. Maybe it's written into my genes, because apparently, I love the stuff.

I kept thinking I had no expectations of this trip, but it turns out I did. I have a day left here to answer Babcia's unspoken question, but I have no way of finding out how it all fits together. All I *really* know for sure is that there's an elderly woman named Emilia somewhere here in Poland who regularly visits what might just be an empty grave with my grandfather's name on it.

Back home, Babcia is only getting sicker. It sounds like Eddie is in freefall. Wade is juggling a million balls at once, and some are inevitably falling. Callie is drowning under more responsibility than any ten-year-old should ever have to face.

And I'm five thousand miles away, in Poland. Achieving nothing for any of them.

"So…" Zofia says lightly. "What should we do with this day, then?"

I'd almost forgotten she was there. I grimace as I meet her gaze.

"I'm sorry, Zofia. I'm going to rearrange my flight and head home today if I can."

She tilts her head, staring at me thoughtfully.

"You're disappointed. I understand that."

"There just doesn't seem much point in staying. Whatever it was Babcia wanted me to find out...we seem to be at a dead end, and back home, she's getting sicker so..."

"I do a lot of this family history stuff."

"I know."

"Sometimes, I have customers who travel from all over the world trying to track down their ancestors, and they get here, and they can't find *anything*. The whole country was messed up after the war. Birth records, death records, bodies...stories...all kinds of things were lost and can't ever be found. But there's one thing that can *always* be found." She raises her gaze to me, then smiles gently. "That's the experience of having tried. You've never been here before, Alice. You're probably not coming back, right?"

"Probably not," I admit. My throat is suddenly tight at the thought of the missed opportunities that fly right by me with every second I'm here.

"Your flight is when...tomorrow?"

"Yes."

"You have a hotel room. Me. A car. And a *full day*. Let's *use* them?"

"But...my grandmother...and...my family..." My voice grows husky, and I pause to clear my throat. "My kids. Eddie is...they aren't coping without me, that's all."

"Alice, I don't have kids yet, so you go right ahead and ignore me if I'm way off base here but...I just have this feeling that whether you go home today or tomorrow, the outcome is probably the same. You're going to slot right back into your life and carry them all, and a week or two from now, everything will be back the way it was. And when you look back at this amazing trip, all you'll have to remember are the failures. Okay, we can't figure out what your grandmother wanted you to find—I know that's upsetting and disappointing but...maybe instead you can

just experience a little more of the country that produced her."
She slides the napkin off her lap and dumps it on her plate, then
stands and shrugs. "My two cents, as the saying goes. I'm going
to go put gas in my car, and you take some time to think about
it? If you decide to stay, I have some ideas how we can kill the
time. Or I can take you to the airport if you want. I'll be back
soon and you can let me know what you decide to do."

She gives me one last little smile, then leaves the table. I sink
back into my chair and look around the hotel dining room. People sit in small groups, eating, laughing, smiling. All of those ac-
cents and languages blending together into one generally excited
din. Aside from a group of men in the corner in suits, everyone
else is wearing casual clothes today—mostly active clothes too.
I wonder if everyone else here is on holiday. I wonder if I'm the
only person in this room who is here, but not *really* here.

It suddenly seems completely, brutally unfair. I'm doing something I dreamed of for years. Yes, this trip hasn't gone as I'd
hoped it would. I wanted to go home with answers—instead,
it seems inevitable that I will walk away having only uncovered
more questions.

I let myself face the full depth of my failure. It seems that I
have to accept that Babcia is going to pass away sooner or later
with threads left loose that she hoped I would tie for her.

It feels so unfair that after all of the love she's given me, this
one thing she's asked of me is something I just can't give her. I
want to sulk. I want to run home and spend her last days with
her begging her forgiveness. I *don't* want to give up, but it feels
like I have no choice. What else is there left to try? What more
would she want me to do?

The answer comes in an instant.

She'd have me stay.

Babcia would never want me to feel so guilty. She'd never
want me to sulk, or to throw away this opportunity. I *know* if she

was here advising me right now, she'd give me a haughty look and she'd point to the door. I can hear her voice in my head.

Go see some of my country, Alice. You're probably not going to get another chance.

She'd have me look around this country she once loved so much and soak it all in. She'd have me take the downtime and resist guilt for doing so. She'd cheer me on and celebrate my courage at having tried. She'd tell me that my family would be okay without me for another day. She'd tell me that my rushing back won't make her better, in fact, it would probably be the *only* way I could disappoint her.

When Zofia returns to the lobby twenty minutes later, I greet her with a smile.

"Okay. So we have today. What do you suggest we do first?"

"Mountains or salt mines," she says, without missing a beat.

"Which is better?" I ask her.

"Depends. What do you fear more, heights or enclosed spaces?"

"How far underground are we talking?" I ask her.

"One hundred and thirty-five meters?"

I can't quite figure out the math on the fly to convert that to feet, but I know it's a long way and I hate confined spaces. I shudder and shake my head.

"No thanks. Mountains it is."

Ten minutes later, we're back in the car and headed through the dense traffic and out of the city. Zofia again slips into tour guide mode, pointing out landmarks and historical sights, but this time I make myself focus on her words because whenever I let myself zone out, I think about the situation back home and I feel myself tensing up. Fortunately, Zofia is good at this tour guide gig—and by the time we're out of the city and starting the climb into mountain country, my mind is full of information about the region, like she's conducted a rapid-fire brain dump.

"You must try *ociepek*," Zofia exclaims suddenly, and she pulls the car abruptly into the parking lot of a tiny wooden hut by the side of the road. The structure is tiny—about the size of one of the small bedrooms in my house. There's smoke pouring from the chimney, and five cars already in the car park.

"What is..."

"*Ociepek,*" she repeats, correctly guessing that I've already forgotten the word. "Smoked cheese. Out of this world." Zofia reaches across into her handbag and withdraws her mobile phone, which she switches off.

"Service is all but nonexistent out here," she warns me. "Best to turn it off now or your battery will be drained from all of the roaming."

"Oh," I say, and I hesitate, because I ended *all* of my conversations late last night on a terse note. "But my family might need me..."

"We will be back here by about 6:00 p.m. You can talk with them this afternoon their time?" she suggests. I look down at the phone, then sigh and send a group text. I flush with embarrassment when I realize I can send exactly the same thing to Mom, to Wade and to Callie.

I won't have much coverage today. If you need me I'll be back in range by about 1pm your time. We can talk tonight. I'm really sorry about yesterday, and I love you.

And then I follow Zofia into the hut, where I indeed am impressed by the squeaky, smooth taste of smoked *ociepek*. The vendor winks at me and insists I also try his homemade lemon liqueur—which tastes exactly like lemonade when it first hits my tongue, but scorches the back of my throat like vodka. Zofia and the vendor laugh at the way my eyes widen, and then they laugh harder when I thump my chest as the liquid burns its way down.

We are straight back in the car and Zofia is zooming through the traffic again, stopping only to show me some impressively styled wooden huts and a breathtaking vista from a lookout, and then we keep moving on all the way to the town of Zakopane. It's high in the mountains—so high that, despite the summer heat, I can see snow on some of the peaks of the mountains behind it.

We stop for lunch and I pick up some souvenirs from the stores in the town center: necklaces fashioned with Polish amber for Callie and Mom, a sippy cup that says *Zakopane* for Eddie, some authentic Polish vodka as requested by my Dad—and a second bottle for Wade, who surely deserves a drink after what I've put him through this week. When I think we're finished, Zofia steers me back toward her car.

"The town is cute, *sure*," she says with a grin. "But what I *really* brought you here to do is the cable car."

It's midafternoon by the time we reach the cable car station, and I'm taken aback by the insanely long line waiting to ride it. But Zofia asks me to wait at the end, then disappears into the crowd. Ten minutes later she returns.

"Good news," she says, motioning for me to follow her. We walk all the way to the front of the line. "You get to skip the line! Just one thing you have to promise me."

"Sure?"

"When you get to the top, go for a walk—enjoy the view—take your time. But do *not* come back down until you've stopped at the restaurant for a glass of wine. It's pretty much the law," she says, then she winks at me, and farewells me to take the journey to the top alone, because she's convinced a Japanese tour guide to let me slip into a spare slot with his group. That's how I find myself standing in a cable car, hundreds of feet above the earth, squeezed into the little space with a dozen Japanese tourists and their guide.

It's a two-stage journey to the peak, but ten minutes after we board, we are almost to the top of an immense mountain. The

English announcement in the cable car tells me it is two thousand meters above sea level.

"That's 6,500 feet," the Japanese tour guide offers me helpfully, and I give him a grateful smile. I leave the group at the cable car and begin the walk up the last little part of the mountain to the summit. There's dozens of people making the journey in each direction past me as I walk, but the tourist traffic ebbs and flows. Just as I reach the very peak, there's a break in the hikers, and for a few magnificent moments, I'm actually totally alone.

A sign tells me that the valley on one side is in Slovakia—and the valley below where Zofia awaits is in Poland. The mountains are so high, the valleys below so low—and the shades of vibrant green against the white snow-topped peaks and the milky blue sky is so breathtaking it actually leaves me feeling a little emotional. I rotate slowly—taking in a 360 degree view of one of the most stunning vistas I've ever seen.

Three days into this trip, it hits me that despite the disappointments, this has been a wonderful experience, and I'm actually lucky to have lived it. Maybe I won't be going home with any distinct answers, but somehow, the chance to connect with the roots of my grandmother's life has been satisfying in a way I'd never anticipated. And having *survived* this trip—failures and all—has bolstered a confidence I didn't actually know was shaken.

Wade has given me a real gift this week, despite the struggle of it back home and my own struggles here. I can't wait to tell him how much of a revelation it has been to do something like this—standing on a mountaintop for no reason other than the sake of the experience. This moment is an investment in myself. I'm giving myself permission to make a memory that benefits *no one* but me. I love being a mother, and I love being a wife. I even love being a daughter and a granddaughter. But as I stand here on the mountaintop, I'm not any of those things.

I am simply Alice, and for one breathtaking moment, I'm completely present.

I don't just drink a glass of wine at the restaurant. I linger over it, then I drink a second, and when I get back down to Zofia—I tell her one glass was for me, and one was for her. She laughs, and then she hugs me.

"You're finally getting the hang of this 'travel' thing, Alice."

As we pass the cheese huts on the way back into Krakow, I realize that I still haven't turned my phone back on, so I fish it out of my bag and hit the power button. It takes a few minutes to locate the tower, but when it does, a flurry of text messages hits the phone. There are the inevitably chilly *thanks for letting us know* messages from my husband, daughter and mother in response to my warning that I'd be off-line. Then, a series of completely unexpected texts arrives.

Alice, this is Lia—Emilia's granddaughter. Please call me back on this number as soon as you can.

Alice, it's Lia again. I have been trying to call you all day. Please tell me you are still in Poland. Call me urgently.

Hello Alice, I am very scared I have offended you and I am really sorry if I did. The policeman was my husband—I just wanted to scare you, I wasn't really going to have you arrested. Please call me back.

Then finally:

Alice, this is Agnieszka Truchen. I am so sorry about the mix-up at the clinic yesterday. I hope it's not too late for you to speak with us—please call me on this number immediately if you are still in Poland.

"Lia *and* Agnieszka have been trying to call me," I tell Zofia, through my shock. Zofia looks at me in surprise, but there's no time to discuss it, because I've already lifted the phone to my ear to call Lia back.

"Alice?" She greets me breathlessly on the first ring.

"Lia, yes, sorry—it's me. I've been out of cell range today."

"But are you still in Poland?"

"Yes, yes I am—why? Did you—"

She interrupts me, and her words are rushed with urgency, "Can you come to Krakow? Tonight? I can come pick you up if you need transport. I'll come to wherever you are."

"I'm on my way there now—my hotel is there." I pause, waiting for an explanation, but when the silence starts to stretch, I prompt her, "What's going on, Lia? You said you couldn't help me."

Lia draws in a deep breath, and I can hear the remorse in her voice as she mutters, "Well, *I* still can't. But my grandmother would very much like to meet with you."

CHAPTER 37

Alina

We'd so hoped that the camp would be, at least, comfortable, but we were sorely disappointed by the reality we encountered. It seemed to me that the whole world had run out of resources in those days, because everywhere we went, people were starving and filthy and miserable.

The camp at Buzuluk was no different—in fact, it was all of the suffering we'd grown somewhat used to, but now intensely concentrated. The entire purpose of the camp was to prepare newly freed Polish citizens to contribute to combat with Allied troops—but there were no weapons to train with, far too few uniforms and *far* too little food. Everyone had lice—even Saul and I within a few days—and there was no controlling them, because there was no way to bathe, let alone wash our clothes or hair. The day we arrived, we were told pesticide was on order to treat the lice. When the shipment came on the train a few weeks later, there was a single carton of chemicals provided—enough to treat a few dozen people, as if that would make any difference at all in a camp of nearly eighty thousand by that stage.

And by then, I was *indeed* cursing Tomasz for the cast, because between the lice and the itch beneath the plaster, I was even itchy in my dreams.

Saul was quickly put to work in the medical clinic as Doctor Tomasz Slaski—no one questioned his age or asked to see his qualifications. I was deemed "injured" because of my ostensibly broken wrist, and was assigned to help supervise the orphaned children during the daytime. I protested this at first, having such limited experience with children. But everyone had to do *something*, and I had no other skills to offer.

I'd expected all of those orphaned boys and girls to be miserable and weepy. Instead, they played and laughed and ran—demonstrating a resilience that astounded me. I quickly came to enjoy that work and made friends with the older women in the same role. I was especially fond of Mrs. Konczal, who had been an opera singer before the war, and she'd sing the most beautiful songs with the children when we needed to calm them down for the informal lessons we tried to offer. It was hard but rewarding work, and each afternoon when I finished my shift, I'd feel a sense of intense satisfaction that I was doing something worthwhile for the camp. I couldn't wait for Tomasz to arrive so I could introduce him to the children. I couldn't wait to see the pride in his eyes when he saw the contribution I was making.

Saul was in his element within the clinic—having quickly taken command of what passed for a "surgical" ward in the infirmary, but his work was so much more taxing than mine. I tried to keep a close eye on him, checking in with him every day without fail—even though sometimes that meant I'd have to wait hours for him to finish with his patients. The nurses got used to me sitting in their makeshift office, and soon when I arrived, I'd chat with them and even help where I could with paperwork. I so admired the way that Saul carried himself in that place, and I could easily picture Tomasz filling a similar role once we landed somewhere and he finished his training. With virtually no supplies and endless patients to care for, Saul was always patient and unfailingly gentle—the compassion and empathy he had for his patients astounded me. When he told me about his day, he'd describe his work as if his patients had done *him* the favor in letting him treat them. And perhaps they had, because despite the difficult conditions, Saul certainly seemed to thrive in knowing he was useful again.

"You wait, *Hanna*," he'd tell me. He was constantly reminding me of my new name, because I was constantly forgetting to answer to it. "Once your Tomasz gets here, I'm going to take him under my wing again and by the time the British come for you, he'll know more than most professors."

We settled into our roles as the weeks passed, but we still met over dinner or breakfast every day. The itch beneath the cast was *maddening* by then, but Saul had made me promise not to scratch beneath it with a twig as I was tempted to do. Instead, he found a ruler in the administration block and for a few wonderful minutes a day, he'd slide it carefully beneath the plaster and with utmost care, he'd rub the skin for me.

"We have to be so careful not to disturb the film canister," he murmured to me one day, as he intently concentrated on the task. "And we also have to be doubly sure not to break your skin, because if you get an infection in there—we *will* have to take the cast off. Don't try to do this yourself. Promise me."

"Okay," I said, lost in the sheer relief of the ruler against my skin.

"Good," he said, and he laughed at the blissed-out expression on my face. "Same time tomorrow?"

Sometimes when we were alone, he talked about Eva and Tikva, about the tender months he had with his daughter, about the happy years he shared with his wife before the war. Other days, we'd talk about my parents or my brothers, or it would be my turn to share a happy story about Tomasz. I thought the sharing would help the longing I felt—but somehow, it made it worse.

"Tomasz should be here any day," I'd whisper, when the emotion swelled and tears threatened.

"Any day now." Saul would smile confidently, and I'd feel bolstered, reminded of the plan, reassured that everything was still on track and things were going to be okay. But the periods of sadness came and went anyway, especially as it gradually dawned on me that unless Tomasz had news of my parents' welfare when he arrived, I had to assume, and then *convince myself,* that they were dead. When the grief took hold, it was Saul I talked to, and Saul who offered words of comfort. He became a dear friend to me, and I could completely understand why Tomasz thought so highly of him.

"Hang in there, my friend," he said to me one day, when we'd been in the camp for some weeks. "Any day now, Tomasz will arrive, and then the British will come, and you'll begin the life your parents likely dreamed of for you. A very wise young woman once said that I had to believe I was meant to survive, and now that I'm here and I am helping these people, I can see that she was right…" We shared a sad smile, and then he added, "It will be the same for you and Tomasz."

"You seem happy here."

"As happy as I'm ever likely to be in what is left of my life. Wherever the camp goes, I'll join them." Saul shrugged. "I have heard we will be evacuated to Persia soon because the camp is not prepared for the winter…but whether it's there or here or even the moon, I think maybe my place is helping these people."

"Despite the fact that the Polish army wouldn't have even allowed you to join this camp if they knew you were Jewish?" I said, a little incredulous at Saul's willingness to forgive.

"When the time is right, I'll be honest about who I am—my name *and* my heritage, and you'll see what I knew all along. When a man is a patient on an operating table, and there's only one person in the room with the skills to save his life, that patient will instantly forget that he used to be a bigot."

I laughed weakly, but then I had a sudden thought. "I'll miss you if you do stay on. I wish you would come with me and Tomasz instead. Perhaps we would all be able to settle together in England—wouldn't that life appeal to you instead?"

"You and Tomasz will have a wonderful life together," he assured me. "And it's a life you've more than earned. I won't tag along—a fresh start will do you both the world of good."

Saul had become a good friend to me—an ally when I otherwise would have been alone. It made me happy then that he was thinking about his own future again—even if his eye was still on the war. I was just glad that he seemed to have found a light at the end of the tunnel of his grief, because in those early days when he was all but catatonic at the loss of his wife and child, I'd thought such a thing impossible.

It seemed to me that almost *everyone* was sick in the camp, and I was no exception. We'd been in the camp for almost two months, and I'd had a stomach flu on and off for much of that time. Some nights, I'd try to eat whatever scraps were set out before us and I'd manage only a mouthful or two before the sickness resurged. I actually felt lucky—I was always able to tolerate at least water, and Saul assured me that as long as that was the case and I could keep my food down at least once a day, I would be okay. I knew that half of the beds in the infirmary at any given time were patients with acute diarrhea, and when they became dehydrated, they usually died.

All I could do was eat when I could, and wait for it to pass. At breakfast one morning, I looked down at the slightly moldy bread we'd been served and had to push it away before I retched. I felt miserable that day, and I drew in a deep breath and tried to remind myself this was all only temporary.

"Tomasz should be here any day," I said, and I waited for Saul to echo the reassurance he always provided.

Instead, though, he said suddenly, "Eva and I really didn't intend to fall pregnant with Tikva." I looked up at him in surprise, momentarily distracted from my nausea, and he shrugged. "War is not a time when people plan to bring a child into the world, especially not the situation we were in. But we loved each other, and all we *had* was each other so it was natural for us to express that. And I really thought we were being careful...but these things happen. Would you like to know how I discovered she was pregnant?"

"How did you realize?" I asked him. Saul smiled sadly.

"We were traveling from Warsaw with Tomasz—we'd been on the road for a few weeks, hiding where we could, eating what he could find for us—he was so much better at scavenging than me. One day, he trapped and caught a *duck*. Can you imagine? We roasted it on a fire, and it was like manna from heaven, Alina—oh the taste and the texture, my God." He pressed his knuckles to his mouth like a delighted child, and I laughed. "It was a *miracle*. Tell me...when was the last time you ate roast *anything*?"

I laughed weakly.

"I can't even remember."

"Exactly. And there we were, hiding in a cave of all places, and your Tomasz provides us a feast like that. We were all so excited—but Eva lifted the duck meat to her lips and put it on her tongue, and then she was ill. She said the taste was divine, but the texture turned her stomach, and she couldn't understand why," he said. The joy had faded from his face, until his gaze was distant, but then he turned it upon me. "Alina, do you understand why I am telling you this story?"

I gaped at him, and then there was a rushing sound in my ears, and I knew I was going to be sick again. But it was even worse than that this time, because my whole body seemed to turn to jelly and Saul caught me as I slid from the chair toward the dirt floor of the dining tent. With help from one of the stronger men from the dining hall, Saul carried me outside into the fresh air. He sat beside me and rested his hand on my shoulder, and as soon as we were alone again, he said, "I didn't mean to shock you. Forgive me."

I hadn't cried in all of that time—not in the truck, not on the

train, not even when I sacrificed Mama's ring, not in the camp.
I had become a braver version of myself than I'd ever realized
was possible but *this*?

This was too much.

I'd not had a period since we left Poland, but my cycle had
been unpredictable throughout the whole war, so I hadn't missed
it. But Saul was right—even when we did get food, I'd been
far too sensitive as to what I could stomach. And just like Saul
and Eva, Tomasz and I had thought we'd been careful—but
we'd been dizzy with the joy of *finally* being together, and we'd
leaped into our sexual relationship with less care than we probably should have.

"Mama will be so angry with me. And Father. And the people here will judge me—"

"No, they will not," Saul said. "Because Tomasz will marry
you."

"But everyone will *know* before then, Saul." And then for the
very first time, I spoke aloud a thought I'd been too terrified to
give voice to until that moment. "He should be here by now,
shouldn't he? What if he's not even coming?"

"If he was really here, what would he do?"

It took less than a heartbeat for me to answer that question.

"He would marry me. He was *going to* marry me. He promised me we'd find a priest the very day we arrived, but…"

"Then, Tomasz will marry you. Today." I stared at him
blankly, and Saul's expression softened. "Alina, I will stand in
his place just for now, because that is exactly what he would
want me to do."

And later that day, that's exactly what he did.

There was much excitement about our wedding among the
people we knew in the camp—"Tomasz" was building quite a
reputation as a surgical miracle worker—and strangers brought
us gifts. There was a perfect little wildflower from a woman

Saul had treated weeks earlier, a luxurious new blanket from one of the camp administrators and, best of all, some *soap* from Mrs. Konczal—all of the staff of the orphanage had banded to- gether to barter for it. We went to the dining hall for our dinner meal, and by some miracle, the cooks had found a fresh sausage. Saul and I shared it, and it was such a gift and a blessing that for a moment or two, I was moved to deep gratitude by the effort and the generosity of our friends. For a few minutes I forgot how broken everything was, and I let myself feel happy because I felt so loved and so accepted.

But then Mrs. Konczal approached us again, a huge grin on her face, her hands clasped before her chest.

"We have another surprise for you. For your wedding night."

And with rising dread, I followed her to a tent that had been moved apart from all of the other tents—no small feat given the entire camp was overflowing with humans desperate for shelter. This was a small tent, fit only for two.

"Surprise!" Mrs. Konczal said proudly.

"Thank you, Mrs. Konczal," I said. My lips were numb. I could not look at Saul—I couldn't even force my eyes to shift in his direction. Mrs. Konczal kissed my cheeks, then Saul's, then she wished us a good night and left us be.

I crawled onto the mattress she'd placed on the floor of the tent, rolled onto my side and burst into tears.

"I'm so sorry," Saul said desperately. "Forgive me, Alina—this was never my intention, I didn't think they would—"

"He's not coming, is he? What if I'm all alone with this baby?"

Saul sat beside me, and he rested his hand over mine and gave a gentle squeeze.

"Here is the thing, Alina," he whispered softly. "War breaks us down to nothing more than our most selfish will to survive— but when we rise above that instinct, miracles can still happen. I helped Tomasz, Tomasz helped me, *you* helped me—in more ways than you can ever know. And now, at last and in this small

way, I am grateful for the opportunity to help you in return.
This, my friend, is how we find the best of humanity during
times when the *worst* of humanity may seem to have the upper
hand. You are not alone—you won't be, not for a single moment
until Tomasz arrives. I traveled from Warsaw with Tomasz—
I have seen firsthand that his drive to be with you is relentless.
This time will be no different, and until that moment when
Tomasz arrives to take his place, no matter *when* that moment
comes, I will care for you and your baby as if you are my own."

Everything changed after that day. Saul and I were moved
into a married couples' dorm—and there was no way for us to
avoid sharing our bed on an ongoing basis. We'd suffered more
awkward intimacies on the journey to that point, but sharing a tiny single bunk with a man who was only a friend was
not something I relished. But the cold was coming in, and the
summer tents were not nearly enough shelter, so soon enough
Saul and I were relying on each other's body warmth to keep
us from freezing. Every single night, he'd wrap me in his arms,
and right beside my ear I'd sense his lips moving as he prayed
without making a single sound.

Saul kept his promise. He nurtured me, constantly going out
of his way to find me foods I could tolerate—and that was no
small task in a camp where food was a scarce commodity. He
arranged for my work duty to be transferred to the office of
the infirmary clinic, where I spent my days in a heated room,
sitting down and filing away patient records and chatting with
the nursing staff. Some days, when the kitchen served up a meal
I could stomach, Saul would insist I eat his share—and if I refused, he would force me to, lifting the food to my lips in exactly
the same fashion I had done for him in the crate on the truck.

Had Saul not married me, I would have become a pariah; un-
married mothers bore an intense stigma even during wartime.
Had Saul not cared for me, it's possible I'd have starved early in

the pregnancy, when it was so difficult to eat and he worked so hard to ensure I did. I'd had the cast on my arm by then for months, so it was filthy and uncomfortable and starting to crumble at the edges. Other doctors in the infirmary had started to suggest it really should come off, and it was Saul who provided excuse after excuse why I needed to wear it "just a little longer."

Saul was there for me and my baby when Tomasz could not be. I knew that no matter what happened after that, I'd be grateful to him forever.

Soon, we'd been in the camp for almost three months. My rounding belly was almost filling out against my trousers, and the sickness had finally passed. I was in the infirmary filing when I heard someone calling for Saul from outside. Of course, they were calling *Tomasz*, because that's what we called him in the camp—even me, by necessity—something I'd never felt comfortable with.

This voice was urgent—and alien. Saul was in the makeshift theater then, so I went out to see what the fuss was. I didn't recognize this soldier's uniform or the language he spoke. All I knew was that at the end of every sentence, he said a butchered version of the most beautiful words I knew.

"Thomas Slas-kee?" the man said, and I pointed toward the theater room, but the man pointed toward the administration block of the camp, and then he said, "*British? Brytyjski?* Thomas Slas-kee?"

Suddenly I understood—this man was British, and *he had Tomasz.* Clearly the delay in Tomasz's arrival was because his plan had changed—he'd met up with the British somewhere else, and was finally back to get me! I squealed and I started to run to the administration block. I made plans as I ran. I would throw myself at him. I would smother him with kisses. The camp administrators would be confused because they thought I was married to someone else, but I couldn't use restraint—I *couldn't*. Once I saw Tomasz, I would never, ever let him go, not ever again.

There were more men in strange uniforms outside the admin block, and I approached one and asked desperately, "Tomasz Slaski?"

He looked at me blankly for a moment, then his eyes lit up, and he nodded and looked at me expectantly. And we stared at each other—each waiting for something. I quickly became impatient with him and moved on to another soldier, but got much the same result when I said Tomasz's name.

"Hanna," a deep voice said behind me, but it was *Saul*, not Tomasz, and I turned back to him frantically.

"They have Tomasz, Saul!"

"Hanna," Saul said again very gently.

"Have you seen him? He's here some—"

"Alina." I froze, startled at Saul's *loud* and unexpected use of my real name. His gaze softened. "These men are British—they are here delivering the uniforms, and they are looking for *me*. Do you understand? They have come to *collect* Tomasz, like we planned."

I stared at him, trying to process the implications of this. Finally the terrible, terrible reality of my situation struck me.

Tomasz should have arrived by then.

Tomasz had *not* arrived, and we hadn't made a contingency plan.

"I have to stay," I blurted, shaking my head. "I can't leave— he must still coming—he must be on his way—"

Saul caught my forearm and he pulled me into the administration block, and then into a room all on our own. He rested his hands on my shoulders, and he stared right into my eyes.

"You have to calm down and concentrate," he whispered. "You have to think this through, very quickly. We've come so far with that film, Alina. That cast has been agonizing for months and you've endured it—for this moment. Tomasz is not here, but I am *sure* he's still coming—he will not stop when he gets here and finds we're gone. People at this camp will tell him where we went and he will find you. But... I can't...". He broke off, suddenly frustrated. "Alina, if you stay here in these conditions, the chances of you and your baby surviving are slim to none, especially if I go with these soldiers—and I feel like I *have* to. How can I *not* tell someone about what is happening at home? How can I betray my wife and my baby and my people by wasting this chance to help?"

An hour later, I was sitting in the back of a transport with Saul, on our way to an airfield where I would board a plane for the very first time. We had no bags to take with us—the suitcase was long gone, and our only possessions in the world were the clothes we were wearing on our backs and the tiny leather shoe that Saul was still carrying absolutely everywhere he went, tucked into the waistband of his undergarments.

CHAPTER 38

Alice

Emilia Slaski is now Emilia Gorka. She's retired from a very successful career as an artist, and she lives in a surprisingly luxurious apartment block with a view of Wawel Castle, just a half dozen blocks from my hotel. When I knock on the door to her apartment, my stomach is churning, and the anxiety only worsens when the door opens and Lia is there.

"I'm really sorry," she says. "I was just trying to protect her."

"Let them inside, Lia," another woman chastises from deep within the apartment, and Lia steps aside. I suspected we shared a likeness from the thumbnail photos of her online, but there's no question now that I'm related to Agnieszka Truchen. We share the same green eyes, and her hair is gray, but we have the same hairline, the familiar widow's peak at the center. She approaches me and takes my hands between hers. She's frowning, though, staring at me hard—and there's an awkward moment where she just stares at me and doesn't say anything, until she shakes herself and says, "It really is a pleasure to meet you."

"Likewise," I say, and she smiles. "And this is my guide, Zofia." The woman nods toward Zofia, but then we fall into a lengthy silence again. Agnieszka is staring at me, but now she looks quite stricken. I'm confronted by our likeness too, but I don't understand this prolonged awkwardness at all. "You must be Agnieszka?" I prompt.

"Yes, I'm Agnieszka Gorka-Truchen. I'm sorry," she laughs softly. "I just didn't expect you to look…" She trails off, then glances at me again, her eyes widening all over again, as if she can't believe what she's seeing. "Lia," she scolds. "I can't *believe* you ever doubted her."

"I could *see* she was related," Lia mutters. "But I told you, I thought she was here looking for money, and then I really didn't want to upset…" She trails off, and they're both staring at me, until I start to feel incredibly self-conscious. I gently pull my hands back and smooth my hair down. Agnieszka clears her throat, then explains, "Forgive us, Alice. Lia just didn't explain that you're *so* familiar, that's all. Please—come through to the sitting area. Mama is so very anxious to meet you."

Zofia and I follow her through to a large sitting area, lined with bookshelves and furnished with heavy, antique furniture. Seated in one of the deep leather chairs is a tiny elderly woman. Her hair is carefully set; she's wearing heavy makeup and a set of ornate jewelry that's almost as big as she is. She gasps when I step into the room, and I smile at her, but I kind of want to gasp too, because I actually look more like this stranger than I do my own grandmother.

I kind of figured I might share some physical features with my distant relatives here in Poland—but in this case, it's so much more than a passing resemblance, and Agnieszka's odd reaction when she saw me is starting to make sense, because I'm staring hard at Emilia like Agnieszka stared at me. Emilia stares right back, shock in her eyes—those eyes that are so uniquely colored, the same striking green that Eddie and I share.

Emilia reaches out her hands to me, and I see that they are shaking. I approach her hastily, and then because she's sitting so low, I have to crouch to let her take my hands. Her skin is soft and wrinkled, just like Babcia's, and she stares up at me in wonder—then her hands lift, until she's cupped my face in hers. Soon, she's crying—two heavy tears roll from her eyes and into the lined skin of her cheeks and onward, down toward her neck. She starts to speak in Polish—rapid-fire words loaded with those sounds that still seem so alien to my ears—and I'm not even sure who she's speaking to or if she's expressing happiness or sadness.

"Is she okay?" I ask Agnieszka, who has taken the seat beside her. Agnieksa's eyes have filled with tears and she nods.

"She is overwhelmed. She's not sure how this is possible. You are *obviously* my uncle's grandchild. Tomasz," Agnieszka murmurs. "Mama is saying that you could be her twin when she was younger. But—Tomasz died in 1942, before he could marry Alina, so we're not really sure how she came to be pregnant by him."

"Oh," I say, and I frown and shake my head. I feel *so* awkward, because I can't imagine it's going to be easy for Emilia to hear the news that her brother did *not*, in fact, die during the war. But it needs to be done, so I draw in a deep breath and say, "I'm really sorry but that's just not right. Tomasz—my Pa—only died last year. He had a very long, very happy life in America."

There's suddenly a flurry of rapid-fire Polish—Agnieszka, Emilia, Lia and Zofia all taking turns firing speech at one another, while I stare back at Emilia as she cries and strokes my face. As the conversation progresses, they each raise their voices a little—and to my ears it sounds like an argument. They all fall silent abruptly, and Zofia touches my arm and says gently, "Alice, could we video chat to your grandmother, do you think? Emilia would like to see her."

"Did you explain that she will be able to understand their Polish, but can't speak back to them?" I say, pulling gently away from Emilia's hands to glance at her. Zofia nods.

"I explained that. Emilia said she'd hop on a plane and go to America now if doctors weren't all idiots, including her daughter. She's not allowed to travel because of her health," Zofia murmurs softly. I flash Emilia a smile, because that sounds exactly like something my grandmother would say, then I withdraw my mobile phone from my pocket.

"Are you going to FaceTime her?" Lia asks me, and I nod. She seems desperate to please now—a complete 180 degree turn from yesterday at the clinic. "Then let me get the big MacBook. Her eyesight isn't the best. The bigger screen will help Babcia see."

At first, I think she's talking about *my* Babcia—but then I realize she's talking about her own—and of course that makes sense, but it's also kind of shocking after a lifetime of being the *only* person I know who has a grandmother called "Babcia" instead of "Grandma" or even "Nanna." I place a quick voice call back to Mom. She's at her chambers, but she agrees to go to Babcia immediately.

"Who is this we're speaking to?" Mom asks me, somewhat suspiciously.

"We got through to the mysterious Emilia Slaski," I tell her. "Pa's sister."

"I thought you said it was a dead end," Mom says.

"It was," I say. "The dead end opened up again."

"Are you sure it's the right person?"

I laugh weakly as I stare at Emilia.

"You'll understand when you see her."

While we wait for Mom to drive to the hospital, Emilia touches up her lipstick—her hand shaking as she raises it to her lips, but stilling as she uses it, and then she orders Agnieszka and Lia into the kitchen, where they prepare tea and a light supper for Zofia and me.

And the whole time, between ordering her family around in a matriarchal way I know *all too well* from my own Babcia and preening herself for a decades overdue reunion, Emilia stares at me. At one point, she reaches out and touches my forearm, then recalls her hand and shakes her head, as if she can't quite believe what she's seeing.

"She doesn't seem upset to find out her brother was alive

for all of that time," I whisper to Zofia, who winces and says, "She doesn't believe he was. Hopefully this call will straighten things out."

Then the text comes from Mom.

I'm with Babcia now. She's very alert today and I think she understands what's happening. I'll answer when the FaceTime call comes in, so go ahead whenever you're ready.

"Ready?" I ask Lia, who speaks to Emilia in Polish. I pass the laptop to Lia, and we hear the familiar sound of the call connecting. Lia lines the camera up on the lap-table so that her great-grandmother's face fills the screen. When the call collects, Emilia gives a gasp of recognition and delight, and then on a slight delay, a mirrored gasp travels over the line from Florida.

"Alina! *Duża siostra!*" Emilia cries, and she reaches for the laptop and holds the screen between her palms. Her eyes fill with tears, and I shift so that I can see the screen. Babcia is propped up in bed, the stark white of the hospital pillow behind her, but she leans toward the camera on the iPad. There's no mistaking the unadulterated joy on her face.

"She called her 'big sister,'" Zofia whispers to me.

Emilia starts to speak in Polish but she's speaking *incredibly* quickly. I look to Lia in alarm.

"I'm not sure my babcia is going to be able to keep up with her," I whisper. Lia says a few hesitant words to Emilia, who rolls her eyes and says something to Babcia. Babcia rolls her eyes too, then gives an exasperated nod.

Zofia stifles a giggle.

"Emilia just told your grandmother that the young people assume they are stupid because they are old, and asked her if she can understand."

Emilia speaks again, with much less force behind the words now—her tone is so gentle she could have been speaking to a sick child. Even so, the words flow in a steady and determined stream, and I wait for her to pause so I can ask Zofia for a translation, but no pause comes. After a while, I realize that I'm the only person in the room here in Krakow who isn't struggling to hold back tears.

"Zofia?" I whisper urgently. Zofia shuffles to sit on the armrest of my chair, so she can whisper in my ear.

"So—firstly, Emilia's adoptive parents were Alina's sister and her husband—Truda and Mateusz. She says Alina saved her life, then found her a loving family that gave her a better life than she could have hoped for. She tells Alina that Truda and Mateusz survived the war and lived to a happy, fulfilled old age. Now Emilia is thanking her, and oh, that's lovely…she's exceedingly grateful to your grandmother, and she's thanking the Blessed Mother for this chance to say thank you. It's just beautiful."

There's more Polish now, but this time, Emilia is directing it at Lia and Agnieszka and Zofia.

"Okay," Zofia says, softly. "Now she says that Tomasz had been working with the Zegota Council…" At my blank look, she explains, "The Polish government in exile set up a group to assist Jewish people during the occupation. Tomasz had been helping several groups in hiding, including a young doctor and his family… Emilia thinks the doctor's name was Saul."

"Saul Weiss?"

"I think we can assume so," Zofia says absentmindedly, because she's focusing hard on Emilia. "Right, so Tomasz had organized a way out of Poland for himself and for Alina, but when the day came for them to go, Saul and his family were discovered by the Nazis. It seems they had been hiding with a farmer, and the farmer had betrayed them all, Tomasz included." Emilia begins to speak again, and I have to watch my grandmother's heartbreak right there on the laptop screen, almost as if it's a slow-motion stream. She's not wailing, she's not sobbing, but her face has crumpled and her tears flow as constantly as

Emilia's words do. Zofia sighs sadly. "Saul's wife and baby had been killed…"

"Eva and Tikva…" I whisper.

Emilia is quietly crying now as she speaks, looking into the camera toward my grandmother.

"Tomasz had already planned an escape—he had agreed to act as a courier, to take a canister of film across the border and to meet up with some English soldiers. Alina was to travel with him, but Tomasz refused to leave once the Nazis learned his identity. He was concerned for Emilia and her adoptive parents, because at that time, the Nazis had been executing the entire families of those who aided the Jews. This meant that Alina had to go without him, and to take the film herself."

"Wow," I say. I glance back at the screen, and see my grandmother is still silently crying.

"Emilia says she was not at all surprised when Tomasz told her what Alina was doing, because Alina Dziak was the bravest girl she knew." Zofia speaks to Emilia for a moment, then tells me, "It is like I told you at the grave—it was almost impossible to leave during the occupation. Alina had to be smuggled out of the Third Reich, across the Eastern Front and into Soviet territory, and then somehow she made it *all* the way to America."

"She's a tough lady," I whisper. "Even so…that's amazing. What was on the film?"

"Tomasz didn't tell her, but Emilia figured it out much later. She thinks it was photos from Auschwitz." Zofia pauses, listening a moment as Emilia begins to speak again. "Ah…so then they decided that Saul would go with Alina. Emilia…ah…she thinks that Saul probably took Tomasz's identity papers too…"

It takes me a moment to process the implications of this. But then it hits me like a punch to the stomach, and the shock is so intense that I can't even breathe. But there's no time for me to linger in my panic, because Emilia is still talking and Zofia is still translating. I have to immediately refocus my attention on the conversation at hand.

"After Alina and Saul had left, Tomasz came to Emilia's home early in the morning and he woke her family up. She says he was very distressed and in a desperate hurry. He gave Emilia a message for Alina, then he told her adoptive parents to flee immediately. After that, he ran to turn himself in."

"*Why* would he do that?" I whisper. Zofia and Emilia talk for a moment, then Zofia turns to me again.

"Tomasz knew so much about the Jews in hiding in the area. He knew the Nazis would be determined to find him, and inevitably, that would mean checkpoints on the roads." Zofia's eyes flick from Emilia's face to mine. "Emilia says he was quite frantic—he'd tried desperately to think of an alternative, but the only way to be sure the Nazis wouldn't search Alina's truck as it left the district was to end the manhunt…and there was only *one* way he could do that…" I bite my lip, glancing hesitantly at Babcia. She is sobbing, and my mother is hovering helplessly beside her. Emilia continues in a hoarse whisper, and Zofia translates, "Emilia says now that it is an honor to finally deliver her brother's message…that he'd be waiting for Alina on the other side because, even in death, he would keep his promise that they would be reunited."

I look at the MacBook screen. My grandmother's jaw hangs loose, and she lets out a moan of sheer grief that makes me sick to my stomach.

"Alice," Mom says flatly, and the screen shifts to her *very* pissed-off face. "What the *Hell* is going on?"

I know Mom can't hear Zofia. Emilia's impassioned declarations are loud; Zofia's voice is soft and close to my ear.

I'm going to have to tell her. I'm going to have to tell her.

"Mom," I say unevenly. "Please, just give me a moment."

"But she's so upset—"

Emilia lets loose with a string of frustrated Polish, and Agnieszka says urgently, "Ah—perhaps your mother could put the camera back onto your grandmother?"

"Mom! Please," I beg, and I can't help it—I start to cry. "This is important," I choke, through my tears. "*Please*, Mom. Please."

Mom gives a growl, then the lens refocuses on Babcia's face.

"One more minute, then if someone doesn't tell me what's going on, I'm ending this," I hear Mom warn.

Emilia is momentarily silent now, giving her friend a chance to process what she's heard. Babcia's grief and heartbreak are written all over her face, but as I stare at her, those emotions shift just a little, until finally, she looks something like *relieved*. Emilia speaks again, and this time, her words fall more slowly— finally, Zofia can keep up.

"She asked Alina if she was okay…" Babcia nods, then waves her right hand, indicating for Emilia to continue. "She's telling your grandmother that after the occupation ended, Tomasz was honored as Righteous Among the Nations—that's the medal we saw on his gravestone."

Babcia is smiling sadly now, nodding—her pride is evident. That's all important and beautiful, but I can't even focus on her just yet.

"But Emilia definitely said it was Saul who left Poland with Alina, *not* Tomasz. Is she absolutely *sure*?" I whisper to Zofia, then a sob bursts from my lips. "Because…the thing is…that means, I will have to tell my mom…"

Emilia looks at me, and she puts her hand on my arm again. She whispers some words to Zofia, who tells me carefully, "Yes, Emilia is quite sure that Tomasz was executed. Mateusz paid a guard to retrieve his body so they could bury him before they left for the city. It was Emilia's idea to take him to the hill—she says she used to catch him with Alina there kissing all of the time, and she knew that was the place where Tomasz was happiest. They marked the grave with rocks, and she returned in the seventies with the headstone once she had the money to do so."

"But why did she never reply to the letters?" I blurt to Agnieszka. "My babcia tried so hard to reach her. She wrote for years and years. Why didn't Emilia respond?"

There's a moment of quiet conversation, then Emilia turns to the camera, and her gaze is stricken.

"We think your babcia sent the letters to the house in Trzebinia," Agnieszka tells me softly. "But even once the war ended, the communists had possession of the house so Mama never did move back there. We didn't even get the clinic back until the seventies after I qualified. So Mama never received the letters, but she wants you to know that she tried so hard to find your babcia. Tomasz had told her that Alina would be waiting in England somewhere, likely using the name Hanna. So once she was old enough to travel, that's where my mama went…"

"She was looking in the wrong country," I whisper.

"Besides," Zofia remarks sadly. "Even though she knew to look for Hanna, she could never have known to look for Mrs. *Slaski*."

I leave everyone else in the living room and walk into one of Emilia's bedrooms. I text Mom to call me when Babcia is settled, and after ten or fifteen minutes, the FaceTime comes to my phone. Mom takes the news of her parentage with the dry-eyed stoicism I'd expect from her, despite the fact that I'm sobbing as I explain.

"I'm worried about you," she says, peering into the camera. "Christ, look at you. You're a mess, Alice."

I laugh weakly and wipe at my eyes.

"It's been a very long day," I say, then I ask, "Is Babcia okay?"

"She's exhausted. I've left her to nap, but she looks so happy. I don't know how else to explain the change in her except to say that your grandmother seems at peace. That's a pretty remarkable thing to gift an old woman. I hope you're proud of yourself and I'm sorry I wasn't more supportive—I guess you could see she needed you to take this trip even when I couldn't."

"Thanks, Mom," I murmur, and I'm grateful for the concession—but I know my mother, and I know it's at least in part a deflection. "But...*you* do seem to be taking this pretty well, Mom."

Mom sighs, then tilts her face to stare up at the roof for a moment. Then she drops her gaze back to the iPad and she says to me, "Dad was *dad*, Alice, and he was a great man. Whether he was really Saul or Tomasz...I was *his* daughter and I never doubted that for a second of his life. I don't know why they never told me, and maybe later, once it sinks in, I'll be upset or angry but...for now...? I'm just sad for Babcia, that she was never able to tell us about what happened back there...that she waited her whole life for closure." Her voice breaks, and she pauses carefully before she adds, "Will you give Emilia a message for me?"

"Of course."

"Please tell her that her brother gave his life for the best man I ever knew," my mother says abruptly. "Tell her that my father loved my mother, and he loved me, and he helped hundreds... *thousands* of children in his career, and he was the best dad and friend and husband and..."

She stops abruptly, then clears her throat again, before she says calmly, "Just tell her that Saul Weiss, if that's who I knew as my dad, did not waste a second of the life he was given. Neither did Mama. Make sure that Emilia knows that the sacrifice her brother made was not wasted."

"I will, Mom," I whisper unevenly. Mom's eyes are filling with tears, and I can tell she's not going to be able to blink them away this time.

I'm not surprised when she says gruffly, "Babcia needs...I need to go. I'll talk to you tomorrow."

I'm on the way back to the hotel, drained but exhilarated—and I think Zofia feels the same, because she's fallen very quiet over there in the driver's seat. It's just after 11:00 p.m. Krakow time, and my phone sounds from my handbag. I realize that I *still* haven't called Wade or the kids, and I flush as I bend to search for it. The message on the screen is not one I'm expecting.

Mommy. I'm about to FaceTime you. Please please please answer but mute your phone, because I don't want the boys to know we're watching them.

I frown as I quickly reply.

What's going on? Is everything okay? You won't be able to see me because it's very late here and I'm in a car.

She doesn't reply—instead, the video call comes in, and I answer it immediately. Callie's face fills the screen and she holds her hands up to her lips, so I mute the call. Then she's walking through the house, and she holds the phone into the doorway of the dining room.

Wade and Edison are sitting at the dining room table. I squint at the screen, but it takes me only a moment or two to realize that they're playing chess. I hear Eddie's AAC, but I can see that it's Wade who's using the screen.

Your turn.

There's a pause, then Wade and Eddie both laugh. Eddie's laugh is tinged with mischief and pride, and Wade's sounds surprised.

"You got me, buddy," Wade says, then he glances down at the iPad and the AAC says, *Good work.*

Eddie takes the iPad, and then he laughs with delight and he claps with sheer excitement as the AAC announces, *Eddie pawn eat Dad pawn.*

The angle is all wrong—and Callie's iPad is too far away for me to be sure—but when Wade looks up at Eddie, I think I can see a glimmer of something new in his gaze. I can't tell if it's affection or love or pride, but the specifics don't even matter.

Wade is using the AAC, and Eddie and Wade are playing *chess*.

It's been a big day—one of the most emotional of my life. But this...this is almost too much. I hold it all together while Callie walks back to her room, and then I unmute the call.

"How long has that been going on?" I ask her. My voice is husky from all of the crying back at Emilia's house, and I brace myself, hoping to dodge the question if Callie notices and asks why. She's too busy chuckling at her father, though, and she grins at me as she says, "Well, a few days ago Dad started trying to teach Eddie the rules so they could play together, but he *insisted* on talking as he did it, so that was obviously a miserable failure," Callie says, then she rolls her eyes. "But then this morning, Eddie found the instructions book in the box from the chess set, and he sat and read the whole thing, then he got the AAC and he asked Daddy to play. Dad *finally* seemed to realize if they were going to play together, he'd need to communicate on Eddie's terms, not his own. They've been sitting there ever since. Dad won the first game easily but I have a feeling he's going to let Eddie win this one. I just thought you'd like to see...you know, since it's a miracle and all that Dad finally listened to us."

"Sometimes," I choke, "Daddy has to see things for himself. I guess...maybe I should have thought of that a few years ago."

"Oh please, Mommy," Callie laughs. "You do enough around here. You shouldn't have to *think* for Daddy, as well. How's the holiday?"

"It's not a hol—" I start to correct her, then I pause. "You know, Pascale, today, I stood at the top of a mountain and I could see into two different countries at once. And I uncovered a secret from your Babcia's past that's so amazing—I can't wait to tell you all about it when I get home. One day, we're going to come here to Europe together, and I'm going to make you try sauerkraut."

"What's that?"

"Fermented cabbage."

"Ew! Mom! Way to make a gross food even *grosser*!"

Zofia and I share a grin.

"It sounds like things are okay there without me," I say to Callie. Her gaze softens.

"Mommy, we miss you. A lot. But...I can't wait to hear all about your trip. And we're doing okay today. Two more sleeps, right?"

"Two more sleeps," I murmur, then I yawn. Loudly. Callie laughs. "Honey bear, I'm at my hotel now so I need to go, but please tell Daddy I'll call him in five minutes?"

"Sure thing, Mom. Talk to you tomorrow. Love you."

"Love you too, honey bear," I say, then she hangs up the call. Zofia parks the car, then she turns to me.

"Glad you didn't go home this morning?" she says, and I laugh softly.

"That's maybe the understatement of the decade."

"Hi, Alice." Wade is wary when he answers my call. He stares into the camera as if it's about to bite him.

"I'm sorry," I blurt, and his eyebrows knit.

"I know, you texted me—"

"No, Wade. I'm *really* sorry." A sob breaks, and now he looks quite terrified. "Eddie needs you every bit as much as he needs me. You've done things with him this week I couldn't have done—and that can only open up his world. I'm *sorry*."

"Ally, I'm sorry too," Wade whispers, then I see the flush creep under his skin. "There were things I didn't understand at all. I get it a bit better now."

"I figured out Babcia's big mystery," I blurt, through my tears. And then, sobbing uncontrollably now, I try to bring him up to speed with the day.

"Alice," he says, when I finally stop with the weepy babbling. "I am so damned proud of you."

Just for a second, all of the chaos inside me eases, and my mind is completely still. I have a great love just like Babcia's great love—and *this* man is it. It's not clean and simple, because our lives are not clean and simple—and it's harder day-to-day to keep that love in our focus, because we have so much else to manage. But right now—just for a moment—the static of managing our kids and his career and the dynamics of our home life has completely cleared, and my love for Wade surges until it's all I can think about.

Right now, I know one thing for sure: if this separation between us was open-ended, I'd be focused on getting back to him until the very moment of our reunion.

No matter *what* that reunion looked like.

Babcia fire Tomasz.

I close my eyes, because I finally understand.

"Wade?"

"Yes, honey?" he whispers.

Babcia fire Tomasz. Finally, I get it. "Fire" doesn't represent passion—it doesn't even represent love. It represents literal fire.

"Babcia wants me to bring her ashes home. She wants me to lay her to rest with Tomasz."

Wade's gaze softens.

"Well, my love...then that is what we will do."

I'm unbelievably excited to see my family, and for the whole flight home, I'm picturing them waiting at the arrivals gate. I imagine running to them and embracing the kids, and everyone is smiling and excited to have me home. I know I'm kidding myself, because with Eddie's disability, an arrivals gate is a challenging place to navigate. The endless sounds and scents and the surging crowd make for a perfect storm of sensory overload, which, combined with the emotional impact of my return, is almost guaranteed to result in a meltdown.

Reality hits when the plane touches down and I turn my phone on—but it's the very best kind of reality.

Honey. I'm not sure how Eddie would go in the busy arrivals lounge, so I've found a place to park and we'll wait for you at the car. I hope you aren't too disappointed.

"Disappointed" is not the word I'd use to describe my feelings as I read that text message. "Proud" and "incredulous" are probably closer to the truth—because Wade has understood and predicted Eddie's reaction, and he's found his own workaround, without a shred of intervention from me.

And I get my moment of overjoyed reunion, because I see the car just as Callie sees me. She's standing by her door, but the minute we make eye contact, she runs at me and starts a stream of high-pitched, excited chatter. This means I get a moment or two alone with her before I even see Eddie, who's still strapped into his seat in the car. Wade is sitting in the front seat. They're both looking at their mobile devices with the same glazed happiness on their faces—Eddie watching train videos, Wade reading what looks suspiciously like a mommy blog. I laugh weakly as I approach the car.

"Hello, you two. Are you even a little bit excited to see me?"

Eddie looks up, and he squeals with delight, then he bursts into tears—completely overwhelmed in an instant. I rush to throw open his door and cradle him against me.

"It's okay, baby, Mommy's home," I murmur against his hair. I breathe in the scent of my son—my beautiful, complicated son—the kid who makes aspects of my life so difficult, but who also is a kind of sunshine and joy I'd never expected. And those difficulties and struggles and that sunshine and joy? I have always wanted to share them with my husband—and maybe, just *maybe* we're getting at least closer to that.

"Eddie, I love you Eddie," Eddie is echoing against my chest, and what else can I do, but to echo it right back.

We go straight to the hospital. Eddie is apparently proud to show his father that he knows how to navigate the way to Babcia's room, so he insists on walking right at the front, holding Wade's hand the whole way. Callie and I walk in the back, as I quietly explain to her what I discovered on my trip.

Then we're at the room, and Babcia and Mom and Dad are all there. Babcia is resting peacefully, Mom is sitting stiffly by her bed, Dad stands behind Mom, his hand on her shoulder.

"Hi, loves," Dad says, and there are hugs all round, until his gaze narrows in on me and he grips my shoulders and he says with mock seriousness, "Tell me you've got that vodka, child."

"I have the vodka," I laugh softly.

"Babcia's been sleeping on and off all day," Mom tells us stiffly. "Yesterday took a lot out of her…she can barely keep her eyes open today."

Eddie climbs up onto the bed regardless, and squeezes in beside her. Even in her sleep, Babcia winds her arm around his shoulders. They lie like that for a while, as the rest of us discuss the trip, Dad's "spontaneous" return, Mom's work schedule, Wade's plastics program and Callie's schooling. When Babcia wakes a little while later, she kisses the top of Eddie's head, reaches for Callie's hand, nods toward Wade, and then her eyes finally land on me.

I walk toward her, and she thanks me a thousand times a second as she stares at me through her tears. Then she's searching around the place with her gaze, until it lands on Mom's iPad, so I shift the kids out of the way so we can "talk."

Thank you. Thank you, Alice.

Babcia happy. Babcia proud.

Alice home now. Alice sleep.

Thank you. Thank you, Alice.

We kiss her cheek and say our farewells, then turn toward the door. As I'm about to leave, the iPad sounds.

Babcia fire Tomasz.

I turn, and Babcia is looking at me with a desperate hope in her eyes. I return to the bed and take the tablet, and my hands are shaking as I type my reply into Google Translate.

Yes. I promise you Babcia. I will take your ashes back and lay them to rest with Tomasz.

When I convert the words to Polish, Babcia's tears spill over, and she fumbles for my hand again.

My grandmother is a ninety-five-year-old woman with a brain injury, trapped in a hospital bed, unlikely to ever leave. But as I look at her in this moment, I don't see the elderly hospital patient—I see a beautiful young woman, madly in love with her fiancé, desperate only to find herself home with him once more.

CHAPTER 39

Alina

Everything worked just as we'd hoped and just as we'd planned, except of course for the very important exception: Tomasz was not there to see it. Saul and I were taken directly to the US embassy in London. Word was sent to Henry's brother in America, and we were told we'd have to wait for his arrival.

In the meantime, we were offered comfort like we wouldn't have dared to dream of during the years of the occupation—clean linen, hot baths, treatment for the lice, more food than we knew what to do with. The staff even arranged a translator for us—and sourced for us a hacksaw.

When the air hit my forearm for the first time in all of those months, I looked down and saw the wrinkled, pale skin left behind, and I sobbed with relief as I reached to scratch it freely.

The cast had fallen into two pieces on my lap, and nestled within the lining was a roll of film as expected—but also, right beneath it, a folded piece of leather—a texture and color I immediately recognized as cut from the corner of an old satchel my father had owned.

"What is this?" Saul murmured, but I shook my head, bewildered. "Did you see him put this in there?"

"I was distracted…" Saul carefully pried the film container from the plaster and handed it to the translator for safekeeping. But as soon as this was done, Saul returned his attention to the cast. He lifted one half, stared down the line of his cut, and smiled to himself.

"Well done, Tomasz," Saul said softly, then he glanced at me. "He knew where we would cut the cast."

He very gently pried the leather out from the layers of plastered bandage, peeled off some residual plaster, then unfolded it. But as soon as Saul took a look inside the makeshift pocket, he passed it to me.

"It's for you," he said softly. "A letter."

He stood then, squeezed my shoulder gently in reassurance, and he left me alone. My hands shook as I opened the leather pocket, and a piece of paper fell out and onto my lap.

Alina,

Perhaps I'm sitting beside you as you open this, and you're laughing at me for doubting for even a second that we'd make it. But war is unpredictable, and life itself these days is risk. I just don't know what's going to happen and I can't bear the thought of us being separated without reminding you of who we are.

Moje wszystko, the love I feel for you has been the fire that fueled my desire to be a better man. Until we are reunited, I will be longing for you, and I won't rest until you are back with me where you belong.

Till that day—be safe, my love.

Tomasz

As I read that letter for the very first time, all I felt was guilt—an immense wave of sadness and regret that threatened to swamp me. *I should have waited for him. I should have stayed.* I pressed my fists over my mouth and pressed hard against a scream that surged as I considered a series of unbearable possibilities: What if Tomasz had arrived at the camp in the hours since I'd been lounging here in luxury in London? What if he was waiting at the gates *even as I left*, locked outside because of the overcrowding? Why didn't I think to double-check that? Why didn't I wait just a little longer? Why didn't we discuss what I should do if he *didn't* arrive before the British soldiers?

But the letter had fallen onto my lap, beside the fragile curve of my stomach, and when I looked back down to it I was reminded of *why* I'd agreed to leave with Saul. It was a reality that did not yet feel real, one that I still forgot myself at times.

Our baby.

If Tomasz knew we had made a baby, he'd have wanted me to do anything within my power to reach for a safer life for that child, even if it meant we were separated for a little longer. And there was no doubt in my mind even then that Saul had been right—pregnancy in the camp was a tenuous prospect at best, and caring for a newborn in those conditions all but impossible.

I had done the right thing, I promised myself. It might be a few extra weeks or months before Tomasz found me, but I calmed myself by refocusing on his promise that he would.

In the week at the embassy as we waited for Judge Adamcwiz, Saul and I made a new plan. We would meet with the judge together, and we'd admit the truth about who we really were. It only made sense—there was no more need for subterfuge, and surely Saul's testimony would be all the more powerful once the judge understood it was actually personal experience.

But beyond the judge's visit, we knew we couldn't stay at the embassy forever, so Saul and I were hopeful that someone would help us find accommodations elsewhere in Britain. Saul would try to reconnect with the Polish army eventually, but until Tomasz arrived, he'd stay to help me find some kind of life here during the waiting.

My morning sickness had resurged since we arrived in London—partly because after years of a starvation diet, the heavy, rich foods on offer were both tempting and cruel to my fragile stomach. The night of the judge's arrival, I was particularly sick, and in the end I spent the evening in our room riding the waves of nausea. Saul had to meet with the judge on his own—but this didn't concern me. If the judge wanted to interview us about the suffering back in Poland, no one could give a better account of that than Saul Weiss.

Saul returned at our room very late that night, but he was unexpectedly pensive, his brow furrowed and his lips pinched. He fussed over me as he always did—tucked me into the blankets and checked that I'd been keeping up my water intake.

"I'm fine, Saul. Lost my dinner but no problem keeping water down," I told him, but then I asked a little impatiently, "How was the meeting with the judge?"

"He is very interested in taking the information I gave him back to his government, but he said they seem determined to turn a blind eye. He's hopeful Henry's photographs will prove useful but…there have been other photos, other information from within Poland has found its way out, and they have been reluctant to act even with evidence…" He trailed off, then sat on the edge of the bed and started to rub his temples.

"Are we in trouble?" I asked him, my voice a bare whisper.

"No."

"Saul," I said, and then I sat up and rested my hand against his forearm. "Something is obviously wrong. Was he upset that we lied about our names?"

"Actually…" Saul hesitated, then he swallowed. He exhaled and looked at me almost pleadingly. "Alina, I didn't tell him."

I looked to him in shock—then searched his gaze, bewildered. "But…"

"He said he's arranged visas for us," Saul blurted. "To *America*."

"America?" I repeated incredulously. I sank back into the pillows and felt the room spin a little. *America.*

"It's nearly impossible for Poles to get into America now, Alina—even for Judge Adamcwiz this was very difficult to organize. Their government is afraid the Nazis are sending spies disguised as refugees so they have all but shut the doors. Please understand—I just panicked when he said we already had passage. And Henry's wife, Sally, has said she will let us live in her home until we find our feet. But the judge said it's up to us—we can quite easily stay here, and there are people here who will help us too. But...*America*, Alina. Your baby could be an American— imagine the opportunities! And it is a world away from all this mess." I nodded, but couldn't bring myself to speak—instead, I stared down at my lap. Saul squeezed my shoulder. "We don't have to decide right now. But the visas are not for Saul Weiss and Alina Dziak. They are for Tomasz and Hanna Slaski, so..."

He trailed off, and I looked up at him.

"You don't even *want* to go to America," I protested weakly. "You wanted to go back to the camp, right? To serve with the Polish army?"

He nodded, then he paused, and when he turned to me, his gaze was intensely serious.

"But...what *I* want does not matter in this moment, Alina. I am not proposing to do this for myself. I made you a promise," Saul said. "I told you that until Tomasz returned, I'd care for you and your baby as if you were my own. And there is *no doubt* in my mind that this is exactly what he would have wanted for you both."

"But how will he ever find me?" I asked weakly.

"Do you really think a little thing like distance would stop him from coming for you? He walked across *Poland* for you once before. Finding his way to a boat to cross the Atlantic will be easy after that."

Less than a month after we left the camp at Buzuluk, Saul and I stood with Frederick Adamcwiz on the deck of the biggest boat I'd ever seen, staring in wide-eyed wonder as Ellis Island loomed before us. I was dazzled and awed and, frankly, terrified.

All I knew about this country were the things that Tomasz had told me, and even at the time, I had hardly believed him. Now, Sally Adamcwiz would travel to pick us up, and we would make our home in a tropical place that had barely any winter, a house so close to the beach that we could *walk* there. I was excited about the possibilities of this new life, and so hopeful—because I knew that Tomasz would find me there, and until then, I had my dear friend Saul by my side. I glanced at Saul then, to find he was staring down into the water in silence.

"Are there Jews here?" I blurted. Frederick gave me a patient gentle smile.

"Oh yes, Hanna. There are many Jews in America."

"And it's safe for them here?" I asked him hesitantly.

"Well, we have some problems..." Frederick admitted. "Especially here in New York, where I live. There have been some issues in recent years with gangs of youths harassing our Jewish people—a few incidents of businesses being vandalized, a cemetery desecrated... But, of course, nothing like what you saw in your homeland. America is a peaceful place, I assure you."

I watched Saul as Frederick spoke. I watched as the blood drained from my friend's face. I watched as his hands against the rail began to shake until he clutched it tightly in his fist to hide the tremble. I watched when he closed his eyes on what I knew was an intense wave of déjà vu.

His calm wisdom had impressed me until that moment, but I had just discovered that Frederick Adamcwiz was incredibly naive. I knew with absolute certainty that small problems in a country can become immense tragedies when left unchecked. It started small in Germany. It even started small in Poland, long before the occupation. It started with a small group of people harassing and vandalizing and desecrating, and it ended with trainloads of my countrymen shipped to furnaces and dumped into a river.

I reached for Saul's hand then, and I squeezed it hard. As soon as Frederick left us to go pack up his luggage, I turned to Saul and I shook my head fiercely.

"You have had your lifetime's share of persecution and suffering, Saul Weiss. Until we are absolutely sure this is a safe place for you, we need to keep your secret."

"I can't go through it again. God forgive me, I can't."

"We will keep it to ourselves until we know this place is safe," I promised him. "It may be some time until Tomasz arrives. You deserve a few months' rest."

We embraced there on the deck—witnesses to a vow to hold on to a secret that we thought we could simply reveal one day. We had no idea of the gravity of that lie. We didn't realize that time has a way of racing past you—that the long hard days sometimes make for very short years. Before we knew it, I was holding my daughter, who was always somehow *our* daughter because Saul took his vow to care for her very seriously from the moment of her birth. And as soon as his English was up to the challenge, Julita's beloved "Da-da" was studying and certifying and working *so damned hard* to support us all, and he was doing it *all* under Tomasz's name.

The day Saul was recertified as a physician in the American medical system was the day he applied to complete a program to become a pediatric surgeon. We didn't talk about the twist on the specialty he'd achieved at home, but we both knew why he'd chosen it. And by then, we were hopelessly trapped within the prison of a lie that had seemed so sensible and so altruistic at the time. My false name was one thing—a small detail I'd eventually adjusted to, something I could have undone at any time if the need arose. Saul's situation was so much more complicated.

It was Tomasz's name on his certificates—Tomasz who was employed, Tomasz who held a lease for our home and later the finance arrangement for the car we purchased.

Tomasz who took a residency at the hospital as a pediatric surgeon.

Tomasz who climbed the ranks at the hospital until he was a consultant, and he was training dozens of medical students, saving hundreds of lives a year.

Only Saul and I knew that the *real* Tomasz was the man with the laughing eyes, the man captured in the photo I found while helping Sally in the days after Henry's death, when we sorted through the enormous collection of duplications she'd amassed from the film he sent home over the years.

And only *I* knew that the tiny shoe Saul kept hidden in the top of our cupboard had actually belonged to his first daughter, his desperately loved Tikva Weiss.

It was *Saul* I shared my home with, Saul I shared my parenting highs and lows with. Saul who shared my bed, because we had grown so used to sleeping side by side since our "wedding" at Buzuluk. The few times we tried to establish separate bedrooms I'd wake to hear him shouting and sobbing in his sleep. Eventually, we accepted the reality of our situation. In some absolutely unique way, we were bonded to one another in spirit, if not in body.

I could not be Eva for Saul, and despite what *every person* in our lives thought, Saul would never be Tomasz for me. Instead, we were the very best of friends—partners in every way except that one which usually defines a marriage. We pined in company somehow—each of us eternally dedicated to our lost loves. And we were happy, and the life we built never stopped astounding me. I reveled in providing my daughter a life where she never had to learn what hunger or oppression meant. I watched as Judge Frederick's yearly visits with books and toys at Christmastime spawned hero worship in Julita. By the time he passed away, she hadn't yet hit puberty, but she'd already announced her intention to go to law school one day—and even more miraculous than that, she had the opportunities to make that dream a reality.

But as blessed as Saul and I were, I always waited. Every night,

I'd look to the window as I fell asleep, and I'd let the hope flicker for just a second, like the flare of a match that doesn't quite take. I'd imagine some unlikely scenario where Tomasz had been imprisoned somewhere, but even after all of these months then years and then decades, he would soon be free and would come for me like he'd promised. Perhaps he'd lost his memory? Perhaps he'd been injured and could not travel.

In my heart of hearts, the only thing that I knew to be true was that Tomasz had promised me we'd always find each other. Distance, time—these things were surely irrelevant against a love as big as ours—one day, he'd appear without warning just like he did last time, and life would begin again in earnest.

I never stopped longing, and I never, ever stopped waiting.

Perhaps it sounds foolish, but the strength of hope I held in Tomasz deceived me. I didn't even think of Saul and I as old until we were very old indeed. I had an adult daughter—a strong-willed, furiously ambitious daughter—but in some ways, I felt like through all of the hard years and all of the hard work, I had clung to the last artifact of that childish version of myself, and the innocent girl inside me was still waiting for her hero to return.

Saul stopped working as a surgeon when his passport said he was seventy, but he and I knew he was seventy-five. He taught at the university for another decade. He loved his work with a passion—that's why I was bewildered when he suddenly decided to retire. He'd hidden the signs so well, but as we climbed into bed after his retirement celebrations, he asked me to join him for a neurological consult. Just a few days later, we had the diagnosis: vascular dementia.

We wept together, and then he took my hands and he asked me to go to the synagogue with him.

"It would be an honor," I whispered, and he smiled sadly at me.

"Thank you, Alina," he whispered, because he had always called me that when we were alone.

"What do you want to tell Julita and Alice?" I asked him. A

shadow crossed his face, a glimmer of uncertainty that almost broke my heart to see.

"They are mine, aren't they, Alina?"

"How could they *not* be?"

He smiled then, a relieved, grateful smile.

"We will tell them the truth, then."

"They will understand."

"How could anyone understand?"

"Then they will, at least, forgive us."

But Julita is a busy woman, and she'd just started on the district court bench. Saul's degeneration happened so fast from there—as if he had held off his demise until he retired, but then it became very real in such a rush. For a few frantic months, I was focused on trying to convince Julita or Alice to join me on a trip back to Poland while I could still go. Then, by the time I realized we *really* needed to tell Julita the truth, Saul was no longer up to such a conversation, and I simply could not bear to do it alone.

Tomasz's last instructions to me were to care for Saul Weiss, and to Saul's *very* last breath, I honored that promise. I came to love him very deeply—and I know he loved me too. That very different kind of love was inevitably the foundation of my life in America, and it was a beautiful life indeed. Even if, to *my* very last breath, I will long for Tomasz—my first love.

My true love.

I'm near to that final breath now, locked helplessly here within my own thoughts—which is why it's utterly shocking that all I really feel in these hours is an astounding peace. It's all because of my beautiful Alice, with those laughing green eyes she inherited from my Tomasz—those eyes that she has passed on to our special, perfect Eddie. It is somehow fitting that it was Alice who found Tomasz for me, because she has always reminded me of her grandfather, the one she would never meet. She shares that same love of learning and knowledge and story, the same sense of compassion, the same ability to dream big despite her circumstances—even if she sometimes forgets she's allowed to do just that.

As I wait for the release of death, I look back on my life and I feel the *one* thing that has been missing for all of these decades. I am at peace, because I *know* that my Tomasz is waiting for me on the other side.

Soon, I will breathe my last and prove him right for all time.

We would always find our way back to one another.

Always.

CHAPTER 40

Alice

I wake up in my own bed to the sound of Wade's cell phone ringing. He's lying beside me, spooning me tight against his body, but as the call wakes him he rolls away to answer it.

"Hi, Julita," he says gruffly, and my already-racing heart kicks it up a notch as he passes me the phone.

"You need to come, now," Mom says stiffly. "It's another stroke, a big one. They've moved her to palliative care. Throw some clothes on and come. Don't waste a second. The doctor said we might not have long."

I'm at the hospital by 6:15 a.m. The staff have turned the lights down low, but even so, it's obvious that Babcia's skin has taken on a gray pallor, and her breathing is shallow. I'm crying before I even reach the bedside. Dad approaches me, then pulls me into a tight embrace. He doesn't speak, but at long last, that's because there's nothing left to say.

Babcia takes her very last breath right at 6:30 a.m. Mom is holding her right hand, and I'm holding her left. There's no struggle at all—no tension in her features, no fight against its hold as death takes her away from us. She slips from life so peacefully that it's hard to accept at first that she's even gone. The doctor joins us and he calls her time of death quietly, reverently. Mom is calm as she washes Babcia's hands and her face, and then we have one last moment with her all together.

Dad is, typically, more emotional about it all than Mom, who remains dry-eyed right up until the time comes to leave the hospital room. Then she turns back to the bed for one last glance, and she suddenly runs back to her mother's body and begins to wail—an animalistic, out-of-control cry that startles me. I'm stunned by this, but Dad offers me a gentle smile and murmurs, "I told you I'd need that vodka."

"Is she okay?"

"I knew this was coming, sweetheart. Your mother has a tough exterior, but her mother was her sun and her moon."

When I hesitate, Dad nods toward the door.

"Go home, sweetie," he murmurs, and he returns to the bedside. "Mom and I will need some time here, and you have your family to tend to."

As I head home, I'm sad of course—but mostly I'm grateful. I'm grateful to Babcia for every moment I shared with her—everything she taught me about motherhood—every hug and every loving gesture and every damned meal she ever cooked me. And most of all, I'm grateful that she entrusted *me* to uncover a little of her story, because I can't help but feel that in finding her past, I found a lost little piece of myself too.

I hesitate on my doorstep. I can hear activity inside, and I know they'll all be awake. It belatedly occurs to me that I'm going to have to break the news to my family. I'm trying to remember— how exactly does one communicate *death* to a nonverbal autistic child? When Pa died last year, we had time to prepare—we talked to Eddie about it with his psychologist there to help us. I wish we could do the same this time, but I need to tell Callie and Wade now, and that can't wait.

I step into the family room, and Eddie is on the beanbag, holding the dreidel before his face and twisting the handle slowly, train videos inevitably on the television in the background. His iPad is on his lap. I walk slowly to the seat beside him, and he looks up from the dreidel toward me. It occurs to me how my absence when he woke didn't seem to faze him at all—and once upon a time, that very same scenario would have guaranteed a meltdown. Still, his green gaze is a little sad, a little concerned, and he clutches the dreidel against his chest and he looks down to his iPad, as if he's scared somehow, but he doesn't know what to say.

"Hi, baby," I whisper.

Eddie sits up properly. He swipes to the AAC and hits the repeat button.

Babcia finished.

And then Eddie looks back toward me, calmly waiting for confirmation. A shiver runs down my spine, and I stare at him, trying to understand if he's saying what I think he's saying. I hear Wade at the door, and I glance up to see a bleary-eyed Callie still in her pajamas following behind him. I know they're both probably desperate for news, but my attention magnetically returns to Eddie. He repeats the words again.

Babcia finished.

I start to cry at that, and I hear Callie's rising hysteria from the door.

"What is he saying? Is he saying she's *dead*? Mommy—it's not true—tell me it's not true! You just walked in the door and you haven't said a word—Eddie couldn't possibly know that!"

I look toward them, and my eyes lock with Wade's. My throat is so tight I don't think I could speak even if I tried, but I don't need to carry our family through this tough moment, because Wade pulls Callie close and murmurs, "There's a lot more to our boy than meets the eye, Callie."

"But how could he *possibly*—"

"I don't know, honey bear," Wade interrupts her gently. "I don't know how he knew, either. But he's been saying that since he got out of bed at six-thirty, so apparently, he *did* know."

"But he can't..." She's still protesting when a sob overtakes

410 THE THINGS WE CANNOT SAY

her, then I guess it sinks in. She covers her eyes with her hands, then blurts, "I'm going to miss her so much."

Wade scoops her up into his arms and joins me on the couch. We huddle there as a teary trio for a minute, until Eddie stands. I smile sadly at him as he stands awkwardly in front of me. He doesn't join the hug. Instead, he reaches his hand out and he rests it against my cheek.

This family of mine is messy and it's different, but in this moment of grief and sadness, we feel closer to a *whole* unit than we have in as long as I can remember. Life has a way of shattering our expectations, of leaving our hopes in pieces without explanation. But when there's love in a family, the fragments left behind from our shattered dreams can always be pulled together again, even if the end result is a mosaic.

This family is a work in progress, but even today in our grief, I'm blessed by a growing certainty that we're moving ever closer to figuring out how the pieces can fit together in a way that works for all of us.

EPILOGUE

I never thought I'd get to return to that hill above Trzebinia, so it feels surreal to be here today—especially with the motley procession I'm walking in.

Eddie is at the front, where he often walks these days. He's staring down at his iPad, and Wade is close behind him. Eddie is a Google Maps master now, and he navigated us all the way from Krakow, leading us to the point on the map we set up last week when we were preparing for this trip.

Callie is walking behind me, with Father Belachacz from Trzebinia and Rabbi Zoldak, who has joined us from Krakow. Beside them, Mom and Dad walk slowly. Collectively, that part of our little group is discussing the economic boom Poland has been undergoing since it joined the EU. Earlier, I heard the priest ask Callie if she was *really* only ten years old.

"Well, yes," she said quietly. "But I do have an IQ in the 150s. It gives me a distinct advantage."

I'm in the middle of the pack walking alone. I'm breathing it all in again and thinking about how everything looks different here on this second visit, now that I'm here to fulfil Babcia's last request. The grass is even greener, the poppies in the overgrown fields that much more vibrant.

I'm carrying close to my chest the little wooden box that

brought us here today. Within it, Babcia and Pa's ashes rest, along with that tiny leather baby's shoe.

Today, the dodgy gates are open, and there are several other cars already here, which surprises me. As we near the clearing, I see that Emilia is surrounded by Agnieszka, Lia and a group of other adults. Some are holding flowers; some have lanterns or candles. Emilia is in her wheelchair, and I approach her and kiss her cheeks.

"So many people," I murmur to Agnieszka.

"It's just my brothers and sisters, and a few of their kids," Agnieszka explains. "I hope you don't mind—Mama said that Alina needed to be honored by our whole family, since not *one* of us would have ever been born without her." As my eyes fill with tears, Agnieszka winks at me. "You're just lucky we didn't bring the grandkids or great-grandkids—that would have doubled the group."

I throw my arms around Emilia's neck at that, and she whispers some soothing Polish words into my ear. Then I turn and I see the plaque that Emilia arranged in readiness for this day. Beneath the engraving that lists Tomasz Slaski's name, several other names have been added:

Alina Slaski 1923–2019
Saul Weiss
Eva Weiss
Tikva Weiss

Now and without any instruction, Eddie settles himself automatically away from the crowd, perching on the flat boulder at the edge of the clearing as if he's done this a million times before. He loads one of the train videos Wade saved for him before we left home, but before I can ask him to, he turns the sound *all* the way down, then looks at me and he smiles proudly.

I'm not sure my husband explained to our son what was expected of him, but that kid has been an angel today. It's funny how, now that Wade and Eddie have *finally* bonded, there's a whole new avenue from Eddie's world to ours—and that's certainly been helpful for our son. He's going to school three days a week now—and on Thursday mornings, Wade goes to work late because he helps with the science lesson in Eddie's class.

Wade and I still approach our relationship with our son very differently, and there is inevitably a tension in that. Wade will *always* want to push Eddie out of his comfort zone, and I'll always want to provide him security and structure—but in the push-and-pull of our very different approaches, we're achieving some kind of delicate balance. I benefit from that, but so does Wade, and most of all, so does Eddie.

Callie takes my hand as everyone automatically shifts into place around the grave site. Without any preamble, the priest begins the short, respectful service we planned.

Father Belachacz was initially confused when I called him a few weeks ago to ask his help today, and fair enough, because the whole story took some explaining. At first I just said that we needed a service for the ashes of my devoutly Catholic grandmother and everything we had of my Jewish grandfather and his *other* family. Once Father Belachacz got his head around it, he said he'd be honored to help us celebrate their lives and he'd figure something out. When we arrived here today, he introduced us to Rabbi Zoldak, who had come all the way from Krakow to assist.

I can't think of anything more perfect or fitting for *these* people than a multifaith memorial service.

Now Father Belachacz invites Rabbi Zoldak to come forward, and he speaks to us all for a few minutes in English—about grief and love and the incredible power of sacrifice. I'm emotional as all of this is happening, but that swells to all new heights when Rabbi Zoldak begins to chant *El Malei Rachamim*. As the Hebrew words rise around us in that place, a tsunami of grief and gratitude hits me, and I can't help but sob. I cry for the grandfather I so adored, and I wonder how he would feel to know that one day, we brought him to rest with Eva and Tikva *and* Alina and Tomasz, in a time when his faith could be celebrated in safety and with respect. Then I imagine Tomasz Slaski, a man I never had the privilege to know—but I don't need to have known him to know that he would have approved of every aspect of this service and this arrangement, and there's no question that my Babcia would have too.

The priest invites me to come forward. I drop my knees to rest against the soft grasses, then I gently rest the box inside the hole in the earth one of Emilia's sons prepared for us. The priest crouches beside me and scoops up a handful of soil, then sprinkles it atop. He repeats this three more times as he says softly, "In the Name of God, the merciful Father, we commit the bodies of Alina and Saul to the peace of the grave, and along with them, the memories of Saul's beloved Eva and Tikva."

Wade takes the hand trowel from my backpack and finishes covering over the box. Later, Emilia's son is going to arrange for this patch to be concreted over, so that we can all rest assured they will never be disturbed.

Then we stand, and it's finished. There's moments of quiet chatter, but then the crowd begins to disperse—returning to Emilia's apartment in Krakow where she is hosting a luncheon for us all. My parents start to wander back toward the van, with Callie in tow, and Wade glances at me.

"You okay?" he asks gently.

"I'm good, actually but…" I clear my throat. "I could do with a moment?"

"I'll take Eddie," Wade offers. But then we both look over to him, and he's settled on that long, flat rock, completely relaxed as he stares at his iPad.

"He's fine." I smile, then I kiss Wade's cheek. "We'll be back at the van in a few minutes."

As Wade walks away, I stare at the plaque and the headstone and I think about the journey of the last ten months. Taking this trip for Babcia opened up the world to me, in ways I'm only just starting to understand now. I started writing down the things I learned on my trip for Callie and Eddie to read when they are older, and the project has taken on a life of its own—I think perhaps I might have inadvertently started writing a book.

I always thought my family needed 100 percent of my energy— but I'm learning that I can give them the full focus of my love *and* take the time to nurture other things that matter to me too. I'm even busier these days, but the curious thing is that I feel much less exhausted.

"Thank you, Babcia," I whisper, as a gentle breeze stirs the branches above me. "Thank you for trusting me to find out the answers for you. I had forgotten I knew how to do that."

Eddie sits up abruptly from his slump, and stares up into the trees around us, searching for something. As I watch him, a strange shudder passes through me.

"Eddie," he echoes. "Eddie darling, do you want something to eat?"

The shudder ripples down along my body again, and then as surely as if her arms have closed around me, I feel Babcia with us in that clearing, and I feel her peace and her love and her gratitude. I close my eyes and I breathe it in, and for the very last time, I whisper, "Goodbye, Babcia."

Eddie stands and he walks across the clearing to slip his hand into mine. I glance down at him through my tears and find he's patiently staring up at me.

Emilia and our distant cousins will be waiting for us back in Krakow, and then over the next two weeks, Wade and Callie and Eddie and I are going to explore this country together. It's not easy for us to be here, so far out of our routine, out of our comfort zone—but we're making it work for every single one of us, because it's important, and because this was always the dream. There will be challenges, there will be disappointments, there will be failures and arguments and mishaps, but that's not preventing us from *trying* anymore.

Our family life is never going to be easy, but that can't stop any one of us from reaching for our dreams. It cost our ancestors too damned much for us to have this life—the best thing we can do to honor them is to live it to its fullest.

★ ★ ★ ★ ★

ACKNOWLEDGMENTS

My sincerest thanks to my aunt, Lola Beavis, who traveled with me to Poland to help with translation and to patiently assist with my research for this book. Thanks to Barbore Misztiel for her hospitality and, in particular, for taking me to visit my grandmother's childhood home. Thank you to Renata Kopczewska for guide services and research assistance, and to Katarzyna M. for Polish grammar/translation advice.

I'm forever indebted to Ashleigh Finch, who offered invaluable expertise and insight into autism spectrum disorder while I was planning this book. I only hope I've written Eddie and his family in a way that does justice to her generosity and courage in sharing her knowledge and experiences.

And finally, thanks to the staff at the Auschwitz-Birkenau Memorial and Museum, the Warsaw Uprising Museum and the incredible POLIN Museum of the History of Polish Jews. They are unique heroes—storytellers tasked with keeping alive the memory of what should never be forgotten.

AUTHOR'S NOTE

Most of my books have started as a whisper of an idea that I have to strain to listen for. In the case of this story, the idea floated past me at my mother's family Christmas party one December a decade or so ago.

I was standing in a crowd of cousins and uncles and aunts, gorging myself on traditional Polish food, as is our tradition at that party each year. It suddenly struck me that our now-large family had once been just a single Polish Catholic couple—my maternal grandparents. Displaced by war, they made a home almost ten thousand miles from the world they'd always known, in a country that was often less than welcoming to refugees. But seventy years later, more than fifty of their direct descendants know only that *new* country as home. Whether we are conscious of it or not, our grandparents' decisions made in wartime changed our lives.

I knew enough about my grandparents' story and the war to surmise that the paths that led them across the world to a new life would not have been easy...although I knew very little of the specifics of that journey. My grandparents both died in the 1980s, and the sad reality is that much of their story died with them. Like many of their generation, they had little time to reflect or grieve even once the war ended. Their focus was on the future, and the physical, emotional and psychological wounds of war were soon trapped beneath the surface of the new life they were forging. The lessons they learned along the way were often lost to time.

I started reading about life for Polish citizens under the Nazi occupation, initially just trying to imagine what my grandparents might have seen and experienced. But as I read about World War II, I was inspired by so many stories of love and survival, even in the face of unimaginable oppression and cruelty. Tomasz's, Alina's and Saul's story became clear in my mind as I marveled at the way that not even the worst of humanity is powerful enough to stamp out grace or hope or love. I decided that to write this book, I'd need to visit Poland to deepen my research, and while I was there, I'd try to discover some pieces from my own family history.

In 2017, my wonderful aunt Lola and I traveled to Poland and spent several weeks exploring and researching. During those weeks, I discovered that inverse to the story I'd long planned for Alina and her brothers, my own grandmother had been taken for forced labor, while her brother was chosen to remain to work the family farm. And just as I'd planned for Alice, I stood on the patch of land that my grandmother's family had farmed for generations before the war, and I peered through the dusty window of the house that had been my grandmother's whole world before Nazi hatred changed her life forever. My aunt and I walked the streets of Trzebinia, where my grandfather was born (image 2), and ate with distant cousins (image 1).

When the time came to use my research to finally write the story, I took my own experiences in Poland and funneled them into this work of fiction. For me, the best fiction always contains threads of the personal. I used my grandmother's family farm as inspiration for Alina's (images 3 and 4). That real-life property is located some distance to the northeast of Trzebinia. I have taken liberties with the location and imagined it much closer to the township, because I so wanted to tell the story of that town. It suffered almost every brutal injustice imaginable during wartime—heavy bombing raids, horrific persecution, the eventual genocide of the local Jewish community, oppression of the Catholic community and executions of civic leaders. Real-life Trzebinia is located just nineteen kilometers from the site of Auschwitz-Birkenau.

I was changed by the experience of connecting with distant roots and having the opportunity to see a little of the world my grandparents knew as their own. And while Alice's family scenario is so much more difficult than my own, I have tried to write her story in such a way that women of many different family situations can relate to her journey. Wherever it was possible, I drew on my own experiences in Poland to inform the way that Alice experienced hers.

As I finished this book, I found myself right back at the original idea that inspired my research all those years ago. Alina's decisions in wartime would change the very world her descendants were born into, and her *story* had the potential to change her descendants' lives...if only she could find a way to tell it. History's most important lessons can be difficult to confront and even harder to share—but we are all richer when those lessons persist through generations. Perhaps more than ever, we need the wisdom our forebears gleaned through blood, sweat and more than their share of tears.

I loved researching and writing this story, and I so hope you've enjoyed reading it. If you did, I'd be grateful if you could take the time to write a review online. Your review really does make a difference—it helps other readers to find my books.

I also love hearing from readers—if you'd like to get in touch with me, you can also find all my contact details on my website at kellyrimmer.com. You can also sign up for my newsletter to receive a notification when my next book is released.

And finally, it should be noted that although this novel is set around historical events, some changes have been made to timelines and details to simplify the narrative.

Me (right) with my aunt Lola Beavis (left) and our cousin Barbore at her home. Lola traveled with me to assist with my research and translation. (*Kelly Rimmer*)

Trzebinia Town Square: this location was the inspiration for the scenes where Aleksy and the mayor are executed. (*Kelly Rimmer*)

This humble house at Wola Żydowska was my grandmother's family home, and the inspiration for Alina's family property. (*Kelly Rimmer*)

The house itself is abandoned, however my cousins live nearby and still farm parts of the land for produce for their families. (*Kelly Rimmer*)

QUESTIONS FOR DISCUSSION

1. Which characters in this book were your favorites? Why? Alina and Alice narrate the story—but is there another character you wish you could have heard from directly?

2. Were you more engaged in Alina's story or Alice's? Why? Were you satisfied with how the two story threads came together?

3. Alina lives a relatively sheltered life. How is her behavior shaped by her family's attitude toward her? How does she change over the course of the story?

4. Alina, Julita and Alice are all very different women within the same family, although each has a unique approach to how she raises her children. Do you think there's a relationship between how each woman approaches motherhood, or do circumstance and personality play a larger role here?

5. Why do you think Wade held himself at such a distance from Eddie? Why did this damage his relationship with Alice so much? And why did Wade and Eddie's relationship change when Alice was away?

6. Tomasz was coerced to serve in the *Wehrmacht* and, in doing so, inadvertently played a role in one of the most horrific chapters in human history. How did this decision change the course of his life and the life of his descendants?

7. What do you think Tomasz *should* have done, when faced with the pressure to comply with the Nazi agenda? Do you think he redeemed himself once he deserted the *Wehrmacht*, or are some acts unforgivable?

8. Do you think Tomasz ever intended to follow Alina, or did he know all along that he'd need to turn himself in after she left with Saul? And if Tomasz had escaped to safety with Alina, would he have been able to leave his guilt behind?

9. Take a moment to reflect on your own family's story. Do you know much about your grandparents' early lives? How have your grandparents' decisions in their youth affected *your* life? What questions do you wish you could (or would like to) ask them about their younger years?

10. Did you learn anything new as you read this book, and if so, what was it?

11. Which scene in *The Things We Cannot Say* affected you the most, and why? What emotions did that scene elicit?

12. Were you satisfied with the ending? Did the story end as you expected, or did you envision a different resolution for Alice or for Alina?

13. What will you remember most about *The Things We Cannot Say*?

CPSIA information can be obtained
at www.ICGtesting.com
Printed in the USA
LVHW100416180322
713725LV00013B/436

9 781525 823565